MRS WHISTLER

Matthew Plampin

THE BOROUGH PRESS

The Borough Press
An imprint of HarperCollins*Publishers* Ltd
1 London Bridge Street
London SE1 9GF

www.harpercollins.co.uk

This paperback edition 2019
1

First published by HarperCollins*Publishers* 2018

A catalogue record for this book is available from the British Library

ISBN: 978-0-00-816364-8

This novel is entirely a work of fiction.
The names, characters and incidents portrayed in it, while at times based on
historical events and figures, are the work of the author's imagination.

Set in Perpetua by Palimpsest Book Production Limited, Falkirk, Stirlingshire

Printed and bound in the UK by CPI Group (UK) Ltd, Croydon CR0 4YY

MIX
Paper from
responsible sources
FSC™ C007454

This book is produced from independently certified FSC™ paper to ensure
responsible forest management.

For more information visit: www.harpercollins.co.uk/green

MRS WHISTLER

Matthew Plampin was born in 1975 and lives in London. He completed a PhD at the Courtauld Institute of Art and now lectures on nineteenth-century art and architecture. He is the author of four previous novels, *The Street Philosopher*, *The Devil's Acre*, *Illumination* and *Will & Tom*.

Praise for *Mrs Whistler*:

'*Mrs Whistler* is a beguiling glimpse of a fascinating world ... this novel is a delight'   *The Times*

'... rific novel . . . It springs off the page, bristling with ... vivid and absorbing portrait of bohemian London ... the love affair between Whistler and his long-... ng but spirited muse'   Deborah Moggach

'... ly engaging . . . a novel that conjures up the ... an art world in rich colours'   *Sunday Times*

'... ghtful book'   *Literary Review*

'... ly imagined historical novel, full of depth and ...   *Sunday Times Culture*

Also by Matthew Plampin

The Street Philosopher
The Devil's Acre
Illumination
Will & Tom

For Sarah

'Maud could tell the whole story, but she will not.'

Elizabeth and Joseph Pennell,
The Life of James McNeill Whistler (1908)

Part One

The Falling Rocket

October 1876

Maud woke to the sound of a piano. The room around her was dark, its heavy shutters closed. Jimmy was standing to the left, framed by a doorway. She started to speak, to ask what was happening, and he darted forward, shimmering slightly as he passed. Angling her head, she watched as he went to the end of the bed, collected together his possessions and packed them into an old leather bag. When this was done, he whipped off his smock, revealing the suit beneath; and there was that glittering again, like golden fish scales. She realised it was tiny flecks of the Dutch metal he was applying downstairs.

'Up,' he said.

The piano was somewhere towards the bottom of the house. It was being played much too hard, attacked almost, the music tangled and all out of time. After a short struggle with the bedclothes – which were the best cotton, far finer than theirs – Maud managed to rise onto an elbow.

'What in heaven—?'

'Leyland has reappeared,' Jimmy told her, cramming the smock into his bag. 'And he is displeased. We must absent ourselves, my girl, *tout de suite*.'

Maud swung her legs over the side of the bed, her toes spreading on the bare floorboards. Her shift was damp with sweat. She smelt rather ripe, an oniony sharpness mingling with the curdled whiff of nausea. Despite the warmth, a shiver prickled up the back of her neck; the shadowy room, empty save for the bed, seemed to drift like a raft on a pond.

'It's after three,' said Jimmy. 'You've been asleep for nearly five hours.' He stopped to study her. 'How are you faring?'

'Well,' she lied. 'Better.'

'Come then,' he said, adjusting the length of lavender ribbon that served him as a necktie. 'Haste, Maudie. Let's be off.'

Maud dressed as quickly as she could. Stockings, petticoat and corset. One of her everyday gowns, the colour of old brick with black lacquered buttons. The fabric felt odd against her skin, stiff and coarse, and her boots were tight, as if they'd shrunk a size while she slept. She gathered in her hair, winding it into a loose, greasy bun. Jimmy waited by the open door with the bag between his feet, wiping Dutch metal from his eyeglass with a handkerchief, wincing as the piano struck a particularly jarring note. Maud eased herself from the bed and went over to him, grinning a little as she looked at that mobile, actorly face; the white forelock resting amongst the oiled black curls; the small, sardonic line etched at the corner of his mouth. His eyes were a bright, sun-bleached blue. Wide at first, they dipped until very nearly closed, like a cat's. He smiled back at her with affectionate impatience.

'My hat,' she said, picking a gold flake from his moustache. 'Think it's downstairs.'

Jimmy slotted the eyeglass into his breast pocket, scooped his bag from the floor and took her hand. Together they started through the house. Even now, moving at speed, her head muddled by sleep and sickness, and that terrible music grinding out in the background – Beethoven was it meant to be? – the pair of them seemed to *sweep* across the expanse of the landing; to *descend* the staircase, lent majesty by that grand marble curve; to *proceed* into the swank hallway below. It was borrowed, of course, wholly counterfeit, but it felt good nevertheless.

They swerved right, towards the dining room. This was Jimmy's realm, where he'd spent much of the summer. He'd been brought in to finish off the original, rather dull decorative scheme – left incomplete, Maud understood, after its designer fell ill – and had decided instead to transform it into something truly astonishing. She hadn't been in there for a day or two, which refreshed the effect – so much so that she slowed to a halt upon the paint-spattered floorboards, her hat momentarily forgotten. It was like entering a pavilion at a great international fair. The wood-work, the many yards of intricate spindle shelving, had been coated with gleaming gold. Much of the wainscot, cornice and ceiling was now gold also, and was being overlaid with a pattern of Prussian blue peacock feathers. And there, on the inside of the shutters, were the birds themselves. The central set had been closed, as if to show them off to a caller. A pair of peacocks perched at the top of the tall panels, their magnificent tails arranged beneath them in a cascade of fronds and scales and glistening discs. They were Japanese in character, ancient-looking and otherworldly. The low light in the dining room didn't place them at the least disadvantage; the gilded wood positively blazed in the gloom, while the blues appeared a rich, fluid black.

That Maud was at Jimmy's side, that she was helping him to do this – his finest achievement yet, sure to open up a whole new territory – made her so extraordinarily proud it brought tears to her eyes. There was bitterness in her too, though, just a hint; for already, before its completion, this splendid thing had become tainted. A week or so earlier, Jimmy had returned home to Chelsea in a state of fizzing agitation, talking of a development; of how the philistines were everywhere, absolutely *everywhere*, even lurking within those one had previously thought enlightened, with whom one had considered oneself friends. Eventually, after much shouting and cursing, the full story had been extracted. Frederick Richards Leyland, the house's millionaire owner, had made an unannounced visit from his base of operations in Liverpool. His reaction to Jimmy's efforts – undertaken without prior consultation, as a marvellous surprise, a gift to the entire Leyland family – had been, well, a touch disappointing.

'He didn't *ask for it.* That was his response. He didn't ask for it and he didn't want it. Not the gold, not the peacocks. Not even your flowers, Maudie.'

Under the original scheme, the dining-room walls had been covered with antique leather, brownish yellow in tone and patterned with spiralling ribbons of summer flowers. When Jimmy had taken over he'd decided that a number of these blooms had to be retouched, with their colours switched from red to blue – and that this task should be entrusted to Maud, in her occasional role as his pupil. It had been monotonous work in truth, with several hundred little flowers to be repainted exactly the same, but she'd done it with enormous care. Learning that it had merely added to the patron's discontent hadn't been pleasant.

'It was like having a lead ingot tied around my neck,' Jimmy had continued, 'and being tipped into the goddamned river. Nine years, Maud. Nine years I have been cultivating that unappealing fellow. Much indeed has passed between us, oh yes, well beyond the scope of artistic patronage. And yet throughout all of this, throughout all of my attempts to school him in art, Leyland has understood, truly *under-stood*, not a single goddamned jot. All that discourse, all that forbearance, all that blasted *time* – squandered!'

The room, however, had to be finished. Of this Jimmy had been quite certain. He wanted London society to see precisely what this shipbroker from Liverpool had chosen to reject. Leyland had gone north again, to attend to his business, and so the slighted artist had embarked upon a last surge of industry. He'd moved to Kensington, living in the vacant, half-furnished house, enduring the scrutiny of an increasingly suspicious caretaker and applying himself entirely to his labour. Maud had come to see him that morning, with food and a couple of clean shirts. It had been her first visit, on account of this lingering weakness in her stomach. She'd hoped it was gone, more or less, but the jolting of the omnibus had left her so wracked with cramps that she'd been obliged to head directly upstairs, to the room Jimmy had been using, where she could rest without disturbance.

But now disturbance had found her out. The piano hit a crescendo, like a crate of bottles cast onto the ground, then, with barely a pause, lurched into another piece. Maud looked towards the hall, wondering how fast they could get away. 'What happened between you two?'

Jimmy released her hand. He'd thought of a few things of his own that he wanted to take with him, and began a rapid survey of the tools and materials that lay about, picking out this and that, tucking brushes and knives and pencils into his jacket pockets. 'A new friend had stopped by. The Marquess of Westminster.'

'Oh, the *marquess*, was it?'

'What can I say? His lordship wished to be shown the room. Word is going around, Maudie, of what has been done here. Everyone wishes to see it, from society and the press. And everyone who comes is quite awed.' Jimmy looked up at the majestic, mystical birds arrayed across the shutters, a trace of reflected gold colouring the whiteness of his throat. 'But then, honestly, how the devil could they be otherwise?'

Maud's stomach groaned; she swallowed, her amusement fading. The smells in the dining room seemed especially pungent that afternoon, the cloying, heady odour of varnish mixing disagreeably with the metallic tang of the Dutch metal.

'Our marquess, however, is not one merely to *admire* – no, my girl, he wanted it for himself. He's taken to me, I think. Told me he liked Americans, and Southerners in particular. Something to do with mental independence. At any rate, he was soon talking of how he would have me let loose on a wing of Eaton Hall. He was ready to make terms, right there and then.' Jimmy frowned; he gave his feathery white forelock a twist. 'But then Leyland showed himself. Fresh from a railway carriage and ready to kill, in that dead-eyed way of his. The marquess's compliments were thrown back in his face. The room, and by extension its creator, were maligned most viciously. And this nobleman, this fine person of taste and manners, was all but ejected from the premises.' He snatched his cane – a length of bamboo, rather longer than was usual – from the corner in which it had been left and marched back to the door. 'I really cannot stay here another moment. We must go, Maud. Now.'

Maud's hat was hanging on the back of a wooden chair, beneath an empty stretch of patterned leather on the south wall. It was straw, tied around with black taffeta; as she put it on, an uneasy sensation tightening around her midriff, she spotted a tin basin on the seat of the chair, used for thinning pigment but presently empty. Best to be safe, she thought, and tucked it under her arm.

Jimmy was beckoning, reaching out for her hand, starting them towards the front door as if they were running for a steamer. It was too much. After only a half dozen steps the basin slipped free, crashing against the marble floor. The lopsided sonata belting up from below broke off abruptly. Jimmy hissed a curse; and leaving the basin where it had landed, they hurried out into the street.

Leyland caught them thirty yards from the house. Jimmy was trying to flag down a hansom, which was proving rather difficult; he'd acquired a reputation among the cabmen of Prince's Gate for pennilessness, for partially paid fares and absent tips, and the first few that went by ignored his hails completely. Maud watched Leyland approach, pulling a little nervously on Jimmy's sleeve, but he affected not to notice until the shipbroker was directly beside them.

'Whistler,' said Leyland, 'you will finish the room.'

Jimmy stood back from the kerb. 'But why on earth would you want that, *mon cher*,' he said, squinting at the dreary sky, 'when you consider it such a calamity? Surely it would be best to start anew, with an artist more suited to your preferences?'

'You are too close to completion. I will see it done, and your price agreed.'

The shipbroker was a tall, straight sort of man, standing a good foot over Jimmy and Maud. A neat dark beard masked a narrow chin, while blank black eyes stared from beneath a broad forehead. He was wearing his standard, somewhat peculiar costume: a black suit and elaborately frilled shirt, with shiny, buckled shoes, like a music-hall undertaker. There was nothing music-hall about his manner, though – he was utterly cold, his voice without expression. Maud had actually met him on three previous occasions, for dinners at Lindsey Row, at which he'd been awkward, humourless, quite unable to blend with the artists, writers and actresses seated around him. They hadn't conversed exactly, but they had spoken. Those black eyes had roamed over her, proprietorial and unashamed. Now he paid her no notice at all.

'We are to make our terms here in the street, are we?' Jimmy asked. He was using his performance voice, Maud noticed, which was rather more high-pitched than normal, with everything exaggerated – the American vowels yet longer and the Frenchified flourishes more pronounced. 'Like men haggling over a horse?'

Leyland waited.

'Two thousand guineas, then. There's my price. That's what I asked you for, if you recall.'

Maud turned away, smothering a laugh. He was joking, surely. The dining room was extremely fine, of course it was – but two thousand guineas? That was enough to buy the bloody house it stood in.

Jimmy was perfectly in earnest, however. 'Four hundred apiece for the three peacock shutters,' he said, 'and a further eight hundred for the rest. Very fair, Leyland, by any yardstick.'

'Do not test me, Whistler. I could have you barred from the house. I could have those peacocks of yours torn out and burned in the garden.'

There was condescension in the shipbroker now. He believed he had Jimmy outclassed, that this was a matter of bargaining, of forming a contract – his province. Regardless of what he thought of the room, the fellow's pride plainly insisted on victory, and the imposition of his will; that his artist be put in his place and led, chastened, back to work. Maud hugged herself, feeling the first spot of rain land upon her cheek. She knew for a cast-iron fact that it would not be as simple as that.

'You are right.' Jimmy inclined his head graciously, as if accepting a fault. 'You are quite right. My apologies. *Bon Dieu*, how appallingly rude of me. The decoration is an out-and-out disaster, after all, as you have ruled – as you have just declared so candidly to the Marquess of Westminster, and no doubt many others. The only honourable course, my dear Leyland, the only course open to me as a gentleman and a person of manners, is for us to take this sum of mine and split it between us. I will pay my thousand guineas, as my share in the dining room, and you will pay yours.'

A cab pulled up, a four-wheeler, the driver seeming to recognise Leyland. He leaned over to ask the destination; at close sight of the shipbroker he thought better of it.

'You are not serious.'

'I want justice.' Jimmy cracked the end of his cane emphatically against the pavement. 'We bear alike the humiliation of this affair, do we not? You for having entered into it so unknowingly; me for having disappointed so very publicly? It only seems right that we should therefore bear the expense in the same proportions. One thousand guineas apiece.'

The figure was uttered with a certain swagger, almost as if it was being attained rather than surrendered. Maud could sense Jimmy's satisfaction; she could imagine him at the head of their dinner table, in fact, recounting the exchange to laughter and applause. Her head was beginning to spin. She wanted badly to sit down.

Leyland looked to his gaudy shoe buckles, digesting this proposal. 'Should I consent,' he said, 'the sum would be my payment to you for the dining room, and a handsome payment indeed. There would be no question of it being half of anything.'

'*Naturellement*,' Jimmy replied, with an obliging nod. 'But I must be allowed the time I need. This is paramount, Leyland. I won't be hurried out or interrupted. I won't have your blessed caretaker always looking over my shoulder.'

'You will have the remainder of the year,' Leyland told him. 'I am leaving for Liverpool in the morning, and won't be returning to London until December at the earliest. I expect industry, though, Whistler. Promptitude.' He glanced Maud's way at last, and she had a keen, uncomfortable notion of how she must appear: half their age, pale and unkempt, hair falling from beneath her straw hat. Not respectable in the least. 'I cannot permit any more of this . . . coming and going. These visitors, whomsoever they may be.'

Jimmy opened the cab door, gave the driver their address and slung in his bag. 'It will be finished soon enough. I have no desire at all to prolong this experience, Leyland, believe me.' He reclaimed Maud's hand. 'I shall take Miss Franklin here home and see her settled, and then return early tomorrow.'

And just like that they were going, leaving the millionaire businessman standing on the pavement in the gathering rain. Leyland seemed to have been wrong-footed. He simply stood there, arms by his sides, as Jimmy closed the cab door behind them.

'One thousand,' he stated, by way of farewell. 'That is the agreement.'

*

'There you have it,' Jimmy declared. 'There you have the philistine, Maud, revealed in his full and most ignoble aspect.' The insouciant act was beginning to slip; Maud could see the anger quivering in his jaw. 'I have to say that the crudity of his methods has been surprising. That business with the Marquess of Westminster, that deliberate inso-lence, was done merely to *tenderise* me, don't you see, ahead of our little negotiation. This is the manner of creature we are dealing with here. A cut-throat professional.'

The cab turned out of Prince's Gate. Rain was falling steadily now; people were ducking into doorways and opening umbrellas.

'You asked him for two thousand guineas,' Maud murmured.

Saying the sum aloud amazed her all over again. She thought of the recent spate of dinners at Lindsey Row, dinners she'd been too sick to attend, held after Leyland's first reaction to the peacocks – councils of war, Jimmy had called them, with Godwin and Eldon and the rest of them. Had this figure been agreed then? There had certainly been a lot of laughter.

Jimmy crossed his hands atop his cane. 'Labour has been carried out, my girl. Payment has to follow. That's how it goes.'

'But – two thousand guineas, Jimmy?'

'Nothing had been agreed. Do your work, my friend Frederick Leyland said, and then let me know what I owe you. That's how it stood between us.'

Maud was annoyed, she realised, beneath her perplexity. She could see this for what it was. Provocation. Cheek. 'So knowing that he didn't care for what you'd done, you decided to ask him for a bloody *fortune*. What good did you imagine that would do?'

'The villain has twenty times that a year,' Jimmy countered. 'Many hundred times it in the bank. Gained, I might add, through business practices of the utmost ruthlessness. And anyway, Maudie, you heard what just happened. I have scaled back my bill. Let a thousand guineas go. It's quite the move, don't you think? The rejection of the yoke. A lesson in the limits of a millionaire's power.'

He ran on for a while, growing increasingly pleased with himself – conceding that the lost money was significant, undeniably, but would soon be made elsewhere, once word of the dining room's beauty had spread among people of true taste. Maud honestly didn't know what to make of it all. She was dog-tired, despite having slept through so much of the day. Once again, also, she was being assailed by unspeakable smells, of the kind that tended to linger in public carriages. Old cheese and filthy clothes. The foul stuff that gathered beneath your toenails. These odours seemed to reach into her, to coat the inside of her throat, to coil around her innards. She stared hard out of the window. They were still a good ten minutes from home – from the broken gate and the grimy front door; from the panelled hallway beyond, leading through to the back; from the small cobbled yard and the outhouse in its corner.

Jimmy had fished his tobacco pouch from his pocket, along with a couple of papers. He rolled them both a cigarette, passing hers over. Maud accepted it, knowing that she could no sooner smoke the damned thing than eat it whole. He put a match to his own and a new aroma filled that tiny, rocking box. Maud liked to smoke, always had, since she was ten years old. Now, though, the smell of it made her think of bitumen and burnt hair, of blood blackening on a butcher's floor, of something poisonous and revolting. The cab slowed, approaching a corner. Her fingers closed around the door handle and she was out, clinging to a lamp post like it was a ship's mast in a storm, swinging around and sliding down, coughing up a rope of treacly, yellow-green bile in the rough direction of the gutter.

It went on for a while, until her convulsions produced only a ghastly croaking sound. Jimmy was close by, perhaps two feet away. Oblivious to the rain, he was sitting on the high kerb, his leather bag beside him, finishing off his cigarette. Behind him was a parade of fine shops, their lamps alight. Traffic was rolling past, all hooves and horse legs and spinning spokes. Their cab was nowhere to be seen.

'Could it have been an oyster?' he mused. 'Or that trout, maybe, that we had the Wednesday before last? River fish, Maudie, should never be trusted. One simply does not know what they've been swimming through. Why, if I were—'

'There's a child,' Maud said.

She released the lamp post and leaned against it, trying to straighten her hat. Her gown was wet through across the shoulders; a cold drip weaved inside her corset, running down to the small of her back. It had been obvious. A sickness that can't be shaken. Constant, deadening fatigue.

The horrible intensity of smells. And the courses, the blasted courses, late now by more than a week. For nearly four years Maud had managed to avoid even the slightest scare. She knew when the lapse had occurred, though – she knew at once. It had been on the morning Jimmy had finished the shutters. She'd come over to Prince's Gate, having not seen him for five straight days; and those peacocks, those extraordinary, mystical creatures, had been there to greet her, seeming to have blinked into existence at the snap of Jimmy's gold-smeared fingers. He'd been up all night and was quite wild with exultation, proclaiming his deep delight that it was her – his *Madame*, his muse, his sacred partner – who'd been the first to stand before them. She was there, he'd said, in the peacocks – could she not see it? The raw elegance in those necks, in those trailing tails? It was hers.

They'd moved closer, arms entwining, talking excitedly of how pleased the Leylands would be when they took up residence there, and the great advancement it would surely bring. She'd glanced at him admiringly; he'd caught her eye and held it, in a kind of dare; and it had happened, right there on the floorboards, amid the pots and brushes and screwed-up bits of paper.

Jimmy was quiet for a minute. Then he flicked his cigarette end into a drain and began to speak about Charlie, his six-year-old son, who was lodged somewhere near Hyde Park in an arrangement that was satisfactory for everyone. This didn't bring much reassurance, however, either to Maud or Jimmy himself. He stopped mid-sentence, pinching the bridge of his nose, thinking no doubt of the money – the thickening wad of bills on the hall dresser; the back rent due on their damp little house; the deal he'd just made with Leyland, and the different terms that might have been reached.

'We'll find an answer,' he said at last. 'We will.'

Maud drew in a shivering breath. She knew what was required of her. The babe would arrive, and the babe would go – to a foster family elsewhere in London most probably. Jimmy wouldn't have children under his roof. He'd made that plain from the beginning: inimical to art, he'd said. And dear God, Maud didn't want it either! She was a model, for goodness sake – training to be an artist herself, with Jimmy's tutelage and encouragement. This could wreck it all. She pressed a palm against her forehead. How could she have been so careless? So bloody *stupid*?

'Edie will help,' she muttered. 'She knows people, I think, back in Kentish Town.'

Saying her sister's name prompted a series of sudden thoughts, each one weightier and more unwelcome than the last. Sooner or later, she was going to have to visit Edie and submit to a barrage of I-told-you-so's. Her slender body, starved with such discipline, would swell up to a grotesque size. Jimmy would have to find another model, a girl who might well be better and end up replacing her for good. And she was going to have to give birth. Lord above. All that blood and pain and madness. She gulped, and gasped; and she leaned over sharply to be sick again.

October 1876

Swooping in through the door of the Knightsbridge telegraph office, Jim snatched up a form and a pencil from the counter and settled himself ill-temperedly in a corner. For a second or two he took in the hushed, assiduous atmosphere, the smell of ink and electrical wire, the tap-tapping of the machines. Then he inserted the eyeglass and began to write.

Have received your cheque at last.

He hesitated. This really didn't do justice to the indignities of the weekend. Scratching together enough coin for basic sustenance had taxed his ingenuity – and he'd give much, much indeed, to forget the disdainful gratification on the landlord's boiled-beef face as another two days' grace had been begged of him.

Pounds I notice.

The pencil, gripped very fiercely, now popped out from between Jim's fingertips, disappearing onto the floor. He bit back an exclamation. This was no good. Already he'd used nearly a third of the available space. A telegram might be immediate, but there was insufficient room for his anger to unfurl its wings. He needed to write an old-fashioned letter, signed with the Whistler butterfly – copied and numbered, as had become his habit in this particular correspondence. Publication, both the threat and the reality, was a weapon he was perfectly prepared to wield. Why the devil not? Let the vindictive philistine be hoist by his own petard. He had a supply of pens and paper at Prince's Gate. The notion of composing a damning missive under its recipient's own roof had a compelling audacity to it; so Jim tore the telegraph form in half, then quarters, then eighths, returned the eyeglass to his breast pocket and strode back onto the Brompton Road.

He quickly became aware that someone in the telegraph office had followed him out. This fellow had fallen in a few feet behind, but was now drawing level, leaning in to peer beneath the brim of Jim's hat. He was tall, substantially built and clad in pale grey.

'Jimmy,' he said. 'Jimmy Whistler, my dear chap.'

Jim didn't slow down. He recognised this voice: the foreign accent, slight but distinct, married rather curiously to a very English turn of phrase. 'The Owl,' he said.

'How—' The man weaved around a street-sweeper filling a sack with dead leaves. 'How are you keeping, Jimmy?'

Looking sideways, Jim saw a long, reddish-brown moustache, a bright enamelled tiepin, and that decoration on his lapel, the folded strip of scarlet ribbon, said to be an honour of some kind from his native land. He knew this man well, or had done: Owl, the resourceful Anglo-Portuguese, an unequalled repository of art knowledge, on familiar terms with everyone. They hadn't spoken, however, in at least five years; Owl remained close to a number of people Jim no longer saw. Whether this was by drift or rift he could scarcely remember.

'You still Rossetti's man, Owl?'

'That,' answered Owl, assuming a regretful air, 'is a complicated question. Gabriel is a blessedly complicated cove. I may as well tell you, however, that it is coming to an end. I fear he and I have done all that we can do. I know that you two have long ceased your intimacy, Jimmy, but I fear for his health. He barely sleeps these days. Why, only the other week Watts arrived at dawn to find him up a tree in his nightshirt. Out on the Walk, this was – practically dangling over the bloody river. He claimed to be counting off the stars. Luckily I was on hand as well. Ended up luring the poor devil down with a beaker of brandy.'

This was Owl, Jim recalled, to the absolute degree. Some men wrote, some painted, some founded factories, or drew up legislation, or commanded troops in battle. The Owl talked. He had a tale for every situation, an endless roll of gossip and indiscretion – things that he really shouldn't be repeating but was anyway, with every detail vividly and enthusiastically imparted.

'Frederick Leyland, they say, is half mad with worry,' Owl went on. 'Watts tells me that he makes a special point of coming round whenever he's in town – to spend time, you know, and discuss how he will arrange Gabriel's canvases in his new London pile. I've heard talk of commissions as well. For the future. Something large.' He paused. 'Are you still engaged on the decoration there? Is that what brings you to this neck of the woods?'

Jim came close to smiling here – not an especially subtle fellow, this Owl – but his amusement was hindered by unease. So Rossetti got Leyland's respect. Rossetti got shows of concern and allowances made, and further work promised to him. And for what? Certainly nothing as glorious as that dining room. Not by a very long distance. Jim's unease grew into resentment. It was quite preoccupying. His eyes glazed over; he clicked his thumbnail against one of the ridges in his bamboo cane. He had to force his mind back to Owl's enquiry.

'Barely,' he replied. 'Today might well see the last of it.' After which, he thought, I shall be gone. I shall flee that blasted place like it was Bluebeard's oubliette. 'I've other things to be doing. My contribution to the Grosvenor Gallery, for instance.'

'Yes indeed,' said Owl. 'Sir Coutts Lindsay's exhibition. I'd heard that he'd approached you.' An eagerness had crept into him, of the sort that preceded the asking of a favour.

'I'd like very much to see the room, Jimmy, if I may. Since we are so close to it. Just for a few minutes, as you apply the finishing touches. What d'you say? Can it be done?'

The two men had arrived at the corner of Prince's Gate; ahead were the Botanical Gardens, the glass roof glittering through a screen of denuded branches. Jim considered the Owl – his languid, humorous eyes, his squarish forehead and rounded chin, the high shine of his expensive-looking top-boots. This was a cavalier, a dandy of the slickest stripe, but his keenness was disarming. That morning, the prospect of showing the peacocks to someone who might value them had a definite appeal. Jim nodded in the direction of Leyland's house.

Although perhaps a foregone conclusion, Owl's opinion of the dining room was expressed with his usual flair. 'Transporting,' he declared, after two reverential circuits. 'A chamber utterly apart from the rest of the world, far beyond its troubles and interruptions. It is like – it is like being at the pinnacle of a lofty tower. Or in a gilded car slung beneath a balloon, floating a mile above London.'

How could Jim, propped against the sideboard, not grin at this? 'Yes, well,' he said, prodding at an empty varnish tin with his cane, 'I'm afraid that the patron may disagree.'

'Leyland? What else can you expect, though, from such a creature? The fellow is callousness made flesh. A shark, old man, of the Great White variety.'

'Why Owl,' Jim observed, 'you appear to know the gentleman.'

'It is impossible, my dear Jimmy, to work on Gabriel Rossetti's behalf and avoid him. There's a fascination between them. A kinship, if you like, despite the obvious differences.' Owl turned back to the room. 'We've done a deal or two of our own as well, over the years. That Rembrandt head, do you remember?'

Jim did. Rembrandt, in his view, had been a rather optimistic attribution.

'You can take a cur,' Owl continued, 'from the alleys of Liverpool. You can give it an ocean-spanning armada of iron-clad vessels. You can wash its hide, and dress it in mountebank frills and silver shoe buckles. And it is still, under it all, a cur. You can see it in Leyland's eyes, very clearly. The way he looks at you as if he'd gladly bite off your damned hand. Did you know that his mother ran a pie-shop, back in his home city? Down on the quay?'

Owl spoke incautiously, without so much as a glance out towards the hall, apparently indifferent to the fact that he was standing in Leyland's house; that anybody could be listening in, as far as they knew, even the cur himself. It was a display, Jim realised this, staged for his benefit, but there could be no denying the nerve involved.

'I'd heard,' he said.

'And yet you were caught out by his reaction to your room?' Owl faced him again. 'Forgive me, Jimmy, but this is no enlightened prince. This is Frederick Richards Leyland. The most hated man in Liverpool. This is the modern British businessman, in all his bone-headed viciousness.'

'I have received a schooling, this past week,' Jim admitted, 'in business wisdom – as Leyland understands it.'

'He has paid you what he owes, though, hasn't he?'

And then, almost to Jim's surprise, he was telling the Owl everything. He abandoned his remote, stoical stance – profoundly uncharacteristic as it was – and provided a full account of his travails, assuming the same confidence, the same disregard for discretion, as his companion, relishing every disclosure and the sympathy with which it was received. The climax, the peak of indignation, was reserved for the events of that same morning.

'So I set aside my material needs – which are grave, I don't mind saying – and hatch a deal that is wholly to his advantage. He tells me to name my price, Owl, so I do, and when this is deemed unacceptable I agree to take only half of the rightful sum – rewarding him, in essence, for his philistinism. He makes me wait for it, of course. Three rather trying days. Yet finally it arrives. *Bon Dieu!* The trumpets sound – the angels sing. I tear open the envelope.'

Owl was listening intently.

'It was pounds. *Pounds*, Owl! We have moved from the guinea of tradition, of honour – with which he has always paid me in the past – to the base sovereign, the payment of tradesmen. My fee was shorn of its shillings, and left fifty quid lighter as a result. I swear I nearly threw the thing on the fire.'

There was some truth to this. At the breakfast table, Jim had waved the offending cheque aloft, holding forth about how it was a vulgar insult and warranted immediate destruction. After a minute, Maud had risen from her chair and come to his side, to offer consolation he'd thought; but instead she'd plucked the crumpled rectangle of paper from his grasp, smoothed it against her thigh and tucked it into her sleeve for safekeeping.

Owl understood, however, in a way that dear Maud simply could not. 'It's the best the brute can do,' he said. 'The one stone he has left to throw. I pity him, almost.' He gestured towards the room. 'This, though – this alone remains the fact. All else is mere anecdote. Our friend Leyland has earned himself much the same place in history as the dullard who paid Correggio in pennies.'

Jim liked this. 'Indeed.'

'So in sum,' said Owl, producing a cigarette case and offering one to Jim, 'your patron works you like a slave. Looks upon your works with no more feeling than a beast of the field. Pays you like a joiner, or a greengrocer, or the man who brings him those frilled shirts of his, and less than half the proper amount.' He struck a match and held it out. 'Jimmy old man, I'd say this room was half yours, half yours at least. To do with as you damn well please. Remove the shutters, these wondrous peacocks, and sell them elsewhere. Enhance the design, if you see fit.'

'Enhance?' Jim, sensing criticism, was suddenly alert. 'What d'you mean?'

Owl lit his own cigarette, untroubled by the sharpness of Jim's tone. 'The shutters are magisterial,' he said. 'It's the only word. Hiroshige has been eclipsed. And the patterns, these feather motifs – again, exceptional, beyond fault. This, however, this leather . . .' He pointed to the panels that stretched behind the shelves and spanned the empty space above the sideboard and fireplace. 'You've made an attempt, I see that. But it doesn't go. The flowers look Dutch, for God's sake.'

He was right. Jim knew it at once. There was a challenge here too, plain as day. *You have been supine*, Owl was saying. *Supplicatory. Is this really how an artist should behave?*

'They are antique,' Jim said. 'Several hundred years old, I'm told.'

Owl shrugged. He puffed on his cigarette. 'It doesn't go.'

*

December 1876

The front door opened, admitting a current of wintry wind; it nosed through the papers scattered across the dining-room floor, lifting the large mural cartoon like the airing of a bedsheet. Jim scowled atop his stepladder. Young Walter Greaves, dispatched on an errand an hour or so earlier, had been instructed most firmly not to use the main entrance. He was shouting out something to this effect when Maud hushed him. She'd been sitting in a corner, wearing her coat, reading one of the art papers; but now she was up, already on her way outside, making for the French doors behind the central set of shutters. He glanced down at her. Several months had now passed, yet he could detect no outward sign of her condition. Her face retained its striking angularity; her figure was as lissom as ever. A small part of him continued to hope that it was a false alarm.

'Jimmy,' she said. 'That isn't Walt.'

Jim cocked his head to listen. From the hall came not the assistant's hob-nailed thuds but the sigh of fine fabric, dragging in folds across the bare stone. Maud left, closing the shutters silently behind her. Jim climbed from the stepladder and crept to the doorway. Mrs Leyland and Florence, the middle daughter, were standing in the unlit hall, little more than dark shapes against the marble. Dressed for travel, they were looking around them in a faintly expectant fashion. A male servant came in and summoned the caretaker from his downstairs parlour. There was a brief exchange, then all eyes turned towards the dining room. Jim pulled back; he considered quickly how he should be found.

The room, thankfully, was brilliant. It had been enriched past hope or prediction by Jim's greatest change: the painting of those awkward leather panels with a deep, obliterating shade of Prussian blue. This had been a mighty feat indeed, demanding every last ounce of his strength and his vision. His hands and forearms were still stained a little, having a greenish, cadaverous hue; numerous aches hampered the movement of his shoulders, his elbows, his wrists. But none of this mattered. His satisfaction with the result was difficult to overstate. In certain sections — and particularly now, under gaslight — the effect was so smooth and intense that it quite confounded the notion of surface, the gilded shelves seeming to float before a field of pure colour. The whole thing was transformative. Entering the dining room changed your mood, the very feel of your skin.

And then there was the mural. Emblazoned across the southern wall — upon which Leyland had once talked of hanging one of Jim's own canvases — this was the feature with which he was most pleased of all. He chose a spot beneath it and darted over, arranging himself next to the sideboard.

The two fine Leyland ladies stood speechless, blinking as people do when brought forward suddenly into the light. They looked remarkably similar at first: the compact luxury of their clothes, the corseted uniformity of their figures, the handsome solemnity of their faces. Leyland, however, was in the daughter as well — those dark, baleful eyes, that regrettably broad forehead — and seemed even to taint her aesthetic responses; for as her mother's initial shock was replaced by a kind of incredulous regard, her own expression grew rather more negative.

'It is every bit as bad,' she announced, 'as it sounded in that wretched newspaper. Father will be furious. He will be *furious*.'

Commendably direct, Jim thought. He'd never seen this in Florence before: how old was she, eighteen? It was hard to keep track. Over the past five or six years he'd painted nearly every member of this family, starting with Ma and Pa and working down from there. Florence's portrait was the least complete of his Leyland pantheon, now stacked out of sight in a corner of the studio. She'd been a difficult subject, querulous and impatient and impossible to impress; and although wholly at leisure she'd granted him only four sittings, of a couple of hours each. Not at all how Jim liked to work. Luckily Maud had been on hand to stand in her place, just as she had done for the mother and elder sister – wearing the three different gowns, occupying the three different poses, with her usual ease.

'My only wish, Miss Leyland,' he said calmly, 'was to give yourself and your family the most beautiful room that has ever been.'

'Did you obtain my father's permission for this? For any of it?'

'I cannot apologise for *inspiration*, Miss, and the paths down which—'

'What of the leather? Did you pause, even, before turning it all blue?'

Flippancy here became irresistible. 'I did wonder for a moment if it would take the paint,' Jim answered. 'But it did, as you can see. Admirably.'

Florence's right hand tightened its grip upon her left. 'Mr Whistler, that leather was salvaged from a ship wrecked with the Spanish Armada. It cost my father a great deal.'

'And it did not harmonise with the rest. There is really

31

nothing more I can tell you, Miss Leyland. The colours, the patterns – they could not be made to work.'

This didn't satisfy Florence, not in the least, but she would argue no further. She informed her mother that she was going to look around upstairs, then strode back through the doorway, calling tartly for a lamp. Mrs Leyland, walking the length of the room, made no reply. Jim sensed that the day's journey had taken its toll upon family concord.

'My husband is in London,' she said, once Florence was out of earshot, 'and will be arriving soon. He left us at the station. Apparently there was a call he had to make.'

'I see.'

'We are not staying here. Frederick has booked a suite at the Alexandra.'

'My dear Mrs Leyland,' said Jim, 'I should hope you aren't. Why, most of the furniture is still in crates.'

'He has had a piano assembled, though, I assume?'

'*Bien sûr.* The poor instrument is beaten to its knees each time he crosses the threshold.'

Mrs Leyland's laugh was a shade too loud. 'As I believe we have observed before, Mr Whistler,' she said, 'he plays just as he goes about everything else.'

Unlike her daughter, Frances Leyland had sat willingly for her portrait. She'd given her time generously – had been reluctant to leave, in fact, even as the day grew dim. It hadn't taken much to prompt an unburdening. Perched on the studio chaise longue, wearing the loose flesh-pink gown in which Jim was painting her, she'd told him of the indifference and sullen silences, the dozens of petty abuses and betrayals – of a marriage warping into something intolerable. Jim had listened with sympathy and close interest, undeniably flattered by this sudden intimacy – yet also savouring the clandestine thrill of access to another man's most private affairs. Naturally, he'd promised to tell no one, pledging himself to a bond of secrecy. An alliance had thus been forged, and was further strengthened as Mrs Leyland's portrait had advanced almost to completion. Leyland had been unconcerned by this friendship, seeming to trust Jim as much as he trusted anyone. He had no inkling, needless to say, of its confidential depths.

Smiling still, Mrs Leyland laid a gloved hand upon her collarbone and looked around again at the absorbing richness of the blue, at the yards of lustrous feather-patterning, at the resplendent birds. 'It is not at all how I expected. It is like walking inside a jewel box. A Japanese cabinet.'

'My intention precisely,' said Jim. 'A *Japanese cabinet*. I am so glad, Mrs Leyland, that you at least can appreciate what I have done. Although, who knows – perhaps dear Florence is mistaken. Perhaps your husband will as well.'

The lady laughed again, at the improbability of this Jim supposed. The sound was caustic, and also strangely helpless. He was considering whether to express regret at how things had gone, or provide his justification, or simply to laugh himself, when he noticed that she was taking her first proper look at the mural behind him.

The two new peacocks faced each other across the

expanse of painted leather, the gilt in which they'd been depicted built up to a low relief. Their bodies were tense, their heads in hard profile; for despite their grace, and the sweeps of ornate plumage that framed them, these creatures were locked in confrontation.

Wonder had wiped everything else from Mrs Leyland's features. 'What is——?'

Jim stepped leftwards to improve her view. 'It is entitled *The Rich Peacock and the Poor Peacock*.'

'They are fighting.'

'The rich peacock would fight, yes. Certainly he would. See the angle of his wing, how he points with it so haught-ily – how he puffs up that great tail of his. How his beak opens to squawk his commands and the eye flashes a murderous red.' Jim glanced up: the eye-bead, twisted that same morning from the band of one of Maud's more flam-boyant hats, was pleasingly ruby-like. 'In contrast, the poor peacock meets this unwarranted aggression with firmness, but also with a noble resignation. With pride of a different type – a *deserved* pride. He steps back, Mrs Leyland. He will *not* fight.' He paused again, regarding this bird's as yet empty socket. 'That eye will be green. The green of peace and reason. Once a suitable stone has been located.'

'Are those – are those coins? Around the rich one's feet – in its feathers?'

'Shillings, madam,' Jim stated. 'They are *shillings*. Shorn, one might speculate, from guineas, leaving but neutered pounds behind. That the rich bird denies, in its meanness, despite the fact that they literally spill from it. That they are nothing to it.'

Mrs Leyland continued to stare at the painting, the reference lost on her. This was a detail her husband had omitted to share. Hardly surprising.

'You may note that these shillings are rendered in silver, as are various other details.' Jim pointed with his mahlstick. 'See the throat of the rich bird, for instance, and the fronds that frill along it so very modishly. And the poor bird – upon his head there . . .'

Whereas the rich peacock sported a golden comb, the poor one had a single plume of whitish silver, jutting out like a unicorn's horn – a forelock of Whistlerian prominence. What the image lacked in nuance, Jim felt, it compensated for in sheer poetic exquisiteness. Every time Leyland used the dining room, every time he threw a napkin over his frill and subjected a table of guests to his leaden conversation, he would see it. *Everyone* would see it. The mere fact of its existence made him want to seize hold of Mrs Leyland and waltz out into the hall.

'Some may claim to detect meaning in this scene,' Jim continued, 'an *allegory*, one might say. On this I could not possibly—'

'Mr Whistler.' Mrs Leyland's eyes were still fixed on the mural. The joke did not delight her – far from it. 'Mr Whistler, do you realise what you have done?'

July 1877

The force of Maud's anger caught her unawares. At first,
lost for words, she went stamping from room to room,
taking it out on the house – on Jimmy's precise and
oh-so-original decorations. She knocked pictures askew and
kicked up rugs, she heaved wickerwork armchairs out of
their places, she shoved down a Japanese screen. He
followed behind, correcting what he could, making vague
attempts at placation, as if even then the greater part of
his mind was elsewhere. After a few minutes of this they
reached the drawing room.

Maud turned abruptly to face him. 'How could it have
got so bad? Why d'you open the bloody door to them?
Don't you know anything?'

Jimmy didn't answer. He'd lit a cigarette and was leaning
back on his right foot, stroking his moustache thoughtfully,

angling himself towards the two tall windows. This was a familiar ploy of his when he wished to stage a retreat. *The artist is unexpectedly inspired*, said the pose. *Shhh! Don't disturb!*

Maud wasn't having it, though, not today. There was a new piece of porcelain by the divan, a squat, blue-and-white vase, shaped like an oversized onion and patterned with oriental flowers. She went over to it and hooked a toe under one side. The thing was easily unseated, but rather heavier than she'd anticipated; too late she realised that it was half filled with water. It rolled away in a wobbling semicircle onto the rectangle of yellow matting laid in the middle of the room, disgorging its contents in irregular spurts. A white lily appeared, coasting off towards the skirting board, and then a pair of plump, back-flipping goldfish.

This got Jimmy's attention at least. The artistic pose was dropped. Maud stood by, flushed with annoyance and the faintest touch of guilt, as he rushed across the room, righted the vase and attempted to save the fish. The cigarette fell from his lips and hissed out in the spillage; his eyeglass swung at the end of its cord, flashing in the dusty sunlight. He was not, in truth, very well suited to tasks such as this. The fish were sluggish enough but he could only catch hold of one of them; the other squirmed off beneath the divan, beyond his capacity for rescue.

'You shouldn't,' Maud told him. 'Keep them in a china bowl, I mean. Down in the dark. How would you like it?'

Jimmy shook water from his fingers. 'Maudie,' he said, 'you've missed so much.'

Maud crossed her arms; she looked around for something else to upset. This hardly needed saying. Six weeks earlier, as she'd taken her leave, he'd been claiming that victory was imminent – the Grosvenor had opened to fanfares and he was poised to recover, in a single swoop, every last penny of their missing fortunes. And yet he'd greeted her today not with news of guineas, of sales and fresh commissions, but of *bailiffs*. The very word knotted her insides. Jimmy, though, had said it matter-of-factly. There was no secretiveness in him; no particular shame either. Two men, he'd reported, had called early yesterday morning, appointed by the Sheriff of Middlesex. He couldn't recall who'd sent them; there were papers in the hall. Although perfectly polite, and better bred than one might imagine, they'd departed only after he'd produced ten pounds in cash, a broken pocket watch and some opal earrings that had belonged to Maud's mother.

'You said we'd be set right. You bloody *promised it*, Jimmy. You said we'd be able to talk things through. Don't you remember? Move the child a bit closer. Find a woman in Battersea, or – or—'

The anger sputtered; Maud's thoughts were straying in an unwelcome direction. The absence. The coldness in the crook of her arm. The sense of something very close at hand, something vitally and profoundly *hers*, that wasn't being seen to. She'd been forewarned; she'd considered herself prepared. And it had beaten her to the floor. Five more days she'd remained at Edie's after the foster mother had left – until her milk had ebbed almost to nothing, and the worst of the bleeding had seemed to be over. *We'll get you all cried out*, Edie had said. Maud knew now, there in the drawing room at Lindsey Row, that five days hadn't been nearly long enough. Jimmy would be sympathetic, of course he would. But only up to a point. They had an agreement – and with bailiffs at the door, any chance of amending it was gone.

'We *will* be set right,' Jimmy said, rising to his feet. 'You'll see, Maudie. I'll buy you those earrings back.'

He misses it, Maud thought. *He misses it by a bloody mile.* Immediately her anger was restored to its full, scalding strength. She found that she was glaring at his hair, so carefully oiled and arranged; she saw herself grasping that single white lock and ripping it out at the root. The urge was resisted, just about. Instead she began telling him exactly *what he was*, drawing on a reserve of the ripest London slurs; and even after all the years he'd lived in the city, and the many battles they'd fought, a couple of these left him wrinkling his nose in bafflement.

The list ran on. Jimmy weathered it with the air of a man marking time, swivelling very slowly on his heel – then coming to a halt as he spied something outside. The drawing room was on the first floor, providing a broad view of the slow, brown Thames and the road that ran along its bank. Suddenly deaf to Maud's invective, he went over to the right-hand window, dragged up the sash and leant out a few inches further than was safe, shouting a name with undisguised relief.

Maud fell into a glowering silence. She'd missed the name and could make out little of what was being said now, but this was clearly a friend. She edged sideways to peer out of the other window. All she saw was hats, a grey topper and a curious affair in rose felt, heading underneath the sill towards their front door. It was not one person but a pair – a couple. And Jimmy had invited them up. He ducked back in, strolled to a sideboard and began rolling another cigarette.

'Stay there,' he said lightly. 'Don't worry – they're really not the sort to object. They're rather keen to meet you, in fact.'

Any control Maud might have had was gone. She looked to the door, sorely tempted to ignore Jimmy and withdraw anyway. Fatigue was fast overwhelming her anger. Her bosom ached – Edie had laced the corset very forgivingly, yet still she seemed to strain against it – and further down, around the base of her belly, a sharper pain was stirring. She could go upstairs. Strip to her shift. Bury herself in their bed. But there were footfalls out on the landing – shapes blocking the line of light beneath the door. It was too late.

The callers made an assured entrance, striding in across the yellow matting. Maud's initial impression was of height and handsomeness, and well-made, slightly unusual clothes. The gentleman trailed cigarette smoke; his companion wore a dark blue jacket that accentuated how very slender and pale she was.

'*The Harmony in Amber and Black*,' declared the gentleman.
'*The Arrangement in Brown*. By Jove, Rosie, she is before us.
Before us completely.'

They advanced towards Maud, regarding her with the
close appreciation you might give a statue or a particularly
interesting piece of furniture. Both were smiling. The
drawing room felt dingier, smaller; Maud became aware of
the rotten-egg smell of summer mud, oozing in through
the open window.

'I mean, it is uncanny,' the gentleman continued, glancing
over at Jimmy. He had a fine voice, warm and deep with
the touch of an accent – Spanish, Maud thought. 'Your
portraits, dear fellow – they are more than likenesses. So
much more. There's a *core* to them, I'd say, a true artistic
understanding. They get to the bottom of the matter. The
essence.'

Maud looked at Jimmy. He could be prickly with praise;
she'd heard him dismiss it, dismiss it with real violence, if
he thought it misguided or insensible to his aims. That
afternoon, however, he simply nodded in acknowledgement, then screwed in the eyeglass and smiled – the kind
of wide, unguarded grin you'd only see in the company of
those he genuinely liked. Two cigarettes had been rolled:
he lit both, passing one to this new arrival. The Spanish
gentleman sucked a last lungful from the butt already lodged
between his fingers, flicked it deftly out through the window
and accepted the next with a murmur of thanks.

'Miss Corder,' said Jimmy, 'may I be so frightfully

unnecessary as to introduce Miss Maud Franklin.' He puffed on his cigarette, making a back-and-forth gesture. 'Miss Franklin – Miss Rosa Corder.'

A hand was extended, in a glove the same pinkish colour as the felt hat. 'Charmed, Miss Franklin, truly.'

Miss Corder's voice was difficult to get the measure of. Respectable, if not quite quality; confident but also unassuming, somehow; wholly in earnest, yet tinted with laughter. Maud had been eyeing her cagily during Jimmy's introduction, thinking that she might well be a model. A substitute. She certainly had the figure for it. Now, though, such fears could be disregarded. Maud had never met a model who spoke like this.

'We know you, of course, from the Grosvenor,' Miss Corder explained. 'The pictures were so very beautiful. Do forgive us if we stare a little.'

Normally Maud would respond to a comment like this with self-effacement – perhaps something like, 'Really I just stood there, that's all' – which would lead to discussion of her stamina, her patience and fortitude and so on, in the face of Jimmy's famously gruelling requirements. That afternoon in the drawing room, however, she managed only a non-committal mumble. She was painfully conscious of their gaze upon her; of her swollen, ill-clad, exhausted body; of her complexion, drawn by stress and sorrow. She took Miss Corder's offered hand. There was a strength in the long fingers that reminded her oddly of Jimmy's.

'I am glad you are back safely,' Miss Corder added, more quietly. 'I hope we will be friends.'

I'm glad you are back safely. Maud met her eye. She saw nothing there but good intentions – a slightly insistent kindliness. This strange pair obviously knew far more about things at Lindsey Row than Jimmy was supposed to have revealed to anyone. They'd been primed, Maud realised, and this amiable little scene arranged in advance. They knew what their arrival had interrupted. They were there specifically to deliver Jimmy from the trouble that was sure to attend upon her return, without their daughter, to news of bailiffs. This was another of his favourite stratagems – to seek refuge in company, drowning any difficulty in the bottomless pool of his acquaintance.

'And this creature here, Maudie—' Jimmy paused for effect, twisting the left point of his moustache, 'is the splendid and most illustrious Owl.'

The Spanish gentleman made no comment on this peculiar introduction. He gave a shallow bow, smoke winding from his nostrils. 'May I simply say, Miss Franklin, that in your presence one feels most clearly the intense and singular charge of inspiration. The Muse's aura hangs heavy in the air. You are part of an exceptional group, Miss – an eternal being akin to Rembrandt's Hendrickje, or Leonardo's Mona Lisa, or the Bourbon princesses of our great god Velázquez.'

Maud laughed, she couldn't help it – a hard, sceptical snort. This Owl was definitely one of Jimmy's people. Beyond that, though, he wasn't easy to classify. His manner was too smooth for a poet or a painter; his looming, leonine person too neat, too well tended for the stage. He lacked the careless superiority of a man of leisure, and a couple of unconventional details in his dress – the spare cut of his dove-grey suit, that red ribbon pinned to his lapel like some kind of military decoration – seemed to disqualify him from the law or most branches of business. There was the foreign aspect as well, the hint of *elsewhere* – could he be a diplomat? A journalist? Maud honestly couldn't tell.

Plainly thinking he'd slipped the hook, and enjoying himself immensely, Jimmy sauntered to the door and called downstairs for John. Maud's hackles rose anew. This low little trick mustn't be allowed to pass unchallenged.

'Do you reside here in Chelsea, then, *Mr Owl*?' Saying the name felt ridiculous, childish; she gave it a mocking emphasis. 'Or did you just happen to be passing by?'

'Putney,' Owl replied pleasantly. He drew a card from his waistcoat pocket and presented it to her. 'We often come this way when travelling to Miss Corder's lodgings in the city. Rosie likes to walk beside the river.'

The card lay face down in Maud's palm. She turned it over and read: *Charles Augustus Howell, Esq., Chaldon House, Putney*. There it was. 'Owl' would be a common pronunciation of this surname in London. It was a very English handle, though, for a rather unEnglish person. No profession was given, she noticed, and no house number or street either; the suggestion was of a squire in his manor. She considered what he'd told her. Their guests were a gentleman and his mistress, with her installed at his convenience in an apartment closer to town – an arrangement almost disappointing in its ordinariness.

John appeared in the doorway. He noted Owl's presence with wary recognition. The servant obviously hadn't let this couple in or shown them up, as might have been assumed. The Owl at least had been to Lindsey Row before and knew his way around. Maud's brow furrowed – hadn't the front door been locked? Did he have a *key?*

'Sherry,' said Jimmy, 'and the last of the buckwheat cakes. In the studio, if you please.'

'No sherry left.'

'A bottle of the Muscadet, then.'

John shook his head.

'The Scharzhofberger? Surely we still have some of that?'

The servant hesitated; he gave a quick nod and made to turn away. Remembering the onion-shaped vase, Maud bent down and gripped it by the lip. A muscle in her midriff contracted; the pain was so astonishing that she nearly cried out. For a second or two, through a lens of tears, she watched the remaining goldfish wriggle weakly in an inch of cloudy water. Then she straightened up, wiped her eyes on her sleeve and held the vase towards the doorway.

'Put this poor thing in another bowl, would you?' she said, keeping her voice steady. 'Something glass. And fetch a broom. There's a dead one under the divan.'

John took it readily enough. He didn't always heed Maud,

but wouldn't risk a fuss in front of his master. Owl, meanwhile, was studying the floor, the boards and the soaked patch of matting, tracing the pattern of splashes with the tip of his cigarette. He went to the divan, dropped to a crouch and reached into the shadows beneath – standing again a moment later with the missing fish in his hand. The tiny body was quite motionless and furred with dust. Expertly, Owl placed a fingertip against it, where the orange flank met the silvery underbelly. He gave it the gentlest of prods; the frond-like tail beat about, and for a second a fin was raised upwards like a miniature sail.

'*Bon Dieu*, it lives!' cried Jimmy, with a short, piercing laugh. 'A Lazarus, what! A Lazarus among goldfish!'

Maud blinked. How long had it been since she'd spilled the fish? Four minutes, five? How could it possibly still be alive? As she craned her neck to see, Owl tossed the fish across the room, towards the vase – a light-hearted lob somewhat at odds with the eerie tenderness of the revival. His aim was true, though; it landed in the water with a hard hollow plop.

'There, John,' he said. 'Never say that I have no gold for you.'

*

A display had been arranged in the studio, a dozen or so of the finest paintings currently in Jim's hands, fixed onto easels or propped against the walls. There were his night-time views of the river, the *Nocturnes*, rendered in bands of luminous, misty blue; the Cremorne Gardens or some-where like it, where half-formed figures drifted in golden fog; a couple of unclaimed, unfinished portraits; and Maud herself, Maud time and again, in an assortment of costumes and attitudes. Over the years Jimmy had painted her in the flowing tea-gowns of the artistic rich, peasant skirts and bodices, and bold modern garments that had fitted around her body like a sleeve.

Maud stayed close to the studio door. The muscle in her side still throbbed something awful. She rubbed at it, and was briefly taken aback by the amount of flesh her corset contained. She glanced at the Owl and his consort. They'd surely be making the comparison now, if they hadn't already up in the drawing room. How could they not, with these paintings arrayed in front of them? They'd be lamenting the speed of Maud's decline, and doubting her ability to recover; and wondering, perhaps, what Jimmy planned to do about it. Humiliation began to enfold her, but she clenched her teeth and forced it away. She wouldn't be shamed by what had happened. She just *wouldn't*. Inwardly, she dared these guests to make a remark. To raise an eyebrow. Anything.

Miss Corder had gone to the pictures, however, lost in veneration. She'd approached a full-length figure – Maud in white and black, her hands set on her hips, as modishly elegant as a Paris fashion plate. Owl, meanwhile, had taken up a position over by the French windows. After declaring Jimmy's paintings beyond approbation, the great art of the age, he'd produced a pencil and a notebook and

47

begun to write. It was a conspicuously businesslike response; he appeared to be compiling an inventory. Maud had been hoping that he might actually be a customer – that Jimmy had got the canvases out so that he could make his selection and furnish them with a few dozen much-needed guineas. She saw now that this couldn't be the case. Customers did not make lists; if Mr Howell had dealings in the art trade, it was plainly on the selling side. His attendance at Lindsey Row was no accident, as she'd realised upstairs, but there was more to it than simply providing a distraction. Some form of arrangement was being set in place.

'Is this all of them?'

'Well, you know . . .' Jimmy was in the middle of the room, smoking his cigarette. 'There are a couple elsewhere in the house. Things being finished off. And there's the Grosvenor, of course. Eight more canvases.'

Maud surveyed the studio again, and this time noticed a couple of absences. Most conspicuous was the portrait of Jimmy's mother. He was especially attached to this picture – and somewhat more attentive to its well-being, she'd heard others imply, than he was to that of its model. Maud hadn't seen it in the drawing room either, or the parlour, or any of the downstairs corridors. Jimmy had moved it well out of the way.

'The Grosvenor paintings are yours?'

'All the important ones. We still have an expectation of sales, a strong expectation. The exhibition has three weeks left to run. Stands to reason that the big buyers will wait until the end.'

Owl was nodding sagely. 'That can be a pattern at shows of this kind.'

This sounded unlikely to Maud. She said nothing, though, as Jimmy was now talking with some candour about how tough things were becoming at Lindsey Row – the outstanding bills, the mounting legal threats, the bailiffs. It was a confession of sorts, a statement of failure, and his spirits dipped accordingly.

'It's difficult, old man,' he concluded, 'damned difficult. Each and every path seems to promise only fresh disaster.'

Maud felt the beginnings of pity. He was shaken. He needed her, in his way – his ally in penury. She hardened her heart, though, directing her eyes firmly towards the uneven herringbone floor. He deserved her anger. It shouldn't be that easy.

Owl stepped in. 'Well, there's a great deal we can do here. These works of yours mayn't have buyers, Jimmy, not yet, but they certainly have value. In abundance. The means are before us to generate nothing less than a fortune. From the paintings, and the copperplates as well.' For all the ambitiousness of his words, his voice was level. Reasonable. 'As for the bailiffs, what can I say? It shan't happen a second time. I can promise you that. We shall build a barrier around you, my dear chap – a barrier of gold two miles high, and every one of these accursed philistines will be shut out for good.'

Maud's doubt must have been showing, for Jimmy approached her, his composure regained, to offer some reassurance. 'The Owl, Maudie,' he said, 'has worked deals that mystify the mind. That send the soul soaring.'

A cigarette was burning between his fingers. Maud plucked it out, deciding right then that she was ready to smoke again, and little caring what these guests might think about it. Jimmy's tobacco was fine, smooth and strong; one puff set her fingertips tingling. She tilted back her head to exhale, holding his eye. 'Like what?'

Jimmy turned to Owl. 'Rossetti's painting, the last one you handled,' he asked. 'That woman, you know, with those monstrous shoulders. How much did you get? It was all anyone talked of for weeks.'

'A gentleman of my acquaintance,' replied Owl, marvellously offhand, 'paid us two thousand guineas.'

Maud coughed on the cigarette, soreness flaring along her side. That was the same sum Jimmy had asked for the entire Peacock Room, as everybody had taken to calling it. The sum he'd been denied. And this fellow was getting it for a single painting. Hope returned, despite her determined wariness; it was breaking through her like a lantern's light. Everything could change. Their debts could be wiped clean away. Jimmy could be made wealthy. They could travel. Their trip to Italy, to Venice, so long postponed now that the idea had nearly lost all meaning, could be made at last. And dear God, they could talk of Ione. Of their daughter. Maud saw her ruddy hands, bunching the midwife's shawl, and those glassy blue eyes; she felt the press of the child's feet against her thigh. She couldn't ever live with them. This Maud accepted. But if there was to be money, a second property could surely be rented nearby – in Chelsea even. A nurse could be employed. Or the foster family moved in. It had to be possible.

'A fair figure,' said Miss Corder, from across the studio. 'Very fair. Why shouldn't he pay that? What is he, a banker? A merchant? He should have paid more.'

'And I could assuredly have got more,' Owl told her, 'had I been given another week. No question of it. But you know how damned impatient Gabriel can be.' He removed his top hat, revealing a head of glossy auburn hair as oiled as Jimmy's. 'Where do things stand with the large picture over yonder? *The Three Girls*?'

This painting had been given only a secondary placing in Jimmy's little display, out of the studio's best light. It featured a simple, Japanese-style composition: three female nudes arranged around a potted cherry blossom, its pink flowers scattered against a backdrop of pale grey screens. One girl stood to the right, holding a parasol and clad in a robe so diaphanous it barely existed at all; another crouched beside the plant as if tending to it, her hair tied beneath a red and silver scarf; and there, at the painting's left edge, was Maud Franklin, rather younger and slimmer and completely stark naked. *In the altogether*. This had been done right at the start, around the time of Maud's eighteenth birthday, before anything particular had happened between Jimmy and her. She'd agreed readily enough. The art had required it, she'd reasoned; such was the bargain a model made with her modesty. Still, despite this firm self-instruction, she'd been a mite startled to discover that she wasn't going to be alone in this picture, the two other nudes having already been laid in on an earlier occasion.

'Three girls was the scheme agreed upon,' had been Jimmy's dry explanation. 'Three *different* girls. At the patron's specific request.'

Parts of it were sketchy, but Maud herself was pretty unmistakable – shown from the side, leaning gently towards the centre of the scene. It had been a hellish pose to hold, even by Jimmy's standards. You couldn't tell, though; the figure had a grace to it, and a sleekness, that now seemed frankly incredible. Yet her earlier discomfort did not return. As their guests looked at this painting, she felt only a sickly excitement at the sums that might be proposing themselves to Owl.

'It's Leyland's,' Jimmy replied. 'As I suspect you are aware.'

'And he still wants it?'

'You know his views on receiving that which he has paid for. How very dogged he can be.'

'But you don't think simply to send it to him?'

'My dear Owl, it is *unfinished*. Can you not see that? It certainly isn't ready to be subjected to any form of general inspection. The same goes for the rest of Leyland's works I still have here. All those blasted portraits, for instance.'

Owl looked about him. 'And where might they be?'

Commissioned back when Jimmy had been counted among the family's most intimate friends, the Leyland portraits had provided Maud with her ticket through his door. He usually kept the one of the wife out for show, being rather proud of it, she suspected; but today, along with the rest of them, it was nowhere to be seen.

'Work upon all Leyland faces has halted, for the time being,' Jimmy said, 'and an alternative berth found for the canvases. Being as they are so big, you understand. There just isn't room.' He grew subtly mischievous, and gave a sigh of mock-regret. 'The truth of it, *mon vieux*, is that having our British businessman in here, all long-limbed and morose – befrilled, you know, with sunken eye, lurking off in the shadows – was proving far too dire a distraction, so I bundled him into the cellar. The painted version, that is. Not the original.'

The Owl and Miss Corder laughed. Jimmy's forgotten cigarette was almost burned out, the ember scorching Maud's knuckles; she dropped it with a wince into a grubby saucer. When she'd left for Edie's back in early May, the Leyland matter had been all but dead. The Peacock Room had been finished with at long last. But she knew their tone. Behind these jokes lay something new.

'What's happened?'

The studio door opened to admit John, bearing a tray with his standard air of mild irritability. Upon it was a plate of Jimmy's American buckwheat cakes, a half-empty bottle of white wine and four smudged glasses. After setting the tray on the edge of the painting table, John stood back and looked to his master, expecting the usual complaint or additional instruction.

'Jimmy,' Maud said. 'What's happened? What've you done?'

Jimmy went to the wine bottle and picked it up. He sighed again, this time at her persistence. 'Nothing, Maudie. I swear.'

*

Maud went upstairs barely a minute after the Owl and Miss Corder had taken their leave. She disrobed and dropped into bed, burrowing gratefully amid the cool sheets, and was filled with the sense, oddly welcome, of laying herself beneath the earth; of dragging the turf over her pounding head, never to rise again. For several days she stayed there, weighted down by exhaustion and a feeling she came slowly to recognise as loneliness. Her body and her mind had been refashioned to receive a child. To care for a child. And it was not there.

The moment of parting was played out a thousand times, the memories pored over and picked through in the hope that some new detail or sensation might be uncovered. Maud had been sitting in a scuffed, high-backed armchair, a mainstay of Edie's parlour. Ione had been dozing in her lap; her own eyelids had started to flutter as well. She'd heard the front door, and lowered voices in the hall, but hadn't thought anything of it. Edie had come in and bade her stand. Then she'd leaned forward, lifting away the child as if relieving Maud of an encumbrance.

'Pass her here,' she'd said.

'It's all right,' Maud had replied, slightly perplexed, in a tone of good-humoured protest, 'I can manage. Why, she's light as a—'

Her sister had already been turning away, though, going back to the door, thinking it best just to get it done – to tear off the bandage with a sudden, unexpected stroke. It was only when the front door closed again, in fact, that Maud had fully appreciated what was taking place. She'd known that the foster mother was due, of course she had, but had assumed this would be after teatime. Later on. The next morning. She'd thought of pursuit. A few groggy, wandering steps had shown her that this was futile. So she went instead to the window, hoping to catch sight of them – to call out and have them stop for a proper farewell. The parlour was to the rear of Edie's small terraced house. All that she'd been able to see was a bare yard. Ione was gone. Her awareness of this had seemed to gather at the top of her chest, pressing in on her until she'd been unable to breathe; until her collarbone had felt like it was about to crack in two. She'd made a sound, a kind of anguished yelp, and dropped back into the armchair. Alone.

With Maud's grief came yet more anger – directed at herself, for her feebleness and her idiocy, but also pretty squarely at Jimmy. He kept his distance, sleeping on the studio chaise longue, no doubt thinking this considerate; and was preoccupied, as always, with his own business. Mrs Cossins, the cook at Lindsey Row, brought up her food and dealt rather grudgingly with her laundry. Once a day, twice at most, Jimmy would appear to ask how she was faring. His bed was huge and heavy, with a frame of dark lacquered wood; buried within it, she would glare out at him, refusing to speak. The words built up, acquiring a terrible pressure, as if they were soon going to explode from her and force a proper confrontation. *How can you care so bloody little?* she'd demand. *How can you want things to be this way?*

The feeling passed. Besides, she already knew full well what he would say. This was part of it, part of the risk they took. He was finding money, somehow, for the fostering – no mean feat. And he had welcomed her back into his household. It was wrong of her, really, to want anything more. The burden was hers. She understood that now. She had to become used to it; to cease to notice it, even. There in that dark bed, with a bead of blood drying stickily against her thigh, this seemed entirely beyond her.

Late one evening, Maud stirred to find Jimmy's younger brother pulling a chair across the rug and settling himself at her side. William Whistler was a doctor of some renown, with a practice in Mayfair, a new wife named Nellie, and a smart house on Wimpole Street. He was a regular guest at Lindsey Row and familiar with the arrangements there, which he'd always appeared to accept without censure –although Maud had never been to the smart house or met the new wife. She sat up, self-conscious and a touch startled, unsure of what to say; then he began to ask a series of matter-of-fact questions about her well-being, and she saw that this was a house call, most probably undertaken at Jimmy's request. Burlier and balder than his brother, with an accent less complicated by other influences, Willie was every inch the respectable professional – rather anonymous in a way, as easy to overlook as Jimmy was not. This was a screen, Maud had discovered, drawn before a life of real incident, of *fearsome* incident, in relation to which his present prosperity stood as a well-deserved reward. While Jimmy had been establishing himself in London, and making his first attempts to have a painting shown at the Royal Academy, Willie had been at war. He'd seen war at its most ferocious and bloody. There was a photograph of him, younger and leaner, in an embroidered officer's coat, serving as a military surgeon in the army of General Lee. Jimmy's pride in this could not be overstated. He remained an unrepentant champion of the Confederate cause – to such an extent in fact that Maud had learned to avoid the subject – and derived a fierce excitement from imagining what his brother had endured.

'Boys, they were,' he'd say, 'mere boys, conscripted from farm and city alike. Brought into those hospital tents by the dozen, injured in ways one can barely conceive – shredded, Maudie, by the Union's shot and shell. And expiring faster than they could be put in the ground.'

Willie himself never so much as hinted at any of this. You could scour his bland, plump face for as long as you liked and find no trace of it. But he had an authority about him, along with his reserve. Maud answered his questions promptly; she could hear a trace of meekness in her voice. He put a hand to her forehead and pressed two fingers gently against her neck to take her pulse. Then he thanked her, rose from his chair and retreated to the landing. Briefly, Maud caught sight of Jimmy, waiting just past the doorway. She heard Willie tell him that there was no cause whatsoever for alarm.

'Could you leave her something?' Jimmy asked. 'For the restlessness – the moods?'

'Not necessary. Miss Franklin is doing well, Jamie. As one might expect from one so young. She'll soon be fully restored, I should think.' Willie paused. 'She would benefit from some diversion, though. Perhaps you might consider taking her down to Hastings.'

This was not an innocent suggestion. Jimmy and Willie's elderly mother lived in Hastings, lodged in a cliff-top boarding house overlooking the sea. Willie had found the place, had handled the move and was footing the bill. He seldom saw Jimmy without mentioning how much the old woman longed to have him visit her; how the train was quick, three hours was all; how a trip there need only take a day, with some planning. Maud had met Mrs Whistler several times. She'd actually been residing at Lindsey Row when Maud had first come to stand for Jimmy, a domestic situation that now seemed unthinkable. It had surprised her that this singular gentleman, foreign in so many respects, could have family about him in London. *Exiles, ain't they*, another model had told her. *The losing side*.

Mrs Whistler had left the city within a few months, at Willie's urging – the smoke and endless fogs were bad for her health, he'd said – thus clearing the way for Maud to take up the role of *Madame*. Jimmy did venture down to see her a couple of times a year. Willie made it plain that he didn't think this was nearly enough.

Maud lay motionless, listening closely, her feelings set at a degree of opposition. Such a journey would certainly be difficult. She found, though, that she wanted to see Jimmy's mother again. She wanted him to take her. Apart from anything else, it would be interesting to find out what tale he'd spin. She'd be cast as a follower, she supposed, as well as a model; a chaste disciple, convalescing from some unnamed illness, brought along by her kindly mentor to benefit from the sea air.

Jimmy wouldn't hear of it. 'Now is not the time, doc. She's damned tired. You've seen it for yourself.'

'Mother likes her,' Willie persisted. 'She asks after her sometimes. She knows that she still features in your paintings. I'm sure you could tell her more or less anything you pleased.'

'I cannot leave London at present, even for a day. Not with things the way they are – the Grosvenor and so forth.'

'Jamie—'

'We can do better, I believe. Wait here a moment.'

There was a shuffling of feet and a sigh from the doctor. The bedroom door began to open. Maud closed her eyes, pulling the sheets up to her chin, feigning sleep. She heard Jimmy's boot creak on the loose floorboard by the bed; she smelled oil paint and tobacco. His fingertips touched the counterpane, just above her shoulder.

'Maudie,' he said, 'I've had a thought.'

*

The Harmony in Amber and Black was a full-length female figure and breathtakingly slender: Maud's figure as it had been around two years before, shaped by a corset that she hadn't been able to wear since Christmas. The pose was simple, front facing with the arms at the sides. It had been made soon after she'd taken up residence at Lindsey Row, commissioned by Frederick Leyland as a portrait of his daughter Florence. The gown was close-fitting and modern, cut from a tawny chiffon that Jimmy had captured most skilfully, drawing out the tone with the sharp whiteness of the ruffed collar and cuffs, the black bow at the breast, and the neat black gloves, which melted, very nearly, into the hazy blackness of the background. Since she'd seen it last, however, a few months previously, the portrait had undergone a rather crucial alteration – for where the face of Florence Leyland had been was now that of Maud herself. This was why Owl had mentioned the *Amber and Black* upon meeting her the week before. She hadn't realised exactly which painting he'd meant until a good while later. It hadn't seemed terribly important – a mistake, most probably. Who, in all honesty, could keep track of Jimmy's titles? He certainly couldn't. Maud often thought that their principal purpose was to sow confusion.

And yet it hadn't been a mistake. She hadn't sat for this, or seen Jimmy at work on the canvas. It must have been done from an older drawing, or from memory – and recently, while she'd been away. He'd made the change especially for its exhibition in the Grosvenor Gallery.

'Heavens, Miss Franklin,' said Miss Corder, in the manner of someone intending to be overheard. 'You are with your sisters.'

Maud thought of Edie, toiling in her husband Lionel Crossley's book-keeping office; of her widow's peak and ink-stained fingertips; of the tearful reluctance of their farewell. But Miss Corder meant the paintings, of course – *The Harmony in Amber and Black* and the other one. The Owl's consort was about six yards away, across the Grosvenor's west gallery. It was the largest room in the place, as big as a decent-sized dance hall, and fitted out with great extravagance. White marble statues stood against crimson damask; a long skylight was set into a barrelled ceiling of midnight blue, studded with golden stars. Even against such a background, however, Miss Corder made for an arresting sight. Her jacket was a bright silver-grey, impossibly tight, and trimmed with deepest green, while her hat had a brim nearly three feet wide, upon which lolled an enormous creamy orchid.

'A hallowed moment,' she continued. 'Muse and master-pieces reunited. Such a rare privilege for us all.'

People were turning around. The Grosvenor held a wealthy-looking, vaguely artistic crowd, wandering and murmuring before the paintings that had been chosen for display. These were present in much lower numbers than was usual, arranged on the walls only one or two canvases high. The Whistler contribution had been hung over at the right end. The surrounding pictures, so dense with shapes and colours, and the luxury of the gallery itself, made Jimmy's look strikingly empty: pure, in a way, both peaceful and mysterious. But after only a couple of minutes, it was already plain that they were receiving a rather different sort of attention to the rest. There were smirks, whispered remarks and snatches of suppressed laughter. Jimmy's paint-ings were being mocked.

Maud started towards the velvet curtains that had been hung across the entrance. Miss Corder moved to intercept her, and they met awkwardly in a hot square of sunlight.

'I'm leaving,' Maud said, trying to step past. 'Tell Jimmy I'll be waiting at home.'

'You are too modest. Why, without you, without your particular talents, these works simply would not exist. Your strength and grace has permitted—'

'I know,' Maud interrupted. 'I know.'

This had been Jimmy's proposal, in place of the seaside: a visit to the first exhibition of the Grosvenor Gallery. Maud hadn't been keen. Rising from the bed, preparing a bath and dressing in something appropriate for the Grosvenor's Mayfair address had all seemed like a desperate chore. She was very aware also that the predicted change in their fortunes had failed to arrive. The undertaking was proving a disappointment, for Jimmy at least. He'd been insistent, however, so eventually Maud had agreed. She'd told herself that this was the life she had chosen; that if she was to be Whistler's *Madame*, she had to keep abreast with Whistler's affairs. Only after they'd left the house – her garments kept loose in certain areas and discreetly reinforced in others – had Jimmy revealed that he wouldn't actually be going to the gallery. Miss Corder, who'd called the week before, was to accompany her instead. He had something important to attend to, he'd said, and would meet them later at the Café Royal, an old haunt of theirs. This disclosure had been carefully timed. A hansom had already pulled up; she'd been climbing inside. It had been too late to turn back.

Miss Corder had been standing ready at the Grosvenor's entrance. She'd kissed Maud on the cheek and told her how extremely well she was looking, then paid for their tickets with a ten-shilling note. Maud had followed her up the broad marble staircase, trying to accept her fate and muster some enthusiasm. Now, though, she'd reached her limit. She was tired out and sore. She was cross with everything. She was heading off to bed.

Her companion stayed close, blocking her path. Miss Corder's face was as unaccountable as the rest of her – really rather plain in a way, with its prominent nose and heavy, slightly protuberant lips; yet something was there, cleverness perhaps, or nerve, that lent it an odd appeal. A beauty, even. Her eyes, lilac in the sunlight, held a query; then they flitted away, back to the gallery, and her brow knitted with displeasure.

'These people here don't understand,' she said, the volume of her voice unaltered. 'They don't look at the paintings for themselves. They have been drinking from a tainted source, you see, imbibing foolishness and conceited ignorance, and it has clouded their vision. Clouded it quite fatally.'

Those nearby were staring openly now, umbrage adding to their curiosity, as was surely Miss Corder's intention. Four years with Jimmy had schooled Maud thoroughly in this variety of anger: the kind that insisted upon making a public display and clashing hard with that which had provoked it. Something here made her pause, however. Early the previous morning, the day after Willie's visit, she'd been woken by the sound of Jimmy shouting, really shouting, down in the studio. He'd been alone, as far as she'd been able to tell. The words 'impudence' and 'imposture' had kept recurring. Sensing that an explanation might be at hand, she asked Miss Corder what she meant.

The lilac eyes widened. 'You don't know. Of course you don't. He can't bear to tell you of it, most probably. Your Jimmy has been maligned, Miss Franklin. Attacked in the crudest manner.'

She turned, moving her face out of the sun, and pointed

a green-gloved finger at a nearby canvas. It was one of the larger *Nocturnes*, a couple of years old now – the *Gold and Black*, did he call it? – showing fireworks launching and falling over the river. A rack of livid white-orange hissed in the darkness, while banks of black smoke rolled off to the left and right, laid against the blue night like the silhouette of a mighty forest, and red-gold sparks drifted above in long, scattered trails. The handling was loose, even for Jimmy – the darks smeared on, blocked in; the lights barely more than raw dabs of colour.

'A notice has been published,' Miss Corder announced, 'and much circulated, in the art press and beyond. A famous critic, keen for attention it would seem, has penned something far beneath him, beneath any right-thinking person – an assault, essentially, intended to blind his readers to this painting's obvious virtues. Fortunately, Charles has been on hand to offer Jimmy advice. If he hadn't, I scarcely dare to imagine what might—'

She stopped talking, distracted by a trio of young gentlemen, about their age – smart types, city fellows – who were grinning by her shoulder.

'Custard,' said one, indicating a falling rocket.

'Gulls' droppings,' offered another.

'Who was the critic?' Maud asked.

'Ruskin,' said Miss Corder shortly. 'And you can see right here what his authority has licensed. Stupidity Miss Franklin, has been allowed free rein.'

With that she swivelled another quarter-circuit and

launched herself into battle, informing the young gentlemen that they were plainly insensible to art, hopeless cases indeed, embarrassing themselves further with every utterance; that they might as well take their tweed and their watch-chains and their primped whiskers and go back to their desks, in whatever godforsaken office they scratched out their existences.

Ruskin. Maud knew the name, of course; it had an association of stature, of the kind you might see spelt out on book spines in austere, golden letters, or heard being dropped into conversation as a display of knowledge. She hadn't read any of it herself, but gaining the fellow's ill opinion was surely a serious reversal. She wanted to ask what had been written, but Miss Corder was caught up entirely in her skirmish.

Thrown at first by her vehemence, the young gentlemen had rallied, rather pleased to have any form of attention from such a woman. They declared that the *Nocturne* was plainly the work of a drunkard, a staggering sot, and not very much work at that. Pictures of this type, one of them continued, might well appeal to ladies of a – they exchanged glances, starting to laugh – *bohemian* persuasion, but to the wider population they were nothing but a joke, an act of imposture, as Mr What's-his-name had asserted.

Imposture, thought Maud. There it was.

Miss Corder listened, nodding as if some deep suspicion was being confirmed, the orchid bobbing atop her vast hat. Then she gestured contemptuously at the opposite side of the gallery, towards a spread of large paintings with a good deal more people gathered before them. All by the same hand, they had the look, from a distance, of stained glass.

'That is more to your taste, I suppose – old Ned Jones?' she demanded. 'That is *excellence*, is it, all that laboriousness, all that misspent labour? Is that English art? Is that honestly what we deserve?'

Maud studied these paintings more closely. The colours had a delicate glow, as if the pictures were lit from behind; the forms were flawlessly arranged and drawn. She could see a row of beautiful angels bearing large crystal balls. Half a dozen women kneeling by a lake, gazing at their own reflections as if entranced. St George in his armour. Every one of them had virtually the same face – both the men and the women, and the ones who were neither men nor women. Their expressions held only the merest hints of thought or feeling. The effect was mildly unnerving. When considered next to the work of this Mr Jones, it could well be true that Jimmy's pictures would not seem pure and peaceful, but crude. Lacking somehow. This notion came to Maud unbidden and it startled her with its disloyalty. She made to look back towards the Whistler display, for reassurance; and instead spotted attendants in livery, closing in on them from opposite sides, censorious glares on their faces.

Miss Corder was growing yet more impassioned and voluble about the various deficiencies she'd observed in the other artworks of the Grosvenor display. Maud was wondering whether she should interrupt, to point out the attendants perhaps, when her companion withdrew abruptly from this somewhat one-sided debate, casting not so much as a parting glance at her chortling adversaries.

'Come Miss Franklin,' she said, starting towards the curtained entrance, and the wide stairway beyond. 'I believe we're due at the Café Royal.'

*

Outside, the heat was starting to lift, a breeze snapping the shop awnings taut in their frames. Miss Corder walked along New Bond Street with a pronounced, leisurely sway, her hips swinging out a couple of inches with each footstep, unperturbed by either the clash in the gallery or the manner of their exit.

'Ned Jones,' she said. 'Good God. Or *Burne*-Jones, as we must call him now. Charles knows the fellow. Used to know him. Even back then his style was said to be ponderous and overworked. All those hard lines, all that intricacy. And for such a wretchedly insipid result. But I suppose I should hope that the popularity of his pictures grows yet further. The blasted things would be easy indeed to replicate.'

Maud frowned a little, and began to ask what was meant by *replicate*, but Miss Corder was crossing a side street, moving around the back of a carriage, out of earshot. While Maud bent to gather up her hem, Miss Corder was just letting hers trail where it would, dragging through the summer dust. They were drawing stares – being unaccompanied and rather conspicuous – none too pleasant, some of them. The attention fell upon Miss Corder like sea spray on the prow of a gunboat.

'I understand why you wished to leave so soon,' she said, when Maud caught up. 'To be honest, Miss Franklin, I can only stomach brief visits myself. The Grosvenor is a worthy venture, all things considered. It provides a place of exhibition to the occasional true talent, like your Jimmy. But I cannot help thinking it corrupt. They do it by invitation, you know, rather than merit. Amateurs, friends of Sir Coutts Lindsay and his wife, shown alongside proper artists. It is a game, a game for the rich.' Her lip twitched. 'But works are shifting nonetheless. They are going for hundreds of pounds, if Charles is to be believed. I am beginning to think that I should have tried to get something of my own in there.'

There was a pause. Maud looked at a bolt of burnt-orange silk arranged in a draper's window. 'You're an artist,' she said.

'More than that,' replied Miss Corder, lifting her chin. 'I am a professional, Miss Franklin. I make my living at it. But I am also a woman. And my father was a lighterman, down at Rotherhithe. And so I am kept always at the margins. Versatility is demanded of me, if I am to survive – a versatility that I'll bet Mr Millais or Mr Leighton, or Lady Butler even, would struggle to summon.' She stopped, checking the fervour that was returning to her voice. 'But of course you know all this. You are an artist yourself. Charles says that Jimmy rates you highly – that he had you at work on the Peacock Room, in fact, repainting flowers. Before he brought the scheme to its final form.'

'Before he covered them all up, you mean. Painted the whole thing blue.'

Maud was embarrassed, and faintly annoyed; Jimmy knew she didn't like him telling people about her attempts at art – boasting about them, as he couldn't help but do, despite having obliterated her painstaking labour at Prince's Gate with barely a second's hesitation. She'd protested about this, just once, trying to sound as if she was joking.

'I had to Maudie,' he'd answered simply. 'It didn't go.'

'That was necessary,' Miss Corder told her. 'A sacrifice, you might say. Charles tells me that Jimmy regards you as a pupil as much as a model. That he'll have your pictures selling before the decade is out.'

Maud felt herself colouring. She stared down at her boots. 'I don't know about that. I've barely begun.'

'The best models,' Miss Corder continued, 'often have a painter in them as well. I have always thought this. It refines your sense of what's needed. Of what it is to stand on the other side of the easel. And I must say that you are in the very best place. Jimmy Whistler is the finest teacher – the finest protector that you could ask for.'

It was rare indeed for Maud's situation to be met with such approval. Edie, so careful in her respectability, didn't even like to think of it. The other models she knew regarded it simply as a deft manoeuvre, a tidy bit of luck. How could she help feeling a flicker of affinity now with Miss Rosa Corder? Perhaps it wouldn't be so bad to talk of art with a professional woman painter. Someone unmarried and young, and without social advantage. Someone who seemed interested in *her*, furthermore, and who could surely offer guidance when she felt able to work again. Questions began to occur also about Miss Corder and the way she lived. The pictures she'd painted, where they'd been shown and to whom they'd sold. Her own protector, the Owl.

Miss Corder was talking herself, though, expanding upon her admiration for Jimmy and of her sense of the war that had begun, between the forces of artistic righteousness and a broad, determined coalition of enemies. It was being fought on the walls of the Grosvenor Gallery apparently, and in numerous other places besides, with this Ruskin review being merely the latest offensive launched against them. Maud thought of that strange moment down in the studio – the suggestion that there was fresh trouble with the Leylands. It had slipped her mind until she'd stood before the *Harmony in Amber and Black*. They started down a lane and the wind picked up, overturning a metal pail and sending it rolling noisily across the pavement. Miss Corder paused; Maud saw her chance.

'What of the Leylands? What's going on there?'

'Oh, nothing,' Miss Corder replied, without much interest. 'You mustn't worry. A couple of accidental meetings between Jimmy and the wife, at the houses of mutual friends. The husband wasn't best pleased. He still considers Jimmy and himself to be at odds, it seems.'

Not a word had passed between Jimmy and Frederick Leyland since the previous winter. The shipbroker had responded to his reworked dining room – to the Prussian blue walls, and the mural, with its spilled silver shillings and puffed-up, befrilled peacock – only with silence. They had been left to wonder, a very deliberate form of torture. The decorative scheme remained intact – that much they knew. But no more.

Maud had other questions, a long list of them; Miss Corder was back on the Grosvenor, though, and the dismal quality of so much of its display, a topic that sustained her without interruption until they reached Regent Street. It was packed solid, traffic inching and creaking around the dust-hazed Quadrant. Miss Corder weaved along the busy pavement, leading Maud beneath the red and white striped canopy that shivered above the entrance of the Café Royal. Jimmy's preferred table was off to the side, next to one of the broad front windows, providing a commanding view of both the restaurant and the street. It was large, able to accommodate double their number, in case any notable passers-by were waved over to join them. Jimmy was at the head, listing things on his fingers; Owl sat to the right, nodding in understanding as he reached for his glass. The two women went in. A smart, portly waiter was there at once, asking their business in a heavy French accent.

'We have come to meet our husbands,' Miss Corder told him. 'They are over there, by that window.'

'Husbands,' the waiter repeated. He took their hats, though, standing aside to admit them. Maud saw Miss Corder's orchid smear pollen across his black silk waistcoat.

Both men rose at their approach. Jimmy's eyeglass dropped out; Owl set down his drink. There were kisses and embraces. Miss Corder sat on the seat opposite the Owl, with her back to the window. Maud joined her gratefully, nearly groaning aloud in relief, kneading her aching knees beneath the table. She'd walked further that afternoon than she had in the previous month.

The Café Royal was decorated in the Parisian style, with tall mirrors in ornate, gilded frames, tabletops of veined marble and a black-and-white tiled floor. It was about a quarter full, perhaps slightly less; waiters roamed about the empty tables, polishing cutlery in the pre-supper lull. At that moment it seemed to Maud a haven of airy comfort and tranquillity. She smiled at Owl, at Miss Corder, and they smiled back at her; and there was a tiny flash of strangeness. The scene was that of four friends, four dear friends, settling in for a celebration. Yet she barely knew this pair. She'd met them only once before. Jimmy had mentioned that he and Owl had been on decent terms a few years previously, prior to her arrival at Lindsey Row, and had recently renewed their association. But this hardly justified all the confidences he appeared to be piling on the fellow.

The flash faded. A flute was placed in front of her and filled with sparkling wine. The day's exertions had left her utterly parched. It was nothing short of beautiful, that glass: tall and delicate, frosted with moisture, the wine golden in the light of the declining sun. She picked it up, chimed the rim against Miss Corder's, and Owl's, and Jimmy's, and drank deep – almost half the contents in one gulp.

'And now, Maudie,' said Jimmy, 'you must tell, in precise detail, sparing me nothing,' – here he screwed the eyeglass back in, and fixed the blue eye behind upon her with semi-comical intensity – '*What. You. Thought.*'

Maud had been furnishing Jimmy Whistler with opinions for a while now. For one who courted disfavour, who made out that he revelled in it, he could be acutely, damnably sensitive. Snide phrases penned in seconds by some newspaper critic were branded forever on his brain; there were a couple that Maud was pretty certain he would be reciting on his deathbed. Her actual views, therefore, were unimportant. She knew what he needed from her, and she supplied it without thinking.

'Wonderful,' she said. 'It was wonderful. The hall was yours, Jimmy. No contest.'

The moustache bristled with satisfaction. Miss Corder spoke up as well, poised and formidably eloquent, reporting on the crowds, the regrettable popularity of Mr Burne-Jones, and in particular on the reception of the firework painting – the *Nocturne in Black and Gold*.

'The philistines were out in force,' she said. 'They were

reciting Ruskin's words before the picture. He has given licence to ignorant disdain. A refusal to look, or to see.'

Owl was shaking his head. 'I tell you, Jimmy, the old goat's been beyond the pale for a good while now. But this is a step further still. Ad hominem, as the lawyers say. Actionable.'

Jimmy was grave. 'You aren't the first to say this,' he said.

'What was in it?' Maud asked, by now rather anxious. 'What did he write that could be so bad?'

They shared a look; then three indulgent expressions were turned her way.

'You deserve to know,' Jimmy said. 'I'd hoped I could spare you, but this may now be unavoidable. It was brief. Published in that peculiar private paper he puts out. But picked up since by everyone.' He spoke slowly, assuming a terrifyingly steely smile. 'The fellow wrote that my poor picture approached the aspect of wilful imposture.'

Maud gripped the stem of her flute. This was Ruskin's own phrase, she could tell. The dreadful notice had plainly been memorised in its entirety.

'He wrote that I was a coxcomb, Maudie. A *coxcomb*. That I was asking two hundred guineas to — how was it put? — *fling a pot of paint in the public's face*. That the *Black and Gold* displayed only what he felt qualified to term *cockney impudence*.'

At this Maud let out an involuntary laugh, a flat, nervous whinny. 'You're no blessed *cockney*, Jimmy.'

Owl was grinning too. 'It is absurd,' he said. 'Completely absurd. And actionable, as I say. In the course of my life, I have learned a thing or two about the law, and there is no doubt in my mind that you have been libelled. He attacks your person, my friend. Your character.'

'The rogue denies me my fundamental right,' Jimmy stated, 'to call myself an artist. He says my work is not art. This is why no one buys. But what right do they have to pass judgement in this manner? These self-appointed critics, these ignoramuses, these blasted fools? What goddamned *right* do they have?'

'None,' said Miss Corder. 'None at all.'

Owl nodded in sympathy. 'You must go to court, Jimmy. I have said this to you several times now. The public chastisement of John Ruskin for the abuses of his pen is long overdue. And there must be compensation for the damage he has sought to inflict.'

'That he has inflicted already,' said Jimmy.

'Compensation?' Maud asked. 'You mean – you mean money?'

The Owl turned to her in an attitude of apologetic explanation. 'I know Ruskin, Miss Franklin. Better than any man alive, I should think. I was his – well, I suppose you might call it his private secretary, back before my association with Gabriel Rossetti. I undertook many missions on his behalf, and became familiar with every part of his affairs – some dark regions, Miss. And he has grown yet more strange since. The lunatic's beard. The demented air that attends on his manners and his writings. It is said—'

'Owl,' Jimmy interrupted, dragging on his cigarette. 'Not now.'

'He must pay,' said Owl, changing tack. 'He can afford to, certainly. His father traded in wines, he traded very well, and left his only child rich indeed. The wretched fellow squats up north somewhere, among the Lakes, atop a veritable mountain of gold. It is your duty, old man, if you ask me, to have some clever lawyer relieve him of a portion of it.'

Jimmy seemed to see the sense in this. 'We are down, I won't deny it. To be completely honest, *mon cher*, we suffer still from the lack of Leyland's thousand. That is the root of the trouble. Most of what he paid was already owed, you see – it's long gone.'

Leyland. Maud sat up. 'The *Amber and Black*,' she said.

Again all three of them looked her way, curious and vaguely condescending. A connection had been forming in the back of her mind, since the walk over from New Bond Street. While visiting Lindsey Row in the years before the Peacock Room, Frederick Leyland would surely have seen the *Amber and Black* when it had Florence's features. And then he would have seen it again in the Grosvenor Gallery.

'I saw what you did to it. To Leyland's daughter. You scraped off her face.'

They laughed hard at this, did Jimmy and the Owl, slapping their palms against the tabletop and stamping their boots upon the floor. It was more than Maud had expected, a lot more, and it knocked her off-course. She found herself smiling too, even as she tried to raise her voice over the uproar.

'Something else has happened, hasn't it, Jimmy? Why would you do that?'

'You see the eye on this one, my dear Owl! A goddamned *painter's* eye, it is! Nothing escapes it. *Rien de tout!*'

And somehow, before Maud could say anything else, she was under discussion as an artist for the second time in an hour. Jimmy trotted out a little legend of his own devising, in which the eighteen-year-old model Maud Franklin, soon after her arrival at Lindsey Row, had happened to discover an album of Japanese prints. The detailed studies of flowers within had inspired her to such a degree, he claimed, that she'd picked up the brush at once, and displayed an obvious gift for it. Owl said that he would very much like to see her latest drawings; as did Miss Corder, who declared that Maud simply must visit her studio on Southampton Row, within the week if it could be arranged. The attention and encouragement flattered Maud to the point of giddiness. Her skin flamed radish red, perspiration stippling her brow. Frederick Leyland and the *Amber and Black* quite left her mind.

'I haven't done anything for a while,' she said, as her glass was refilled, 'you know, on account of – of being away and . . .'

They told her that she must reapply herself at the first

opportunity. That it was her responsibility to humankind. To leave such a talent unused, they said, was an unforgivable waste. She had to paint.

Maud nodded, and sipped, and promised that she would.

*

Dusk was shading the grand bend of the Quadrant by the time they decided to eat. As always, Jimmy insisted upon everyone having the same, with him ordering: *Homard en Croute*, a favourite of his. Maud would have eaten this gladly, but Miss Corder's sylph-like form, snaking against the table beside her, served as a stern admonition. She had to recover her own figure as soon as possible, so she picked at the little pie, trying to look like she was making a start on it, breaking a hole in the buttery crust and prodding at what lay beneath.

Owl's serving, in contrast, was gone in moments. Noticing Maud's reluctance, he offered and then engineered a discreet swap of their dishes. It was a mystery, how he managed to eat such quantities while talking – for talk he most certainly did. Even Jimmy stayed quiet, or mostly quiet, to hear him. In that impressive voice of his, he began to tell them of a certain period of his youth – always brought to mind, he claimed, by the taste of lobster. He was Portuguese, as it turned out, not Spanish as Maud had assumed; or rather a half-Portuguese, the son of an English wool merchant and a noble lady of Oporto.

'Their final child,' he said. 'No fewer than thirteen others preceded me. My father expired, in fact, not long after my birth.' The cause was exhaustion.'

Left destitute, his widowed mother had moved out of the city with her six youngest to a village down the coast. There, some years later, the teenage Owl had supported them all by diving for treasure. The *Barbosa*, a mighty galleon from the time of King Alfonso VI, had been wrecked just offshore, the hull lying untouched in shallow waters. And so, an India rubber air tube clenched between his teeth, he'd set about groping through the seaweed-coated timbers – braving the snapping jaws of monstrous eels, the tentacles of octopi and heaven knows what else – returning to the surface only when his fishing net was filled with gold doubloons.

'On occasion, in the *Barbosa*'s innermost crevices, I would encounter these gigantic lobsters. These turquoise levia-thans, like creatures from dreams or the paintings of madmen. I see you laughing there, Jimmy Whistler, but you wouldn't have laughed if you'd been in the water beside me. You'd have spat out your air tube and screamed like a horse.'

Jimmy was rolling a cigarette and smirking so hard he dislodged his eyeglass.

'I swear the blasted things were two feet long,' Owl continued. 'The size of a small dog, and deuced lively with it. Spines like you wouldn't believe. Claws the size of coconuts. I'd wrestle them up from the wreck, through the surf, to the beach where my mother and sisters would be waiting. Often we'd make a fire in the sand and roast the beast in its shell. Feast on it before the sunset. This,' – he held up a forkful of pinkish flesh, the last of Maud's pie – 'can't really compare.'

'We should go,' said Miss Corder. Her eyes were dark with love; she reached between the dishes for Owl's hand. 'You should take us – the three of us. We could find a house on a cliff-top, overlooking the ocean. The wild Atlantic. Think of it, Carlos. Think of what Jimmy could paint.'

The Owl – *Carlos* – agreed. 'A fellow's shilling goes far over there,' he said. 'Damned far. Why, we could take a castle. Live like royalty.'

Right then, with a newly refilled glass raised to her lips, this struck Maud as a truly brilliant idea. Why on earth *shouldn't* they? Venice had been the plan, the promise, but elsewhere could surely be as good, especially in such en-livening company. The land of Carlos the Owl. She very much liked the sound of it. She glanced at Jimmy. Eyeglass reinserted, cigarette lit, he was studying the Portuguese with wry affection.

'We'll be expecting lobster every night, Owl, you know,' he said. 'You'd better bring along your bathing suit.'

They toasted their expedition, several times over and with much laughter. The last traces of formality fell away: Miss Corder and Miss Franklin were shown the door, with Rosa and Maud taking their place. Various far-fetched arrangements were made. Goals were set, both artistic and gastronomic. A warm camaraderie enfolded the table.

Shortly afterwards, as the dishes were removed, an unspoken communication passed between the men. They excused themselves and rose, disappearing into the rear of the restaurant.

'Cigars, most probably,' said Rosa, looking over her shoulder, out at the street.

Maud emptied her glass. She was feeling pretty damned tight, in truth, having drunk a good deal and eaten next to nothing. She fell to staring at Rosa's hair. It was tied up in a plait, the coil as elaborate and perfect as a carving in a church. Until then it had simply seemed a yellowish shade of brown. Now, though, in the candlelight, Maud could see something much paler in it – a lustre that was almost metallic.

Abruptly, Rosa turned back to the table. Her eyelids lowered a fraction; she gave Maud a look of fond assessment. 'You are brave,' she said.

'Beg pardon?'

'To have done what you did. What was needed. All by yourself. And to be here again, at his side. It is very brave.'

Maud saw her meaning now, and her woozy happiness – all the pleasure she'd been taking in this place and this singular couple, so convivial and ambitious and full of spirit – went in an instant, vanishing as if it had never been, leaving her with the cold and simple fact that she was sitting there in a swell restaurant, pickling herself in sparkling wine like she hadn't a care in the whole bloody world, while her child, her *baby*, was away several miles to the north in the care of a woman who could be *anybody*, who could be *anything*, who could be about to bake the infant alive in an oven and there would be nothing, absolutely *nothing*, that she could do about it. She put down her glass. She felt panic rising. It quivered inside her, urgent and hopeless. It bolted her to the spot.

'You mean with my daughter,' she said. 'You mean with Ione.'

The smallest crack ran through Rosa's self-possession. She'd plainly thought they would discuss Jimmy – the importance of loyalty or something. Not this. 'Yes,' she said, 'your daughter.'

'I chose the name. Ione Edith Whistler. On my own. While I was – just after. I had to tell it to Jimmy. He hadn't—'

Maud was going to say that he hadn't asked what the name might be, that she'd given him three days to do it and he hadn't, so she'd snapped and simply *told him*, shouted it at him in fact; but recounting this, trying to untangle it all for the first time, proved too much. She slumped forward onto the table, pressing her cheek hard against the marble. A slick of liquid – tears or wine, she couldn't tell which – made her head slip an inch to the left.

'I thought I could just leave her. I thought it wouldn't matter. I—'

Rosa eased her back upright, wiped her face with the cuff of her silver-grey jacket, and proposed that they take some air – walk down to Piccadilly, perhaps. Maud was signalling her assent when the men came back into view on the other side of the room. They were speaking loudly in French to the head waiter, talking over each another with much gesticulation. Maud followed their approach with a prickle of resentment.

Jimmy noticed at once that something was wrong. 'What's this?' he said. 'An excess of cheer?'

'She's tired,' Rosa told him, 'that's all. A little weak still.'

Sliding his wiry frame onto the seat beside her, Jimmy plucked Maud's hand from her lap and squeezed it between his. 'Is everything well, Maudie?' he asked, gently as you like. 'What's the difficulty here?'

Maud reclaimed her hand. 'Nothing,' she sniffed. 'Honest.'

July 1877

Lord's Cricket Ground, Jim swiftly decided, was a charm-less spot on which to pass a fine summer's afternoon. It was little more than a broad, dull lawn, a few streets away from Regent's Park, hemmed in by depressing terraces and withered nursery gardens. There was something, perhaps, in the contrast between the luminescence of the sportsmen's white costumes and the smooth green carpet upon which they played, but brief observation of the game itself – much milling about, punctuated by sudden thwacks and shouts, and frantic, inexplicable rearrangements – demonstrated to Jim that he would never understand or care for cricket, even if he lived to be a hundred years old.

He was there, of course, for a very particular reason, wholly unrelated to sport. By the day's end he was deter-mined that Whistler would be reinstated as the *cher ami* of the Leyland family. He would be the confidante of the wife, of the children, and of the husband too. Once again there would be dinner invitations, and visits to the opera, and trips up to Speke Hall, the Leyland country pile. And he would be allowed access to his Peacock Room, for the first time in half a year. He would be able to make a full and proper photographic record of what he'd done there, and expunge this corrosive suggestion of imposture once and for all.

The first encounter, nearly a month earlier, had genuinely been one of chance. Mrs Leyland had been seen across a drawing room, in a dress of powder blue, listening with the slightly pained attentiveness of a polite person enduring a tedious conversation; yet looking, it had to be said, tremendously well nonetheless. Indeed, the intelligence in her face, its beautiful tenderness, had made Jim's breath catch very slightly in his throat. There had been a certain caution in him as they'd spoken. The saga of the Peacock Room was still much discussed in society. Many, he understood, were inclined to view him as a vulgar, self-promoting vandal, a foreigner with no understanding of honour or manners, who had traduced his patron's trust; reacted with petulance to a generous fee; disregarded and then deliberately contradicted Leyland's wishes, slathering valuable antique leather in bucket-loads of blue paint. And of course – perhaps most seriously of all for these blasted English – it was claimed that he'd made a gentleman's home into an exhibition hall, with press nights, newspaper reviews and an unending procession of visitors. It had seemed entirely possible that Mrs Leyland might want nothing whatsoever to do with him.

But no. The connection forged during the painting of her portrait had survived. Her smile had been dry, faintly teasing; it held a memory of jokes, subtly shared, at the expense of those around them.

'Should I strive for *rapprochement*, madam?' he'd asked. 'Is there hope?'

'It will be hard,' she'd replied, 'most certainly. You know what Frederick is like. But there is always hope, Mr Whistler.'

A fortnight later they'd taken a drive in the Leyland carriage. It had been extremely pleasant, with much gossip and laughter, like old times almost – but only Mrs Leyland had been there. Jim had the sense that the rest of them might be avoiding him, or even unaware that the meeting was taking place. As he'd left, however, she'd mentioned this fixture at Lord's: two Cambridge colleges, one of them her son Freddie's, meeting during the summer recess to play for the relief of a pauper school in Maida Vale. The whole family would be present, she'd added. He'd understood her at once.

In the days afterwards, Jim had convinced himself that it was in fact a very natural progression towards the restoration of goodwill, somehow both rapid and agreeably unhurried; and when the envelope had arrived bearing the orderly, sloping hand of Frederick Leyland, his immediate thought had been that the wife had spoken with the husband. That she'd brought him round. That their rift was to be mended and the philistine tamed right there and then. That the value of the Peacock Room had been recognised even, and the Leyland commissions might conceivably resume.

The letter inside had been short, a dozen lines or so – headed with a 'Sir', finished off with a 'yours truly', both clear signals of war – and it had stopped Jim like a clock. The two of them, Leyland had written, were publicly known to be in a state of absolute and enduring opposition. In riding out with his wife, Jim had taken advantage of *the weakness of a woman* – yes, those really were his words – and had placed her in what he termed *a false position before the world*. Any further contact had been prohibited.

For a week Jim had stewed, occupied by Maud's return from her confinement, and nagged by a most unwelcome sense of having been outmanoeuvred – of the Peacock Room being gone for good. Then, while out at the Café Royal the previous evening, he'd consulted with the Owl, whom he'd been keeping apprised of the situation. As usual, the Portuguese had been able to see in an instant that which eluded less nimble minds. His advice had been unequivocal.

'Why, my dear chap, you must attend the cricket ground. Mrs Leyland is a tactician. One would have to be, with a husband like that. She has engineered a final opportunity for you to say your piece. The *perfect* opportunity, I might say. No, no, Jimmy – you must attend. You must go before him. It is the only way.'

So there Jim was, clad in white cotton duck and a straw boater, ready to patrol. His plan was to remain at a distance for a while, assessing the Leylands' mood and selecting the optimum moment for his approach – perhaps just after Freddie had scored a wicket or whatever they were called. There would be a great cheer; he would stroll up, applauding with hands raised, calling out '*bravo!*', and as one the family would turn towards him. Mrs Leyland would beam and beckon for him to approach. Her husband would be rather less pleased; Jim was confident that his wife would have worked on him a little, though, upbraiding him for that outrageous letter and laying out the situation in a manner so reasonable and objective that even the British businessman would heed it. He'd be flushed, furthermore, with his son's sporting success – the son who'd always held Jim in such amity and regard. The fellow would have to give Jim a chance. A decent hearing, out there on wholly neutral ground. Yes, Owl was right. It really was ideal.

But a problem soon arose. This confounded game took up an unreasonable amount of room, two or three acres by Jim's estimation, obliging the spectators – of whom there were a good number, a few hundred at least – to cluster thickly around the edges. It made the careful scouting he had in mind completely impossible. He was in amongst them from the start, these wealthy families and crowds of well-to-do youths, stuck beneath a shifting lily pond of parasols, unable to see more than a few yards in any direction. He might stumble across the Leylands entirely by accident – the timing of their reunion, and the climate of his reception, determined only by the whim of the gods.

Fortune, however, was on Jim's side. Halfway around the cricket ground's circumference, between caps and boaters and a variety of summer hats, he spotted the Leyland girls, perched atop a mustard yellow landau to get a better view of the proceedings. There was Florence, looking characteristically truculent; she would have seen the *Amber and Black*, he supposed, on the wall of the Grosvenor. Some appeasement would be required there – an explanation, somewhat disingenuous, of the artistic necessity of the change. Fanny, the eldest, was next to her, in a cream gown with a dark stripe. A woman of twenty now, she was out in society, being touted around for the purposes of marriage. And on the end, closest to him, was Elinor – Baby, they all called her – the youngest, but along with the others looking noticeably older to Jim's eye – about fifteen, he guessed. She had been his most devoted companion of the three, always making him gifts of flowers and hopeless scraps of needlework, and he had applied himself to her portrait with special dedication. The child had been taken in blue, like Gainsborough's boy, with a result almost equal to his painting of her mother.

The sisters had arranged themselves upon the open-topped carriage in a charmingly *jejune* attempt at elegance. Their attention was very much on the game and their elder brother's performance in it – and rather pointedly *not* upon the gaggle of students who stood nearby, talking loudly and larking about, doing all they could to draw the young ladies' notice. Jim smiled, recognising both roles; and then Baby — whose display was a touch less committed than that of Florence or Fanny — noticed him standing there. Her indifferent expression screwed up into an antagonistic little pout.

It was a spear, quite frankly, driven into Jim's heart — yet another wound to an organ pretty much riddled with perforations already. He wanted to appeal to her somehow, to launch into an old jest perhaps, or recite a favourite rhyme. The girl was nudging her sisters, though, alerting them; and Florence was shuddering, yes, actually *shuddering* at the thought. Neither would so much as turn in his direction. Very well. So this would be difficult. It was foolish, really, to have thought otherwise. Jim carried on towards the landau, inserting the eyeglass. His cheery hail went unacknowledged.

Mrs Leyland was at the carriage's near end, standing alone between its back wheels. Her fine, fashionable clothes — a light grey gown trimmed with delicate ruffles, tied behind with a bow of cerise satin — contrasted with her apprehensive bearing and the hard lines beneath her eyes. But she at least was pleased to see Jim, noticing his arrival with a sudden, unguarded smile. Relief, he thought.

'Well, how about this,' he declared, looking around him and wondering where Leyland was — watching at the front maybe, at the border of the pitch? Perhaps a well-timed approach was still feasible. 'All these years in London, in

England, and never once did I dare to imagine the, ah – the sheer *glory* of this game.'

'I wasn't sure you'd come,' she said.

'My dear Mrs Leyland, how on earth could I not?' Jim glanced up at the girls; they continued to ignore him, to ignore them both, acting as if completely absorbed in the match. He lowered his voice. 'Did you happen to hear that your husband wrote me the most astonishing letter, after our excursion the other day?'

Mrs Leyland maintained her smile; her eyes spoke of something else altogether. 'He informed me of it,' she said. 'And took no little pleasure in the revelation.'

'Such a heinous misunderstanding. I confess that it left me bewildered.'

'I told him it was nothing,' she said. 'A ride in a carriage only. That it wasn't defiance or deliberate rudeness or what-ever else. But he wouldn't heed me. He never does. He scarcely credits me with the mental capacity to walk down the stairs.'

'He's turned the children against me, I think.'

'Of course he has, Mr Whistler. That is how it's done. That is how you are cast out. Why, he's managing to do the same to me, even as he leaves me with them all to go about his business. These pressing appointments that he has. He creeps off the instant we arrive in London, you know, then reappears back in Liverpool a week later as if this was a perfectly respectable way for a husband and father to behave.'

There was applause; Jim joined in, despite having no idea who he clapped or why. He could only think that Leyland *was not there*. The family had plainly come to Lord's without him. Was this a last-minute alteration? It didn't seem so. Mrs Leyland appeared to have invited him along knowing that her husband, the man with whom he needed so keenly to speak, would not be present.

The cricketers were walking off, heading into a low pavilion at the head of the ground. From conversations around them, Jim gathered that play had stopped for luncheon. The crowd broke apart, drifting in its different directions. Mrs Leyland opened a parasol and took his arm. She led him away from the landau at some speed, towards the long rectangle of paler grass in the centre of the pitch.

'One of his women,' she said, when they were a distance from her daughters, 'came to our house. Can you believe it, Mr Whistler? To our *house*, up to the very door. With an – with an infant. *His* infant. After money, unsurprisingly.'

Mrs Leyland's grip had become ferociously tight; Jim winced a little, both at the pressure of her fingers and the obvious extent of her distress. What, though, could he reasonably be expected to do? The thought occurred – ignoble, yes, but impossible to help – that if his strongest ally in this family was really in serious danger of exclusion herself, then the Peacock Room was truly lost.

'You've known all along, haven't you? His infidelities. The women he keeps around town.'

Jim gave a slight shrug, avoiding her gaze. He had a

plain sense of escalation, of something growing far beyond him into regions that were really quite unknown, where wit and style and nerve would not even begin to address the problems at hand. He felt a desperate need for a cigarette.

'Naturally you have. Dear God. I know the way you men talk to one another. The great licence you allow yourselves.'

She was right, worse luck: Leyland had shared a fair deal about his women, usually late at night at his club or in some restaurant or other. This talk hadn't taken the form of confession or anything like that, or even of boastfulness. It had been closer to a *dare* – as if Leyland, aware of the familiarity that existed between the painter and his wife, had been challenging Jim to make an objection. Needless to say, Jim had not. They were men of the world, the pair of them, and this particular millionaire had seemed then to contain a deep vein of future commissions.

'I am bound, my dear Mrs Leyland, by many ties. It is not my place to—' Jim hesitated. 'Know only that I value your friendship. More than I can tell you. If there is anything I can do, anything at all, to be of assistance, you must tell—'

He stopped again, as it occurred to him now that this could actually be why she'd encouraged his efforts to repair their connection. The marriage, ailing for years, was entering its final collapse. She needed an accessory. A berth, perhaps. A route out of the Leyland fortress that enclosed her so completely. The current of this whole episode, as he'd conceived it, had been him rejoining the family, via Frances Leyland – not her leaving it via him.

How did this reversal make Jim feel? Well, flattered certainly. Also consternated, as he had not the least idea how he would manage this, whatever it might turn out to be, in practical terms. It would add immeasurably to his own roster of trouble, in every conceivable area. And alarmed. Yes, most definitely alarmed. It was one thing to clash with a man in the field of art, where your own rectitude, your superiority in both taste and sophistication, could be taken for granted. But this, assisting in the end of his marriage – the removal, quite possibly, of his wife – was something else entirely. Suddenly he wondered whether Leyland already had suspicions. Whether this lay behind the extraordinary venom of that letter. *The weakness of a woman. A false position before the world.*

Jim's offer was never finished. Reaching the centre of the ground – where three sticks were wedged into the turf, serving some obscure sporting function – they came to a halt and simply stood together in the sunshine, arms linked still, both struck mute by the enormity of what had been touched upon, and the panicked flailing of their thoughts. Jim looked back towards the landau. The Leyland girls had alighted from it and were talking with one of the cricketers – an especially tall fellow with a slope-shouldered, vaguely diffident stance and longish auburn curls spilling from beneath his cap. It was Freddie. Even at a distance, Jim could see clearly what was happening. The poor lad was being press-ganged into an unwelcome task. It wasn't hard to guess what it might be. Soon afterwards, he started in their direction.

Mrs Leyland released Jim's arm and began talking loudly about the garden at Prince's Gate, and how much the new plantings were suffering in the heat, until Freddie arrived before them. Over the years, Jim had gone to some pains to cultivate a friendship with the younger Frederick Leyland, developing a tone both worldly and avuncular. The boy was every last inch his mother's son – the same doe eyes, the same hint of vulnerability. Without a word to Jim, he trotted out some transparent nonsense about Baby having a headache, which apparently necessitated an immediate return to Kensington. He'd be all right, he added; one of the chaps would be sure to offer him a lift at the end of the match. Mrs Leyland met Jim's eye very briefly and started to walk back. Jim made to follow – rubbing his forearm to restore the circulation – and found Freddie, sweet, loyal Freddie, deliberately blocking his path.

'Now see here, Jimmy,' he said. He paused to lick his lower lip; he crossed his arms and then uncrossed them again. 'Jimmy, we can't have this. We just can't.'

Jim affected ignorance – blamelessness. 'Have what, my dear fellow?'

'Jimmy.' Freddie sounded almost pleading now. 'I can't go against the governor. You must see that. Don't force matters further. Please.'

'I meant,' said Jim, 'to drop you a line about us going

on a jaunt into town. I mentioned it to Godwin and he said – you'll like this, I think – *he* said that—'

Freddie was shaking his head. 'I can't. Not now.' He girded himself, like a man about to swallow something unpleasant. 'Listen to me. You must not approach my mother again. In any fashion. And you must not write to her either. I – I really don't think I can be any more clear about it than that.'

Jim looked into his pink face, so blessedly young; at the battle underway there, the reluctance and the resolution. 'Surely not,' he murmured. 'Come now, Freddie. Surely not.'

The boy would say no more. He turned away and went after his mother – standing guard over her effectively, until she was in that landau with his sisters, the horses had been brought back up and they were departing the cricket ground. Despite all that had transpired – the pails of Prussian blue and the duelling peacocks, the roadside confrontations, the assorted barbs and slights – it was only now, as he watched the Leyland women being driven off into the dusty city, and Freddie cast one last look over at him before rejoining his fellows, that Jim fully understood the irreversible nature of this situation. He was shut out forever. An enemy.

Lindsey Row felt cool and dark after the sun-blasted cricket ground, and the sweltering box of the cab. Maud was suffering still from the dinner with Owl and Miss Corder. The aim had been to lift the girl out of the dumps in which she'd been mired since her return, and in this it had appeared to succeed — until her disintegration in the later stages, at any rate. Jim had all but carried her back to their bed; and the mumbled, accusatory questions she'd slung his way had indicated plainly enough that this particular difficulty was far from finished with.

Now her brown eyes followed him from a parlour armchair. 'Where've you been?'

Jim sat opposite, dropping his boater to the floor. His clothes were stiff with dust and dried sweat. He had an overbearing sense of mental obstruction — of a great many things trying to fit through the same small aperture at the exact same instant.

'Cricket,' he said. 'A match at Lord's.'

'You don't care about *cricket*, Jimmy.' Maud's face was pale but attentive. She was a clever soul, his *Madame*. She knew that something was up.

'There was a plan,' Jim told her, 'for the betterment of our position. But it came to naught. It may have been — well, it may have been something of a misstep.'

This wasn't enough. 'Rosa Corder,' she said, 'talks of conflict.'

'Yes, well, conflict may be coming.' Jim tried to rally. 'But we'll prevail, my girl. Things will improve. There are several other strategies under consideration. The Owl, you know, is a most resourceful and well-connected fellow.'

And then for some reason he began to tell her about lithography, and the Portuguese's proposal that he make a series of lithographic Nocturnes – coloured prints of the river and its bridges, made ingeniously by sketching with crayon upon tablets of damp stone – which would surely amount to a stream of gold so steady and plentiful it might as well be coming in through a pipe. As he went on, he got a disconcerting sense of how he must appear to her. There will be a taxing period, certain friends had warned him, after a woman surrenders a child. It cannot be avoided. No matter what she has promised, no matter the arrangements that have been reached, no matter how unified and durable the two of you were before, there will be distress. Lingering distress. Resentment.

Maud rose while he was talking and went to leave the room. He reached for her as she passed but she was walking too quickly, brushing against his outstretched fingers.

'Why will *nobody*,' she said, 'ever tell me what's bloody happening?'

July 1877

Maud was turning at the end of the banister, on her way to the dining room for breakfast, when she met John coming back from the front door. He presented her with a small bundle of letters, along with July's *Art Journal*. It amused him, when Jimmy was out of earshot, to act as if there was a kind of collusion between them, as if they were on the same level, Whistler servants together. She did her best to ignore it.

'There you go, Miss,' he said with a wink. 'Bumper crop today. Pass it on, would you?'

Jimmy was dressed, smoking, the eyeglass in, his plate and cutlery pushed aside to make room for a sketchbook – in which he was setting out a pattern, similar to the overlapping feathers of the Peacock Room, but with butter-flies woven into it as well. He stopped at once and without a word or glance applied himself to the post, sorting through the sheaf deftly and slightly secretively, like a card sharp assessing a hand. Maud sat across from him and reached for the blue-and-white coffee pot. As she poured, past the steaming arc of coffee, she noticed that he'd opened up one of the letters and was reading it with absolute attention; the colour of his face was changing, growing deeper, and his posture altering also, as if to accommodate a physical discomfort.

The cup was overflowing, the surface of the coffee level with the brim, a sheen of dark liquid spilling across the pagodas and cranes that decorated its side. Maud put down the pot and looked at the letter more closely. It was one sheet only. There was no black border, at least – no one had died – although Jimmy's manner as he read on suggested that the news was equally terrible. She wanted to ask what it contained, what was so very wrong, but knew that it was always best to wait. Gingerly picking up her cup, she was about to sip away the surplus when he leapt to his feet with such abrupt force that he knocked over his chair. She started, splashing hot coffee over her wrist and onto the tablecloth. He was out of the room already, collecting his hat and cane from the hall stand. The front door opened and closed, then opened and closed again. She heard his boots running back; he rushed to the dining table, to the letter, which he'd left on his sketchbook. Grabbing a pencil, he scrawled something upon it, in the top corner.

'Jimmy,' she said, rising from her chair.

'I'm going into town,' he told her. 'I have to talk to Anderson Reeve. Take this downstairs, would you? To the studio. Put it with the others.'

'The others? Jimmy, what in blazes—?'

'There's a box on the sill of the garden window.' He was heading back to the hall. 'I've been too supine again, my girl. Too goddamned supine!'

The door slammed, with finality this time. Maud saw him through the window, surging down the path and out along the pavement. She stood for a few seconds, coffee dripping from her fingertips, allowing the atmosphere to settle; then she reached over for the letter.

It was from Frederick Leyland, from his house in Liverpool, and a colder, more savage letter would be difficult to imagine. Jimmy had been seen walking with Mrs Leyland, apparently, at Lord's Cricket Ground – where he told Maud he'd been the week before. This was a final straw for her husband. He stated that Jimmy was incapable of gentlemanly conduct, and that if he found him in Mrs Leyland's company again he would give him a public horse-whipping. Maud covered her mouth; she almost laughed aloud. A *horsewhipping*. It was like a scene from a play, a melodrama, or a novel set long in the past. That someone would actually threaten to do it then, in London in 1877, seemed absurd. There could be no mistaking the letter's sincerity, though. Leyland was serious.

Maud's next thought was for Jimmy, and what he'd stormed off to do. Would he be so foolish as to confront

Leyland – to test the fellow's resolve? Of course he would. Should she give chase, then – catch him on the threshold, urge him to step away? No, that would never work; and besides, he had too much of a head start. She read the letter again. This was the new trouble with Leyland that he would not admit to her, and it had nothing to do with artworks or that blasted room. It was about the man's wife.

Above Leyland's address, in the top corner, was the number fourteen. This was what Jimmy had returned to the dining room to write. Maud recalled his instruction: *put it with the others.* She went down to the studio. Jimmy was bad with letters. Usually he had no system of arrangement or preservation, piling them on mantelpieces, on sideboards, on the floor, to be gathered up like so much litter and thrown away. But there it was: a small wooden box, plain in design, containing letters from Leyland, drafts of Jimmy's replies and a couple of telegrams, numbered from one to thirteen. These papers told the whole sorry story, from the dispute over the dining room to this current chapter: the attack and counter-attack of two very different voices. Jimmy's flippancy was startling, as were his efforts to divide up this family, to draw distinctions between the husband and the wife; whereas his adversary remained scrupulously formal, his language rigid and brittle – cracking as the quarrel worsened to reveal a real viciousness beneath.

Maud returned the letters to the box; she pressed down on the lid as if trying to hold them in. The house around her was quiet. She looked up, out into the garden. John was sitting by the gate, smoking a small pipe, idling in the absence of his master. Behind her, she realised, across the studio, the portrait of Frances Leyland had been put on an easel – returned from the cellar, if it had ever been there. The subject was turned away from the viewer, her hands clasped at the base of her back. She was part Japanese maiden, part medieval princess, the diaphanous, pinkish fabric of her gown heaping upon the chequered matting like a train. Jimmy had taken her in profile, head angled to the left, her rich brown hair – a similar tone to Maud's own – wound up loosely on her head. It appeared the pose of a moment, but Maud remembered very well the dreadful ache you'd get in your neck after six straight hours of standing like that. She'd never really seen Mrs Leyland in person. There'd been that time at Prince's Gate, when Jimmy was finishing off his mural; but she'd been in shadow then, merely a lady sweeping into a hallway. Here she looked rather melancholy, gazing at the pale blossoms dotted beside her as if lost in reflection and regret.

It was a fine work, rightly considered one of Jimmy's best. Maud had seen it before, of course, dozens of times. Now, though, she did find herself wondering why the painting was still in his possession, as it was surely finished and should be with the family – with the husband who'd ordered and paid for it many years previously. They were friends, Jimmy and Mrs Leyland. This she knew. There was a long-standing friendship with the whole family that was several years older than his connection with her. But had she been missing something here, something really rather obvious? Was it there in the portrait – in the sympathetic, faintly adoring way that Mrs Leyland had been painted? Was Jimmy actually in love with this woman?

The jealousy was devilishly sharp, a hot blade against the skin; but even as Maud flinched, a part of her was qualifying, setting out the broader view, warning herself against over-reaction. What could she expect here at Lindsey Row, in the end? What could she ever really be to Jimmy Whistler? No promises had been made, as Edie so liked to remind her. There was little feeling that they were building towards anything, towards any kind of change. She'd just sent their child for fostering, for heaven's sake, so that their circumstances could stay the same. Their child. That sweet scrap. Hers for minutes. Now in the care of strangers.

And what would she be left with? What would she be without Jimmy? A compromised woman. An artist's model, her best years already gone. An aspiring painter who couldn't even bring herself to pick up a brush. She dropped onto a rickety, paint-flecked stool, head sinking to her knees, dull with despair once more.

This would not do. She would not be led down this path. She sat up straight, wiped her eyes and made a determined effort to order her thoughts. John was gone by now – as was Mrs Cossins, off on her errands. The house was empty. Raised in a tenement, sleeping three to a bed, Maud had always savoured these stretches of solitude at Lindsey Row.

She'd read, or draw; leaf through Jimmy's albums of Japanese prints, with their blossom-blotted branches and firework displays and tall bamboo bridges, or his many boxes of photographs; or simply watch the light move through the empty rooms. That day, however, she felt blank, without appetite or inclination. She forced herself to think of art. The sky was overcast, muting the garden's colours, so she decided instead upon a self-portrait. This, according to Jimmy, was an exercise quite essential to a painter's growth – to his sense of what he could do and where he was heading. *Rembrandt*, he'd say, as if the name was an argument in itself. *Velázquez*.

Maud chose a sheet of red paper and a piece of chalk, put a wicker chair before a mirror and considered her face. She'd thought herself prepared, but still saw the shift in her own expression – the dismay. The eyes had a bruised squint; the skin was pallid, waxen; yet the problem ran rather deeper than that. Sad, she thought, setting down her materials. I look profoundly sad.

She stood at various windows. She went upstairs and sat on the bed. The summer sun broke through the clouds, the floor growing bright around her feet; and the notion arrived, sudden and irresistible, of travelling north. Of finding Edie, in Lionel Crossley's office or wherever she might be, and learning the address of the foster family – Edie had it, Maud was sure, even though she'd never admitted as much – and visiting her daughter. This could happen. It would be so simple. She'd let a month pass. More than a month. They were both in this same city. They were a mere handful of miles apart. Why shouldn't Ione know who she was – why shouldn't she be held by her mother? She might be smiling by now. She'd surely smile at her.

Maud wasn't aware of having made the choice to go – only of being at the end of their path, pushing open the gate in a hat and a jacket that did not match, running the coins in her pocket through her fingers to check she had enough for the fare. Glancing downriver, she saw a lone woman about twenty yards along the Row, over at the rail, gazing out at the water. It was Rosa Corder, clad in a bright coral gown. Maud was in no mood to talk with her. She'd been tight at the Café Royal that night, but not so much that she had no memory of what Rosa had said about Ione – about the fostering, and how it had been so *necessary* and so *brave*. The Owl's girl had acted like she knew everything about Maud and the decisions that had been made. Looking back now, it had the feel of trespass.

Rosa didn't seem to have seen her, so Maud hurried away up the cobbled slope to the end of the Chelsea Embankment, and followed Beaufort Street over to the King's Road. The omnibus stand was a few blocks to the east, close to the workhouse. Maud was already beginning to flag, her muscles protesting, but she walked towards it with everything she had. The long, straight street was quiet in the sunshine, with a sparse early afternoon crowd ambling along its pavements. A number eleven appeared ahead, wheeling in from the direction of Brompton, its flanks loud with notices for soap and matches and the latest cut of glove. Maud chased it for twenty or thirty yards, drawing level as it approached the stand. As she climbed arduously aboard, she noticed a vivid drop of coral, not far from the top of Beaufort Street, practically thrumming against the dusty shopfronts.

She handed over her tuppence and ducked inside the cabin. The two facing benches were empty save for an elderly couple, dressed in modest, much-mended clothes, the man fast asleep and snoring. The windows were open, but it was still oppressively hot, thickening the usual smells of dung, sweat and sawdust. They pulled away. Maud sat down opposite the couple, sliding along to the end; she caught her breath, turning this way and that on the bench, looking outside. Seeing no coral, she relaxed a little. It had been a coincidence, that was all. Rosa had probably been on her way from Putney, and would now be looking for a different omnibus to take her on to the West End. Maud's mind returned to her task. It was Thursday, which meant that Edie would be at her husband's neat little premises on Inkerman Road, just back from the high street, with a ledger open before her. She would walk in. She would say what she wanted, and hear no opinions on the matter. And then she would go to her daughter.

At Sloane Square there was trouble with a coal wagon. The omnibus halted and stood still; insults were slung between the drivers, briefly waking the slumbering man opposite, and prompting some scandalised whispers from his wife as the language deteriorated. Then Rosa Corder appeared at the cabin's entrance, her gown bringing a rich blush of colour to the varnished wood, altering the quality of the light. She must surely have come down the King's Road at a healthy trot – the coral dress was indeed dusty in places and its armpits a touch dark – but she settled onto the bench beside Maud as if she'd been waiting at the corner in a state of perfect leisure.

For a while the two women didn't speak. Others came aboard, taking places around them. Neckties were loosened and newspapers shaken open. Maud thought that perhaps she'd just stay silent. Surely Rosa wouldn't ride with her all the way up through Piccadilly, Euston and Camden Town. She'd see that she wasn't wanted and she'd disembark. Mind her own business.

'Forgive me for following you,' Rosa said eventually, as the omnibus eased its way into wider, busier streets. 'I was approaching your door when you left. I've had an idea – I was on my way over to tell it to you. Why don't we make an expedition together, with our sketchbooks, out to Hampton Court or somewhere? An artistic colloquy, it would be, of a sort. What do you think?'

Maud said nothing. She didn't even look Rosa's way. They rounded a corner and sunlight swept through the cabin, laying a scorching band across her face. She raised a hand to block it.

Unconcerned by this lack of a response, Rosa was now peering through a window at the long shed of Victoria station. 'I must confess that I don't know this route,' she said. 'It goes . . . north, doesn't it?'

And at that Maud was up, pushing past the knees of the elderly couple and worming between the bodies packed around the entrance. She felt damp fabric pressing against her, and the slippery flesh beneath; a beard dragging across her shoulder; someone's breath washing warmly over her neck; and then she was out, released onto the grand, curving street that ran away from the railway terminus towards Hyde Park Corner. She unbuttoned her jacket and pinched the top of her dress, peeling the material from her clammy collarbone. There would be another omnibus she could catch up there. But she had to be quick.

After a dozen yards or so Maud looked back – and sure enough, there was Rosa Corder, hopping down from the number eleven as it started to move. So it was to be a chase. Maud went faster, gathering up her skirts; she considered breaking into a run. Ahead, Hyde Park Corner was a great revolving ring of dust and noise. She reckoned that she could glance against its left edge and shoot off into the park, among the trees, along one of those endless diagonal paths. Lose Rosa. Recover herself a little, in the shade somewhere. Head over to Paddington and resume her journey to Kentish Town. To Inkerman Road. To Ione.

But it was no good. Maud simply couldn't manage it. She was still too weak; too strained and ridden with aches. Her lungs burned. She tasted blood, she was sure it was blood, in the back of her throat. By the time she reached the gateway to the park her limbs were lead, barely hers to command. She had to stop – to stagger out of the sun and lean hard, panting, against one of the fluted columns that fronted the gatekeeper's lodge. Rosa was there in less than a minute. Maud realised that it hadn't actually been any kind of chase at all. Her pursuer had been hanging back, biding her time, a cat stalking a crippled bird.

'You mustn't,' Rosa said. 'Please believe me. You think that this is something you have to do – something that will help you. But it will not.'

Maud wiped the sweat from her eyes. She waited for more.

'This life requires us to endure certain things. To adapt to them.' Rosa moved closer, joining Maud in the shade. She was speaking more softly than she ever had before. 'I can tell that you are strong, Maud, and that you are determined. You have made this place for yourself, with Jimmy. I couldn't bear to see you squander it.'

Maud glowered at the sandy ground. She felt neither strong nor determined. She felt like she was slowly melting. 'Squander it,' she repeated.

'There are different ways of living. This is becoming ever more clear. We might need these men, but we need not be defined by them. Not forever.' Rosa was nearly touching her now. 'Charles has a wife, you know, over in Putney. And an infant daughter, born in the spring. It suits him to be married. To be established. And I get the best part of him, there's no question about that. It is rather like having a different room in the same house. Would I swap rooms with Kitty Howell? Would I give up my studio and devote myself to rearing children, and worrying about linen, and arguing with the cook? I would not. I am an artist. *We* are artists.'

Maud looked off into the park. She kept quiet.

'It is difficult when a child is involved. I know it is. But it has to be this way. Maud, you have *Jimmy Whistler*. That really is an unbelievable thing. He is certain to rise. To overcome his enemies. And the better his position, the better everything will be. For both of you.'

Maud eyed her doubtfully. 'I'm going,' she said.

She moved from the column and selected a path, thinking again of Paddington. She was weary, though, deeply weary; and Rosa was still there too, slowing her further it seemed, causing what remained of her impetus to leak away. Fairly soon she came to see that it would not happen. She would not visit her daughter, not then. She would not hold Ione in her arms. The journey to Kentish Town, which had seemed nothing ten minutes earlier, telescoped out to an impossible distance. The afternoon was starting to grow old, besides – the sunlight becoming richer, deeper in tone, losing some of its glare. The moment had passed.

Maud veered from the path and sat beneath a tree. The grass around it was long and cool, tinted blue in the shade. She wanted to cry, perhaps; to curl up and sleep. She covered her face, welcoming the darkness, breathing heavily against her damp palms.

Rosa sat next to her. 'You must bide your time, Maud,' she said, 'that's all. You must be patient.'

*

After a while they began to talk. Maud knew that she was being teased out, that Rosa was trying to foster an alliance between them, but found that she was too tired to care; that it soothed her, in fact, to speak of the latest difficulties that were rapping at the door of Lindsey Row. Why in heaven's name should she keep it all secret anyway? Jimmy wouldn't be. He'd be telling everyone he could. Rosa was listening closely – and she knew a fair bit of it already, of course – so Maud gave her the entire story, the whole frightful swamp of the Leyland letters, right up to that morning's threat of a horsewhipping. This last part still left Maud thoroughly perplexed. Rosa merely nodded, however, as if it was an entirely predictable development.

'Leyland believes his honour is at stake,' she said. 'The situation has advanced. Mrs Leyland is involved now. I'd heard this might be so.'

Maud stared ahead. The morning's jealousy was resurfacing; she could feel it standing in her eyes. 'What've you heard?'

'There's a rumour that they were preparing to elope. Charles thinks Gabriel Rossetti is the source. He's been seeking to end Jimmy's connection with Leyland from the outset and has been dripping all sorts of poison into his ear.'

Maud didn't know what to say to this.

Rosa looked at her. 'It is nonsense, Maud. What on earth could Jimmy possibly find to admire about Frances Leyland? What has she ever seen, or said, or done? The woman is an adornment only, a millionaire's brood mare. I suppose she must be lonely. Ill prepared for the heights her husband's riches have raised them to. It is tragic, in its way. Mrs Leyland is friendless, derided everywhere for her lack of breeding, of manners – all those petty attainments that wealthy people prize. Jimmy alone has responded to her with decency. With kindness. No wonder that she clings to him as she does.'

Maud realised that this dismal picture was being drawn for her benefit. 'I don't *fear* her, Rosa. Never for a moment have I—'

Her denial faltered. Could Jimmy do such a thing – run off with a married woman, the wife of a prominent businessman? It would be a full-blown, shout-it-from-the-rooftops scandal. A lifetime's worth of trouble. But this was Jimmy Whistler. Trouble may well be part of the appeal. Maud had decided that he'd directed her to his Leyland correspondence with the deliberate intention that she should read it – to understand the battle he was fighting. Now it occurred to her that it could just as easily have been a form of confession, designed to prepare her, in some small part, for the overturning of her world.

Rosa saw her uncertainty. 'Jimmy values you, Maud. This is plain. For a painter to be with his model is hardly unusual.

But for the model to move into his house, to have a part in his domestic affairs as well as his artistic ones, to serve as companion, and as hostess . . . Yes, I believe he values you highly indeed.'

Maud nodded. She could see this. She'd known that her arrangement with Jimmy would be different. She'd known from the minute it began. They'd been laughing together in the studio, about something or other; he'd murmured an invitation, wryly offhand; she'd stepped down from the model table and accepted straight away. *Submitted*, some might say, but they'd be wrong. It had been a union. A meeting of desires. She'd been perfectly sure that she was safe; that it wouldn't end with abandonment, or destitution, or any of the other things Edie liked to predict. She'd seen it in him, seen it clearly, for all his quirks and posturing. They were joined.

But how much reassurance could this supply, honestly? Rosa was right. There were things she had to endure. Conditions and limitations. It could never be complete.

'How did Jimmy respond?' Rosa asked. 'Was there thunder?'

As Maud tried to frame a reply, she recalled an odd detail – something Jimmy had said just before his second exit, after numbering Frederick Leyland's latest threat. *I have to talk to Anderson Reeve.* She hadn't paid it any mind at the time, being too occupied with his great agitation and the letter that had provoked it. This Mr Reeve was a regular guest at Lindsey Row. Rotund, well groomed and somewhat older, Maud considered him a sober sort – and sobering also, as he was often required to pour cold water on all manner of hot-headed schemes. For Mr Reeve was Jimmy's lawyer.

*

The two women returned to Lindsey Row to find a dinner in progress, assembled hurriedly in the latter part of the day. It was a 'smoker', as they termed it, an occasion attended by gentlemen only and characterised by noise and an accumulating sense of chaos. Maud and Rosa were hailed, however, and offered elaborate words of homage – lauded for their beauty and grace, and the light they threw upon an otherwise dingy gathering. There was a general insistence that they join the party, their day clothes and slightly dishevelled appearance (in Maud's case at least) being dismissed as unimportant. Seats were found at opposite ends of the table.

Maud recognised Jimmy's mood. He had something to reveal and needed an approving audience. The guest list contained no surprises. Edward Godwin was there, and Matthew Eldon, along with Alan Cole from the museum, Bertie Mitford and a few others; and in a far corner sat Owl, clad in his grey suit, with that red ribbon pinned to his lapel and a cigarette between his fingers. A couple of them were on their feet, engaging in a spot of amateur dramatics, as Jimmy put it – enacting the moment when a certain befrilled British businessman attempted to carry out the horsewhipping of a notable and tirelessly audacious

American painter. Leyland, played by Bertie Mitford, stood upon the Chelsea pavement, drawing back his weapon; while Eldon, as the spry artist, hopped about, dodging the blows; then the whip's end snagged on the extravagances of the frill, tangling it around the persecutor's face and causing him, finally, to topple into the river.

Everyone roared and bayed, thumping the table until Maud feared for its legs. The morning's letter, she sensed, had been the sole subject of conversation thus far. When the laughter had subsided and the actors returned to their seats, Jimmy first apologised for the absence of victuals – temporary only, he assured them, his menu having posed Mrs Cossins with a couple of unforeseen challenges. Then he laid his eyeglass on the tablecloth and said that the hiatus did at least give him a chance to announce a rather significant development. Grins widened once more. This was bound to be good.

'In the spirit,' he went on, 'of my recent confrontations – the David and Goliath style of encounter that you fellows know I favour – I will be marching off to court for a battle of the, ah, *legal* variety.'

'Ruskin,' said Eldon. 'Has to be.'

Jimmy inclined his head in acknowledgement. 'I went to the Strand to speak with Anderson Reeve – who I have to say remains the brightest little lawyer in London – and he believes there is a suit to be brought.' He paused for a second or two, making a tiny adjustment to his knives. 'Libel. You all saw the notice, I assume.'

'Savage,' said Mitford. 'Irresponsible.'

'Yes, a poor show indeed,' added Cole. 'Ruskin, I fear, has passed the point of reason. Of fairness. Many are saying it.'

Maud drank some wine. She remembered the angry discussion in the Café Royal – the talk of recompense. Having an idea where this might be going, she looked to catch Rosa's eye, but to no avail. The other woman's attention was fixed entirely upon the Owl.

Godwin alone was doubtful. A lofty, dapper gent, an architect Maud had been told, he was a touch greyer than the rest of them, and tended to adopt a schoolmasterly air when with Jimmy and Eldon and the others. She'd mentioned this once to Jimmy, who'd laughed hard; 'Edward Godwin,' he'd said, 'is no deuced *schoolmaster*, I can promise you that.'

'A Goliath indeed,' he said. 'John Ruskin's influence, James, is difficult to understate. As is his petulance and his petty nature. This could inspire him to ruin you absolutely. To be written about in such a way must smart, that I understand, however—'

'It does not *smart*, Godwin,' Jimmy snapped. 'I have been painting for upward of twenty years, and am well past the point where the views of some splenetic journalist can injure my feelings. This here,' – he tapped his forearm – 'is the hide of a rhinoceros. No, the issue in this instance is *reputation*. I cannot have these hopeless fellows, these philistine millionaires and backward-looking critics, treating me with such open derision. This goddamned Ruskin does not simply attack my art. He attacks *me*. He calls me an impostor. He says that my work, my *Black and Gold*, the product of all the knowledge that I have attained, is but *a pot of paint flung in the public's face.'*

Loyally, the party shook their heads, grumbling with disapproval.

'He is blind,' said Rosa. 'As receptive as a rock on a riverbed.'

'And of course there is the money,' Jimmy added, to laughter. 'There's a hole in my finances, ladies and gentlemen, to the tune of one thousand guineas – thanks to the intransigence of Mr Frederick Leyland, our extraordinary British businessman. And thanks now to Ruskin, I have sold not one canvas from the Grosvenor, nor am I likely to in the weeks it has left. Nor, if we are honest with ourselves, in the foreseeable future. He has injured me, so he shall make up the shortfall. I have conferred with Anderson Reeve. We will seek one thousand guineas in damages. With costs, *naturellement.'*

He reinserted the eyeglass and looked over at Maud, supremely pleased with himself and expecting admiration. He plainly felt that this was the answer – the way in which their difficulties would be ended. His guests were delighted, for the most part. They began to talk of victory, of the rewards it would bring, and the great interest it would surely create for his paintings.

Godwin remained the dissenting voice. 'You seem to believe,' he sighed, 'that you are pitting yourself against some meek curate who pens the odd review for *Blackwood's.*

A harmless old sheep who will hand over his cash with barely a murmur. But this is John Ruskin. His *hide*, I would wager, is every bit as thick as yours. He'll argue this case to the hilt, and will employ the most capable advocates to help him do it.'

Jimmy made no reply. Instead he looked to his right, ceding the floor to Owl. The sleek Portuguese had stayed quiet up until now, gazing off appraisingly at the framed prints and painted fans that were hung across the walls; waiting for his moment, as it turned out, to stroll forward into the spotlight.

'I know Ruskin,' he said. 'Better than most, I think. I can offer an insight into how he might defend himself here.'

The company's curiosity was tempered with something rather like caution. Maud sensed a pulling back, a packing away of mirth; Owl plainly had a reputation of his own. Unconcerned, he started to talk, embarking upon a thorough demolition of England's most famous art critic. Ruskin, he claimed, was a dying star, a force in terminal decline, frail in both mind and body. Once the master of London's exhibition halls, he now had to be escorted around them like an aged relative on the rare occasions that he left his retreat in the Lake District – where he lived as a recluse, his eccentricities growing more acute by the day.

'And do you know who took him to the Grosvenor Gallery on this occasion? None other than Ned Jones and his wife, the fragrant Georgiana, whose works he went on to praise with as much warped fervour as he calumniated poor Jimmy here. There are connections, you see. Reasons behind the reasons. I also find it interesting that Mr Burne-Jones has recently discovered a new and enthusiastic purchaser,' – here he paused for effect, as Jimmy himself might have done, drawing on his cigarette – 'in the shape of our old pal Frederick Leyland.'

Maud attempted to set all this out in her head, this little conspiracy Owl was proposing; one or two of the necessary links appeared to be missing. The table around her seemed equally unsure.

Jimmy, however, was nodding strenuously. 'Yes,' he said, 'yes, that *is* rather interesting!'

'You were Ruskin's secretary, Howell, is that correct?' asked Godwin. 'Before you became . . . that which you are presently?'

'Secretary,' Owl replied, 'in the very broadest sense.'

And then he told them the most astonishing story – the one Jimmy had curtailed, Maud guessed, when they were in the Café Royal – of how John Ruskin, at the end of the previous decade, had consented to give drawing lessons to the young daughter of a family friend, a girl of barely more than ten years of age, with whom this august figure had managed somehow to *fall in love* in the fullest and completest sense, as a man falls in love with a grown woman. The sorry fellow had used his position of great respect and trust to woo this child, and get the poor innocent creature to agree to wed him more or less the day she came of age.

'When the parents got wind of what was going on, of

course,' said Owl, 'the drawing lessons came to an abrupt halt. The young lady was sent to Ireland, to be sequestered at a family estate. The end of it, you might think.' He took a gulp of wine. 'Not so, unfortunately.'

The Owl – then a younger, more impressionable man, and much in need of his employer's goodwill – had been dispatched to rural Ireland with a begging letter. Charged with placing it in the girl's hands, and bearing back her reply, he'd been given over two hundred pounds in cash to offer as bribes. The estate was closed to him, naturally, and he was hopelessly conspicuous among the peat-cutters and goatherds, so he'd disguised himself as a labourer. Waiting until the girl was alone, picking wild flowers in the grounds, he'd approached her slowly, the letter held aloft, and performed the task that had been assigned to him.

The table sat in disbelieving silence. Owl blew out a single delicate smoke-ring, awaiting the question.

Maud obliged. 'What – what happened?'

The Portuguese chuckled. 'Dearest Maud, what the blazes d'you think? She recoiled as if I'd handed her a dead frog. She read it in moments, damn near sobbing with the strangeness of it all, then passed it back to me, this declaration wrung from the deepest chambers of John Ruskin's heart, and told me that she could not grant him what he desired. Not now or ever. Sanity had been restored, you see. His influence shaken off. The child was a child once more. And it struck me too, most forcibly, like a bolt from above, as I stood there in the Hibernian gloom – clogs on my feet, a hessian collar sanding the skin off my neck, this innocent trembling before me, bravely rejecting the perversity I had travelled several hundred miles to lay before her. What, Charles, I asked myself, have you become a party to? What might he require of you next? I returned to London and ended our association forthwith.'

Owl sat back, swirling the remains of his wine about in his glass and tipping it down his throat. For once, for nearly half a minute, Jimmy Whistler's dining table remained absolutely quiet.

'Why do I tell you this distressing tale, my friends? Simply to show to you the kind of man John Ruskin is. His desires are not our desires. His judgements are not our judgements, or those of any right-minded person. He has deviated from the path of reason. This needs a full public airing. This *writing* of his needs to be called what it truly is, and the injustice of its effects corrected. Jimmy needs to be compensated. Of course he does. Ruskin has the cash, of that I can assure you. And I'd say that he should be made to donate a slice of it to our worthy friend here.'

Maud was persuaded. She looked around her. The company's earlier circumspection was gone. Everyone was raising their glasses, Godwin included. She quickly picked up hers as well.

Jimmy sprang to his feet, the eyeglass dropping out. 'The suit!' he cried. 'Ladies and gentlemen, let us toast the suit!'

*

The lawsuit was soon famous, discussed in the art journals and the various venues of artistic society, almost to the exclusion of everything else. Maud gathered that much of this was unsympathetic to the plaintiff. Jimmy Whistler was called a capering fool, a nuisance, an unserious man seeking merely to draw attention to himself and his work – to stage an advertisement, in essence, like the vulgar and dishonourable foreigner he was. The only way to combat such talk, Maud was told, was to talk oneself, and more loudly; to paint over it, layer upon layer, in tones more arresting and truthful.

And so the dinners began. Jimmy had been obliged to restrain himself for the past year or so, due to lack of funds. Now, though, with a thousand guineas surely on the way, and a righteous cause to fight, all reserve disappeared. New suppliers were found; new lines of credit opened. Lindsey Row was filled at least twice a week with lavish five-course dinners and the late Sunday breakfasts for which Jimmy was renowned. Mrs Cossins marshalled an unending parade of dishes up the narrow staircase from the kitchen: grilled soles and fricasseed chickens, wild ducks and salmons, French crêpes and all sorts of unlikely salads, followed by pastries and ices and flans. Empty bottles crowded the yard. The usual names appeared frequently, but they were mixed in with a staggering medley of others – a long list of influential acquaintances deemed ripe for recruitment to the Whistler cause.

Before each of these occasions a frank conversation would

take place to decide whether or not Maud should be present, in deference to the sensibilities of Jimmy's more respectable guests. Increasingly it was decided that she should not.

'Better to err on the side of caution,' he said, 'where toffee-nosed types are concerned. This is all primarily for show, Maudie, you understand. A duty rather than a pleasure.'

Exiled to the top of the house, Maud would mostly lie and read on Jimmy's bed, simmering with vague humiliation; to be subjected afterwards to half-recalled witticisms and his distracted, boozy caresses. There could be no mistaking the process, however. Jimmy was attempting to draw a battle line through the art world of London. She'd listen out on the landing as the story of the Peacock Room was related for the umpteenth time, along with the juiciest passages from the Leyland correspondence. The lot of Leyland's wife would be reflected upon sadly; and then, to restore their cheer, he'd embark upon his new favourite pursuit – reading out excerpts of John Ruskin's criticism, from volumes purchased especially for this purpose, in order to dismantle them line by line, refuting suppositions and exposing inconsistencies with ferocious glee.

Those who attended these gatherings were given the very best of him – premium Whistler, his energy and wit unflagging. Tours of the studio were made, with *The Three Girls* and the now notorious *Nocturne in Black and Gold* – recently returned from the Grosvenor, along with all the other unsold pictures – set out for viewing. He would even provide live demonstrations of his art, portraits sketched in chalk and oil, something he had previously abjured. And his reward was the keenest, most affectionate appreciation. All manner of things were predicted for him: certain victory against Ruskin; a fresh launch to his career, as a sought-after portraitist to the wealthy and fashionable; even a commission from the Crown, from the Prince of Wales, to decorate a royal property.

There on the landing – or later in his arms, the moustache rubbing against her shoulder as he snored – Maud allowed herself to think of how everything might be changed, and her spirits rose again in the up-down pattern of hope and dejection that was life with Jimmy Whistler. *A different way of living*. That was what Rosa had said. She just had to wait.

*

Coal merchants, however, would not wait. Fishmongers would not wait. The landlord would certainly not wait. Even Jimmy understood this. He was meeting often with Mr Reeve now, as the summer slowly burned itself out and the city began to cool. The suit became real. Legal terms abounded in Jimmy's conversation. Writs had been served, Maud heard; a statement of claim prepared. Reports reached them of Ruskin's reaction – one of relish, apparently, equal almost to Jimmy's own, the celebrated critic promptly appointing some grand old firm to represent him.

No one seemed able to estimate when the trial might actually take place, though, or the damages be paid, or the flow of lucrative new commissions begin. Maud grew a little nervous.

'*C'est rien,*' Jimmy would say to her. '*Rien de tout.* My dearest Maudie, you mustn't worry. You forget that we have the Owl.'

Much was said at Lindsey Row about the Owl's abilities. According to Jimmy, the fellow's business acumen was simply remarkable, and his contacts extensive; his art-dealing was imaginative and resourceful; his gift for spotting over-looked opportunities was entirely unrivalled. Thus far, however, his contribution had consisted of attending a great many of Jimmy's dinners – the breakfasts he was incapable of making in time – at which he would spin his tales, eat enough for three, offend at least one of the other diners, and then fall asleep in the drawing room, taking his leave at some point in the night.

Just as Maud was beginning to grow sceptical, the Portuguese appeared one morning with Rosa on his arm, quite unannounced, much as they had on that first day a few months before. Both, again, were exquisitely dressed, with the same attitude of genial inscrutability; but Maud knew them a good deal better now and could detect a specific purpose. Unusually, Jimmy was in, and they all met in the hall for a lively round of embraces and declarations of friendship. Maud and Rosa shared a confidential smile, a clasp of the hands; then the Owl swooped upon her, kissing each cheek and complimenting her fulsomely on what he termed 'the pace of your restoration'. She thanked him for this with a shy grin – only to furrow her brow very slightly as they started up the stairs.

'So, Jimmy,' said Owl, 'where is it?'

Was this another artwork, to be added to Owl's inventory? Jimmy didn't reply. He took them to an unused room at the back of the house, looking out over the garden; the obvious place, Maud had once thought, for a child. She'd only been in it a couple of times. Rubbish was piled all about: packing crates and boxes, stepladders and broken easels, old discoloured folders bulging with drawings and letters. He pointed off into a corner. A machine of some sort, made from wood and blackened iron, sat almost hidden from view. Owl quickly cleared a path to it, indifferent to the cobwebs that clung to his fine fawn suit, and beckoned the rest of them over. It was like a mangle, this thing – a long roller mounted in a frame, turned by a wheel on the side, with a wide, flat surface set at waist height. The Portuguese had a bottle, produced from beneath his jacket. There was a smell of fermented oranges as he flicked a splash of the spirit within onto the flank of this contraption, leaving a long dark star on the dusty wood.

'A tradition from my homeland,' he said. 'We must anoint the press. It will bring us luck. Here – the artist drinks first.'

The bottle was passed to Jimmy, who lifted it to his lips with a flourish, throwing back his head; the liquor sloshed about behind the tinted, brownish glass, but Maud couldn't actually tell if he'd drunk any. Rosa did, though, a hearty slug, downing the stuff without a shiver and handing it on to her. It was strong, floral and faintly cloying; she sipped and coughed, covering her mouth with her sleeve. Owl went last, taking in a great sucking gulp. He fell quiet, briefly, savouring the moment; then he gave Jimmy a sideways look.

'Are the plates still down in the studio?'

Maud swallowed, trying to get rid of the drink's taste. This neglected press was for making prints, she realised, like those Jimmy had hanging around the house, in stairways and corridors mostly: views of East London, of the docks at Limehouse and Bermondsey. They'd been done a good while ago, during his first years in London. It was a form with which he'd grown tired, he'd told her, despite being highly regarded for it. In the course of one of his inspections, it was now revealed, Owl had come across the original plates and had been astounded. Completely bowled over.

'More so,' he added, after another pull on the bottle, 'than with any of the works our dear Jimmy has stowed here. For a painting is a painting. It has a value, one places it with a buyer, the coin is paid and there you are. Done with. Prints, though, exist in *numbers*. They can be placed all over town, in a variety of premises. They come in series, do they not, when produced by an artist of any sense at least – series that all self-respecting collectors will want to complete. And of course they make a man's work known like nothing else. They *circulate*. In short, my dear Maud, they are gold. There is gold here, beneath this roof – gold in abundance, merely waiting for us to gather it in.'

The plates were retrieved from a cupboard down in the studio. There were around thirty of them, each eight inches by five, and wrapped individually in lengths of flannel. The two sash windows were thrown open to flush the room of smoke and dust. Jimmy and Owl then started fussing with the press, prodding this and testing that, assessing the condition of the mechanism: rather rusty, it seemed, in need of some repair.

Maud unwrapped the flannel on the topmost plate. The copper was still a deep, fiery orange and very clear, reflecting the underside of her nose and the slight bloat that lingered around her chin. Upon it, etched in lines of extraordinary delicacy and precision, was a rickety row of weatherboarded warehouses; the harsh pattern of masts and rigging; a gnarled sailor, perched in the foreground, looking on with a clay pipe jutting from his mouth. In the corner she noticed a small signature – just 'Whistler', written simply, very different to the elaborate butterflies with which his canvases were now marked – and beside it a date: 1859. She placed her fingertip against it, pressing until she felt her skin sink into the tiny, scratched numerals. She'd been but two years old.

Now, under Owl's direction, their labours began. Rosa and Maud readied the room: clearing space, sweeping the floorboards and constructing a work surface from two crates and an unhinged door. Jimmy sat in a corner and checked the plates – a slow task indeed, for poring over these early works caused him to sink into a kind of reverie – while Owl himself went out for supplies. He returned an hour later with a ream of heavy paper and a dozen cakes of ink, and also engine grease, various tools and pads of wire wool. Then he removed his jacket, rolled up his sleeves and set to work on the press. By early afternoon the machine had been thoroughly cleaned and returned to full operation. Owl demonstrated the action. The wheel spun slowly, almost carried by its own weight; the roller rotated and the flat panel slid through beneath. All in one polished movement.

Next, the Portuguese vanished into the lower floors of the house; and when he came back up Mrs Cossins was with him, somehow drafted in to help. Indeed, they were joking together as they climbed the stairs, the cook letting out a hoarse gurgling sound that could only be laughter. Maud was impressed. In the years she'd lived at Lindsey Row with Jimmy, the old woman had shown no interest or affection towards anyone save John the valet, to whom they thought she might be related; and certainly never to Maud herself, being of the openly stated opinion that the master's *Madame* had used deceit and wantonness to leapfrog life's rightful order. Yet here they were, Mrs Cossins' sheep-like face arranged into a smile so broad and genuine that the broken veins on her cheeks could almost be taken for a girlish blush. Owl was complimenting her *compote de pigeons*, saying that he had never tasted its equal – that she could surely depart this shabby abode and set her sights on the best addresses in the city. Jimmy made an indignant exclamation. There was more laughter.

Owl and the cook were carrying basins of water and lengths of cloth, which were then placed atop the door-table. After receiving a couple more compliments, Mrs Cossins withdrew. The Portuguese promptly set about running a length of twine above their heads, from the top corner of a window frame to a stretch of picture-rail above the door, and then arranged the four of them into a work-shop. Maud and Rosa were charged with dampening the paper in the basins and hanging up the prints when they were done; Owl was to grind up the ink cakes, mixing the resulting powder into liquid, while Jimmy applied it to the plates, painting it on with the greatest care and expertise; and they were all to take turns on the wheel.

This part Maud loved. The easing in; the peak of effort, of force; the sense in your palms, your wrists and arms, of *impression*, of the metal rectangle being forced into the paper, of the ink taking and the image being forever marked upon it; and then the easing off again, the bed of the press gliding out the other side – and the new proof being peeled off the plate and held up to the light. There was wastage, Jimmy being rather out of practice and the rest of them rank novices, but by the day's fading the line above them was like a length of bunting, filled with sheets from one end to the other. Maud counted them off, with no little pride: sixteen proofs of a saleable quality.

Dinner that night was especially fine, with an entrée – they noted – of *compote de pigeons* and bottles from a fresh stock of wine, Jimmy having discovered a new merchant prepared to offer him credit and ordered in with his standard abandon. Maud had devised an approach, after her experience at the Café Royal. She would take a single glass and eat a third of each dish, and a third only. It was extremely hard, though, not to drink at the same pace as the others, which meant that her allotted glass was gone long before the first course arrived, and was refilled by Owl without consultation. The compote, also, was so good that she'd put more than half of it away before she realised; so she thought *to the devil with it* and ate the rest. Tomorrow, she told herself sternly, smiling over at Jimmy. Tomorrow you eat nothing at all.

The conversation returned repeatedly to the prints. Their little party was aglow with a sense of shared achievement – of having found the solution, or part of one at least.

'Why, we could do this every week,' said Owl. 'Twice a week, if you find it necessary. By Jove, my dearest friends, we might as well be printing out pound notes. And it's just the beginning. The print is your future, Jimmy Whistler. I see it driving you onwards, as coal propels the great locomotives. You will race across countries, old man. Entire continents.'

'I only have so many plates, Owl, you know.' Jimmy

demurred. 'It isn't a medium to which I've devoted much time in recent years.'

'He means reproductions,' said Rosa. 'Copies of your paintings. You've never engraved your works, Jimmy, have you?'

'Copied myself, you mean? Good heavens, dear woman, I simply could not. No, I am not one of those *reproducing artists*. A chicken can only lay the same egg once.'

'Have you thought, then, of having another do it? Charles has many talented friends in this field.'

'I know men,' Owl qualified, 'who know men, if you follow me. You own the copyright on your works, don't you? I can certainly see some of your paintings, the *Carlyle* for instance, finding an enthusiastic market. Or that portrait of your mother you showed a few years ago at the Royal Academy.'

Jimmy moved in his chair, mildly discomforted. Maud recalled that this particular painting had disappeared from view on the day of Owl's initial inspection. She hadn't seen it since, in fact. He ventured that a portrait of his mother was surely of limited interest to the wider world. Absolutely not, replied Owl. It was a masterpiece, startling in its originality and beauty; the forms, the tones, would translate so well; the process would be speedy indeed, and the rewards enormous. Jimmy remained unconvinced. He repeated the chicken remark.

Owl switched subjects, encouraging Rosa to talk about Newmarket, where apparently she used to have a studio, making decent money painting portraits of horses and jockeys for the local stable-owners. The mood had altered, though; the laughter was less free, the wine slightly sour. A crucial change had occurred, a tiny weight added to one side of the scale that had thrown off the balance completely.

After dinner they went back upstairs. Maud led the way into the dark printing room, carrying a candle. It felt like a discovery. The windows were still open, the line of etchings shivering in a faint draught. The candle's light made the sheets seem very thin, almost transparent, and the inked images upon them so absolutely, indelibly black that they appeared momentarily to have separated from the paper and to hang suspended in the air. Maud ran her eye along the line, over the quays, the heavy harbour posts, the rows of barges and tall ships, marvelling anew at their clarity – the forms as strong, she thought, and as true in their arrangement, as photographs.

Owl and Rosa stepped around her and started taking down the proofs. The Portuguese had a folder that Maud hadn't noticed before. The prints were laid inside, then Owl wrote in his little notebook, inventory entries she supposed, and took them all over to Jimmy for inscription with the butterfly 'W'.

'And there we are,' said Owl, when the last was done. 'The 1877 impression of Mr Whistler's renowned Thames series. Twelve signed etchings. There's a man on Pall Mall, a most respectable dealer in prints named Graves, who will damn near tear off the arm that offers him these. Two quid a proof isn't unreasonable, I don't believe. I'll go to him first thing tomorrow – return to you with the tin, Jimmy, before the day is out.'

Lord Almighty, thought Maud, that's *twenty-four pounds*. Twenty-four pounds in a single afternoon. This would shoot down a half dozen of their outstanding bills straight away. Ward off any future calls from the bailiffs. Perhaps even enable the recovery of her mother's earrings. She turned to Jimmy, starting to laugh. He was smiling too, sort of, leaning wearily against the doorframe with an arm bent up behind his head. She could see the doubt in him – a suggestion that he felt compromised somehow. That in his sense of his progress through life and art, he'd just taken a small but ignoble step backwards.

Owl and Rosa left soon after. There were embraces again, and kisses, and promises of better times ahead; and then they set off at a brisk pace towards the centre of town. Jimmy was suddenly exhausted, unable to string two words together or observe his usually comprehensive ablutions. He merely removed his trousers, necktie and collar, and collapsed into bed. He was snoring inside a minute.

Maud undressed, standing her corset in the corner, and washed herself; then she lay down beside him in her shift and looked up at the bed's black oval canopy. A barge bell rang out on the river. Her breath slowed; her skin cooled. Do you know, she thought, I might just go straight to sleep. I might be spared my usual stretch of fretting and regret. Yes – there it was, that soft slide, that untethering of the thoughts; a greater ease, indeed, than she'd known since her return.

Then it came, like a switch rapped smartly across the thighs. She stared up again at the black canopy. They'd printed off sixteen, she was sure of it. Owl had said twelve. That's what he wrote in that little book of his: twelve signed etchings.

But they'd printed off sixteen.

*

Jimmy had already gone when Maud awoke – off to continue preparations for the suit, she assumed, as had become his habit. She headed out into their small garden, to savour what would surely prove one of the year's last warm days. A strand of ivy, the leaves dark and heavy, curled across the back wall. She considered it for a minute, then went into the studio for chalk and paper. The next few hours were spent sitting on an upturned bucket, buried in the slow summoning of a study. The result was not good, not by any means; she kept it only for reference, stowed away where no one would see it. But it was something. She was drawing once more.

It was well into the evening when Jimmy came home, released into the house like an over-excited terrier, skittering through the hallways and across the landings, yapping out her name over and over. 'Something really quite marvellous has been done,' he declared. 'Something *magical*. I can – I can scarcely believe it. I almost have to damn well pinch myself. Come, we must – you must – you must fetch your hat. You must see it, right this minute. You absolutely must.'

As she was marched up onto Cheyne Walk, pulling a shawl around herself, Maud mentioned the missing prints. Jimmy was dismissive; it was plain that for him the activities of yesterday were already in the distant past.

'An error,' he said. 'It's easily done with prints, God knows.'

'There were sixteen, Jimmy. Why would Owl say twelve? How many did you sign?'

'For pity's sake, Maudie, it really doesn't matter. If he did take them for himself, as you seem to think, then it is hardly unjust, is it? We can't expect him to toil away for nothing. One might even call it his compensation. The Owl, you know, is a fellow of rare ability – of *singular* ability. We need him to keep the show rolling onwards.'

Maud couldn't quite bring herself to agree. It was distracting, though, to be outside with Jimmy, walking alone by the Thames at nightfall. They used to do this a good deal in their early days. Together they would take in the settling mists, the lights of the factories and mills across the water, the clapboard hump of Battersea Bridge. He would stop, spying Nocturnes, drawing himself up and gazing out, committing scenes to memory for the following morning's labour. She'd stand close to him, feeling what she'd supposed must be *devotion*; that she had in some important way found her place. These were among her keenest and most precious memories.

It had to be admitted that this particular excursion was rather less leisurely. They were moving fast in the direction of town, Jimmy working his bamboo cane against the pavement like a boatman's pole, as if to provide further acceleration. No more was said about the prints or the Owl. Maud wondered where they could be going – what could be causing this excitement. The houses of the friends who would receive her were all further to the west, or up in Holland Park. Any gallery or dealer's shop would be closed. And they couldn't be heading out to the theatre or a restaurant, as Jimmy would have insisted that they both dress for it, and hailed a cab to take them there. Her one remaining guess was that it must be a new subject. A new view, found out somewhere on the dusky river.

Halfway along Chelsea Reach, however, Jimmy led them across the road, out of the light of the embankment's orderly lamps and into the gathering darkness. They entered a side street, stopping after a few yards. Maud looked around. It was incomplete, this street, half built; the houses that did stand there seemed handsome enough, but were largely unoccupied, and a lot of it was empty space. There was a gap next to them, in fact, behind a tall fence of black boards, upon which had been pasted an official-looking notice.

A deep breath and Jimmy was off. This was Tite Street, he began, a regrettable name but there you were; and right here at its riverside end was where his new house – *their* new house – was going to be built. Lindsey Row, he'd decided, was no longer satisfactory. Some really splendid designs had been put together by Godwin, who'd leased the plot from the Metropolitan Board of Works and found a suitable builder, a Mr Nightingale from Pimlico. The whole thing would be up within a year. The bamboo cane danced about in the damp air, sketching out windows and doorways, angles of elevation and the huge space at the top of the structure that was to be reserved for the studio – twice, three times as large as the one at Lindsey Row and flooded, always, with light.

Maud gazed into the empty gloom above the fence, trying to picture the house that might stand there. 'Heavens, Jimmy,' she said, 'it'll be big.'

And at this her thoughts acquired a momentum that she was unable to halt or influence. Ione was now four months old. Sitting up, most probably. There would be more rooms here. More space. Enough, surely, for a child to inhabit one corner while her artist father inhabited another. Things could be arranged – doors, corridors, staircases – so that he'd scarcely know she was there.

The cane was lowered. Jimmy turned towards her. There was no gas on Tite Street yet, its lamp posts standing dark; his face was little more than an outline. This notion of hers seemed to float between them, like a heart-warming scene from an illustrated magazine – and even as she contemplated it, and felt the sweet ache of it, she knew for dead certain that it could never be. Jimmy was an artist, the increasingly notorious butterfly, and she was his *Madame*, his hostess, his model. Family was not a part of this at all. He began to describe how the house was to be the setting for the next great stage of Whistler: an artistic structure, with art at its very foundations, made for painting and entertainments, which would soon become a site of pilgrimage for would-be patrons. On he went, predicting this and anticipating that: it was all so enthusiastically evoked, so absolute in its cancelling of Maud's own unspoken vision, that it started to annoy her.

'Jimmy,' she interrupted, after a while, 'how much is it going to *cost*? We can't pay the bloody butcher. How in blazes are we to pay for a house?'

'Damages from the Ruskin suit,' he answered smartly, 'will fund it. And a new wave of custom, attracted by the victory, my public vindication, will support a wonderful life within it. And there's the Owl's ventures, of course – the prints, lithography and so forth, that will cover our expenses until the trial is heard and the house brought into being. Glory awaits, my girl, truly it does. Can you not see it?'

Maud remembered what Rosa had said, on the day Jimmy had announced the suit against Ruskin: *the better his position, the better everything will be*. This studio house had to be a part of that. It would mark a definite advancement, just as he claimed: a new and higher platform upon which other things could be built. But what, precisely, and when? Rosa had also said that she should be patient. There on Tite Street, though, before that empty plot, her patience felt limited indeed.

Jimmy lit a cigarette. The flare of the match revealed him briefly, standing there in a dark suit and topper with the black fence behind. Cane resting against his shoulder, he was completely assured, craftily handsome, his eye glinting at the thought of his coming triumph. He shook out the match and drew closer, snaking an arm around Maud's waist.

'Let's go out for supper,' he said. 'To celebrate. I have the tin right here. How about that place you like up by Wellington Square? They keep a decent Moselle, as I recall.'

The cigarette was passed to her, the end slightly damp from his lips. She let it hang in her mouth unsmoked, sliding her own arm around him, attempting to quell her irritation and her doubt. What else, really, could she do? This was Jimmy Whistler. A little faith was required.

Part Two

Arrangement in Grey and Black

Winter 1877

Whistler was on the town. It was happening, finally, as it was supposed to – a steady accumulation of good things. His name was mentioned in every conversation. His endeavours were reported in every newspaper. He went out as much as any mortal man could manage, five nights in the week usually. He dined in Mayfair mansions, Holland Park follies, the smart bachelor flats of Piccadilly and elsewhere; he attended acts of plays, a movement of the odd opera and music parties in parks and pavilions; he haunted restaurants, taverns and clubs of every stripe, scheming with friends and castigating foes. All of this honed his rhetoric to a most satisfying level. You could sell tickets, he told himself. You could speak in a hall somewhere and they'd surely pay to hear it.

The two principal topics did not change. Foremost was

the approaching confrontation with John Ruskin and all Jim had learned about the critic since the firing of that first savage shot.

'Too quickly!' he would cry. 'Our dear Mr Ruskin says that I paint *too dashed quickly!* And yet one only has to open any of his dozens of volumes to find exultation upon exultation being piled upon the Venetians. Upon *Tintoretto*, for pity's sake, the fastest painter of them all. Why, the fellow would cover a half-acre of canvas in an afternoon. And *Turner* – my goodness, he will not be quiet about Turner. A more potent example of undeserved attention is difficult to call to mind.'

'Do you not value Turner, Mr Whistler?' someone would ask. 'Forgive me, but your *Nocturnes* seem to hold a definite resemblance.'

Jim would dismiss such comparisons at once. 'My works resemble old Turner's,' he'd declare, 'as the finest chocolate resembles the droppings of a dog.'

There was always a rather pleasing reaction to that one.

The other great subject, of course, was the Leylands. It was the controversy that would not die; the gift that simply would not stop giving. A sting did still linger there. This Jim had to admit. The children's severance of all connection with him had inflicted a wound far graver than anything doled out by their father. He'd also heard that another painter, a distinctly inferior talent named Morris, had been commissioned to paint Mrs Leyland in his stead. This rascal was reportedly going great guns with the thing, and planned to have it in the Academy show the very next year. At first, it felt as if Jim's own personal territory was being infringed upon – until Godwin helpfully reminded him that it was, in truth, his no longer.

None of this prevented him from playing out the old tales, however, with a couple of new chapters attached. Rather to his delight, Leyland had seen fit to forward him a gas bill covering the period of his occupancy at Prince's Gate, a bit of pettiness that played into Jim's hands so perfectly he was almost thankful to add it to his ever-growing pile. He began to wonder if the fellow was losing his grip on the situation.

To Jim's own entertainments – which were kept up with formidable frequency in that dingy, unsatisfactory dining room, stuck at the rear of that unsatisfactory house, on that unsatisfactory fag-end of a street – something else was now appended: the communal outing, on foot or by carriage, eastwards along the river to Tite Street. Sometimes this would grow into a procession, two or three four-wheelers, with an appropriately carnival atmosphere. Jim would have his cabman park before the plot and would climb up onto the vehicle's roof to describe the bold plan he and Godwin had settled upon. Aided by the cane, he would attempt to convey the stunning starkness of the design, the clarity and simplicity of its lines, the Japanese slope of its roof – to be made with tiles of a deep dragonfly green that would glisten and glow in the London sunlight, precious rare though it was. And the walls beneath would be white. Yes, *white!* None of this muddy red brick for Whistler! No dun timbers or dull stone!

'By Jove,' murmured Owl, his hooded eyes narrowing a little further. 'Our favourite American lodged in his very own White House.'

And thus it was named.

'This has all been approved, I assume,' asked one of his guests, a lawyer he thought the fellow was, on one excursion after a Sunday breakfast.

'Yes, yes,' he answered at once, then puffed reflectively on his cigarette. 'By whom do you mean, exactly?'

'By the Board of Works, Whistler, of course,' the lawyer replied. 'Since the completion of the embankment, they have become known for being rather *exacting* with regards to new structures – the character of the neighbourhood, and so forth . . .'

'Godwin arranged the lease,' Jim informed him airily. 'The terms of the contract. I'm sure everything was agreed then.'

The pace of the construction surprised him, despite the assurances that had been made when he'd started signing things. The exterior walls rose at speed, accreting like some kind of unstoppable natural phenomenon, barely contained by the scaffolding; the rooms within, their dimensions and the placing of their windows, became ever more discernible. The builder, Mr Nightingale, was an efficient, straightforward sort of man, lean and leathery, with a blacksmith's beard and a top hat wrapped in sealskin to proof it against the weather. He could usually be found on site, checking and measuring, correcting the work of his subordinates. Jim liked him immediately. He would make a point of waving a hand or cane in Nightingale's direction and stopping to exchange a few words if the fellow was available. These were conversations trimmed of fat, masculine and gruff, concerning matters of mortar, elevation and joinery, or the hazards of the frost – extremely refreshing after the effete ramblings of artistic society. Jim could really *talk* to these men, he'd always felt, these menial types; he'd none of the awkwardness he saw in Godwin, say, or Bertie Mitford, or Leyland even, who'd started out among them. He could adopt their manners, their essential simplicity, as if he was slipping on a coat. It was a talent of his.

A week or so into the new year, Jim was returning from one of these powwows when Owl – who'd waited with Eldon in the relative warmth of the cab – remarked that at the rate everything was going he'd be hanging pictures on those walls by the spring.

'Conception to residence in less than a year. My stars, Jimmy, it's an endeavour worthy of Caesar.'

Two large chaps were Eldon and the Owl – one this fleshy, auburn Portuguese, the other a strapping flaxen-haired Saxon, albeit running a little to seed – and between them they more or less filled a hackney carriage. While Jim picked his way through their legs, slotting himself beside Eldon, Owl talked on about furnishings, not at the White House but at Lindsey Row. His interest was in the pieces that had no place in the new residence, or could not be moved; the many fittings installed over Jim's eleven years there that the landlord had no claim on and that could be sold, either to the next leaseholder or another party.

'Of which,' he added, 'there is always a plentiful supply.'

Jim had to laugh as the cab started off again, bearing them on to some assignation or other. This was the Owl's great gift, his mind's basic orientation – the wringing of profit from any and all circumstances – and it was proving valuable indeed. He'd come to serve as a lens between Jim and the more practical side of things, supplying an essential focus, making a dense and confounding script fully comprehensible. Each time they met there was a new scheme to be outlined or a new spin applied to the existing ones – a different way to shift art, rake in tin and confound their adversaries.

'Matters various, old man,' the Portuguese would announce, pulling up a chair, 'for the betterment of the show.'

The Thames etchings sold well, for a while at least. As that waned, Owl reminded Jim about his lithograph man, over in the West End, and then mentioned that Graves the printseller did in fact happen to know a fine engraver, a real master of mezzotint, who was prepared to take on the portrait of Thomas Carlyle. Owl was well aware that Jim had his doubts here, a dim yet troubling sense that the replication of paintings might have an inimical effect upon the originals – upon their reputation, certainly, but also somehow upon their *essence*. The pitch, accordingly, came rather harder than usual.

'You do nothing,' Owl said. 'Nothing at all. And the coin comes gushing in like seawater into a holed ship. It positively sinks you in riches. If this one goes to plan, if we like this engraver and what he can do, then all sorts of interesting avenues become open to us. Here's one for starters. The great men of our time. Portraits by James McNeill Whistler. A series of subscription prints.'

'A series? Really, Owl? What pictures would we use?'

'Along my travels,' Owl enlarged, 'and my assorted endeavours for Ruskin – his charitable works in particular – I made the acquaintance of several rather famous fellows. Any one of them could serve as our second instalment.'

'Who are we talking of here, precisely?'

'None other than the Prime Minister. You are looking a trifle dubious now, Jimmy, but I'm pretty sure I could secure a sitting – several sittings. We rubbed along rather well, did Disraeli and I, when I negotiated with him to secure a pension for poor old Cruikshank. He may even wish to buy the portrait – him or some admirer of his. I'll make enquiries.'

In addition to identifying potential sources of custom, Owl provided it himself. Having noticed a small *Nocturne*, the *Grey and Gold* – Chelsea under snow, lit by a mullioned tavern window – that had been painted a couple of years before and left ignored in a corner, he asked if Jim could possibly accept £30 for it.

'A late Christmas gift, it would be,' he explained. 'From Owl to Owl.'

Jim happened to be rather stuck just then, financially speaking, due to certain Yuletide expenses. So he agreed – as it was Owl and as he had the cash with him, or the larger part of it at least. The fellow was immensely pleased, promising to allow the painting's exhibition whenever and wherever it was required; and then, almost casually, he commissioned a full-length portrait of Miss Rosa Corder.

'I can pay you a hundred quid,' he said. 'Please say you will, Jimmy. I mentioned the idea to Rosie a few days back and it's all she's talked of since. She'd give you every last minute of the time you need, obviously.'

Jim was moved by this. So grateful that it left him some-what embarrassed. 'Words, *mon cher*,' he managed to mutter, 'are so dreadfully insufficient to describe what you have become to me. To my endeavours. To my household, and—'

'Jimmy,' Owl interrupted, gently reproachful. 'I am your friend.'

*

Despite his mounting celebrity, Jim remained quite grind-ingly poor. Tradesmen had become more willing to thaw out his accounts, however, or to open up new ones. The bills and writs had also grown less insistent. His creditors seemed to be holding fire, rolling back their cannon. A promise had settled upon him, he realised, and a powerful one at that. A promise of wealth to come.

The statement of claim was published, identifying John Ruskin's calculated and deliberate attempt not simply to object to Jim's painting, but to demolish his name. A riposte came swiftly, Ruskin's lawyers issuing a statement of defence – a formal counter-attack in which they claimed fair comment on a matter of public interest. Anderson Reeve had been disturbed by this, mumbling on about how it was a most unusual step; how it was customary for the other side to wait until they were in court before making such declarations. Jim began to suspect that the solicitor's giant-killing instinct was not quite as strong as his or Owl's. He told the fellow to find his courage – and to bolt it to the goddamned mast.

Reeve shook his head. 'I fear,' he said slowly, 'they may be attempting to stall us.'

'How so?'

'It must be looked at, this statement of theirs. I believe they are seeking to suggest that a trial should not take place. They won't succeed, of course. But I'm afraid it will mean a delay.'

A nefarious turn indeed. These legal men truly were the vermin of the earth. They seemed to know about his situation, about the White House – the payments for which he'd soon be liable, along with everything else – and that *delays*, and the accumulation of further costs, might force him to call the whole thing off, simply because he couldn't afford to proceed any further. But how might they have learned all this? Jim's immediate thought was Leyland. He could be the only real suspect here. The shipbroker certainly had his connections, on the Board of Works and who knew where else. He had surely extended the hand of – well, if not exactly friendship, then fellow suffering, as one who had also tangled publicly with this troublesome painter. Strategic advice had been dispensed. Sensitive information disclosed.

Hopes for a spring trial and a settlement before the summer – before the completion of the White House and the delivery of Mr Nightingale's monumental bill – started to strain, to creak and stretch like an overloaded rope, the plaited cords snapping one by one. Then, on a bright morning in late winter, Reeve rode out to Lindsey Row and made the decisive cut. Jim was down in the studio, attempting to select works for the second Grosvenor show – reflecting as he did so on the dizzyingly rapid pace of life, how he was still ensnared by issues thrown up by the first blasted exhibition, how it so often felt that he was hurtling, yes *hurtling* towards his dotage, and the tomb soon thereafter. He turned to the solicitor with a pained, preoccupied smile.

'Ruskin's health has collapsed, Whistler.' Always prone to talking rather too quietly, Reeve was now practically whispering, as if he imagined they might be overheard; Jim was obliged to come a few steps closer. 'Details are scarce, but word is that the man has gone mad. Completely out of his mind.'

Jim stared; he nearly laughed. 'Absolutely not.' For a few

seconds he was overwhelmed. 'I – I mean, he's faking. Mad? Just now, at this precise moment? How very deuced *conveni-ent*, Reeve! Well – we must have it tested. Dispatch our own doctor for an independent diagnosis. Where is it he's cowering? The Lakes, up in the north? My brother, Dr William Whistler of Mayfair, he'll do it. He would and he damn well should. I'll send a telegram, shall I?'

Jim was serious, in deadly earnest, but Reeve chuckled as if at a dark joke – and then went on to make it extremely plain that there was nothing to be done. That honour forbade it.

Owl came by not long after. Rather to Jim's amazement, this news did not surprise him. 'On the cards, old boy, to be perfectly frank. Very much on the cards. A diseased brain, old Ruskin has – with regards to the fairer sex, obviously, but in other regions too. I recall that he had an acute sensitivity to light, if you can believe it. Reflections, in particular, would unnerve him. Flames on silver, or varnished wood. He told me once that he felt them some-times to be alive. To be spectres, echoes of the dead. I have wondered, you know – as he detested actual fireworks on account of this, and would go to great lengths to avoid them – if this particular foible played a part in his, shall we say, *emphatic* reaction to your painting . . .'

This hardly mattered. The fact of it was that word of the blasted critic's descent into delirium was well and truly out, released over London like a flock of pigeons; and Jim's brief period of triumph, of being so very much *on the town*, underwent the first of what was to prove a long series of diminishments. There were rumours that the suit had been dropped – how could it hope to proceed when the would-be defendant was said to be gibbering around his Cumbrian flower garden dressed only in a nightshirt?

Jim went about debunking these rumours as best he could, asserting that it was all a trick by Ruskin's people, a deception born of fear. In truth, though, he was experiencing a degree of fearfulness himself. The critic's collapse would hold everything up, which in turn would mean an almighty lag in his income. For perhaps the first time, real penury loomed over Lindsey Row. The prospect was akin to dangling out above a yawning chasm, sudden and bottomless, your stomach wrung like a rag, the blood thumping thickly in your neck, your mind blank and raging. It was panic. There really was no other word. And just one solution existed. Jim knew it – the only path out of this unholy fix.

He had to work.

*

March 1878

Miss Corder arrived very much set on black. She was dressed in black, head to toe, and asked for the black velvet backdrop; and as she helped Jim hook it up, she spoke of her deep admiration for his portrait of Frederick Leyland – the subject notwithstanding – which employed a similar black-against-black arrangement. He wasn't aware that she'd seen this painting, which had been banished to the cellar for some months now. She talked away enthusiastically, however, declaring that his skill with black, with its minute shifts and shades, was perfectly unrivalled. What choice did he have after that?

Before long Maud heard them, wandering in from whatever she'd been doing. Miss Corder was most pleased to see her, and eagerly requested any advice she could offer on modelling. They practised as Jim prepared his materials, striking attitudes, trying out various anglings of the head and hips. It pleased him, the amity that had developed there. The unaffected regard that Miss Corder showed his *Madame*, and the way Maud smiled a little bashfully to hear it. The natural intimacy of their conversation. It made everything easier.

Miss Corder stepped up onto the model table, a low podium perhaps a foot high. A pose was agreed and adopted, and the basics swiftly laid in – the face and shoulders, the line of the back. Eldon appeared in the early afternoon, somewhat tipsy, saying that he'd been passing by. He installed himself upon the studio chaise longue and was soon applauding Jim's every stroke, clapping his hands above his head and calling out 'Bravo!' Maud giggled; Miss Corder's composure slipped. Jim couldn't resist playing up to it. He darted back and forth before the canvas, as if filled with a furious creative energy. He harrumphed and muttered and exclaimed. He swapped about brushes and colours for the sake of a single dab.

The result, predictably perhaps, was pretty hopeless. Jim crossed his arms and cocked his head, memorising its errors, then went to a cupboard for his broad-ended knife – and to cries of protest from Eldon and Miss Corder, he set about scraping the canvas clean, stripping off the half-dry pigment in soft, rubbery ribbons.

'He does that,' Maud told them, 'all the time.'

They made for a merry little band, though, the four of them, and could see no reason to break apart as the day waned. Jim shared his plans for the evening: a trip to the West End to attend to an easy bit of business, supper somewhere, and then on to the Gaiety in time for the final act of *The Grasshopper*. Eldon was wholly at liberty, as was Miss Corder, the Owl's present whereabouts being unknown. So, once Jim had changed, a four-wheeler was flagged down and off they went.

Jim's business was in the heart of theatre-land. The cab dropped them just by the Strand, at the top of Wellington Street. It was quiet, cobwebbed with fog, performances well underway in all the major houses. With his cane, Jim pointed towards the Lyceum – or rather to the small parade of shops beside it. One in the middle still had its lamps lit. Stencilled across the window in a gentle arc was *Thomas Way & Son: Fine Printmakers*.

'Are you quite sure that we won't be a nuisance?' asked Miss Corder as they approached.

This hadn't occurred to Jim at all. 'Goodness, no,' he replied. 'Absolutely not.'

Jim had always liked offices, workshops, that sort of place; not actually to *work* in, of course – heaven forbid! – but he found the air of efficiency and order peculiarly reassuring, so alien was it to him. Upon his entrance, the two fellows named on the window hurried out from the back to shake his hand, murmur their greetings and compliments, and say what a pleasure it was to remain open past their usual hours to receive him. Thomas Way was a bandy, bright-eyed spaniel of a man; and his son basically himself as a youth, no more than eighteen years old. Both were in ink-stained aprons, bless them, with printers' tools tucked in the front pockets and those little green visors upon their brows. The artist and his retinue plainly left them rather awestruck, and if they did feel any unseemliness at having Maud there, or Miss Corder, they didn't dare show any sign of it.

'Mr Way,' Jim informed his companions, 'is a master lithographer, the best in London. And therefore the world. He is poised, *mes amis*, to save me.' He swept his arm around the office – the display cabinets, the framed prints on the wall, the machines just visible to the rear. 'His form, this great medium of the lithograph, will save me entirely.'

Jim's arm finished its sweep upon the shop counter, indicating a mounted print, unframed, standing on a desk-easel: a *Nocturne* in ink, an original work. The Thames was shown in the full serenity of night – an unbroken expanse of water, stirred by the faintest ripple, the darker ridge of the opposite bank, a single chimney against the immaculate sky – all of it done with only soft jades and a note of shimmering blue. The lithograph, with its panels of stone and grease crayons, was one branch of print-making about which Jim could be genuinely keen, and he was proud indeed of this first attempt. It had been drawn a week or so before, in a single sitting – from memory, as was his practice – right there in Way's office, at a desk in the back, with the printer and his son in reverential attendance. He couldn't help noticing, however, that dear Way was beginning to look rather uncomfortable. The printer's smile was flattered, unmistakably, yet a touch queasy as well. Leaving the others to admire the *Nocturne*, Jim took Way aside and enquired about subscriptions – the true purpose of his visit, after all.

The terms had been extremely reasonable, perhaps too reasonable: signed proofs at one guinea each, unmounted prints at half a guinea. This had been done at Owl's urging, shortly after he'd first brought Jim to Way's office and made the introduction.

'A modest start,' he'd said, 'is vital. We must make the things accessible, get them *out there*, you know – and then slowly restrict supply, increasing our prices as we go. Basic commerce, old man. Basic commerce.'

Owl had also assisted with the circulars, providing several hundred names on top of those that Jim and Way could summon, creating a great roll-call of London's print collectors. Success had seemed guaranteed. Now Jim gripped Way's shoulder, in a gesture of confidence and confidentiality.

The man's muscles were like ropes; all that print-pulling, he supposed.

'What news, Way?' he asked. 'How many so far?'

Way couldn't meet his eye. 'We've had three in the past week, Mr Whistler. Since they was sent out, that is.'

Jim didn't understand – was this some printer's abbreviation? 'Three score, you mean? Three dozen?' He paused. 'Three hundred?'

The fellow shook his head. 'No, sir. Three.'

Jim released him. There was a ghastly cramping sensation gathering inside his chest, like the clenching of a fist. 'Three,' he said.

'Others may come,' Way told him, a little desperately. 'I've known it happen. Word may get around. You mustn't lose heart, Mr Whistler. We are just beginning here. Mr Watts has been in, several times, talking of the *Piccadilly*. It may be that once your images are in his magazine, interest in them will increase.'

'*Three*,' said Jim again, rather harder and louder. He heard a sneering note in his voice this time, directed at Thomas Way, artistic pygmy that he was, and his depressingly ordinary premises; at himself and the failure that dogged him. That clung to him like a bad goddamned smell.

A minute later they were outside, Miss Corder taking them to a restaurant she knew of nearby. They went to a table and ordered, the women chattering in a determined fashion that made it plain they'd deduced the nature of Way's news. Jim said next to nothing. Eldon filled his glass, but he did not drink. The food arrived, a rack of beef; Jim could barely stand to load his fork and lift it to his mouth. The meat was matter only, devoid of flavour and nourishment. He managed less than a quarter of his portion.

'Jimmy,' Maud whispered, 'shall we go home?'

He glanced up. Three worried faces were leaning in on him. This served as an immediate corrective. What man could stand to be *pitied*, on top of the rest of it?

'No,' he said. 'Of course not.' He pushed his plate away and removed the napkin from his collar; he brushed a crumb from the deep black of his dinner dress. 'It is the *Grasshopper*, Maud. It is the end of the run. Whistler must be in attendance.'

This production was a farce of the broadest kind, a speciality of the Gaiety – penned originally in Paris, Jim had been told, to mock artists and the disordered lives they led, and to take a couple of more targeted shots at those painters the papers had begun to call *Impressionists*. Adapting the piece rather hurriedly for the London stage, someone at the Gaiety had decided that Whistler, and Whistler in isolation, was the local equivalent. Jim's reaction to this had been one of open glee. He'd been to see the thing a half dozen times over the course of its short run, always in company, drawing as much attention to himself and his enjoyment as he could.

Certain of his friends had been mystified by this. 'But it is mockery,' they'd say, 'and such a mediocre script. The jokes are so stale. How can you bear it?'

'You must understand,' he'd explained, 'that something of this nature should be *owned*. Taken into one's possession. This draws the venom from it, you know, every last drop. And it is proof of real distinction, after all. *Mon chers*, it is proof of fame.'

On this final night, however, the Gaiety's cavernous, gaudy hall was more than half empty, the stalls dappled with vacant seats. Many of Jim's circle who'd vowed that they'd be present were not, as far as he could see. Even Godwin – who was often at the Gaiety, prowling about for actresses – was nowhere to be found. Nonetheless, Jim managed to prop himself at the front of their box, the eyeglass inserted so that it would flash in the stage lights, in order to laugh loudly – and not entirely kindly – at the parts that concerned him. Despite the numerous times he'd seen it, he couldn't say with any great certainty what the plot involved. Two young friends vying for artistic prominence? A girl who wished to paint disguising herself as a man to improve her chances of success? Perhaps. It hardly seemed important. His scenes, as he thought of them, were in this last act. At one point, a full-length caricature was wheeled out – with bamboo cane, white forelock and eyeglass – to be venerated by all onstage as a likeness of the master. At another, a crude parody of a *Nocturne* was made to serve as two different paintings by the ingenious conceit of being turned upside down.

Eldon laughed along with Jim, with the same sardonic heartiness; he really was the best follower one could wish for. Maud, hanging back in the shadows, let out the occasional groan. Miss Corder, however, was contemptuous, quite nakedly so. New to *The Grasshopper*, and made fractious by wine, she took against its liberties in the very fiercest manner. She scowled and sighed. She tutted and heckled. And then, at the conclusion, to Jim's enormous delight, she rose from her chair and she damn well *booed* it. She booed the actors individually, and she booed the ensemble when they lined up for their final bow – throaty honks of disdain that one wouldn't imagine a young woman of her build and apparent refinement was capable of producing.

'I will never understand those,' she announced, as they prepared to leave, 'who actually take pride in their damned ignorance.'

April 1878

Jimmy's voice was shrill, signalling exasperation. Maud had been heading through the studio, towards the double doors and the garden beyond, where he'd been for most of the morning. Now she slowed, hanging back. Someone had joined him; they were talking through the situation at the White House. The equation Jimmy had sketched for her that night on Tite Street – the series of debits and credits that would carry them through the construction and the trial, to the golden uplands beyond – had already been shown to be unworkable. This had caused disgruntlement and dismay, the occasional moment of wild terror, and much, much discussion. Maud wasn't completely sure that she wanted to hear it all again.

Owl was standing there in his grey topper, set against a backdrop of seething greenery. He looked rather out of his element; brushing away a shaggy tendril that was dipping over his shoulder, he began repinning his crimson ribbon, his Order of Merit or whatever it was, nodding as he did so. To the left of him were several of Jimmy's canvases, propped in the sunshine – *mellowing*, as he would have it, after a spot of touching up ahead of their transportation to the second Grosvenor exhibition. It was to be a more modest showing for Whistler this year. Maud could see a *Nocturne* and two full-lengths set up by the garden wall, tilted like sunflowers upon their easels, the images partly obscured by the crackle of light across the varnish.

Jimmy was out of view, off somewhere to her right. He was holding forth with great vehemence about the delays caused by the recent interference of the Metropolitan Board of Works. One of their architects had objected to the character of Jimmy and Godwin's design, apparently, declaring it to be too plain.

'Like a dead house, they are saying. A *dead house*, Owl! They are insisting on changes, the most vulgar additions, before they'll grant the lease.' Jimmy made a sound, partway between a growl and a sigh. 'I blame Godwin. It pains me to say so, *mon vieux*, but I do. This is his realm. These are his people. He should have anticipated it. Acted to forestall it.'

'The Board of Works,' Owl demurred, 'are difficult buggers at the best of times. I'm not sure——'

'I shall do what I can, *naturellement*. Spread word about town. They have no idea, I think, who they've picked as an enemy here. I've dined with a couple of the very top Board of Works fellows – or their wives, at least. There'll be an angle.'

'That's the spirit, old chap. You must stare it in the eye.'

'It's a campaign, you know,' Jimmy continued. 'A campaign against me. For he knew the very minute I obtained the plot. He has his spies, no doubt, on the Board of Works, who are seeing to it that these ridiculous obstructions are placed in my path. Palms have been greased, *mon cher*, and greased well. Why, I'd be surprised if this damned Board architect hasn't been bought entire.'

Owl hardly needed to ask to whom Jimmy was referring. The hand of Frederick Richards Leyland was seen everywhere. Several seasons had passed since the horsewhipping threat, the better part of a year; it had seemed, for a while, that Jimmy's sense of grievance was diminishing. But then news had reached him that Fanny Leyland – being something of a prize, a girl both pretty and staggeringly rich – was engaged after but a single turn about the course, to some dullard in naval insurance, a widower older even than Jimmy. He'd been particularly stung by the fact that the family had celebrated this happy event in the Peacock Room – exactly the sort of thing he'd envisaged when he created it, only with himself numbered among the most honoured guests. Now he began reeling off his various nicknames for his foe, a nearby rhododendron bush shaking as he swiped at it.

'British businessman – befrilled barbarian – counting-house rat! He means to bring me down, don't you see, by whatever means he can. The graceful slur of the Peacock Room must be avenged. The sympathetic ear I lent his poor wife must be sliced off and tossed on the fire. Dark wheels are turning, Owl. Sinister machinery is being brought to bear. He was behind this accursed Ruskin business – egging it on, if not originating it. And I am inclined to think that it was his influence that doomed the first lithograph. A whispering campaign, you know, amongst those who might otherwise have been disposed to buy.'

Owl seemed to agree. He looked at the canvases for a moment, the *Nocturne* especially; then he turned towards the house and spotted Maud lingering at the edge of the studio doorway. She stepped outside at once, trying to appear as if in motion. Jimmy was pacing on the lawn. He looked extraordinary that day, clad in a yachtsman's suit of blue serge, worn with his best square-tipped shoes and his straw boater; an outfit smart yet individual, casual yet not informal. The reason was a newspaperman, dispatched from a new magazine called *The World*, who was calling at eleven to interview him about his paintings and the way they were made. There had been much rehearsal and preparation, on everything from costume and decor to what precisely he would say. A quiverful of lines had been readied, potent phrases that he planned to loose, ever so casually, in the journalist's general direction. Owl was there in the garden, Maud presumed, to offer some last-minute guidance. She attempted to adopt a more friendly expression.

'What of the Leyland paintings that you still have?' Owl

asked. 'All those portraits, for instance?' He gave Maud the very slightest of sidelong looks. 'Or that glorious painting of the three girls? If any of these were to be made available, I'm sure that I could have my people bring about—'

Jimmy cut him off with some impatience, informing him that yes, those canvases did remain in his hands, but they were *unfinished*, quite unworthy of display or engraving or anything else; and they had been paid for, furthermore, a number of years previously. Maud was watching him closely. This testiness told her that something was underway, right then and there – that Owl's visit wasn't about *The World* at all.

On cue, John appeared at the back gate, in his shirtsleeves, trying to manoeuvre a thin crate in from the lane. Owl stepped forward to speed things up, taking hold of one of the lower corners; John cowered a little, almost as if he expected the urbane Portuguese to clout him around the ear. The crate was carried into the studio and laid out on its back. Jimmy watched, chewing distractedly on a thumb-nail. Maud had listened to him talk on endlessly about this *World* article, what a great puff it was, and the splendid figure he must cut. Unwittingly or not, the Owl was threatening to knock him off-course.

'What's going on?' she asked.

Jimmy didn't answer her. John crossed the studio, walking fast, heading up into the house, while Owl sauntered back to the lawn, making for a small leather bag that had been lying at his feet. He bent down to open it, pulling it towards him, metal objects jangling within. Out came a length of dark, oily iron, hooked at one end. He straightened up, weighing the thing in his hands. It was a crowbar.

Maud crossed her arms. Almost without realising it, she took a step that placed her between Jimmy and Owl. She liked this man – how could you not? – but she was surprised by how easy it was to mistrust him. She hadn't forgotten those prints. There was a readiness in the Portuguese, she reckoned, to act without permission.

'All right,' she said, 'what the *devil* is going on?'

There was a short silence. Owl looked past Maud, to Jimmy.

'He's taking the *Carlyle*,' Jimmy said. 'It's all agreed, Maudie.'

And then Maud saw it, at the rear of the studio, waiting to be packed away in Owl's crate – one of Jimmy's few well-received works, its silver and fawn tones dulled by shadow. The old gentleman – a famous scholar, she'd been told – was shown from the side, grey-bearded, sitting on a simple kitchen chair. His coat was across his lap, his hat perched upon his knee, and a gloved hand set atop his cane. Maud always thought that he looked ready to hurry off; as if he'd mistakenly given too much time to the sitting and was keen to be gone.

'Taking it where? For sale?' This didn't seem likely; Jimmy would certainly have said something. 'For engraving?'

'Soon, yes,' Owl cut in. 'Very soon. My man Graves has a mezzotinter in mind, and a fine one at that. Mr Carlyle .

over there should be with him by the summer.' He launched into his standard assurances regarding the tin that would soon be pouring in.

'But it isn't going to him today,' Maud interrupted. 'Is it, Owl?'

'There are great things on their way,' Owl said. 'That is definite. But by heaven, Maud, they aren't here yet. Our British art collectors may not see the value in these pictures, dense as they are, but plenty of others do. They see the value and they will advance good coin against it.'

Maud stood quite still. 'So you're pawning them, then,' she said. 'You're going to put Jimmy's paintings in pawn.'

'Security,' Owl qualified, adjusting his hold on the crowbar. 'They are serving as security. It is a testament to what Jimmy has achieved, really it is. We've raised a tidy sum in a matter of days.'

'But *pawning* them, Owl?'

The Portuguese's smile hardened just a fraction. 'The show is afire, my dear girl. I don't need to tell you this, I'm sure. The flames leap high indeed, and we must fight them in any way we can. Those works over there in the studio have real worth, buyers or not. And so we must send them out to earn.'

Maud thought of the heaped bills back in the house; of the various promises that had been made. She turned to Jimmy. He was standing very straight, wearing a pained wince. 'Surely it can't be that bad,' she said, without much hope.

He began to polish his eyeglass on his lapel. 'I am presently being sued,' he told her, 'by a cheesemonger.'

'It will be a great joke,' Owl said, 'before very long. You'll see, my friends. A colourman I know up in Bethnal Green agreed to give sixty quid for the *Carlyle* on the bloody spot, with the most reasonable terms. We'll have the tin in under a week. You are fortunate, from this point of view, to have so many significant works at your disposal. Why, just imagine what could be raised by the notorious fireworks. Or one of those marvellous full-lengths of Maud here.' There was a sly pause. 'Just imagine what we could get for the *Mother*.'

Jimmy's laugh was empty and irritated. 'You are becoming predictable, *mon vieux*. How many times must I tell you? That picture has been damaged. It needs work.'

The portrait of old Mrs Whistler had appeared in their bedroom several weeks previously. There was no damage to it that Maud could see. She'd wondered as to its placement; it was not the most agreeable location for it, in all honesty. She saw now that it was being hidden.

'Damp, I think,' she volunteered. 'The whole left side will have to be scraped.'

Owl hesitated. 'I understand your reluctance. Your attachment. Why, if I were capable of producing such an image of *minha querida mãe* . . . All I can tell you is that it would be temporary. A month or two only. Until you have your damages from Ruskin, and other things besides – and then it would be back here so damned quickly, you wouldn't even—'

'No, Owl.' Jimmy spoke with unusual firmness. 'You are my friend. My only true friend, I think sometimes. But this I can't allow.'

The Owl accepted Jimmy's ruling with a shrug and a good-natured downturn of the lip. He retreated to the studio, out of the sun, and prised the lid off the crate in a manner that suggested he'd done it before. In a few minutes he had the *Carlyle* snug within it, packed with wads of oilskin. His bag, it turned out, also contained a hammer and nails; as he sealed the painting away, knocking each nail all the way in with just two or three long strokes, Maud turned again to Jimmy, thinking to ask a quiet question about the *Mother*.

'Not now,' he said.

His task complete, Owl picked up the crate, managing it perfectly well alone, and carried it past them to the lane. Maud saw the roof of a cab behind the wall. She realised that it must have been waiting there the whole time.

A few seconds later the Portuguese returned, a cigarette in his mouth, to reclaim his leather bag and bid them farewell. 'Do consider the others, Jimmy,' he said. 'The *Nocturnes* and so forth. They could be out in the city, old man, earning you decent coin. Fairly soon I shall be in the position to buy a couple more myself, and it shall be my honour to do so. But I warn you that the remainder of the month could prove rather lean.'

Owl reached into his inside pocket with a businesslike air. Jimmy's neck craned very slightly, as if in anticipation;

Maud noticed a hint of distaste, of self-disgust, upon his face. Out came a worn leather pocket book, capable of holding much, but currently holding little. Owl produced a banknote from it, though, folded twice – how large Maud couldn't tell, but the thing looked like it had passed through the hands of half of London. He extended it towards Jimmy, held between middle and forefinger. It was plucked away at once.

'Get the roof on,' he said.

'I beg your pardon?'

'This house of yours. Get the roof on and there won't be a damned thing those Board of Works men can do. If the two of you are living there – if you are receiving their wives for your breakfasts and lining them up to be painted in your magnificent dance hall of a studio, then any objection will be solidly after the fact. Impossible to take seriously.'

Maud directed a dubious glance at Jimmy – who was rolling his banknote into a tight tube and turning it over thoughtfully between his fingertips. Neither of them spoke.

'The Board of Works is a rascally foe, but one must show the blighters no fear. This is essential. Take my own case.'

The Owl's case. Maud had heard much about this from Rosa. It was a situation that could only befall this particular person. In recent months it had transpired that the Metropolitan District Railway needed to knock down Chaldon House, the Howell family's residence in Putney, to clear a path for their westward line. A piece of the direst ill fortune, you might think, but the Owl had immediately scented opportunity. An offer had been made by the railway people, and a good one at that; but Owl, much to Rosa's admiration, had rejected. This, he'd told them, was home. The home of his wife and baby daughter. And so it was to go to court.

'The word now is that I can expect to be awarded several times the original sum. Which means clover, old man. Clover for us all.'

Jimmy didn't see it. 'What is the parallel, Owl, precisely?'

'Simply that you must never, *never* accept things at their first stage. It is a game, old chap, for these officials and legal types. Fortitude. Obstinacy. Nerve. These are the qualities that are rewarded.'

With that the Portuguese departed, dropping Maud a shallow bow, telling them both that he'd be round again in a couple of days; and then, while climbing into his hired carriage, he shouted 'Get the roof on!' over the wall.

Maud and Jimmy stayed on the lawn. She looked up at the sun. The hour of *The World* interview must be drawing close. Jimmy was shaking his head, slotting the banknote into his breast pocket. She asked if it was an advance on the pawn. The question annoyed him; he informed her that it was in actual fact a first instalment for the sale of the copyright on the *Carlyle*. Eighty pounds he was getting, along with a half dozen proofs.

'You sold it to Owl?'

Jimmy glowered at her, catching the doubt in her voice. 'What is copyright to a painter?' he demanded. 'It is a phantom, girl, a simple nothing. A speculation on a shadow. It will buy my supplies. It will cover our expenses. Beat back the creditors, for a while at least. Tell me, what else should I have done?'

He fell quiet, taking a long breath, a hand at his brow; then he came over, four steps across the grass, removing his boater and leaning against her, fitting his head into the crook of her neck. They both apologised, speaking over one another. She could feel the apprehension in him, and the fatigue – the absolute absence of desire. This was how it went with Jimmy. While soaring high, his every touch was tense with ardour; his every thought, when they were alone, aimed at bringing about her disrobement. And accordingly, when in the dumps, he was but a husk – a despondent child, a tired old man.

It didn't last. He knew full well that the time was approaching; that the man from *The World* was at that moment most probably walking over from the Battersea Bridge pier. Pulling away, he gave his spirits a restorative shake, like a dog fresh from a river. The blue yachting jacket was straightened, the boater angled just so atop the black curls, the eyeglass slotted in. Then he tried out a couple of his favourites from the lines he'd prepared.

'As music is the poetry of sound,' he said, 'so painting is the poetry of sight.'

The meaning here seemed a touch obscure. The poetry of sight? Maud wrinkled her nose; she gave him an ambiguous nod.

'Art should be independent of all claptrap.'

That was more like it. The low mist dissolved, revealing a smile so very wily and pleased with itself that Maud couldn't help returning it. Jimmy swivelled on the heel of those square-tipped shoes, towards the soot-streaked house and the open sky beyond, extending his arm in the style of a great orator.

'Art,' he announced, 'should be *independent* of all *claptrap*!'

*

July 1878

'There's nothing to worry about,' said Jimmy, as the train juddered to a halt. 'Mommy likes you, Maudie, very much. And she is the soundest judge of character that I know. Unaffected by spite or censure, or indeed any base sentiment whatsoever. I'll simply tell her that you are now my pupil – that you have stepped down from the model table and are drawing for yourself. All above board. She won't suspect for a second.'

He rose and left the compartment, battled briefly with their umbrella, then handed Maud out into the morning drizzle. The station at Hastings was triangular, built into a split in the line, its platforms bending apart with the track. Across its point lay the town, mud-brown and dull, half lost in fog. Beyond, the sea was a blurred grey band, almost the same tone as the sky. Maud hadn't been to the coast since she was a child – a single excursion to Brighton at the age of ten. Jimmy, in contrast, was a veteran traveller; he'd sailed oceans and crossed continents, numerous times. Sight of the rainy Channel didn't even register in his mind. Even now, after everything, Maud tried not to appear too callow — too curious about the view before them. She adjusted her hat, tilting it an inch, and asked how far it was to the boarding house.

'Two miles,' he replied, 'or thereabouts. This way, this way.'

They found a cab on the street outside, an ageing four-wheeler. It skirted the town, making for a low hill on its western edge. The miserable weather lifted a little, a shaft of sunlight cutting through the banked cloud. Maud watched the colours change in the waters below and the white lines of the waves running up the wide beach. The cab lurched over the cobbles; the tip of her nose rubbed a mark on the dewy window.

'It is really something, isn't it,' Jimmy declared, 'to free oneself from London and its worries? Push it all out to arm's length for a while.'

This was the reason — one of the reasons — for their expedition. Dr William Whistler's suggestion was finally being acted upon, almost exactly a year after it had first been put to Jimmy. Maud was to be drawn from the doldrums into which she'd drifted around the time of Ione's first birthday. The sorrow had settled upon her like a bad cold — like a physical ailment she couldn't shake off. Once more, that which she thought she'd contained, that she'd managed to control, showed her that she'd done nothing of the sort. Jimmy had observed this slump in his *Madame's* spirits – and a corresponding lull in her attention to his own vicissitudes – with concern. He'd recognised that something should be done to alleviate her woe, even if he did not seek to discuss the cause of it. So here they were in Hastings.

After a quarter hour's travel the cab arrived at a smart boarding house. Jimmy ushered Maud inside, straight up a broad central staircase to his mother's cluttered but scrupulously clean sitting room. They were greeted by a strong smell of lavender and beeswax, and the sight of Mrs Whistler rising from an armchair to receive them – assisted by Willie, who'd travelled down alone the previous evening.

Maud was not, of course, the principal attraction. It happened to be the 11th, Jimmy's own birthday. He was forty-four years old, a fact which caused him acute distress. She was under strict instructions not to mention it or do anything to mark it. The date was kept secret from his circle, even from his closest friends. His mother and brother, however, were determined to celebrate. There was a gift, a tiepin in the shape of an American eagle, that Jimmy would never wear in a thousand years; a rich fruitcake of a kind he abhorred; and singing, a string of sweet little songs from their native land, delivered in the old lady's whispery warble, underpinned by Willie's flat, ironic baritone. Jimmy bore it with good humour; he grinned, and offered thanks, and managed to eat part of a slice of the cake. Looking at the three of them, at their expressions and the way they talked to each other, Maud could see something that ran back to the brothers' beginnings, through a number of very different situations.

Jimmy, though, was still Jimmy. He'd brought along a sheaf of clippings from newspapers and magazines, which he presented to his mother with a flourish once the singing was finished. Her head dipping heavily upon her neck, she tried to follow his finger as it directed her towards the choicest features. There was the profile from *The World*, declared a triumph by everyone who mattered: a comprehensive statement of his position. And here was a cartoon – a comic sketch of her own son! – published in *Vanity Fair*, which had gone so far as to name Whistler as one of the 'men of the day'. Jimmy was particularly proud of this cartoon. The artist, a fellow known only as Spy, had shown him in a light brown overcoat, his body a whippet-thin curve, with all his attributes in place: cigarette and cane, forelock and eyeglass, topped off with an arch twist of the lip. Maud had heard others call it grotesque, but to her it captured a certain side of him with an almost uncanny sharpness.

Setting the cartoon aside, Mrs Whistler listened patiently – or absently, Maud couldn't quite tell – while her eldest son recounted an ideal version of his life, purged of all trouble and uncertainty. The Ruskin case was to be a public vindication, and a great advertisement to boot. The new house – the *White House*, he took pains to point out, like the presidential abode – was to be a marvel, the talk of London, and she must visit it as soon as could be arranged. Not a word was said of the mysterious delay that had prevented them from actually taking up residence there. Maud passed by this White House all the time; although still wrapped in sheets and scaffold, it looked fit for occupation, as far as she could tell, like a cake waiting only to be slipped from its tin. Nothing could be moved over, though, not yet, for reasons Jimmy was reluctant to discuss with her. She'd gathered that he'd overreached himself again – done things he shouldn't have, been rebuked by the authorities and then ignored the amendments they'd required, leading to some kind of impasse.

Maud herself was brought forward next, out from her place by the door. As she approached and took a chair by Mrs Whistler's side, those dark, moist eyes grew bright and a look of genuine pleasure broke across that softly sagging face. It had been nearly five years since they'd last seen each another. Mrs Whistler's first enquiries were about Maud's father, seriously ill when last they'd met (through drink, although Maud hadn't revealed that), and dead now for several years.

'Forgive me,' Mrs Whistler murmured when she was told; like Willie, her American accent was a good deal purer than Jimmy's. 'Do forgive me, my dear. I am so very sorry.' She took Maud's hand and gave it a bony squeeze, lowering her head and closing her eyes. 'Lead me in thy truth,' she said, her voice firmer. 'Lead me in thy truth, and teach me.'

Maud glanced around. Willie sat stolid and inscrutable. Jimmy, leaning back in his chair with his legs crossed, gave her a wink.

'Lead me in thy truth, and teach me,' Mrs Whistler continued, 'for thou art the God of my salvation. On thee do I wait all the day.'

The brothers said an 'Amen' – certainly the first time Maud had ever heard Jimmy use the word. She echoed it a second later.

'You are an orphan then, Miss Franklin,' Mrs Whistler continued, relentless in her sympathy. 'You are reliant upon the Lord alone. Upon His holy guidance. As my boys will be, soon enough.'

No, they said, hush; you are well, all is well; you will be here a decade from now.

Mrs Whistler ignored them. 'And you are so young still, Miss. At the outset of life, the – the threshold of woman-hood. Is it enough, this painting Jamie says you do? Is there a living to be made? For a woman, I mean?' Her grip on Maud's hand tightened again. 'Will it support you until you find a suitor, and are married? That will not be very long, I believe.'

Maud blinked; she almost laughed, but Mrs Whistler's gentle earnestness kept her in check. The old woman really, truly *did not know*. She hadn't the first clue.

Jimmy stepped in, holding forth for a while on Maud's particular talents, and the broader changes of the age. There were more works by women on the walls of the Royal

Academy every year, he told his mother, and at the Grosvenor Gallery too. Why, his own table had hosted a veritable procession of fine female painters. Lady Butler had been, as had Mrs Jopling . . . Here he ran out of examples and returned to generalities.

As he talked on, a question rose in Maud's mind – something that had been with her throughout the day, just beneath the surface, but now rapidly came to eclipse all else. What would Mrs Whistler make of Ione? Of the simple fact of Ione? How might she react if she discovered that she had a year-old granddaughter – a helpless, beautiful babe to be held and cherished and loved? The idea had an irresistible rawness to it. It was like something desperately sore that you are told not to touch, but touch anyway, and find yourself savouring the pain. Mrs Whistler as a grandmother. Why, she'd be perfect.

Except of course that she very much *wouldn't*, at least not to poor Ione. For all her kindliness, the old woman could barely open her mouth without delivering a bloody great ream of scripture. An infant born out of wedlock would occasion only embarrassment. Suddenly Maud was angry, a tremor building behind her inane, aching grin. She longed to pull her hands from Mrs Whistler's. To leave that suffocating room and head directly to the railway station.

Jimmy was still talking, winding back inevitably to himself. He'd picked up a small bronze bust of a bearded gentleman and was considering it idly as he spoke of society portraiture and the riches it would offer once he was installed on Tite Street.

His mother waited for him to finish – to round off a list of the aristocrats and celebrities whose custom he reckoned he could secure. 'And then, perhaps,' she said, 'you might be loyal enough to take your genius back across the Atlantic.' Her voice was surprisingly forceful. This was obviously a favourite idea of hers. 'Back to our beloved native land. I shall not see it again in this life. This I know. The short time allotted to me on this earth shall be passed beneath this roof, where I am very comfortable and thankful to be cared for. But my heart would go with you, Jamie. My heart would go with you.'

Jimmy returned the bust to an incidental table with some discomfort, setting the bearded gentleman so that he faced the patterned wallpaper. 'The arts in America are in their infancy still, Mommy. I have tried, you know, in the past, to interest sales agents over there, dealers and the rest, but the results were hardly encouraging. I could – well, I suppose further enquiries could be made. We could give the tree another shake.'

Willie stood, clapping his hands on his thighs, putting an end to his brother's squirming; then he bent down to retrieve his bag, brought with him from London, saying that it would be best for him to conduct his examination of their mother before luncheon.

'Jamie and Miss Franklin might like to brave this uncertain weather and go for a stroll,' he added. 'For a quick birthday lesson, maybe, in theories of marine painting.'

The doctor was teasing them, Maud saw, for the stilted

little act they'd put on, and she coloured hard as she set about extracting herself from Mrs Whistler's grasp. Jimmy, however, appeared to find the suggestion amusing. Hopping from his chair, he proffered his hand with elaborate courtesy.

'What say you, Miss Franklin?' he asked, an eyebrow twitching theatrically. 'Shall we take the air?'

*

The hall at Lindsey Row was so filled with packing crates that the front door would only open halfway. It was some time after ten and the house was dark from top to bottom, John and Mrs Cossins having long since headed off to wherever it was they went. Willie had travelled back to London with Jimmy and Maud; it had been agreed that he would come in for a brandy, to restore him a fraction before he returned home to his wife. Jimmy coaxed a candle alight and led them through. Two crates were outside the dining room that hadn't been there when they'd left that morning; nailed shut, they were the size, more or less, of paintings.

The three of them settled in the parlour. The brothers lit cigarettes and poured liquor, lowering themselves into armchairs, while Maud, under a storm-cloud still, perched on a large box of crockery and crossed her arms. The rest of the day had proved trying. Her coastal walk with Jimmy had been curtailed by a downpour. The conversation at luncheon had mostly revolved around reminiscences of the brothers' childhood in Russia, where their father had worked as an engineer on the railways. Mrs Whistler had contributed little, eating almost nothing, retreating into herself. After the meal, she'd granted Jimmy an hour to sketch her in drypoint, on a small copper tablet that he'd brought along in his jacket pocket. He'd promised to send her the first successful print that was pulled from it; to write to her the very next week; to visit again before the end of summer. And then they'd gone.

Having availed themselves of claret at the luncheon table, the brothers had slept for a good stretch of the train journey. Maud had gazed out balefully at the rainy countryside, allowing thoughts she would normally suppress: the resentment of youth against age. Jimmy was forty-four. Exactly twice as old as her. When he'd stood at her point in life she'd been new-born, a babe in arms. She'd begun to watch him as he dozed, his head swaying with the carriage, seeing the deep lines around his eyes, the way the skin was starting to fold against his collar, the whitish grey that streaked his curls like paint.

'Five years,' said Willie now, staring at the candle. 'That's at the outside, mind you. It could well be less.'

Jimmy took the hint. He re-crossed his legs, frowning at his cigarette. 'See here, doc,' he said. 'I try, really I do, but things are damned hard at the moment. I put on a brave face for the Mother — but the show, *mon frère*, the show is most terribly afire. Time is at a premium. There simply aren't enough hours in the blessed day.'

'The *show*,' Willie repeated, faintly mocking. 'You speak

of time, Jamie, of your time – but like I say, she has no more than five years remaining to her. You must exert yourself, brother. You must visit more frequently, and you must write. You really must. For your own sake, do you hear? Your remorse will be most bitter if you do not.' The doctor took a drink. 'She enjoyed this afternoon so very much. Meeting Miss Franklin again, and hearing of your efforts to school her. Seeing your clippings. Learning of your adventures.'

'Well,' Jimmy said, 'one does like one's Mommy to see that her first-born does not toil in *complete* obscurity . . .'

'She knows that there's trouble, though,' his brother added. 'She's no fool, Jamie. Not the ins and outs of it all, perhaps, but she can tell that you struggle.' Here he looked over at Maud – studying her, it seemed. She'd noticed him doing this before, earlier in the day. It made her uneasy. 'She knows that there's a want of money, whatever you might claim. That bills are going unpaid and yet more being run up.'

'There are schemes afoot,' Jimmy said, a little defensively, 'a number of them sure to yield cash in abundance. You've met Howell, Willie. You've learned what kind of fellow he is. He has the measure of the situation.'

The doctor hesitated. 'My feeling is that you must rely upon your own self before all others. Even friends like this Mr Howell. You're selling something, aren't you brother, in the end. You're asking people to buy your productions. To pay a good deal for them.'

Maud could guess where Willie was heading. It was a well-trodden path, and a futile one at that. Jimmy made no comment; he looked away, smoking his cigarette.

'So I've got to ask: where's the harm in giving them some of what they want? You said it yourself in *The World* – about that painting in the Grosvenor Gallery, the tavern in the snow . . .'

'*The Nocturne in Grey and Gold.*'

'Yes. That's the one. This is what I wonder, though – would it really be so difficult for you to paint in another figure or two? Provide a small tale perhaps, unfolding there on the pavement? Your skill is beyond dispute, Jamie, so why not profit from it? Just to sell a few paintings. Just to kill off a few of these debts.'

Jimmy turned back to him, his expression quite blank. 'A spot of Dickens – is that the sort of thing you mean? Trotty Veck and his rosy-cheeked Meg, clasping hands before a *Nocturne*? How's that sound?'

Willie, already regretful, set down his glass. 'It was a suggestion only. I am tired. God knows, I surely wouldn't have spoken otherwise.'

'Willie,' Jimmy said. Maud thought that he might leap onto his chair – he'd done this numerous times in the past – but he stayed put, teasing up the white lock, his eyeglass glinting scornfully in the firelight. 'I care nothing for the tavern. Not a red cent, d'you hear? Not for the figures who may be coming or going, or pissing in the alleyway behind, or fighting over a girl, or any damned thing. All I know is that my combination of grey and gold is the basis of the picture. That is its core and its one aim. To pretend otherwise would be indecent, a vulgar trick. The picture must not depend upon a story, or a moral, or some point of local interest. What was it I said to *The World*? You told me you'd read the article.'

'Jamie—'

'Art,' Jimmy very nearly shouted, 'should be *independent of all claptrap*. It should stand alone, quite alone, and not confound the artistic sense with notions of pity, or patriotism, or love, or—'

'I know, brother,' Willie broke in, rising from his chair. 'I know. Christ alive. We've been through this already today. I just don't see why—'

But Jimmy would hear no more. He bounded off upstairs without another word. Maud and the doctor looked at one another. Willie was unperturbed; he was well used to Jimmy's displays and knew how swiftly the tempest would disperse. Not knowing what else to do, Maud showed him rather awkwardly to the door; and in the hall, as she reached for the latch, Willie laid a hand against her upper arm.

'My dear girl,' he said softly, glancing behind to check that Jimmy really was gone, 'is all well?'

This query was expected, sort of, but it knocked Maud off-guard nonetheless. She mumbled her affirmatives, a couple of halting sentences, wondering how much Willie had been told about her recent sadness. He nodded, plainly unsatisfied, but he let her be. Fitting the hat on his head, he touched a forefinger to the brim and headed out to the embankment.

Jimmy was in their room, at the top of the house. His mother's portrait was propped atop the chest of drawers opposite the bed, an oil lamp sputtering close by, in hiding from the Owl and his pawn-shop crates. The painting was large, four feet by three at least, and strangely, strikingly composed. Mrs Whistler was in the drawing room, as it had been when Maud first arrived: the walls grey and the curtains black, patterned with silver. She was shown from the side, seated on one of the dining chairs with her feet upon a low stool, her sweet old puss set in hard profile like the face on a coin. Maud sat on the end of the bed; her hands, planted behind her upon the counterpane, slid an inch or two across the green satin. Jimmy was over by the window, his eyes on the picture, and for a minute they considered it together. Having bade the sitter farewell only a few hours earlier, Maud noticed now the extraordinary care that had been taken with the likeness, which was unusual for Jimmy: the effortful painting of her lace cap and the way it trailed across her black-clad shoulders, the great tenderness of it all.

'Looks like she's waiting for something,' she said.

There was an exasperated exclamation and a bang, as if Jimmy had just stamped his foot. 'You too, eh? Hang it all, Maudie, I spoke of this in *The World* as well – of this picture, this exact matter! You listened to me practise the blasted words, girl! It is an *arrangement in grey and black*. That is what it is. *All* it is. *Bon Dieu*, I am surrounded by incomprehension, from the fools in the Grosvenor to my very closest allies.' He strode between Maud and the *Mother*, lunging out onto the dark landing and dropping from sight, thundering back down the stairs. 'I am damn well buried in it!'

*

The front door was dirty, mud and soot streaking panels that might once have been a soapy grey. Maud shielded her eyes against the sun and looked again at the '93' stencilled on the pane of glass above it. This was the right address. She knocked again and peered in through the street-facing window. Pictures stood about – the corner of something set upon an easel, others propped against a wall – but Rosa Corder didn't appear to be at home. Maud leant heavily against the door, Southampton Row rattling on around her. Streets like this one made Chelsea feel like the open countryside, and swank too; it was so very crowded, jam-packed with aggravation, everybody spoiling for a chance to sink their teeth into somebody else. She couldn't think why Rosa chose to live there.

The telegram had arrived at eleven, from the office on the King's Road. Mrs Cossins, answering the door, had reported disbelievingly that the message was for Maud, and that she was required to sign for it and hand over thruppence for the delivery. She'd been amazed herself, in truth.

Her sister and aunts always wrote. Why would they do this instead, and spend the extra pennies? The answer had come to her the next instant. It must be Ione – Edie was wiring to tell her of an emergency with Ione. The child was dying, or dead already. She'd been laid low by disease. She'd fallen down the stairs. She'd wandered into the road and been trampled by a horse.

Maud had scrambled through the house to take the message. The relief had been a shock, a cold, unbalancing blast of wind that had sent her reeling into the doorframe, followed perversely by a single second's disappointment. The telegram was from Jimmy, and had nothing whatsoever to do with her family up in Kentish Town or the daughter they'd given away.

Read almost as an afterthought, this telegram had drawn her into a crisis quite unlike the ones she'd imagined. Early that morning Jimmy had left for the Albemarle, a swell hotel on St James's, to finish off a two-day commission from *Vanity Fair*. The editor had thrown him a scrap of work on the back of this much-trumpeted 'man of the day' business, to help see him through to the trial – which, like the move to the White House, was always imminent, always at the point of arrival, but never actually there. It was an etching, a street view taken from the hotel's elevated terrace to accompany an article on fashionable London. Jimmy had been full of talk of its excellence the previous night, and how it would mark the beginning of a most profitable connection – *Vanity Fair* being like an orchard, in effect, through which he merely had to stroll, plucking fruit from the branches.

This telegram, however, had struck a rather different note. *Tin needed at Albemarle*, it had read. *Quid Plus. See Owl – Eldon – Cole – Watts. Urgent.*

Maud hadn't the first idea where to look for Eldon or Watts; indeed, she barely knew who Watts was. The one address she had was that of Alan Cole, a cripplingly shy fellow who worked at the South Kensington Museum – a post he only held, according to Jimmy, because his father had set the place up. She'd learned where he lived a month or so before, when Jimmy had proposed that she accompany him over there one evening to dine.

'Won't he mind?' Maud had asked.

'What, Cole? No, of course not. I'll send a note ahead, but there's really no need to worry. He knows you, Maudie. He knows you are my pupil, and everything is perfectly decent.'

It had quickly turned out that mousey little Alan Cole *had* minded. He'd minded very much indeed. Jimmy's note had received an immediate reply, prohibiting Maud's attendance in the strongest terms. He'd gone anyway, and there was no indication of any awkwardness between the men regarding the matter; but if he honestly thought that Maud was going to present herself at the fellow's door and ask him for money – no matter how much or for what purpose – he'd have to think again.

Owl had his place in Putney – Chaldon House, the

doomed, sprawling pile that, due to the legal screws he was applying to the Metropolitan District Railway, was going to enrich him beyond measure. Maud reckoned it would be easy enough to find. The odds were even of catching a gentleman at home on a Saturday morning, especially a married gentleman with an infant daughter. This was the Owl, though. He was seldom where you expected him to be. And Putney was a good few miles in the wrong direction.

Then Maud had thought of Rosa. Owl might well be with her, but even if he wasn't, Jimmy's devoted disciple would surely do whatever she could to aid him. Maud knew the address. They'd been talking for many months of her visiting, of her working there for an afternoon or longer, although nothing had yet been arranged. She'd pulled on her jacket and started for the omnibus.

It was becoming plain, however, that Rosa wasn't in. Maud didn't have time to wait; she undid a couple of her jacket's small ivory buttons, wracking her brain for other possible sources of emergency cash. There were those two printers, she supposed, the father and son, with their prem- ises beside the Lyceum Theatre. Jimmy had approached them the previous autumn, asking for their assistance and tutelage – and now they too were his followers, acquired in that effortless way of his, devoted both to his art and his example. This matter here, though, was as delicate as it was urgent. It needed to be kept contained. Should these people learn of it, their view of Jimmy would be affected

– diminished perhaps. And word might get out. It wasn't worth the risk.

Maud returned to the pavement. The journey into town had been especially cramped and stifling. Her shift clung wetly to her skin. She was famished, sluggish, her head starting to throb. But this had to be dealt with. She followed Southampton Row to its end, turning right onto High Holborn. The change of street – wider and busier, festooned with advertising boards – for some reason brought the name of Anderson Reeve to her mind. That could be it. The lawyer would help them, and in absolute confidence. He often saw Jimmy on Saturdays, at his offices down on the Strand. She'd posted many letters bearing the address. She could very nearly remember it. Three digits, there were. Maybe four.

The crowds on High Holborn were dense and noisy. Smells clogged the air – ordure and axle-grease, rotten vegetables, the ripest, thickest sweat. Maud couldn't concentrate; she could scarcely breathe. She swerved into a narrow alleyway, out of the current. This brought her to a blind court, no more than fifteen feet square and half filled with barrels; rising up in the distance was a wing of the British Museum, another block or so away, hazed by a bank of sunlit dust. She leant against a wall, feeling the cold of the bricks, their slight dampness, through her clothes. The reek of the streets furred her mouth, making it hard to swallow. She pressed a hand to her breastbone and something bubbled inside, deeper down, squeezing between her innards. There was a ghastly sense of suspension, of imminence; then the first prickle of nausea.

It passed. Maud gasped and coughed, and cast a furtive look around her. Am I going soft? she wondered. Have the years in Chelsea with Jimmy Whistler been washing the city out of me?

A smart young gentleman had stopped at the lane's mouth. Clad in a grey top hat and pale grey coat, he was attempting to look casual, as if merely passing the time, but it was clear enough that he'd been following her. He was gravely out of place, dressed for a garden party or a ride in the park; there were a couple of daintily wrapped parcels beneath his arm, for goodness sake, as if he'd been out shopping for trifles. Then he peered to the side, along the street – and Maud saw that this was Freddie Leyland, son and heir to Jimmy's great foe. Maud had met Freddie once at Lindsey Row, very briefly, when he'd come by to fetch Jimmy for a night in town with Eldon and a couple of others. The fellow had been another paid-up acolyte, positively basking in Jimmy's company, and had treated her with careful respect, as one close to the great man. Yet he'd cut Jimmy along with the rest of them, cut him dead, and showed no inclination to speak to her or even glance her way. His whiskers were threadbare, she noticed, still those of a youth; his brow was creased with consternation.

A woman walked into the alley. The gown was a different style – dark blue, closely fitted and understated to the point of severity – but there could be no mistaking that this was

Mrs Leyland, the lady from the portrait. Freddie's mother. She approached without ceremony, and little of the grace with which Jimmy had imbued her. Maud stood up, away from the wall. You look older, she thought. You look like you could use a good night's sleep.

'I am afraid, Miss,' Mrs Leyland began, rather louder than was necessary, as if gathering determination, 'that we have not been introduced.'

Maud eyed her coolly. And when *exactly*, she wanted to ask, would the two of us ever have been bloody well *introduced*?

'You know who I am though, I believe. I have something for your — for your master.' She slid an object from her sleeve and held it out, dangling from a fine chain: an almond-shaped locket, solid gold, its cover etched deftly with a curling vine of ivy. 'This belongs to Mrs Whistler, your master's mother. An heirloom, she told us. Irreplaceable. It was left at Speke Hall when she came to visit, a number of years ago now. You would have been only a child. My own daughters were children.' Mrs Leyland looked away. 'We've often talked of returning it, but the opportunity has never presented itself.'

Maud didn't move. This all sounded rather unlikely. 'Mrs Whistler went up to Liverpool?'

Mrs Leyland ignored her. 'I feel very strongly that it should go back to the family. I cannot possibly give it to your master in person, not with everything that has occurred. Nor could I use a servant and have my husband find out, as he always seems to do. I am sorry for imposing upon you in this way, truly I am — for following you up here from Chelsea as we have done. It is strange, I know. But I could think of no other course.' She shook the locket very slightly, impatiently almost, as if it were a little bell for the summoning of service. 'Please take it, Miss. It would bring such comfort to my mind.'

As Maud reached out, Mrs Leyland slipped her other hand around the younger woman's wrist; she gripped it hard, harder than you'd have thought she could, and drew them a few inches closer together.

'It is the only way, also,' she added, speaking rapidly, her voice half as loud yet about ten times as fierce, 'that I could convey a warning to him. They are meeting. My husband and the allies of Mr Ruskin. Mr Burne-Jones, the painter. Mr Taylor of *The Times*. Ahead of this trial, this ridiculous libel action. In the dining room, no less, before those peacocks. Some kind of scheme is being put together, of this I am certain. Something to finish him off. Do you understand me? He must *desist*. He must withdraw from it, withdraw from it all. Depart for France, or America even. He must leave it well alone. A trial is *what they want*.'

Mrs Leyland released Maud as abruptly as she'd taken hold of her. She stepped back, corrected her hat and started towards her son, who was still standing as lookout.

'It is done,' she told him.

Freddie offered his arm and they left the alley. Maud waited a few seconds, steadying herself; then she went after them, stopping on the pavement to scour the crowds and the traffic. There they were, across the street, climbing into a hired carriage. You almost had to admire it. Mrs Leyland had staged a two-fold deceit, enabling her to slip through a double layer of scrutiny. For the servants at Prince's Gate, the butler or anyone else, it had been a simple shopping trip, taken in the company of her son, with his parcels acting as corroboration. For the son, meanwhile – who had broken with Jimmy so obediently – it was a final act of severance, a last trinket returned, with the outcast artist uninvolved.

Maud looked at the locket, the gold flushed with the colour of her palm. She opened it up. The tiny chamber within was empty: no lock of hair, no beloved face scissored from a photograph. This was the cost Mrs Leyland was prepared to pay to deliver her message – which Maud did not then pause to ponder at any length as she had realised with a great giddying rush of exhilaration that nestled right there in her hand was the answer to the day's dilemma.

A minute later she was walking into a pawn shop, tucked away in a lane off Great Russell Street. Goods were clustered along its shelves, toys and musical instruments and a travelling library's worth of books. What wall space remained was filled entirely with hack paintings, popular prints and the stuffed heads of various animals, labels hanging from their antlers and fangs. The broker sat behind his counter, display cases to his left and right, scratching his chin with the obligatory air of world-weariness.

'Italian,' Maud said brightly, as she presented the locket. 'Over two hundred years old. Been in the family for generations.'

Life with Jimmy, and indeed her own rather precarious childhood, had left Maud well versed in the games of the pawn shop. The broker's sigh, slightly over-heavy, and the deliberate unconcern with which the gem glass was removed from his eye, told her that this piece was worth serious coin; as one would expect, quite frankly, coming from the Leyland household. He could sense the hurry, however, beneath her play of high spirits, and offered only two pounds. It didn't matter. *She had the bloody money*. There was no time for an omnibus or a cab – at this point in the afternoon the fastest way over was to walk. Maud stowed the banknotes, readied her elbows and pushed out into London.

It took ten minutes to battle through the tangled alleys to St Martin's Lane, and a further five to follow its crooked course down to Trafalgar Square. After that it was a straight dash westwards, into the districts of the easeful rich. Muddled ochres, faded blacks and crumbling reds were replaced by the greys of well-tended stone. The multifarious crowds thinned and the air grew clearer, less malodorous – and hushed, it seemed, by a kind of communal decorum. Hem in hand, Maud puffed along Pall Mall, past the elegant façades of clubs and learned institutions, disregarding the looks cast in her direction. At the Tudor palace she stopped to catch her breath. St James's lay to the right, running uphill into Piccadilly; and there was the Albemarle, standing tall and grand in a long line of similar structures. She squinted up at the terrace where Jimmy would be working and wondered what exactly she might say – with her dusty dress and jacket, her disordered hair, her fourth best hat – to convince them to let her inside. As she approached the entrance, however, she spotted him across the street, propped against a lamp post as he smoked an idle cigarette; so over she went, through the traffic, beaming with the jubilation of a runner reaching the finish line.

'Got it,' she panted as she arrived at his side, nearly colliding with him. 'I've – I've bloody well got it.'

'Why, Maudie,' he said, not quite looking back at her. His voice sounded odd – a hollowed-out attempt at levity. 'You came.'

'Course I did. I've got the money. And you'll never—'

'You're a good girl, really you are. But it's too late. The worst has occurred.'

Maud's face fell. 'You mean you lost the job? The devils didn't pay you?'

'What? No. No, I didn't lose—' Jimmy hesitated. 'Well, I suppose that rather depends how you look at it. Old Tommy Bowles from *Vanity Fair* arrived at the Albemarle to find Mr Whistler being badgered by a waiter for the sake of twelve shillings, which he clearly did not have. The impression, I fear, was of ignoble poverty. Of want, of failure. Their man of the day was made to look very much like a man of yesterday instead.'

'He paid you though, this Tommy Bowles?'

'Well yes, he *paid*, naturally he did. The plate was wonderful. That was beyond argument. And he could see that I had a bill to settle. I daresay he found the whole situation rather entertaining. A tale was played out, my girl, there for a seasoned journalist merely to observe. News of Whistler's destitution will no doubt be spreading about town as we speak. It will be the talk of dinner tables for weeks to come.'

Maud, still recovering her breath, felt the ache of admonishment. 'I tried to get here, Jimmy. I did the best I could.'

Jimmy stood upright, grinding out his cigarette beneath the toe of a fine black boot. 'It wasn't *Owl*, by any chance,' he asked, 'who provided you with the money?'

'I didn't know where he'd be. I thought—'

'I wrote to him on Thursday, you know, specifically to prevent this from coming about. *Thursday*. I asked him to stop at the hotel before Bowles's arrival. When I have etchings to be sold, or when he has some plan for my paintings, the fellow is ever-present. But when I need bailing out, Maudie, when it is a matter of actual goddamned necessity, he's a mirage. A man made of mist. A door one knocks on without reply.'

This made Maud think of Southampton Row. 'I did call on Rosa. Nobody was home.'

'She wouldn't have had anything anyway,' Jimmy snorted. 'Why, she works less than I do.' His anger was guttering already; he looked downcast, in fact. 'Who was it, then? Little Theo Watts? Eldon?'

Maud remembered Mrs Leyland's grip. The things she'd said. *He must desist*. What good would it do, telling Jimmy of this now? He'd pretend to be unsurprised. Unworried. Then he'd become agitated, chewing at his fingernails; and then enraged, shouting and strutting, vowing this and that, plotting all kinds of foolery. And he absolutely would *not* do what his rich friend had urged. No, passing on Mrs Leyland's message would surely make everything worse. It was best left for another time.

'Eldon,' she told him. 'Caught him at the Grosvenor. He'd mentioned to me that he was going again.'

This appeared to satisfy. Promptly losing interest in the Albemarle and the humiliation he'd suffered, Jimmy declared himself to be ravenously hungry. A late luncheon was proposed. Maud knew very well that this would be paid for with the locket money, two pounds that could be more usefully spent elsewhere. She lamented her appearance, in the hope of putting him off. The point was taken, but only so he could bear it in mind while selecting a venue.

'I believe we shall head to Frascati's. They know me there, and will think nothing of a little disarray. You've been before, of course.'

Maud hadn't. At first Jimmy didn't believe her, then he declared that she was in for an exquisite treat which would rescue the day completely. The wines there were merely serviceable, it was true, but one went for the *bouillabaisse*, which really had no rival in London. He set his topper at the preferred angle, planted the end of the bamboo cane on the pavement before him, and raised his arm to hail a hansom.

Frascati's was on Oxford Street, a distance only of a few hundred yards, but Jimmy Whistler would never walk if he had the means to do otherwise. Maud resigned herself to the luncheon, being too tired – peculiarly, overwhelmingly tired – to resist. It was the heat, she guessed, coupled with the afternoon's several shocks and exertions. En route, through the stop-starts of the afternoon traffic, he asked about the Grosvenor, where she'd supposedly met with Eldon. How had it seemed? How had people been reacting to his paintings?

Maud's answers were the same as always: the canvases looked brilliantly bold, she told him, and were causing much astonishment and incomprehension. These lines were surely becoming stale through repetition. Her delivery was also rather less than lively. Jimmy didn't seem to notice, though, nodding through her recitation before informing her once again that the controversy over his *Black and Gold* was still devilishly sharp one year on; that John Ruskin's calumny was still the talk of artistic society; that the much-delayed trial, which would certainly be scheduled within the next week, would still serve as a monumental reckoning.

'We'll thrash them, Maudie,' he concluded, as Frascati's appeared outside the window. 'Every last one.'

With that he swaggered across a strip of sunlit pavement

and into the deep shade beneath the restaurant's awning, immediately striking up a conversation with the uniformed fellow on the door. Maud followed. A warm welcome was being extended and the plate-glass door eased open, revealing a lavish interior of marble and gold leaf. She caught an unexpected glimpse of her reflection – the grubby, rather ordinary dress, the scuffed boots, the faintly dazed expression – and wished she'd put up more of a fight. She didn't even have an appetite; the hunger that had gnawed at her on Southampton Row had vanished entirely.

It was too late now. They made to go in, stepping towards the threshold – and the atmosphere of the place flooded out, engulfing Maud in the odours of fine cuisine. The salty tang of fish. A great brew of herbs and vinegars. The cloying richness of melted butter. That unpleasant pressure from earlier returned; it grew acute, a good deal more acute, its reason suddenly obvious and inevitable and approaching at a full bloody gallop. She turned back to the street. Jimmy was directly in her path. She moved left and he was left; she moved right and there he was there as well; so she abandoned ceremony and hefted him aside, weaving out into the dazzling sunshine and the horrible, unavoidable realisation of what was about to occur. Halfway across the pavement her balance failed, and she barely succeeded in stumbling to the kerb before she vomited.

A minute passed. Maud, on her knees, gazed blankly at the soupy splash below, already drying upon the dung-caked cobblestones. A tear dripped from the end of her nose.

Sourness was rising inside her once more, a boiling knot of it, almost jamming her throat. As she tried to breathe, to manage this second discharge, she realised that Jimmy was at her side. He was standing with his hands in his pockets and the bamboo cane under his arm, concern vying with embarrassment, grimacing a little at the familiarity of it all.

'*Bon Dieu*,' he muttered. 'Not again.'

*

August 1878

The original notion was for a dinner split neatly down the middle. Two courses in Lindsey Row, with the appropriate toasts and valedictions; a gentle procession along the stretch of the Thames Jimmy thought of as his own, past Battersea Bridge and onto Chelsea Reach; and then two more on Tite Street, in the singular glory of the White House. Mrs Cossins, however, greeted it with disbelief.

'How in blasted buggery,' she protested, 'am I to cook a dinner for twelve—'

'Fourteen, dear woman. The final tally, I believe, is fourteen.'

'—in two different houses, two different kitchens, half a bloody mile apart? I mean to say, sir, I could do it, if you're absolutely set on such a thing, but the result would surely be a disappointment. Lukewarm. Indigestible. It's up to you, I suppose.'

The banquet itself was therefore sited at the new residence, with Lindsey Row made the venue of the guests' reception only. Drinks were served, the best champagne, acquired by Jimmy from a vintner off Sloane Square – a man ignorant, crucially, of his impressive customer's precise financial circumstances. A few platters were left in the dining room, upon which were little bits of bread and pastry, with foodstuffs and sauce arranged artfully atop them. This was a French notion, Maud was told, going back to the previous century. Canopies, Jimmy seemed to call them. When she offered them around by this name, however – *care for a canopy, Mr Irving?* – there was laughter; Jimmy embraced her where she stood, tray in hand, and told her she was perfect.

Maud hardly cared. She couldn't bear even to look at the wretched things herself; anything she ate came straight back out again. Her stomach was wholly empty, her body dragging a half-second behind her brain. It was like a weird, lucid drunkenness; she was both there and not there, drifting through the hours like a balloon. They could laugh all they damn well liked.

Once everyone had arrived, the party set about making a last circuit of the house. They raised their glasses in each room, saluting the activities that had been pursued there, artistic and otherwise. Jimmy grew quite sentimental.

'I have lived here,' he reflected, 'longer than I have lived anywhere else. It is rather sad to think that soon I will be here no more.'

'The relinquishment of one's burrow,' Owl concurred, 'does bring on a particular melancholy.'

Maud had watched the men come with their van and carthorses, labour away for the better part of a day, and then drive a towering, tottering load off along the embankment. As she walked around now, though, she was surprised by how much of the furniture was still there, including several of what she'd taken to be Jimmy's finest pieces. A couple more – a large sideboard from the dining room, and that great lacquered bed in which her present predicament had most probably come about – had been sold to the new tenant, she understood, or taken for restoration under Owl's supervision.

The studio, similarly, contained a couple of dozen paintings. Three full-lengths were up on easels, put out by Jimmy that afternoon. In pride of place was the portrait of Rosa Corder. She was shown in profile, her pale skin forming a crisp, glowing line against the black velvet backdrop: it was a pose of grace, style and a certain authority. Jimmy had scraped off the paint and restarted many times, adjusting every aspect, but was finally close to completion. On either side of this canvas were a couple from that first fateful show at the Grosvenor: the actor Henry Irving in the character of a Spanish King, and one of Maud in her old fur jacket. *The Arrangement in Brown*. Jimmy had deliberately chosen paintings of people who were present, and the rest of the party was soon urging them to strike the poses of their pictures, to allow for a comparison. Mr Irving relented almost immediately. A tall, handsome man with a plain enthusiasm for display, he adopted a lofty regal attitude and recited a few of his lines – pretending not to hear Owl's loud suggestion that he consider making an offer for the work.

Rosa went next, swivelling to the side, lifting her chin and placing a hand on her hip. My friend, thought Maud sardonically. She'd found herself smarting – not entirely reasonably, she knew – at Rosa's failure to be home that afternoon. It had taken on the aspect of a profound disappointment. They hadn't spoken so far, beyond a quick greeting. She resolved to be chilly.

Like Maud, Rosa was wearing a summer gown of muslin and lace rather than the darker, heavier clothes Jimmy had painted them in, and she was holding a champagne glass rather than one of her wide-brimmed hats, but otherwise you had to admit it was a pretty decent imitation. She couldn't stay still for long, though, being too aware of the attention, too ready to laugh, dispelling the elegance completely.

'You see the trouble I caused,' she said with a guilty grin. 'Poor Jimmy. It must have been very tiresome.'

Maud was last, her ill temper overtaken very slightly by a desire to show how it was done. The pose was of a type Jimmy had favoured a few years previously, rather like that of the Frances Leyland portrait. She linked her hands behind her back, turned and started to step away; then stopped and looked over her shoulder, towards the rest of the party but not actually *at* them, emptying her features of thought or feeling, as Jimmy insisted upon when he worked from her. It was simple really, tedious more than anything. As a minute ran by, however, and she did not move, an admiring murmur gathered among Jimmy's guests.

'There it is,' declared Rosa, proudly it seemed. 'There is a true model.'

The others agreed; they even gave her a round of applause. Maud dropped the pose, flexing her arms, and immediately felt the sickness beginning to build. Jimmy was talking now, explaining some aspect of his technique, so she stepped away, over to the French doors, staring hard at the sun-browned garden.

'Miss Franklin, are you – do excuse me, but are you quite all right?'

Matthew Eldon had followed her over, concern upon his wide, guileless face. Maud's lie about borrowing the two pounds from him had obliged her to admit Eldon into her confidence, to a certain degree. She hadn't revealed the true source of the money, saying simply that she needed him to cover for her, and that it was to help Jimmy; she then told him about her condition, to arouse his sympathy. This had been more than enough to secure both Eldon's cooperation and a pledge of secrecy, winning her a new, somewhat overly devoted ally. She did her best to distract him, insisting that there was no cause for alarm and asking questions about the other guests – in particular Ellen Terry, star of the Lyceum, who was over on the far side of the studio. Taller than most of the men, this celebrated lady was dark blonde and about thirty years of age, dressed in a fashionably cut gown the colour of autumn honey. The actress had arrived with Mr Irving and had yet to stray from his side, but this plainly wasn't due to shyness. She was looking past him as they talked, surveying the rest of the party with large, calm eyes.

Eldon grew confiding, giving her a lopsided smile. 'Well, you know the story there, don't you?' he murmured. 'Jimmy invited Miss Terry along for Godwin.'

'But Godwin—' Maud bit her lip in confusion. The architect had been pointedly omitted from this gathering, on account of what Jimmy regarded as his failings over the White House – his feeble defence against the Board of Works. 'Godwin isn't here.'

Before any more could be said there was an eruption of claps and whistles in the centre of the room. Jimmy had raised a hand, to signal an announcement.

'The artist,' he said, 'will now quit the studio. Dear room, site of such striving, of such triumph and such bitter disappointment – I bid you adieu!'

With that he started down the passageway to the hall, saying farewell to everything he passed. The panelling, so warped and stained! The banister knob, so exquisitely carved to resemble – what was it, precisely? A nut? Some kind of sprout? The doorstep, trodden upon by so many hundreds of feet, clad in everything from hobnail boots to the finest dancing slippers!

The party collected its hats and jackets and made to

depart. It seemed to be happening quickly now, after so much waiting and delay – in a rush almost. Through that front door they went, the hinge creaking as always, for the very last time; down the path, crowded by leaves and snagging branches; out onto the pavement beyond. Maud's feelings, there beneath the plane trees of Lindsey Row, were desperately mixed. She was keen to be gone from that narrow, gloomy terrace; to be gone from it all, she sometimes thought. Yet the life that awaited her downriver – and the house within which it would be played out – was uncertain indeed. She paused, the procession forming around her in the light evening mist; and Rosa Corder was at her side, taking hold of her arm and kissing her cheek, telling her again how marvellously she modelled. *You hold the moment.* That's how she put it. *You hold it completely.*

Then Rosa was asking about a set of Maud's own studies that she'd seen the last time she called, a fortnight or so before: begonias, taken in chalk, the petals red and white like slices of radish. Had Maud found time to do any more? Had they been taken already to Tite Street? Might they be brought out once they'd arrived there?

Maud held firm. 'I came to your studio the other day,' she said. 'To Southampton Row.'

Yes, Rosa replied at once, Charles had told her of this. She embarked upon an explanation of how Owl and Jimmy had somehow missed one another out on St James's, and then Owl had been obliged to leave for King's Cross, to see to a pressing piece of business; how Owl was wracked with remorse at the thought that he might have let them down; how the porters at the Albemarle had—

'Where were you?' Maud interrupted. 'You told me you worked every Saturday. I needed your help. We both did.'

Rosa appeared chastened, for a second; yet when she apologised, her voice held little contrition, as if she felt Maud was being irrational but didn't wish to argue. Before any more could be said, Owl remarked somewhere up ahead that they should all be on their guard for creditors, for that pesky cheesemonger perhaps, lest they try to bring down Jimmy Whistler while he was on the move. The artist, finding this notion rather less amusing than his guests, redirected them towards a more comfortable subject: his imminent legal victory over John Ruskin.

'We do not yet,' he announced, swinging his cane, 'have a date for the trial. But my goodness, such an army of supporters we are recruiting! So many of the really major painters! All of them will be coming to the White House to dine, and to inspect my works. To be shown precisely what is at stake here.'

'What of Ruskin?' someone asked. 'Any word from him?'

'*Rien de tout*. Word was going around that the old goat was actually relishing the prospect – that he wished to discipline me in public, would you believe, for my crimes against art. But this was months ago. Now he simply hides away among his lakes, allowing his various lickspittles to quibble and dodge, and go about the task of assembling his doomed defence.'

Mr Irving spoke up, volunteering a theory that the venerated critic, fearful of public confrontation, was preparing to flee to the Continent. This prompted a rush of opinion and ridicule; Maud barely listened, thinking instead of her encounter with Mrs Leyland in that alley off High Holborn. She'd yet to tell anyone about this. It was paralysing, a proper dilemma, made a little worse by each passing day. If she told, it would only inflame everything further, and rob Jimmy of his balance; if she didn't, she might well discover later on that she'd kept back a vital fact. *They are meeting*, the shipbroker's wife had said. *Some kind of scheme is being put together*.

There were cheers, and a short round of applause; Maud lifted her head to see that the White House was coming into view. Scaffolding gone at last, the pristine brickwork looked bright and sharp in the low light. As they drew closer, Maud's predisposition to like what she saw grated slightly against the actual reality of it – for it was an odd jumble, this house, with a multitude of small, irregular windows and strangely placed doors. It wasn't even clear where the different storeys might begin and end. The rest of the procession were praising its originality, saying that there was nothing else like it in London, which was certainly true; Maud noticed, however, that Jimmy himself was less exultant than might have been expected. Having brought this thing into being in the face of all manner of practical objections and obstacles, he now seemed unable to take pleasure in it, seeing only the compromises he'd been required to make. These he pointed out and criticised with some passion, in particular the carved panels, vaguely floral in character, that had been set around the windows; and the new elevation, which meant his splendid green roof tiles could no longer be seen from the front.

'We were forced, *mes amis*, forced under threat of demolition, to embellish a building already complete in every sense. To gild our perfect white lily.'

The party entered through a low door – possibly the front door, it was difficult to tell – and was soon split apart so completely that it seemed almost a function of the design. Maud found herself wandering through a string of what appeared to be parlours, running along the front of the house. The structure was shallow, barely more than a room and a half wide. The ceilings were low like the door, and the passages narrow; the walls were ivory, mustard, robin's egg blue. It was even more sparsely furnished than Lindsey Row, some rooms containing no more than a rug and a pair of simple chairs. A Japanese effect, Maud supposed.

Rosa remained at her side. 'How in God's name,' she said, 'are you supposed to *live here?*'

Maud couldn't contain her grin; although it faded quickly enough when they found, amid the warren of corridors, the smallest, steepest staircase she had ever seen in her life. She imagined herself in the months to come, with swollen ankles and heavy belly, having to scale this thing simply to reach her bed. Rosa took it three steps at a time, beckoning for her to follow. They went up to the top, to the studio, which occupied the entire third storey. Maud saw that the whole building had been arranged around it. The floors were stained dark brown, and the walls painted a cool, pinkish grey; the ceiling was higher than downstairs, but still not particularly high; the windows were all on one side, in a row, washing the long room with dusky light. At one end was propped Jimmy's huge mirror, taller than a man, and at the other was the model table. After the poky studio at Lindsey Row, the sheer distance between them seemed incredible.

Rosa walked off on a wide circuit. Maud stopped just inside the doorway, however, the fullness of it all striking suddenly against her. Jimmy had had a house built – a house built from scratch, from nothing. They were living on credit, in debt to a great long laundry list of Chelsea tradesmen. Each hour that passed held the threat of the bailiff's knock. So much was unknown, conjecture, based only on their best hopes. Yet he'd *built a house*! These walls, these floors, these windows, arranged in such an original manner, would have to be paid for, every last one. And then there was her new circumstance. Many expenses would be involved in that. Tears stung her eyes; nausea burned at the back of her throat; and for the first time she began to think, really *think*, of what it would be to give birth again.

Maud had always considered herself to be brave. She'd never been one to run from a barking dog, or a bully twisting ears on a street corner. But no amount of courage was sufficient for what lay ahead of her now. Much of Ione's birth had passed in a fog of chloral. Her limbs had been rubbery and unreliable; the lamps too dim, then too bright, blotting across her vision; she'd seen the blood on the midwife's hands, her forearms; the baby slick and wailing, dark with colour against her bone-white thigh. The drug had not been enough, however, to spare her from the pain. She'd been warned of it – had witnessed it, even, in her own mother – yet still it had managed to catch her utterly by surprise. It had left her broken, trampled all out of shape, squeezed and split like a spent paint-tube. She'd been thankful to live, thankful too that the child had lived, when so many didn't. She'd fought to set herself right; to recover her strength and accept the bargain she'd made. And yet here it was once more. It would be upon her in no time.

Rosa was there, holding up a handkerchief to mop at Maud's face, her streaming eyes – guiding her to the centre of the room, encouraging her to sit cross-legged on the floorboards. Later on, she couldn't quite work out if she'd revealed what had befallen her or if Rosa had guessed, but she was as sympathetic and as reassuring as you could wish for. She understood, she said; it was bad luck, that was all. Maud was resilient and wise. She would survive it.

How could Maud not grab at this, grab at it with both hands? How could she not be grateful? So Rosa had not been there to help on the day of the Albemarle – what of it? She knew Maud's life. She knew why Maud chose to live as she did. Maud spoke of her fears; of the oily tide of debt that was closing around their heels, rising up their calves; and then of Mrs Leyland's warning. This last one was begun on impulse, but felt right straight away. Maud saw that she had to tell somebody – and who better, honestly, than Rosa Corder? It got muddled in the telling, emerging largely backwards; she'd just reached the ruse about the golden locket when Rosa cut her off.

'You must forget Mrs Leyland,' she said. 'Put that woman from your mind.'

Maud hesitated. 'But it can't be nothing, can it? She took a risk to meet with me, Rosa, a grave risk. If her husband had found out, she would've been in the most—'

'He knew. Dear Maud, it was probably his idea. They want Jimmy to lose his nerve, don't you see? To spare Ruskin what he deserves. And they want Jimmy to suffer – to be deprived of his justice in the name of petty vengeance, of spite and wounded pride. It's that dreadful hack Ned Jones, you know. He's the link here. Charles says that he's an old confidante of Ruskin's – and the new favourite artist of Frederick Leyland. Quite a coincidence, wouldn't you agree?' Rosa let out an impatient sigh. 'If Mrs Leyland remains such a friend to Jimmy – if she is so very *worried* for him, despite everything – I wonder why she has never stood up to her husband and made the brute see reason. I wonder why she doesn't do that instead of delivering useless warnings.'

Maud recalled those savage letters – *the weakness of a woman* – and the great urgency in Mrs Leyland's grip. 'So you truly believe it was all a – a trick? That they're in league?'

'All that matters,' Rosa replied, 'is that Jimmy will win. Ruskin will be made to pay. This house will be the site of a new beginning. For Jimmy Whistler, for you, for every one of us who follows his example.'

Thinking of how things would be in the White House brought Maud back to her child. Her second child. Jimmy's attitude had been measured. Things would proceed exactly as before. They would even place the baby with the same family, if it could be arranged. Maud had agreed – what else could she do? She had wondered, though, exactly how many times she could go along with this. Was she to fall pregnant every year, every other year, for the next decade? The next two decades? She couldn't say with any certainty when it had happened this time. There had been many instances throughout the spring, before his optimism began to wane, when (she realised now) she'd given only the most cursory consideration to the point in the month. She frowned at the stained floor. Had she grown careless? Could it have been, in some peculiar way, deliberate?

'Do you wish him to marry you?'

Maud looked up; she had a sense, unnervingly clear, of having been found out. Marriage was not discussed at Lindsey Row; she'd never expected it to be. She'd never wanted it, in fact, considering wedlock to be a great symbol of the loveless, stifling propriety she'd vowed early on to avoid, as best as she was able. Even when Mrs Whistler had mentioned it the other week, in that sitting room by the sea, it had seemed rather laughable – something that could not and should not ever happen. Right then, though, sitting raw-eyed and nauseous on the studio floor, she had to admit that it didn't seem laughable any longer.

'I don't – it hasn't—'

Rosa leaned in closer. 'Perhaps I should ask why you would want him to.'

Now Maud's mystification was complete. 'What do you mean?'

'There are alternatives. Other paths. This is becoming ever more clear.' Voices could be heard down below – Jimmy and the two actors sharing a joke with much exaggerated laughter. 'Take, for instance, tonight's guest of honour, the acclaimed Miss Ellen Terry.'

Rosa then spun the tale of a child prodigy, married at sixteen to a man thirty years her senior, whose eye she'd had the misfortune to catch while on the stage. It had been a dismal union, from which she'd been rescued by none other than Edward Godwin. After their elopement she'd lived with him out in the country for several years, much as Maud lived with Jimmy, and had borne him two children; yet now she was married again, to another gentleman. Furthermore, she was experiencing a theatrical resurrection that few could have predicted, under her own name and based entirely upon her talents.

'Our Miss Terry is more famous today,' Rosa concluded, 'and more admired, than she has ever been.'

Maud sniffed, trying to swallow her sickness. She remembered what Eldon had said at Lindsey Row – his connection of the actress and the architect. 'She – she really had Godwin's babies?'

'A boy and a girl. They live with her, here in London. Godwin and Miss Terry don't care to meet one another any longer, though. Too much has changed. Securing her attendance tonight, you might say, was Jimmy's way of informing Godwin that he himself was not welcome.' Rosa took Maud's clammy hands in hers. 'Why marry? That's the lesson here, don't you see? Moral types may mutter and grumble, but who gives a single fig for them? Why restrict yourself, and what you might do? Children are not the end, Maud. Not in the least. Money is coming, enough money to throw the world open. I can see a future well away from London. We'll be artists together, you and I. Charles and Jimmy can come with us, or they can remain behind. We'll take a place in the countryside. Or away in Portugal, like we talked of at the Café Royal. A villa by the ocean. We'll paint for our living. And our children will play in the gardens around us while we work.'

Maud glanced at Rosa. She was smiling, her lilac eyes narrowed, completely serious. Maud's earlier doubts were quite gone; she was now close to deciding that Rosa Corder was the best, the very dearest friend she'd ever had. Overcome by this vision of Portugal, so vivid and beautiful and just so utterly bloody *perfect*, she began to sob again.

The voices were on the staircase now. Rosa made no effort to rise. She wrapped an arm around Maud's shoulders and gathered her in. Maud found her teary face pressed against Rosa's gown; it smelled of paint and dust, edged with the subtlest scent of roses.

'It will happen,' Rosa said, her lips close to Maud's ear, as the first people entered the studio. 'You'll see.'

Autumn 1878

What was it about the Owl that made one forgive him so much upon sight alone? There in Reeve's office, four floors up in a rather swank block just back from the Strand, Jim had thought that if the fellow did actually deign to appear, he might experience a degree of annoyance, of resentment perhaps; that it could even impair the progress of their discussions. Yet when that familiar silhouette slid onto the smoked glass panel of the office door, he felt nothing but gladness. He was on his feet, introducing Mr Charles Augustus Howell to the barristers as an expert in *objets d'art* and the London market who had generously agreed to assist with the plan of battle, and apologising for having begun the meeting without him, even though Owl was more than half an hour late. It really wasn't like Jim at all.

The meeting was proving a testing affair, though, fast

sapping away the triumph and excitement that had carried him through the past week – for they had a *date*, a date at last for Whistler vs Ruskin. The trial was to occur early in the Michaelmas sittings of the Court of Exchequer, which according to Reeve meant mid-November. Only a month or so off. This was the first proper council of war, with the legal team assembled, and Jim's initial impression of his barristers had been encouraging. Sitting on the other side of Reeve's expansive desk were Parry and Petheram: a serjeant-at-law, no less, and his junior. There was an interesting contrast between the busy little solicitor, flanked by his weighty volumes and heaps of papers, and these more languid courtroom men – that of beasts bred from the same stable, broadly speaking, but for an entirely different kind of race. Parry was in his mid-fifties, with a lugubrious, bloodhoundish face and the pot-bellied physique of the bona fide scholar. He was an advocate of renown, Jim understood, a real barnstormer, much given to the impassioned appeal – to eloquence of an imploring nature, irresistible both to one's sympathy and one's common sense. The junior, Petheram, was sparer in every regard, pale and red-headed, his thin features suggesting a cool, unhampered intelligence.

Their view of the case, however, was another matter. The whole trial hinged, they believed, on the presentation of Jim to the jury as an artist of unquestionable status, possessing both professional dignity and expert ability.

'You are,' Parry had said, 'you will excuse me, sir – a rather singular character, and one that has been subject to a great deal of attention of late. Written up in *The World* and *Vanity Fair*. Parodied, I am told, at the Gaiety Theatre. Known widely as a Frenchified American who sees people principally as harmonies of colour – is that correct? Who dries his paintings out in the garden, and signs them with a butterfly. Who decorates his houses and clothes his person in a wholly, ah, *original* manner, with little regard for prevailing fashions . . .'

Here Petheram had spoken up, in the cut-crystal tones of the nobility. 'They will attempt to portray you as a charlatan, Mr Whistler. A man whose attitudes and habits mark him out as an aberrant clown, not to be taken seriously, and who is thus deserving of Mr Ruskin's censure. Our task is to establish the significance of your art. Its contribution, if you will, to the societal good.'

This had sounded a little lifeless to Jim. His vision, first and foremost, was of *confrontation*. John Ruskin had recovered from his extremely convenient affliction and was said to be back in the National Gallery, bothering the Turners. He wanted the old viper dragged to court and held to account – before London, before *everybody*. Reeve hadn't been wildly pleased about this, saying that nothing was guaranteed where Mr Ruskin was concerned, but Jim had hardly heard him. He was growing afraid that his libel suit had all but disappeared from the public mind, as had surely been the enemy's intention; or that it had simply become a joke, or even an opportunity for some lesser men from the Royal Academy to make a demonstration against him.

'I've heard that one of their number,' he'd said, 'this ghastly hack named Marks, actually intends to present himself in court with easel and brushes, ready to produce a *Nocturne* in five minutes as an illustration of my imposture. As if art was a question of *time*, of the hours put in – like painting fences! Or breaking rocks!'

Parry and Petheram hadn't been particularly interested in this; indeed, they'd rather wanted to stress that Jim himself had shown his art on the Academy walls, as an indication of his pedigree. If paintings were to be brought into court, they'd asked, as looked likely, could he produce the picture that had been exhibited – the portrait of his mother?

Jim had declined to answer. This was a sore subject. As the clamour of bills had intensified, the draper, the boot-maker, even the blasted photographer piling in – along with a new levy called the *income tax*, a most ungentlemanly notion – Jim had assented at last. He had given the *Mother* over to Owl, and it had gone to his man on Pall Mall, Mr Graves, accompanied by the barely complete portrait of Miss Corder and two *Nocturnes* – leaving behind an absence so total, so damned *yawning*, that he scarcely dared think of it. Of course, these were only the latest works to take flight. Another tranche were in a place on the Strand, near Way's premises; not a pawn shop, Owl had insisted, not at all, merely a reputable dealer in fine pictures who happened to offer credit in exchange for collateral. Jim had tried self-deception – the paintings were going out into the world, being put on display with cash involved, which was nearly as good as a sale – but he couldn't hope to succeed. The sums were paltry, nothing close to what was warranted. There was a feeling beneath it, too, something agitating and provoking and rotten right through. Desperation, he suspected.

Instead, Jim had suggested they mention the Peacock Room, his greatest work, which had been admired by all sorts of famous and influential people. But again the barristers had been reluctant, plainly regarding Jim's dealings with Frederick Leyland as a beehive they did not want to poke. James Whistler the professional painter was what they wanted. There must be no hint of previous disputations.

It was at this point, thank God, that Owl made his entrance, scattering ash upon Reeve's oriental rug as he hung his topper and overcoat on the stand, then sweeping through to settle himself in a chair that complained very slightly beneath his bulk. He was wearing that crimson ribbon on his lapel, and a pair of resplendent blue and yellow checked trousers that seemed to flash against the office's dreary tones. Taking a long drag on his cigarette, he popped open a jacket button with his thumb and raised his eyebrows in expectation.

Jim felt reinforced. There was no other way of putting it. Here was someone who would understand the precise attitude they needed to strike. This was remarkable, really, as punctuality and the *Mother* were by no means his only causes for complaint with the Owl. Foremost was their

Disraeli venture, much discussed and anticipated, which had collapsed into farce. Letters had been written and the expedition made out to the grand house at Beaconsfield, so that artist and subject could agree their terms. After a long wait in a vestibule, Jim had finally been granted an audience. While he'd been making his first painterly assessment of the great politician – the bulging cranium, the oiled, steely hair, the gimlet eye – Disraeli had informed him, with the distant calm of a Sphinx, that he'd changed his mind. He was extremely busy at present, he'd continued, and would be sitting for no more portraits. Of Mr Charles Howell, of pensions for Cruikshank on behalf of Mr Ruskin, he'd denied all knowledge. An apology had been made, in an indifferent sort of way. And then the meeting had been terminated.

Jim had been left feeling a double fool. The Prime Minister had clearly let him undertake that journey – a waste of an entire day, and nearly five shillings in fares – as a reprimand for his impudent approach. For his presumption. For which *Owl*, with his apparently baseless tales of previous acquaintance, and his unlimited confidence in the scheme's chance of success, had been completely responsible.

They had been due to assemble at Miss Corder's that evening. Jim had rehearsed a castigation on his way back to London, a real flaying, but the Portuguese hadn't been around to receive it. Miss Corder, so disarmingly reverent as usual, hadn't the least idea where he might be. There'd been no sign of him anywhere for over a week. Then, quite characteristically, he'd strolled in uninvited to a dinner at the White House as if nothing whatsoever was amiss. He'd been full of optimistic predictions about the trial, the *Carlyle* mezzotint and much else. The enquiry about Jim's trip to Beaconsfield had finally been made across the dining table, before the company – thus obliging Jim to spin a tale where he and Disraeli had sparred good-humouredly in the great man's study, recognised one another as the artists they both were, in their respective fields, and parted with expressions of mutual esteem, despite the lack of a result. This had met with general amusement, and had made any scolding of the Owl effectively impossible. It had been a classic move, in short, played so smoothly it had taken some effort not to admire it.

'We were just about to say, Mr Howell,' said Petheram, 'that witnesses, in our opinion, will form a critical part of this case. We believe that Mr Whistler should concentrate his energies upon those immediately involved with the production and sale of artworks. Artists, naturally, but also art dealers. Critics from the newspapers. People who know how the market can be influenced.'

'The more accomplished the better,' added Parry.

'Well,' said Jim, 'there are many dozens who will come forward. My table has hosted the greatest artistic minds in England. Leighton will surely help, as will Tissot. Sir Joseph Boehm.'

Anderson Reeve was nodding in approval. 'We should

make haste with our subpoenas. Ruskin's people are already preparing their own witnesses, with Mr Burne-Jones foremost among them. He's said to be offering advice on how best to proceed – sympathetic parties, angles of attack and so forth. I hear that he volunteered himself in the earliest days of the action, partly through gratitude for—'

'I know Ned Jones,' said Owl. 'Rather well, as a matter of fact.'

There was a brief silence.

'Mr Howell once worked for Ruskin,' Jim explained. 'He was in the rascal's employ for the whole Pre-Raphaelite circus, just about. Isn't that so, Owl?'

The Portuguese gave one of his magnificent shrugs. 'Jones and I certainly had our dealings. A number of years back, we're talking here. He's spoken of as a master these days, gentlemen, but I saw the man behind it all. Behind the sickly, wax-work angels and the wooden fables. And that, I think, does not change.'

Parry's initial curiosity had turned to doubt. 'I am not sure that this pertains—'

There was no stopping Owl now, though. He had a story lined up, a favourite of his; and even these barristers, these professional talkers, could not halt or redirect him. The office was told of how, after a period of warmest amity, this artist had taken quite strongly against the young Owl – envious, most probably, of the great trust that had then existed between the famous critic and his secretary. Burne-Jones had begun to undermine him at every juncture, to sow poisonous seeds of suspicion in the suggestible Ruskinian mind. Things had quickly reached the point where action was called for.

'Now, Ned Jones had a wife. Do you know, I believe he has her still. The fragrant Georgiana. The strength of their bond was the stuff of legend – an example to us all. Our Ned, though, crafty chap, had another lady love as well, a Greek beauty of some renown, whose features made repeated appearances in his works. To the point of eeriness, in fact. I need not go into the details of the affair. You are men of the world, I'm sure. Suffice to say that it was a sorry business. Poor Ned was obsessed – both with his Greek muse, and with keeping his infatuation secret from his dear wife.' Owl leaned forward. 'Yet it so happened – purely through the vagaries of fate, you understand – that one afternoon these two ladies were in the same drawing room at the same time. A confusion of dates it was. You know how these things have a way of coming about. I was on hand – again, strictly by chance – and resolved to avert any awkwardness by making an introduction. And I have to say that we were all getting along rather splendidly until old Ned appeared in the doorway, to see his saintly white and his sinful black quite mixed up together.'

'Why Owl,' asked Jim, 'whatever did he do?'

'Jimmy, my friend,' Owl replied, 'he fainted. The scrawny little wisp fainted dead away. It was a test, I'd say, of his resources – his manliness, if you like – and he fell insensible to the hearth. Knocked his bonce on the way down as well.

Cracked it hard against the mantelpiece.' He pressed a fore-finger to his temple. 'When it rains, he still feels it here.'

Jim let out a high, derisive laugh. The legal types stayed quiet, however – either containing their mirth or unamused. Dear Reeve, now Jim looked at him properly, actually seemed a mite *embarrassed*, almost hiding behind those papers of his. Honestly, these Englishmen and their codes – what one was permitted to say and what one wasn't. Jim would never understand, nor would he care to. The sense of a *faux pas*, in fact, served to enliven him, to bring him really to himself for the first time that afternoon. He asked Owl for a cigarette. Once this was lit he strolled over to the fireplace and studied the coals, poking one on the periphery with his cane; then he turned on his heel to face his team. He felt himself growing before them, filling up like a sail.

'So this is the calibre of our opponents,' he declared. 'How the devil can we possibly lose, gentlemen? Ruskin shall be brought before us and we shall trounce him. We shall strike a blow for art.'

'Hear, hear,' said Owl. 'Absolutely right.'

'Once again, Whistler,' said Reeve, his voice rather small, 'I must tell you that I cannot *promise* that Ruskin will be present. His lawyers will not confirm that his health is sufficiently restored to enable—'

Jim held up a hand. 'Do what you can, *mon cher*,' he said. 'That's all I ask. Do what you can.'

*

25 November 1878

As a battlefield, Jim supposed that the Court of Exchequer would serve well enough. Arranged around a large square table stacked with the lawyers' papers and books, the bench was set at the far end, with the witness box off to one side. The ceiling was ecclesiastically high; the windows, set above oak panelling, held dim panes of stained glass – coats of arms and other such things. There was an aura of ancientness, of authority, and a marked absence of light. Rembrandt – yes, it was all rather like one of the later etchings of Rembrandt. The chamber was rather smaller than Jim had envisioned, however; and if these two facing groups of legal men and witnesses were armies, then one, the enemy's, was missing its general.

Too unwell, the weaselly lawyers had said. Too frail still to submit to the ordeal of the trial. The courtroom was full, crowded with personalities most varied in their stripe and hue; but John Ruskin, the noble author of *Modern Painters*, *The Stones of Venice* et cetera, was made conspicuous only by his goddamned absence. Before they'd begun, before the first bewigged gasbag had risen to speak, there was a very real sense that the entire undertaking had been a confounded waste of time.

'Hang it all, Reeve,' Jim murmured, casting a look of subtle disappointment in his solicitor's direction, 'why in thunder didn't you *do something*?'

Reeve, deep in his papers, didn't notice. After so long

a wait, after so many delays and obstructions, it was shaping up to be a day of such disappointments. The witnesses, for instance. Jim had secured William Rossetti, a decent and responsible critic, to counter the damnable Ruskin; the painter Albert Moore, a real brick, with whom he'd once shared a studio in Bloomsbury; and one other who was rather less easy to account for, a strange, malodorous specimen named Wills. This fellow was an artist, supposedly, unknown to Jim – another client of Reeve's, subpoenaed by him only two days before when it had become clear that no other option remained. Jim was thankful, for Rossetti and Moore at least, but he couldn't help thinking of these men as offcuts. As last resorts. His witnesses should have been a parade of the great and good. Frederick Leighton had been unavailable, though: at the palace being knighted, the word was, an excuse so absurd and impossible it simply had to be believed. Tissot and Boehm – friends of many years' standing, and true allies he'd thought – were rather harder to explain. Indeed, neither man *had* explained, not in any adequate manner, merely displaying a deep and unswayable reluctance to become involved. Something else was at work here. Jim was certain of it.

And then there were his paintings. With much expense and fuss, a small exhibition had been prepared in a room at the Westminster Palace Hotel, just over on Victoria Street, using pictures wrested from the hands of Mr Graves and others – the *Carlyle* and the *Mother* among them. This had

234

been done to provide a full demonstration of Jim's gifts, properly lit and displayed; of his irrefutable right to call himself an artist. Yet already, at the outset, the judge had ruled that it could not be visited. Escorting the jury across the street, he'd said, would cause too much disruption. The Grosvenor paintings were there in court, it was true, stacked off to the side, to be produced as evidence, but the enemy was surely ready for them. Waiting with knives sharpened.

One element that Jim had known he could rely upon was his audience: the fashionable, the artistic and the gentlemen of the press. He'd recognised many of those who'd filed into the courtroom. These were people he'd dined with, and laughed with; and there was an air of levity right then, as the trial began. Everyone seemed to be expecting an entertainment. This was all well and good, in a way; Jim liked to entertain. But rather a lot was at stake here. He was beginning to suspect that this was not very widely appreciated.

Overall, therefore, it could be said that Jimmy Whistler was feeling at a definite disadvantage. This had not been helped particularly by Serjeant Parry, his champion down there on the courtroom floor, whose opening statement had included a full reading of Ruskin's review, in all its bludgeoning, plug-ugly efficacy. *The ill-educated conceit of the artist. Wilful imposture. Flinging a pot of paint in the public's face.* There'd been an intake of breath, of course – shock at the wickedness of it, the sheer baselessness of it – but also titters. Jim had heard them distinctly, off by the doors. *Titters*.

A flunkey over by the bench stood up and intoned Jim's name. Parry, he realised, had finished. He was being called into the witness box. Carefully unhurried, he eased himself to his feet, sauntered along the pew and through a low gate; and then he was up there, before the court. *Art was in the dock*. He'd tested this phrase out on Reeve, in the cab on the way over – which had prompted the lawyer to explain that actually there was no dock, that this was the Court of Exchequer – that no one was on trial, properly speaking.

'Oh, but they are, *mon vieux*,' Jim had replied. 'That they most certainly are.'

Parry sat, ceding the floor to Petheram. Jim straightened his jacket, feeling a strange distance both from himself and the proceedings – this long-awaited moment he now occupied. As the junior guided them through the background of the case, asking about his exhibition history in England, the first show at the Grosvenor and what he had shown there, and the dramatic decline in his sales since, a real and surprising effort was required to frame his replies. His eye kept wandering off into the gloomy vault behind, members of the audience seeming to volunteer themselves for his notice. Old so-and-so's made it here, he'd think – and great heavens, look who's sitting just behind him . . .

A few minutes in he spotted dear Maud, lodged right at the back, her cheeks flushed scarlet. Even from across the chamber, through all the hats and ribbons, he could see how large she was getting. She was six months gone now by his estimation, reaching the point where movement was becoming difficult, along with much else – including their coupling, for which he'd felt an unexpected enthusiasm in the past week. An act of *mounting* had been necessary, in effect, not unpleasant in its deviation from the standard method, but rather lacking in dignity for them both. Why, only the night before—

'Will you tell us,' said Petheram, 'the meaning of the word "Nocturne" as applied to your pictures?' He'd realised Jim's distraction, bless him, his voice acquiring the slightest edge.

Jim inserted his eyeglass and set himself firmly in the present, feeling his pulse throb against his starched collar. He focused on the barrister – the black of his robes against the red-brown panelling behind; the pale, pinkish triangle of his face, crowned by the tight chalky curls of his wig. This was all rehearsed, naturally, the lines practised over and over with the legal fellows, with Maud, with Eldon and Alan Cole, and he delivered the expected answer, neatly wrapped and tied up with string. In a measured voice, he explained that the word 'Nocturne' was employed to indicate an artistic interest alone – to divest the picture of any outside anecdotal interest. A Nocturne was an arrangement of line, form and colour, and that was all. The same applied to his use of the term 'arrangement'.

'There is no suggestion,' he concluded, 'of an actual link

with music. Very often have I been misunderstood on this fact.'

The courtroom fell to murmuring. Jim leaned lightly against the front of the box, his right arm laid along the top, tapping the wood with his forefinger. This was good. Exactly right. *Corrective*. He found he was relishing the prospect of the next question – of supplying another succinct and brilliant response. Petheram, however, was turning to the judge, who was looking on with a vaguely benign expression that could have held deep understanding or its opposite. There was a nod; and then the junior was sitting back down again, shuffling his papers, reading a note that had been passed to him by Reeve. One of the others was standing, one of the blasted enemy – their chief, in fact, Sir John Holker, the Attorney General of England. This was an impressive title, but the fellow struck him right then as a plebeian of the most gormless variety: eyes half shut and peering, a nub of ruddy chin receding into a baggy neck, the mutton chops fluffing out like those of a confounded farm-hand. *Sleepy Jack*, Jim's people called him. It seemed a sound fit indeed.

No. This was the game. Jim just managed to contain his impatience. Amidst all the advice he'd received, all the schooling, some words of Owl's stood out.

'It's not about you and him, Jimmy. It's about the *jury*. Their cove will be trying to skew you from the outset. To present you as he wishes you to be seen. This you really mustn't forget.'

Jim now gave the jury a good stare, and by Jove he could not pick out a single deuced thing about them. They were civilians, twelve damnably ordinary men, quite distinct from the wealthy artistic types in the public pews – property owners from Kensington and Chelsea, he'd been told, but unexceptional in every way.

Sleepy Jack began. The pace and shape of their dialogue was very different, right from the outset: light-hearted, the questions deceptively straightforward. Laughter came to meet Jim's every utterance – to meet *Holker's* every utterance, for God's sake, the feeblest scraps of lawyerly wit eliciting veritable gales of mirth. It became rather unsettling. Jim thought he could detect apprehension there, as if a good number of the audience could perceive the path he was being led along – the destination that this Sleepy Jack had in mind.

It was an obvious one, in truth, predicted by Parry and Petheram almost in its entirety. With monstrous, plodding tediousness, the Attorney General established that Jim's paintings had unusual titles and were widely considered to be *eccentric*, like their creator; that they were stood out to dry in the garden, something he appeared to think highly odd; that the *Nocturne in Black and Gold* – the firework painting that had so infuriated Mr Ruskin, and brought about this trial – was a finished piece, on sale for two hundred guineas, which the artist deemed to be a fair price. His tone, at times, sailed uncomfortably close to insolence. Jim had been warned of this as well.

'Provocation,' Parry had said, 'is often a barrister's goal. A fit of temper on the plaintiff's part, an admonition from the judge perhaps, can easily be turned to the benefit of the defence.'

Jim, therefore, remained completely cool: slightly distant, elegantly baffled by Sleepy Jack's deliberate bumpkin blunderings. Before very long they arrived at the question of *work*: the equation of hours toiled in relation to pennies earned that so entranced the simple-minded. There was a satisfaction in old Jack now. He believed that he could see the mechanism of his little trap enclosing poor Whistler, its jaws clamping shut around the artistic ankle.

'Did it take you much time to paint the *Nocturne in Black and Gold*?' he asked. 'How soon did you knock it off?'

Knock it off? The laughter of the audience acquired a note of disbelief. Setting a hand on his hip, Jim paused for a second or two, as if thrown by Holker's vulgarity. 'I beg your pardon?'

The Attorney General was unapologetic. 'How long do you take,' he said more slowly, 'to knock off one of your pictures?'

So be it. Jim stroked his moustache; he looked up at the courtroom ceiling. 'Oh, I "knock one off" in a couple of days, possibly – one day to do the work and another to finish it.'

Sleepy Jack's satisfaction grew into triumph. He turned towards the jury, swapping his blockheaded glibness for indignation. 'You ask two hundred guineas for the labour of just *two days*?'

And there it was: the enemy laid wide open. Jim wanted to laugh – to hop up onto the edge of the witness box and crow like a cockerel. He did no such thing, of course. Instructing himself not to rush – not to speak too quickly, or seem too eager – he faced the public pews. The air was taut with attention. He drew in a breath. Adjusted the eyeglass, firming its place in the socket.

'No,' he replied, offhandedly almost, 'I ask it for the knowledge of a lifetime.'

The applause – dear Lord, the applause was like a great thundering deluge of rain, immediate and wildly enthusiastic. It awoke the judge to startling effect; he began banging away with his hammer, frowning most imperiously, threatening to clear the court if those present insisted upon turning it into a common theatre. The claps subsided and the cross-examination resumed, but Sleepy Jack was on the back foot now, his sureness visibly diminished – and in the minutes that followed Jim worked the blackguard to his will.

Was Mr Whistler aware, Jack enquired, that the critics were against him? This invited a particularly honed reply concerning the absolute goddamned *redundancy* of critics – men who produce this commentary, this supposedly informed opinion, upon a science that they do not practise themselves. Would Jack respect the legal views of a man who was not a lawyer? Who had never studied law? Of course he wouldn't. The principle was the same.

'I hold that none but an artist can be a competent critic,' Jim told them all. 'None but an artist.'

Holker had no counter to this. He opted instead for a side-step, wheeling out the one great weapon the enemy believed he had left: the direct examination of Jim's paintings. Parry was up at once, dear fellow, trying to prevent it – and to resurrect the notion of the jury processing across the road to the Westminster Palace Hotel and the exhibition therein – but to no avail. At first, it went as expected. The canvases – or the *Nocturnes*, at any rate – were carried in by stewards evidently more used to exhibits of a sturdier nature: *manhandled* was the word. One was mounted on the bench upside down; another, on its passage through the room, was knocked rather hard against a gentleman's head, to the vocal amusement of those nearby. Jim had no option but to maintain his pose, looking on from the box with dry resignation and a certain detached horror. There was no escape from this. He was pinned in place, awaiting their worst efforts.

Once more, the approach was banal to a degree both reassuring and dispiriting. The *Blue and Silver* was examined first – the one that included a portion of Battersea Bridge. In the darkness of the court the painting was reduced to a mere shadow of itself. It was impossible, frankly, to form any estimation of it; there was barely enough light to identify the damned thing. The judge weighed in now, still rather too awake after the earlier commotion, peering at the canvas propped beside his chair with an innocence every bit as bad as Sleepy Jack's clumsy malice.

'And which part of the picture,' he enquired mildly, 'is the bridge?'

Through the laughter, Jim attempted to explain that the work was not intended as a *portrait* of Battersea Bridge, but rather as a moonlit scene; that its subject, properly speaking, was colour. The balance and harmony of colour.

'As to what the picture represents,' he said, 'that depends upon who looks at it. To some it may represent all that I intended. To others it may represent nothing.'

Again, the line was spoken with deliberate coolness, exactly as rehearsed; this time, though, the courtroom's response was muted by puzzlement. Jim found that this pleased him rather more than their applause.

Sleepy Jack was right there, of course, lumbering onwards, pressing what he imagined to be his advantage. Away he sniped, attempting to steer Jim through every part of the composition, pointing at it rather too closely with his thick forefinger. What is this part here – a fire escape, perhaps? A telescope? Are those supposed to be *people*, up on the bridge? The poor fellow's flippancy was marked now by a streak of genuine umbrage, as if something he felt should be fixed in place, readily comprehensible, had been allowed to drift free – a sacred equation crossed out and cast aside.

'They are,' Jim told him, 'just what you like.'

*

Maud was in a small room at the White House's rear, the intended purpose of which Jim had quite forgotten. She seemed to have selected it on the basis of size, having pulled an armchair right up to the grate and the two pebble-like coals that glowed within. Swaddled in a heavy shawl, she was working a pencil against a notebook by the light of a solitary candle – drawing something, it seemed. She set it aside upon seeing him, smiling wearily and beckoning him in for a kiss. Her mouth was dry; her grip upon the back of his head a touch harder than was necessary.

Jim wanted to know everything. He'd been praised throughout the afternoon and evening – in the courtroom, after he'd left the witness box; in Reeve's office, once the day's business was concluded; in the dining room of the solicitor's club, where the Whistler team had taken their supper – and he felt a keen need to be praised again now, upon his return to hearth and home. Maud's account was neat, emphatic, almost as if she'd been practising it. He'd been brilliant, running rings around the opposition. Their witnesses – Mr Moore, Mr Rossetti and the other fellow – had provided staunch support, the work of true friends. Ruskin's bullying brute of a barrister had been made to look properly foolish. It was so close to what Jim wanted to hear that for a second he was almost suspicious. Her expression was sincere, however. Proud.

'Sleepy Jack couldn't get a thing to stick, could he?' he reflected, propping himself against the mantelpiece. 'Not a deuced thing. Is Mr Whistler a serious painter? He is. These are serious and original artworks. Are they worth what he asks for them, even the *Black and Gold*? They are, every penny. Especially the goddamned *Black and Gold*.' Despite his tiredness, the fiery hum of it all started to come back, and he heard his voice quicken as he rolled a cigarette. 'I hesitate to say it, Maudie, lest some mischievous spirit decides to fox everything, but my feeling is that we may be set for victory. It is Reeve's feeling as well, and the barristers'. Everyone is confident that tomorrow will go our way.'

Maud was relieved, plainly; she sat back in her chair, pulling her shawl around her. 'Fingers crossed,' she said.

'How did it appear from where you were? The place, the people? Frightfully busy, wasn't it? I could see you, you know, when I was up in the box. Your shiny red face, away there at the back.'

This prompted a contraction of the brow, then a slight pout of annoyance. 'It was devilish warm in there, Jimmy. And this . . . this is like having a hot-water bottle strapped around your middle.'

Jim lit the cigarette and considered the size of her. Inwardly, he cursed the timing once more; but when, in the life of Whistler, would be an opportune moment for such a mishap? Another babe to be fostered. Another set of associated expenses. Another few months with Maud miserable and moping, of limited use as a model. She would surely miss the second as she missed the first. Did *he* ever think of this child already born, the girl? Every once in a while, perhaps, as he thought of his son, little Charlie: his absent flesh, out there in the world, following whatever path it would. But he couldn't feel guilt, or responsibility, or anything like that. Whistler was an artist, not a father. He was not given to paternal things.

'No one saw you, did they?' he asked. 'Dinner guests and so forth, I mean — gentlemen you've met?'

'I did as we agreed. Arrived just as it was starting. Left as soon as it was over. Rosa and Eldon were with me.'

Rosa Corder. 'I don't suppose that there was any sign of the Owl?'

Two days before the start of the trial, in the absence of other candidates, it had been decided that Charles Augustus Howell — an art dealer, after all, of some prominence, with no formal connection to Jim — could be useful on the stand. He had, of course, eluded every attempt to locate him. Jim's hope had been that he might present himself at court, ready to testify. The trial was an all-hands-on-deck occasion — perhaps the ultimate example of such a thing. Surely Owl would see this. That court, those few hundred beings, was supposed to represent the better part of Jim's entire acquaintance: everyone he knew, or at least everyone who was on his side. Over the course of the proceedings, he'd compiled a mental list of who was there and who wasn't; and the Owl, his friend and cherished co-conspirator, had been foremost among the latter.

'He's busy with his own case, I think,' said Maud. 'The railway company.'

Jim was well aware of this, but it was difficult indeed for him to accept that there could be a greater priority than the battle against Ruskin — which was, properly speaking, a battle against incompetent criticism at large. Against the forces of ignorance and injustice. Their mutual foes. He smoked, and sighed; then frowned at the red-brick tiles around the fireplace, noticing that Mr goddamned Nightingale hadn't set them quite straight on the left edge.

Maud stood with a groan and a short, squeaking fart. She lifted up her candle, causing their shadows to leap and dip as she moved it to the mantelpiece. Jim felt her hand on his shoulder – the heat of her palm, and the shiver in it. He smelled sweat, and gas, and strong tea.

'You beat them back today, Jimmy. Without his help. You saw them off.'

'Owl's the fellow, though,' he murmured. 'Should the fires lick once more, you know, at the curtains of the show. Should anything go amiss.'

'It won't. You'll go in there tomorrow and you'll beat them again.'

'Tomorrow is their turn. The witnesses for the enemy.'

'Your men are ready, though, aren't they? They know what to say?'

Jim looked at her. She was doing her best, her jaw set and her eye firm, but he could see this for what it was. She was supplying his need, as she always did. Doubt took hold, like a cramp; it began to tighten. She drew him in for an embrace, all but wrapping him up in her shawl, nuzzling cat-like against his shoulder; and there it was, jutting into his midriff. It always surprised him how far the bulge came to protrude. How very hard it was. Did he recoil, without thinking, by the slightest amount? She stepped back the next moment, at any rate, and shot him an unreadable glance as she took the cigarette from his hand. After a single puff, she flicked the end among the coals, then turned towards the doorway and the dark passage beyond.

'Let's go to bed,' she said. 'I'm done in.'

26 November 1878

The corridor was broad and long, vaulted in a grand, churchy sort of way, and filled with a well-heeled crowd, waiting to be summoned back into the courtroom. The lanterns overhead had been lit while they'd been out; there was an odour of cigar smoke and perfume, laced faintly with sweat. Maud recognised a number of the people there from the dinner table at the White House, from the theatre and elsewhere; she stuck to the arrangement, though, hanging back in an alcove, hidden from general view. Rosa stood beside her, dressed in a tricorn hat bound around with crimson gauze and a black, close-cut coat, its sleeves embroidered with butterflies – in solidarity, she'd said. She turned, enclosing Maud's hands in hers. Her gloves were a smart and spotless black; Maud's a kind of mottled cocoa, worn to a shine along the knuckles.

'We will win,' she said. 'Never fear. They'll find in Jimmy's favour. How could they do otherwise? He'll have his damages, the whole thousand. And a stand will have been taken, Maud, on behalf of art. A blow will have been struck.'

Maud nodded; she'd heard this a hundred times over the course of the trial. She'd still to catch her breath properly, and her knees were aching worse than ever. The walk back from the coffee house had all but finished her off. She worked her hands free. 'Owl's not coming then,' she said.

Rosa couldn't deny it. She supplied the standard regretful explanation concerning his case, the preparations it required, and the fortune that was at stake. Maud had expected this but was disappointed nonetheless, not least because of the upset it would surely cause Jimmy. Rosa went back to her talk of the coming victory, and how it would deliver a sound rebuke to these critics, these hollow men who thought they could sling any ignorant muck they chose, from Mr high-and-mighty Ruskin to the grubs on the penny papers. Then, rather abruptly, she stopped.

'Dear Lord,' she said.

Maud followed her stare. The lady was standing beneath a pointed arch, perhaps twenty feet away. She could only be glimpsed between the hats and heads, and the clouds of tobacco smoke, but it was Mrs Leyland. There could be no doubt of that. She was flanked by her elder daughters, the three of them refined and faultlessly fashionable, grouped together as if in conference. They were attended by an older, rather grave-looking gentleman Maud took to be Fanny Leyland's fiancé.

'This is your chance.' Rosa's voice was cold and controlled; her eyes were alive with excitement. 'Maud, this is your chance to speak with Frances Leyland. To tell her what you think of her, and that wretched husband of hers as well.'

Maud's arm drew instinctively around the curve of her stomach. 'I really don't think—'

Rosa had her by the elbow and was attempting to steer her in the direction of the unsuspecting Leylands. 'You can tell her that you know. You know why she tracked you down that day. And you can tell her that she *failed*.'

'No.' Maud anchored herself to the patterned tiles, leaning like a reluctant mule. '*Rosa.*'

After a short tug-of-war she broke away, retreating to a side passage. It was darker in there and nearly empty, her footsteps echoing against the stone.

Rosa was close behind. 'I don't understand. It's the *ideal moment*. Just before Jimmy's final triumph. Why, it's positively poetic.'

Eldon appeared at the top of the passage. He glanced from one woman to the other, visibly debating whether or not to get involved.

'Look at me,' Maud panted. 'Heavens, Rosa, even if I wanted to, even if it would be of the least help or use, I could hardly – I couldn't just—'

She gave up. The child was stirring, as if hearing itself referred to. She slipped her hand between the buttons of her coat. A bony part pressed against her palm, and there was a sense, very briefly, of the curled body and the head, of the angle at which it lay. Out in the main corridor a bell rang, signalling the imminent return of the jury. The murmuring of the crowd redoubled; it started to shift, funnelling into the courtroom.

'We should get back,' said Eldon. 'This minute, really.'

As they left the passageway, Maud peered over at the Leyland ladies; they were moving, heading for the courtroom doors along with everybody else. The three women were occupied wholly by their own conversation – which was of a different character than Maud had first assumed. The two daughters actually appeared to be giving their mother a proper earful, their pretty faces pinched with ire. Mrs Leyland remained impassive, plainly too tired, too beaten about already, to mount any kind of defence.

Winter was testing its grip upon London that afternoon, and the Court of Exchequer already had a theatre-like murk; a charge of anticipation was also gathering, as if the curtain was about to go up. Candles had been brought in, but the tiny flames seemed to deepen the darkness rather than reduce it. The chamber was kept a little too hot, as it had been throughout the trial. They went left, to their place on the rearmost pew – selected both for its discreet location and its proximity to the exit, should a rapid departure be necessary. Maud edged in after Rosa, surveying the courtroom as she did so. She saw the Leyland women halfway down, settling themselves with stately grace; the

Grosvenor pictures, the portraits and *Nocturnes* which had endured such indignities during the trial, were propped behind the bench, rubbed down to blank rectangles by the gloom; and Jimmy, the plaintiff, was camped out with his allies in the pew beside the witness stand. He appeared attentive but supremely at ease, idly polishing his eyeglass on a lapel. The black suit was immaculate; the white fore-lock was arranged precisely atop his oiled black curls, like the feather in a soldier's cap. It was a well-practised pose: the worldly genius, surprised by nothing, who met fraught moments like this with no more than a dry smile and a quick remark, before sauntering off into the evening. One of the lawyers made an observation, gesturing towards the pews opposite, where the enemy was seated. Jimmy looked pained, momentarily, some years older and even a touch anxious; then the eyeglass was twisted back in and a rejoinder fired out, and the men around him shook with mirth.

Maud landed upon the pew rather more abruptly than she'd intended. Her lower back protested, prompting a gasped curse; there was pressure on her bladder also, so sudden and intense it felt like someone was sitting on it. Which of course they were. The child twitched, very slightly – was it hiccupping? She kept still, beginning to smile; and there was another tiny start, and another a few seconds later, to a slow rhythm. It really was the queerest sensation.

Rosa was giving her a curious look, as if fearing she'd

lost her wits. 'You mustn't worry,' she whispered. 'They will find in his favour. All will be well.'

Maud didn't respond. Her smile dropped away; she shifted about, biting hard on her lip, nausea fluttering close to her hiccupping child. Down by the table, the jury had emerged and was entering its box. She thought of a dozen different things she needed to ask, to ask urgently, but before she could speak everybody rose in a great rumble of boots. She could hear official voices over at the bench, heralding the beak. Just as she'd mustered the energy to stand, the courtroom was seated again. One of the jurors had remained on his feet, a nervous-looking fellow in a plain brown suit – the foreman, she supposed.

'Are you all agreed?' asked the beak from his chair; he sounded impatient, keen to be finished.

The court was perfectly silent, the universe hanging in suspension. The light seemed to dim yet further; the figure of the foreman grew dark and distant. Maud slipped dizzily to the edge of the pew. She reached for Rosa's hand, getting a good firm hold, and she squeezed it with everything she had.

The foreman cleared his throat. 'We find a verdict for the plaintiff,' he announced. 'With one farthing damages.'

A lively murmur spread through the court. There were a couple of shouts of – amusement, was it? Satisfaction? The bewigged swells down at the front both began talking at once, Ruskin's fellow asserting something, while Jimmy's attempted to interject.

'There,' said Rosa. 'I told you. What did I tell you?'

Maud's voice, when she managed to speak, sounded to her like that of someone else altogether. 'One farthing,' she said. 'One farthing damages.'

'A blow – yes, a blow has been struck.'

The drawl of the beak could be heard, silencing the bickering lawyers before him. 'Considering the view the jury has taken of the matter,' he declared, 'I enter judgement for one farthing for the plaintiff, without costs.'

The gavel sounded, a full stop on the trial. Immediately people began to stand, blocking their view with a dense barrier of millinery. Maud thought of the windows in the White House, the frames already starting to warp on the river-facing side. The studio stacked with unsold works, their numbers reduced only by Owl's endeavours at the pawn shop. The diminished larder, the emptying cellar and the writs heaping up on the Chinese-style bureau in the hall. This surely spelled the end.

'A blow for artists everywhere,' Rosa said. 'A blow for us all.'

Maud turned to her, so elegant and unburdened – so very pleased with this moment and ignorant of what it would actually entail – and was nearly overwhelmed by anger. 'A blow's been struck all right, Rosa,' she spat. 'A – a blow to the bloody *temple* of Jimmy and me – of our——' The metaphor ran away from her. 'Jimmy was due a thousand pounds from that old ghoul, that Mr Ruskin, who can't even be bothered to come in here and – and——' Sweat was everywhere, it seemed, welling from every inch of skin. Her breath was quite gone. She wanted to scream. 'A *thousand pounds*. And we've got a blasted *farthing*. And no costs. That's another bill right there, and a fat one to boot.'

Rosa's expression was sympathetic, yet wholly uncomprehending. She began to stroke Maud's hand. It was promptly snatched away.

'We're *done for*, Rosa, don't you see? We're wrecked, Jimmy and me. We're at the bottom of the bloody ocean.'

Maud had more to say, a good deal more, but the straining of her bladder was now unbearable – the feeling somehow both hot and cold, and prickling torturously. She batted Rosa back and struggled to her feet. Jimmy could be seen across the room, still seated on his pew. He appeared puzzled, and was asking a question of those around him. Dear God, thought Maud as she pushed past Eldon into the aisle, he doesn't know if he's won or not. He honestly *can't tell*. 'I suppose a verdict is a verdict,' she heard him declare as she heaved herself through the doors, and his friends laughed; it sounded forced this time, however, as if coming more from loyalty than actual amusement.

There was a scattering of people along the passage – the first out, young gentlemen mostly. Maud's haste, her condition and her wild look attracted immediate interest. She glared around her and considered bellowing something indecorous. But there was no time even for this. The stark fact of it was that if she didn't continue on her way that instant she would surely release her water right there, in the principal corridor of the Royal Courts of Justice. She went left, continuing at speed along the well-trodden route to the conveniences.

Crashing into the first stall in the row, she fumbled frantically with skirts and undergarments and slung her ungainly frame onto the seat, her thighs sticking clammily to the varnished wood. The stream commenced, hesitantly to begin with but soon picking up. She exhaled hard, closing her eyes; her forehead came to rest against the partition. It was still going strong when Rosa's boots – ripe ox-blood, and so pointed they didn't look like they could hold a human foot – appeared in the gap at the bottom of the stall door. Maud leaned forward to snap the latch across. For a few seconds the only sound was the sharp hiss of urine, then the flow dwindled to drips and Rosa spoke.

'I'm sorry, truly I am. I do understand how this outcome might alarm you. Especially at present, with all you have to endure. But you must remember that Jimmy has friends. Important friends. And he has *genius*. The principle of this ruling, of the jury finding in his favour, will ensure—'

'Money. That's what you said.' Maud stared at her black-stockinged knees; at the acanthus pattern on the floor tiles below. 'Money throws the world open. And now there's to be no money at all.' She thought of Portugal. Of a garden crowded with blooms, stirring in a warm, clean breeze. Of Ione, at five years old or thereabouts, her long auburn hair unfurling against the blueness of the ocean. 'Dear God, I am such a fool.'

'Please do not despair. It will attract custom. It will serve as an advertisement, do you hear? A great invitation for patronage. Jimmy will be earning like never before.'

Maud wasn't listening. She sat upright, fingers splayed across her stomach, and looked around for paper.

*

They emerged to find the main corridor almost full. Maud made to cut through the middle to the nearest set of doors, not really caring any longer who she might bump into or be seen by. Barely a step had been taken, however, when the plaintiff himself streaked past, perhaps three yards in front. The calm perplexity with which he'd greeted the verdict was quite gone; his brow was thunderous in fact, and his pace determined. He was homing in on a target.

Maud ducked back, watching as he made for another side passage further along and the small, slight man who stood there. She recognised this person from the courtroom that morning, when he'd climbed up into the box and given evidence as Ruskin's chief witness: Edward Burne-Jones, star of the Grosvenor, creator of all those identical angels and doe-eyed maidens. There was something of a mismatch between this otherworldly, tranquil art and the man who had made it. Mr Burne-Jones was a creature fashioned by worry. His thin, lank hair was plastered to his head; his grey beard was worn long, four inches past his collar, like that of an anxious little wizard. The evidence he'd given had been less than convincing. Rosa had snorted disdainfully throughout, remarking that the fellow hadn't even had the courage of his philistinism. Despite the bold things he was reported to have said beforehand, at various tables about town – talk of defending the great Ruskin and seeing off the ridiculous Whistler, who scarcely *anyone* took seriously – he'd been toothless and weak, stammering out a series of blatant contradictions, almost as if he'd been trying to serve both sides of the conflict at once.

'Mr – Mr Whistler's paintings are beautiful – they are bew-w-wildering – they are masterly in c-c-colour – they are formless, incomplete – there is g-g-great labour and skill here – they lack f-finish . . .'

What in heaven was anyone supposed to make of that?

Stepping forward, Maud saw that another of Ruskin's fellows stood alongside Burne-Jones. Tom Taylor the newspaperman was a more solid figure than the painter, with cheeks of fiery plum atop a thick raw-cotton beard. Now *his* evidence had just been lazy. He'd merely read aloud from notices he'd written for *The Times*, so-called criticism that once again cited incompleteness and sketchiness as justifications for what Ruskin had written, and which had likened Jimmy's paintings to the gradated tints on a length of wallpaper. Maud had fumed to hear it; and now, as Jimmy closed in, she found herself hoping that he would dish out a sound dressing-down to these two rather wretched characters. Yet at the point of contact, when the assault should rightly have begun, Jimmy pulled up. He swerved from his enemies, feigning a kind of detachment, making a correction to the eyeglass.

Rosa had moved past her. 'Frederick Leyland is with them,' she said.

Sure enough, a tall, black-clad figure was positioned a short distance back from the others. Maud had assumed that Jimmy's great enemy was keeping away, either through animosity or as a show of unconcern; that his wife had decided to attend at least partly in defiance of him. But the moment of the verdict, the delivery of Jimmy's certain doom, had plainly been too much for the shipbroker to resist.

'Didn't I say?' Rosa turned to her, filled with grim satisfaction. 'Didn't I say that there was an alliance here – that Ned Jones was the link?'

Jimmy was trying hard to appear casual, darkly amused, but even from across the corridor Maud could see that his anger would soon be beyond restraint. Around them, people were realising that something was up – that there was to be an encore, of sorts, to the day's entertainment. She started towards him, pushing through the crowd. What could she do to stop this, to convince him to break off? Hang on his sleeve, whisper an appeal into his ear? She came within a few yards of them. Leyland was telling Jimmy mockingly that the trial must have been a dreadful distraction, taking him from works that were surely of the most important and experimental kind.

'As a matter of fact,' Jimmy replied, 'there is much on

the stocks at present, over at the White House. You would have little sense of its aims, of course. Or its worth.'

Leyland had become quite terrifying in his inexpressiveness. 'The White House,' he said. 'Yes, I heard something of the fuss over there. The Board of Works and I have had our dealings in the past. Too plain, they thought it. Too simple. Hardly a difficulty you encountered in my dining room.'

'Different undertakings,' Jimmy shot back. 'Utterly different. *Bon Dieu*, they are quite past comparison.' He hesitated. 'What do you mean by *dealings*?'

This was ignored. 'Still, it must have been disruptive. Your life always seems to be filled with upheaval. With accidents and misadventures. We should not be surprised, quite frankly, that you barely ever manage to put brush to canvas.'

Here Leyland turned from his opponent and cast a look directly at Maud. She'd been slowing down, her nerve faltering. Now she stopped completely, held in place; and Eldon was there, rushing ahead, laying a hand against Jimmy's back. Godwin arrived as well – returned from exile, it seemed, to attend the hearing – and was telling Jimmy that there was a cab waiting, and a party of guests already making their way towards his home. They led him off, warden-like almost, to the nearest set of doors. Her power to move restored, Maud returned to where she'd left Rosa, but could find no sign of the tricorn hat or butterfly coat anywhere in the corridor. This was puzzling; she did not pause to ponder it, however, heading instead through another doorway, keeping as far from Leyland as possible.

The square outside was sunk in a cold, deadening fog. Jimmy was at the kerb, talking with his rescuers – with whom he was furious, predictably enough, for intervening. Hands trembling, he was trying without success to light a cigarette. He glanced at Maud as she approached, but barely seemed to see her.

'I was ready, you know,' he said, dashing the cigarette and match to the pavement. 'Ready to throw it all at him, right there in front of everyone. The bastards, of which he's sired enough to fill a blasted poor-school. The kept women in their apartments, across the goddamned city. The tales from the brothels of his – his *proclivities*.'

'And yet you did not,' said Godwin approvingly. 'You held back. That was wise, James, truly. It was the behaviour of a gentleman. That sort of thing helps no one.'

Jimmy glared at him; and then at the façade of the Royal Courts of Justice, rising up dimly beside them. 'I *held back*, Godwin,' he retorted, 'because there'll surely be a better way of doing it.'

*

The knocks roused Maud at once, giving a fearful part of her a hard prod. She was leaving the bedroom, wrapping herself in a shawl, before she knew properly what was going on. The light was weak, grey, untouched by warmth; it couldn't have been much more than eight o'clock. There was another series of knocks, the same as the first: four of them, evenly placed, imbued with the granite determination of authority. She met Jimmy on the stairs, descending from the studio, nearly running into him in fact; he was wide-eyed and wild-haired, in his outdoor coat to ward off the cold, his fingertips black with ink. When she'd left him shortly before midnight he'd been plotting a tract, and had plainly been working through the night in order to get something down.

A celebration had been the plan, back at the White House: glasses raised, speeches made, plates of Mrs Cossins' *rillettes* passed around. Many of the crucial people, however, had either failed to come at all – in the case of the barristers and witnesses – or had departed before they were more than three bottles in. After a couple of hours it had been just Jimmy, Maud, Eldon and Anderson Reeve. They'd done their best with it, but it was impossible to avoid a sense of impending disaster – of a bone china teacup dropped towards a tiled floor, still intact and perfect as it fell through the air, yet with its destruction rushing up fast.

Reeve had treated them to a thorough post-mortem, unsparing in its use of lawyerly jargon, with much on the bungling of the judge – who, although obviously sympathetic to their side, had utterly confused the jury with his muddle-headed summation, and had read out the Ruskin review several times more than was necessary.

'Drunk, I shouldn't wonder,' the solicitor had concluded. 'Half the blighters always are.'

Jimmy, meanwhile, had fallen into the clutches of a weird mania. Expecting the Owl and Rosa, and both baffled and hurt by their non-appearance, he'd assumed an Owlish zeal of his own. His talk was of the way back – of how to replace the thousand-pound brick that had crumbled from their wall. An exhibition, a one-man show, with a charge on the door, featuring his most famous works. A touring lecture, replete with his best lines. *I ask it for the knowledge of a lifetime. Art should be independent of all claptrap.* Taken perhaps to the halls and theatres of America, where he would play the returning hero. The *conquering* hero. The first true genius of American art. Why the devil not? First of all, though, there would be a special publication. To keep the boilers stoked, as it were. It would be the last word on the goddamned trial; and a canny piece of pre-emption, as one could be sure that Ruskin would belch out some more of his drivel within the month. Or sooner, even – for much as he might find fault with the speed of Whistler's production, in truth his own was equally goddamned rapid!

The knocks sounded again, patient and inescapable. They entered the hall; as Jimmy reached for the latch, Maud had a split-second premonition of trouble.

'Jim—'

Too late. The door opened to reveal a pair of callers, clad in smart but rather cheap-looking coats. One wore a topper, the other something shorter and rounder. Both were lean and tall, with worn-in faces, and what Maud could only think of as a *readiness* about them. She felt an urge to grip hold of Jimmy's arm; to pull him back through the narrow corridors, out of the rear door and over the yard, off into Chelsea.

'What ho, Mr Levy,' said Jimmy cordially. 'You are out very deuced early this morning, I must say. Collecting, are you, for the Church Benevolent Society?'

So they were known; one of them, at least. Maud relaxed a fraction. She tried to smile.

'Good day to you, Mr Whistler,' the topper replied, with the disinterested air of one going about his duty. Then he cleared his throat for a recitation. 'We are here on behalf of Mr Benjamin Ebenezer Nightingale, master builder of Black Horse Lane, who holds against you a debt of six hundred and fifty-five pounds, thirteen shillings and—'

'I was just about to contact you,' Jimmy interrupted. He ran a hand through his hair, fiddling with the white lock, his easy manner slipping. 'Or rather have my lawyer contact Mr Nightingale's. I was quite literally on the verge of it, you know. There's a scheme afoot, gentlemen. A friend who will assist us.'

Maud's alarm had risen again – a blacker, more sickly feeling this time. These men were bailiffs. Of course they were. Six hundred and fifty-five pounds. It was an astoundingly – a *revoltingly* hefty sum. She forced herself to think it through. She had a pretty decent handle on Jimmy's affairs. Benjamin Nightingale. The alterations to the façade; to the elevation. This had been under control. Jimmy had sorted this out. He'd assured her that he'd sorted it out.

The topper – Mr Levy – was unimpressed. His features remained absolutely neutral, but his eyes were a dead well of weariness and cynicism. He heard this many times daily: the miraculous solution, the last-minute reprieve that would allow him simply to tip his hat and return empty-handed to his office. He knew its worth.

'A writ was served you, Mr Whistler,' he said, 'at the Arts Club on Hanover Square, on the thirtieth of September of this year. Nothing of any consequence has happened since. More letters is all. The stalling actions of solicitors. And so the County Court of Middlesex has empowered me to collect money or goods in payment of debts.'

Jimmy's laugh stretched rather too high at the end. 'Excuse me, my dear Levy – goods to the total of *six hundred and fifty quid?*' He made a show of peering past them, out onto Tite Street. 'Did you bring a furniture van, perchance? A pair of drays?'

Mr Levy's answer had the slightest trace of satisfaction to it – that of a functionary given the chance to exercise his power. 'I am authorised,' he said, 'in the absence of any substantial amount of money or goods, to serve a further writ. A Writ of Execution.' The bailiff studied them both for a second, expecting incomprehension. Maud knew very well what this meant, however, and began to speak – only for Levy to talk over her, his voice hardening as he delivered his explanation. 'This permits the Sheriff's office to take possession of your property. Mr Sumner here would live beneath your roof.'

The other man stood to one side, gazing out towards the river. He touched the brim of his small, round hat without looking their way. Maud noticed that a burlap sack, a quarter full with clothes it looked like, was slung over his shoulder.

'His task would be to compile an inventory. To watch what comes here, Mr Whistler, and what goes. To ensure that everything remains in a stable condition, regarding assets and the like, while yourself and your legal gentlemen make your terms with Mr Nightingale. You will be charged a shilling a day for his expenses.'

Abandoning humour, Jimmy began to tell Mr Levy the tale of Charles Augustus Howell versus the Metropolitan District Railway, and those fabled mountains of tin. This, Maud realised, was the scheme he'd just mentioned: Owl guaranteeing his massive debt to Nightingale, paying off parts of it perhaps, from the thousands he was sure to be awarded. Yet the Portuguese hadn't shown up at the trial. Nor had he come to see them afterwards. It seemed a flimsy thing indeed upon which to pin their survival.

For a second, the sense of emergency locked her in place; then she was puffing her way up to their bedroom, heat bristling across her breastbone, to scrabble breathlessly through the cardboard boxes lined on the floor, the chest of drawers, and along the cluttered mantelpiece. This yielded four pounds and seven shillings: everything they had, that was, every last bit of money she'd managed to squirrel away, including one of the pounds from the pawning of Mrs Leyland's locket, which she'd kept back carefully from Jimmy and hidden beneath her shifts. She peered into the carton, once a container for fancy pastries, where she was presently storing her jewellery. Nothing in there was of any real value, sentimental or otherwise – paste, half of it. After poking around with a forefinger, she plucked out a silverish necklace, a couple of copper bracelets and a single earring that might possibly be pearl.

Mr Levy looked at it all like she'd given him a handful of sea-shells. 'Ain't there nothing else?'

'There are paintings,' Jimmy told him. 'I can let you have a full-length oil sketch of the actor Henry Irving, shown at the Grosvenor Gallery in—'

The bailiff was shaking his head. 'I need objects of *demonstrable worth*, Mr Whistler.' He slipped Maud's offering into a pocket and stepped across the pavement, tilting his head to consider the White House itself. 'Queer sort of place, this,' he said. 'But it's large, I suppose. The bills will go up. You'd have Mr Sumner within, sir, and advertisements for sale without. I apologise, sincerely I do, but that's how it would be.'

'Come, Mr Levy,' Jimmy protested, 'surely it won't reach—'

'I know you, Mr Whistler,' Levy continued, 'and I know where you are. So I will accept this advance on your payment, small though it is. But I have to say, if your Mr Howell really is ready to assist you in this matter, he must do it soon.'

With that the bailiffs left. Maud and Jimmy stood in the

hall, waiting until they could be sure Levy and Sumner were out of earshot; then Jimmy moved in for an embrace, his expression one of unadulterated relief. Maud dodged it. She glowered at him. She struck his shoulder as sharply as she could.

'What the devil was that?' she demanded. 'Did you know? Did you know they were coming?'

Jimmy was wincing, rubbing where he'd been hit, but he seemed to accept her assault as deserved – to enjoy it a little, even. Which was absolutely *infuriating*.

'I – Reeve – the trial, Maudie – it was, you must admit, a distraction of a really quite monumental nature . . .'

He retreated to the drawing room, fending off another blow, taking refuge behind an armchair. Maud was caught up in the old rage; the child kicked, a foot nudging the inside of her forearm as if spurring her on. She ran her eyes murderously over the shelves of blue-and-white.

'Stop,' said Jimmy – rather more nervously, as he guessed her intentions. 'Please stop. I understand, really I do. But he will be back.'

This did actually succeed in giving Maud pause. She turned, addressing him with naked, despairing contempt. 'He'll be *back*, Jimmy, before you bloody know it. And he will take our home. Do you understand that? He'll have it sold off. We'll have nowhere. Nothing.'

'Owl,' Jimmy replied. 'Not Levy, Maud. *Owl*. He'll be here within the week. I'm sure of it.' He moved out from behind the chair and took a half-cautious step towards her, with arms slightly extended and hands open – a soothing gesture, as if to calm a restless horse. 'We'll shake this, I promise.'

*

December 1878

Rather to Maud's surprise, over the following weeks it emerged that Mr Whistler's libel suit had been brought purely as a matter of principle. The plaintiff made it known around town that he had not given a single thought either to compensation or costs, being uninterested in money. His only concern had been to protect his status as an artist, and the sanctity of his art. To fight the battle, as he came to put it, between the brush and the pen.

There was a rush of notices in the press – sketches and editorials, a handful of rather unflattering cartoons. And Jimmy pored over it all. Journals were scattered across every room of the White House. Several were French or German; one or two had even been sent over from America. Maud herself had felt compelled to leaf through some of them.

'A *pyrrhic victory*, this fellow says it was. What's that mean, Jimmy?'

'Hard won, my girl. He means it was hard won.'

It was essential, Jimmy explained, for him to know everything that was being said, so that his riposte, the tract he was so busy preparing, would be completely watertight.

So that it would be *invincible*. He could be heard up in the studio, declaiming and remonstrating, strutting about like an actor in the throes of some great heroic role. His brushes, meanwhile, remained quite dry, and his etching needles shut up in their cases.

Evidence did actually appear of wider support, enough that Jimmy briefly considered going back to court – only to be warned against this by Anderson Reeve with emphatic firmness. Still, letters came in their dozens, applauding his performance in the witness box, attacking the judge, barristers and jury for their woeful ignorance, and lamenting the unfairness of the verdict and the rebuke it seemed to contain. Importantly, a few also included cash – in one case a cheque for twenty-five guineas, which Jimmy bore about the house for a triumphant couple of minutes, before hiding it away lest Mr Levy should happen to poke his head around the door.

For this was another result of the trial's notoriety – the opposite side, Maud supposed, of the same tiny little coin. Creditors hummed in like wasps on jam, acting on every variety of Whistler debt: those accrued more recently, since the move from Lindsey Row; the long-standing ones of daunting size; and a miscellany of others, both ancient and forgotten, involving cheeses long since digested, boots already worn out, and the small black piano that now sat up in a corner of the studio which Jimmy was in the habit of forgetting he even owned. They managed to laugh at it, with the first three or four at least, but it was hard to sustain your levity in the face of writs from the County Court. The meaning of it all was becoming increasingly clear. These people knew a listing vessel when they saw one, and wanted to carry off what they could before she was claimed by the waves.

Things grew quite horribly tense. Every knock at the door, every shadow passing across one of the front windows, brought Maud to her feet – by this stage a not inconsiderable endeavour. The house around her seemed to acquire a new flimsiness, as if the walls were made from paper, like those in Jimmy's prints from Japan. It was ever easier to imagine it all simply being broken up and borne away.

Contrary to Jimmy's prediction, the Owl, their purported saviour, failed to reappear. Nobody had seen him from what Maud could gather. He was absent from all his known haunts, missing without trace or clue, as if he'd walked from whatever club or saleroom he'd happened to be in and jumped into the river. Maud received a short letter from Rosa, saying she was obliged to leave town for a while to nurse an invalid brother who lived out at Bray, who Maud couldn't recall her ever mentioning before. Rosa urged courage and fortitude, repeated her rather hollow claim of victory, and gave no explanation for her abrupt, wordless departure from the court corridor.

Jimmy's bewilderment at all this was every bit as great as Maud's – especially when it was reported that Owl had won his case against the railway company. The Portuguese should now be rich, his coffers bursting, and in a position to free them comprehensively from their quandary. Yet he did not appear. With his friends, Jimmy kept up an act of dry composure, but in truth he was growing desperately frustrated. And despite all those who'd crossed or disappointed him, the great range of people against whom he might rail when in public, his private ire would return unfailingly to the same point.

One evening, the noise issuing from the studio grew even louder than usual, loud enough for Maud to haul herself up there to investigate. The Leyland portraits were set against the far wall, the husband and wife side by side, brought out for the first time since the move to the White House. Wearing an overcoat and a thick woollen scarf knitted for him by his mother, Jimmy was bent in front of Mrs Leyland's portrait, cleaning the wide golden frame with a rag. Maud staggered to the old chaise longue in the corner. He didn't seem to notice her. After minute he stopped cleaning and stood back. A single oil lamp had been placed on the stained floorboards before Leyland's portrait. The shipbroker – shown in ruffed shirt and buckles, a hand placed on his hip – was made sinister and a touch cadaverous by the lamp's low, grubby light.

'The word,' Jimmy said, 'is that there has never been such a distance between them. That a fracture may well be on the cards. Indeed, I'd wager that these two canvases here stand rather closer to one another than their models ever will again.'

There was grievance in his voice. Maud glanced around

for that broad-ended knife. 'You aren't going to scrape them, are you?'

'Oh no, my girl,' he replied, malice creeping into him now. 'Not at all. No, I'm going to send them over to Prince's Gate. As soon as I can find coin for the haulage. It is only right and proper that the fellow receives what he has paid for, wouldn't you agree? The happy couple. Their *blissful union*. Immortalised in art.'

So that was it. He was going to use the portraits to needle Leyland, to taunt him with this spectre of his dead marriage. More inventive, Maud supposed, than destruction – although equally unlikely to bring them anything but further trouble. 'Jimmy—'

'The portraits are his. The money – as he himself likes to point out, with his customary charm – was paid years ago. It is the only honourable course.'

Maud peered off into the long, chilly room. Just visible was the large Japanese-style painting, away in a corner, its delicate greys and pinks lost in shadow – her younger, naked self hidden behind another half-finished portrait.

'What of *The Three Girls*, then? Isn't that his as well?'

Jimmy went back to his cleaning. 'That one the rogue can do without.'

'But won't he—'

'He will have his portraits. And good heavens, let us not forget that he has the blasted *Peacock Room*, at a bargain price. He can damn well do without it. These paintings in here are our assets, Maud. They are our salvation. I shall talk them up all over town. I shall get the dealers primed and ready. The guineas, very soon, will be gushing in. You'll see.'

Maud didn't comment, thinking of Mr Levy's talk of *demonstrable worth*; in the days afterwards, though, Jimmy did seem to set about this object with absolute commitment, spending more and more time out in the city – although where, and with whom, and paid for with what, she was unable to discover. And then, in the middle of December, the tract appeared, bearing the simple title *Art & Art Critics*. A humble-looking thing it was, with a plain brown-paper cover – a pamphlet of fifteen pages or so, printed by the Ways at a generously reduced rate. The contents, however, were anything but humble.

Maud made an earnest attempt to read it, honestly she did, yet could only wade her way through the first third before setting it aside in dazed apprehension. *Art & Art Critics* was pungent, positively vicious, heedless both of reason and clear English – being made up of rambling, never-ending sentences that often lost their way altogether. Much of it was to do with Jimmy's favoured notion of painters being the only proper judges of painting, but this was taken off in some decidedly irregular directions. The reviews, collected in the usual fashion, were united in their scorn. Vulgar, they said, unintelligible, utterly inconclusive and likely, in the end, to produce more support for Ruskin. Jimmy had no difficulty dismissing them. Indeed, he delighted in their censure. What would they know, after all? Why, they were the very blasted critics he was denouncing! Would the condemned man rejoice in the executioner's footstep?

Maud kept quiet. Jimmy could be relied upon to assume that her silence held agreement and support. Not for the first time, though, she found herself feeling a sliver of sympathy for his detractors.

*

Despite everything, the entertainments continued. Now they took the form of breakfasts exclusively, with the fare necessarily modest: Jimmy's buckwheat cakes served with molasses and coffee, and a selection of Mrs Cossins' pickles and savoury jams. The host, however, was always at his most amiable and entertaining. The debt Maud had known in her childhood, loaded upon them by her father's determined bond with the bottle, had been a shameful thing, to be hidden away as much as possible. Jimmy's attitude was rather different. He wore his difficulties with a certain pride, as if they were merely the burden of righteousness, to be borne with a shrug and a wry line, and animated readings from *Art & Art Critics*. These his guests applauded, declaring that the pamphlet was perfectly devastating in its anger, its truthfulness and its glittering wit.

Maud's presence was not required. This suited her perfectly well; she was becoming convinced that a good many of these supposed allies were laughing at Jimmy as much as with him. She would draw, if she could find the energy, or read the art papers, or just head to their mattress, which was laid out on the floorboards as the lacquered bed from Lindsey Row had yet to appear. There she would doze uncomfortably for a while, then resurface after the guests were gone, in search of food and somewhere warm to sit.

It was after one of these breakfasts, quite by accident, that Maud discovered Jimmy's plan. An unexpectedly lengthy nap had carried her some way past nightfall. Her descent into the dark hall was particularly awkward; she was reduced to bumping down the ladder-like stairs on her behind. Her head was throbbing, her toes and fingertips frozen. Voices were issuing from the dining room. Surely they can't still be going, she thought, peering in through the half-open door. She kept a careful distance, for there were certain individuals in Jimmy's circle who were unable – for all their artistic sensibilities – to hide their discomfort with her condition and having their host's way of life brought before them so inescapably. These were not breakfast people, though. They were clad in shades of brown, not glossy jet and silver grey. They exuded no sense of wealth or confidence. They were ordinary.

A woman and her child, in winter coats and scarves, were standing over by the fireplace, past a table littered with the debris of a breakfast. The woman was heavy-set, closing in on forty, with something Irish about her; she had the look of a shopkeeper, Maud thought, a grocer perhaps. Had she come in person to ask that a bill be settled? A couple of them had tried that. The child was a short, skinny boy of eight or so, wearing a russet cap – with a pair of very blue eyes and a certain cast to his brow that was immediately familiar.

'You do not need to worry,' Jimmy was saying; he was seated at the table, out of sight. 'Tell Mr Singleton that your funds are secure. I am aware of my duty, dear Jo. I am taking steps to fulfil it.'

Maud drew closer. This was his first *Madame*: Jo Hiffernan, the face in so many of his early paintings, all now fifteen years old or more. And that boy at her side was *Jimmy's son*. Little Charlie. The child was seldom mentioned and never discussed. Maud had gleaned that Jo and Charlie were not related – they were, she saw now, quite plainly not related – but that the boy had become her ward at some stage; that there was an arrangement in place, with payments made and occasional visits from the venerated father.

'I heard of your trial,' Jo replied – Irish was right. 'They says you was finished off, Jim. Laughed out of the place.'

'Come now,' said Jimmy. 'That is hardly an accurate—'

'Mr Singleton is a good man. He will feed us and keep us housed. But I cannot ask him to buy my clothes. To buy new boots for Charlie.'

Jimmy came into view, reaching among the plates and dishes upon the disordered table to retrieve a sheet of thick, creamy paper. 'This,' he said, 'is a mezzotint of my painting of Thomas Carlyle. There are hundreds of them. Hot off the press, as they say.'

Jo Hiffernan considered it without much interest. Charlie craned his neck to look, but the page was already being taken back.

'They're shifting, Jo,' Jimmy said, aiming for reassurance, 'and will soon be shifting more. I have recently conceived of a great scheme, with the help of my associate here. I shall be returning to Paris, directly after Christmas. I have a particular friend there now, you know. A dealer named Lucas – a Yankee, but that can't be helped. He tells me they are all desperate for my work. Even for reproductions, like the *Carlyle* here.'

Maud shivered a little. She knew nothing of this. They'd talked of visiting Paris, of course, many times – those old pipe dreams of which Jimmy was such a master. She thought of the journey involved. There would be a steamer, a proper ship, from Limehouse or somewhere; a Channel crossing; a train over a fair stretch of France. She held her belly. Could it really be done? Was this not the worst possible moment for such an expedition?

Jo Hiffernan was unimpressed. There was a hardness in her, Maud saw; this was someone who knew Jimmy Whistler too well, and had tired of him a good while ago. Information on this woman, her predecessor, was difficult to come by. Few of Jimmy's friends had even met her, as they'd fallen in with him after she'd left, at the start of the decade. It was as if he'd replaced his entire circle.

'Sounds like an adventure,' said Jo shortly, pulling on her gloves. 'A prime bit of fun. Will you be stopping by the

Folies-Bergère, I wonder, with Edgar and the rest of them? Like we used to?'

Jimmy was shaking his head. 'There won't be time for anything like that. Work, Jo, and work alone. I shall hawk my wares with Lucas, and then I shall avail myself of *la ville lumière*. Take some views, you know, on paper and plate. They'll be sure to find buyers. And then there'll be cash aplenty. No further cause for concern. You really mustn't heed what you see in the papers.' There was a change in his voice, a note of forced levity. 'Perhaps, after my return from France, you and I shall go on one of our jaunts, hey Charlie?'

The boy was struck mute by his father's attention. Turning the colour of ripe raspberries, he angled himself towards Jo Hiffernan's ample flank as if he wished it could swallow him entire. Jo wouldn't help, though; she took him by the shoulders and rotated him mercilessly until he was facing the room again.

'I hear,' Jimmy continued, 'that there's a fine show coming to Earls Court – an American show, a circus of a kind.' He snapped his fingers. 'What's the fellow's name . . . some kind of animal . . .'

'Buffalo Bill,' said someone else, from a far corner – a man with a light but unmistakable accent.

'Yes, that's it. Buffalo Bill. What a handle, eh? He's a war hero, I'm told. A killer of redskins. The genuine article.'

The notion appeared to scare the child more than anything. Maud was coming forward now, into the doorway, looking along the room, to confirm that this other person was indeed the Owl; and yes, there he was, feet up on the dining table with his fine boots crossed at the ankle, back among them after a month of inexplicable absence, reading *Art & Art Critics* by the light of a candle. Seeming to reach the end of a section, he tossed the pamphlet aside and addressed the boy.

'D'you not care for soldiers, young Charlie?' he asked. 'Tell me, what is it that you want to be when you grow up?'

Charlie's head was bowed, with his hands deep in his coat pockets. 'When I grow up,' he said, in a voice that was less timid than might have been expected, 'I want to be like my father.'

'My dear boy,' Owl replied, 'you surely can't do both.'

Jimmy laughed despite himself, shooting the Owl an admiring yet reproachful glance, while poor Charlie blinked in total confusion, his blush acquiring a still more fiery hue.

In a matter-of-fact tone, Jo Hiffernan said, 'Jim, there's a girl out in the passage. Eavesdropping, from the looks of it.'

What could Maud do but join them in the dining room? The other woman took her in, the size of her, with something like distaste flickering across her face. No one spoke, not a murmur. And then Jo was leaving – gathering in her ward, pushing him out to the corridor, as if removing him from an unwholesome place. Maud was obliged to retreat into the narrow passage to let them by. Through they went, the boy fixing his blue eyes on Maud as he passed; Jimmy followed close behind, repeating his reassurances; and the three of them – the father, the former mistress and the son – headed to the front door.

In the dining room, Owl had gone back to *Art & Art Critics* and was chuckling as he read – rather ambiguously, Maud thought.

'Dearest Maud,' he said, turning a page, 'do permit me to observe how extremely well you are looking. It rather suits you, you know. Is that polite to say? Rosie will be most pleased to hear that you continue to bloom in such a thoroughly splendid fashion. She's missed you terribly this past month.'

Maud gripped the back of a chair for support. 'Is she still with her brother?'

There was a hesitation, as if Owl was rifling through his memory. 'Yes, I believe she is. Dreadful business. A nervous affliction, they say, quite beyond medical understanding.'

Half a dozen sheets of paper were spread over an empty part of the tablecloth. Topmost was the mezzotint of the *Carlyle* that Jimmy had just shown to Jo Hiffernan. Even by candlelight, it was clear enough to Maud that it held only the faintest echo of the painting. It looked plain, in short, dull and rather flat. It angered her.

'Where the devil have you *been*, Owl? You were needed. We needed your help.'

'What can I say?' The Portuguese raised his hands in

surrender. 'A crew of navvies, dear girl, is presently engaged in knocking down my house. I have had a lifetime's wares to relocate, into venues wholly insufficient for the purpose. But gold is due. That is certain. The case was won, as I believe you heard. I shall be in a position to assist very soon.'

Maud began to ask when exactly this would be, but Jimmy came back in, full of apologies for Jo's surliness – and what was obviously an unintended overlap between *Madames* past and present.

'A fine woman,' he concluded, 'very fine. But she can be rather flinty.'

'Flinty,' said Owl, 'is most definitely the word.'

There was familiarity here, as if Owl had met Jo already, or known her long in the past. Maud wondered how this could be. She had a sense, also, that Jimmy had just handed over money. The pain in her head seemed to constrict; it became so piercingly intense that she nearly swore. She pulled out the chair she was holding on to and sat down heavily.

'Paris,' she said.

Jimmy and Owl exchanged a look.

'Ah yes,' replied Jimmy. 'I'd been hoping to talk with you about that.'

Something in his tone, its forced lightness, told Maud that she'd been mistaken. He was going to Paris alone. Humiliation bit into her, sharp and sudden. It had been ridiculous of her to have thought otherwise. She'd be nothing but a liability in her present state. She tried to be reasonable, to react with a cool, understanding nod. It didn't quite come off. He was going without her. It would be his first trip abroad since she'd arrived in his studio, since their union, and he was going without her.

Jimmy was at her side now, crouching down to comfort and explain. 'It is strategic,' he said, 'purely strategic. Owl is ready to plug the gap with Nightingale, but it may be a week or two still. In which time that rogue Levy might return – take advantage, you know, with the instinctual slyness of his kind. But Reeve tells me that the wretched fellow cannot take possession in my absence. The law prohibits it. So I shall vamoose the ranch. A few weeks should do the trick.'

This did actually seem sensible. Maud gazed down at her stomach, at the way her gown stretched over it, distorting the two-tone floral print. She brushed away the tears that stood in her eyes. 'What – what will I do while you're over there, then?' she asked. 'I can hardly stay here on my own.'

The reply came straight away. Rooms were to be taken in a small hotel in King's Cross – a reputable place, known to Owl, using cash made from the *Carlyle* prints – where she could be snug and safe as the year burned down to its end.

'Your sister Edith,' Jimmy said. 'Or your aunt. There will be space for one of them. In case the, ah, time should arrive.'

Proper thought had been given to this; Jimmy had troubled to learn Edie's name, for heaven's sake. It was to happen. The rooms had probably been booked already. *In case the time should arrive.* Maud could hear herself answering them, consenting to what they proposed, and being given a few further particulars of how it was to work – none of which she could later recall, as she was sinking once more into thoughts of the coming birth. The loneliness of it, in the end. The danger. It was like being tipped over backwards into a soot heap, among the staining, choking smuts. It was like drowning in black ashes.

The men had moved on. Owl was speaking of his admiration for *Art & Art Critics*, for the demolishing power of Jimmy's prose. He opened the pamphlet, located a particular passage and began to read aloud. Maud couldn't listen. She weaved out of the room, and was sobbing before she'd closed the privy door behind her, sobbing so hard and so harshly it felt more like retching. She sat huddled in there for perhaps quarter of an hour, waiting for it to run its course. Then she wiped her face on her shawl and lifted the latch. The corridor outside was icy cold and quiet; the dining room was empty. She listened to the house around her, to the floors above and below. Had something been called out – an announcement made as they'd headed for the door? She couldn't be certain. But Jimmy and Owl were gone.

*

Sharp's Hotel stood off Pentonville Road, a few streets away from King's Cross station. It seemed to Maud a very

285

Owlish sort of establishment. Although not grand, the interior was smart, with a distinct dash of fashion. The staff were smooth in their manner and rather *knowing*, being ready to accept even the blatantly counterfeit respectability offered by Matthew Eldon, who'd been saddled with the task of installing her there, Jimmy being too busy with his arrangements for Paris. Before an understanding manager, he fumbled his way through the story with which Owl had supplied him. She was the wife of his brother, a captain in the 7th Light Dragoons, departed recently for Africa. There was no family in London, and she was too far advanced to travel any distance, so a comfortable berth was required for the last fortnight or so of her confinement. A midwife had been located nearby, in Camden Town; the woman could be there in an hour, Eldon claimed, ready to take charge and transport the mother-to-be back to her house. This was all accepted at once, as if it was nothing out of the ordinary. Payment was made, up until the end of January; thanks were offered, convincingly sincere, for the service of Maud's phantom husband; and then Eldon withdrew, saying regretfully that he had an appointment elsewhere in town. Left alone in the room – a good one, it had to be said, at the front of the first floor – it was hard not to feel that she'd been deposited. Shifted unceremoniously out of the way.

As might have been guessed, Edie found the whole situation both perplexing and somewhat unsavoury. She herself was markedly averse to chance or irregularity; at the age of seventeen, she'd married a man twelve years her senior on account of his steady profession, and was a mother to two boys by the time she was twenty. Previously, she'd been content for the facts of Maud's life in Chelsea to retain a certain obscurity, but the trial had changed this. Mr Whistler was in the papers, and not just the art papers either; her sister's American was now a famous man. Edie could not help being impressed, in a way, which caused her no little irritation. She loved Maud, though, and managed to keep her lip buttoned. Although unwilling to leave her family overnight, she visited most days, sitting for hours with needlework or a novel while Maud sighed and lolled and scratched, attempting with enormous difficulty to apply her mind to anything at all.

Art, she found, was best. There was a definite satisfaction to it at first – amid the sleeplessness, the constipation, the ever-mounting discomfort of that final month when you were really just longing for release – both in the drawings themselves and Edie's surprise at her aptitude. Which wasn't to say that her sister liked them, exactly; indeed, she looked over these modest watercolours – winter flowers mostly, sent up from the hotel desk – with much the same incomprehension as she viewed the rest of Maud's existence.

January passed, and it became yet harder to concentrate. Maud's hand grew unreliable. She wanted simplicity and delicacy, and the impression of easefulness, yet when she set brush to page, none of it was there. She made herself persevere, though, as best she could; and when that knock came on the final morning she was already at her place at the room's round writing table, her paintbox open and her colours mixed, a study of a golden yellow crocus already wandering off in quite the wrong direction. The flower had seemed too weakly defined, the petals meagre and thin, lacking that velvet quality they had – and then all at once it was laboured, overdone, spoiled. Losing heart, she'd fallen to staring down into the street below, looking back to Pentonville Road: the steady march of traffic, its lanterns lit against the miserable day, the blurring fall of sleet.

The knock was confident – three quick raps. Maud started; she turned around in her chair. No one was expected. The breakfast plates had been taken away. Edie wasn't due until the afternoon. It must be someone from the desk, she thought, with a message perhaps. She dropped her brush in the water cup, climbed slowly to her feet and lumbered across the carpet to the door.

Rosa Corder was dressed in turquoise with a black cloak and a small black hat, squarish in shape, a turquoise feather looped at its side. Instead of Edie's tentative embrace – considerate, before all else, of her condition – she was given a hug so fierce that it carried them both back two or three paces into the room, and a great smacking kiss. Rosa then moved away from her abruptly, without speaking. She took off her cloak and hat by the fire, setting them on an armchair – her eyes lingering on the sheaf of Jimmy's letters tucked behind the carriage clock, each one stamped with a claret-coloured Parisian postmark. Hanging from her arm was a little black basket. The heavy sound it made when she put it on the table told Maud that it contained a bottle. Placing a hand upon her slender hip, framed perfectly by the single large window, she angled her head to study the watercolour of the crocus.

Maud found that she was grinning, grinning wide, filled with raw, unreflecting pleasure at seeing Rosa again. The next moment, however, she remembered the weeks of absence; the single, rather cursory letter; the unexplained disappearance in the court corridor. The grin died away. She steadied herself against the mantelpiece.

'How did you get up?' she asked. 'Did the desk not ask your business?'

'Charles talked to them,' Rosa replied, without looking round. 'He sends his love, of course. He had to run off to see a fellow in Clerkenwell about an armoire. Jacobean, they think it might be. We have both been so very busy of late. So much blessed work. Otherwise we would certainly have called on you sooner. It is a relief, I must say, to discover you looking so well.'

'Do you know what's been happening?'

As might have been foreseen, this set her off about the blasted pamphlet. The brush and the bloody pen. The mighty fuss it had caused, marking the beginning of a new bravery, a new integrity, among artists – and how this would do them such good, as disciples of Whistler, who heeded his example and his—

'At the White House, I mean,' Maud interrupted. 'The debt with the builder. The bloody *bailiffs*.'

Rosa hesitated. 'Dear Maud,' she said, picking up the crocus study to examine the one behind, 'you really mustn't worry yourself about all that. Charles's solicitor has been in touch with Nightingale's. Everything is under control. And Jimmy is working hard indeed, I hear,' she went on, 'over in Paris. Charles believes that his sales will soon be completely recovered.' She held up another watercolour sketch: a sprig of leftover holly, as leadenly unsuccessful as the crocus. 'These are very fine, you know. You've been putting your time here to good use. Why, Charles could sell this. I'm sure of it. Any dealer in London would be glad to put it up in his window.'

This praise sounded empty. Maud had done better than these hotel sketches. Rosa had seen them – those begonias, for instance. She sat, lowering herself stiffly into an armchair; feeling doubt now, alongside her anxiousness and her fatigue.

'What happened to you that day? After the trial?'

Rosa pulled out a chair from the table and sat down herself. 'I went to find Mrs Leyland,' she said, as if it were obvious. 'I imagined she would be nearby. I thought I could spell out to her what I knew of her schemes and oblige her to intervene – to remove her husband from the premises.'

This seemed likely enough, if rather naive. 'I really don't think he'd have heeded her, Rosa.'

'Who can say?' Who would have thought that she'd be

part of that loathsome little ploy she tried to spring on you back in the summer?'

Maud recalled their brief tussle just before the verdict, when Rosa had spotted Mrs Leyland in the corridor. 'So you were going to confront her.'

Rosa was unapologetic. 'You are my friend, Maud, my very dear friend, and I'm afraid that if I hear of someone seeking to make you their tool, and cast you in some ridiculous game involving a locket, and secret conferences of the enemy, then I will be seeking to tell them exactly what they are. To the devil with caution, or good manners, or anything else.' She crossed her legs, pinching at the hem of her turquoise gown to set it straight. 'Nothing happened, though. I couldn't find her. She'd gone, I think. Left without him.'

'So you just left yourself. You didn't try to find me or Jimmy. You didn't come round to the White House. You just left.'

'I meant to. I did, Maud. I planned only to stop at home for a minute, to meet with Charles, then come out to you. But the letter concerning my brother was waiting for me there. I had to leave that same evening. He really was very ill. It seemed that he might – well . . .' Rosa took a breath. 'I apologise. I do know that things have been happening, besides the pamphlet. Jo Hiffernan, for instance, paying a visit to Tite Street with a certain young gentleman in tow.'

Maud leaned back in the armchair. 'Owl told you about that.'

Rosa was watching her; she could tell that this encounter had left Maud with some troubling questions. 'He said that Jimmy is awkward with the child.'

'He sees him, though,' Maud answered, a touch too quickly. 'He talks of meeting with him for treats and – and shows and suchlike. He has him lodged with someone he once loved. Not with strangers.' She could hear the distress gathering in her voice. 'Is it because Ione was a girl? Is that why?'

'No,' Rosa said. 'No, it's because of Jimmy. He wouldn't meet the son until the little fellow was over six years old. He told Charles that infants unnerve him.'

Maud was torn between an odd relief – it was good to have a reason, she supposed, even if it was as basic and insurmountable as this one – and annoyance at being observed, and *understood*, and having her own life explained to her. 'He's always said that he can't live with children,' she muttered, feeling that she had to add something, 'on account of his art.'

'The circumstance with Jo Hiffernan is tangled indeed,' Rosa continued. 'It took much strife to bring them to where they are now. Their fragile accord.'

Wearing a slight smile, she went on to tell a tale of Jo and Jimmy, well over a decade old: of an artist and his muse, lovers and friends, who travelled often to France, where they mixed with Jimmy's many acquaintances. Among these were some of the country's greatest painters, and one, a Monsieur Gustave Courbet no less, was rather taken with Jo. He had her model for him while she brushed her hair, all perfectly innocent – but later on, when everything between Jimmy and her was no longer so very wonderful, she came back to France without him, and made a bee-line for the studio of Monsieur Courbet. People talked, they talked up a storm; and then these other paintings began to appear. Nudes they were, but not at all like the one Maud had posed in for Jimmy. The slightest whisper of their subjects, creeping back over the Channel, proved more than sufficient to kill off Jo and Jimmy forever. One apparently showed Jo and another woman lying naked together, wrapped in a passionate embrace. Another, *The Beginnings of the World* Rosa thought it was called, gave a close, unsparing view of Jo's—

At first, Maud listened readily. This was all rather different in character from what she'd been told of Jimmy's younger self, and a part of her was eager for it – for the suggestion that Jo Hiffernan, with her prim retreat from the White House, might be something of a hypocrite. As Rosa went on, however, she grew uneasy. The story had an Owlish quality, both in its intimate nature and its heedless indiscretion. It made her wonder what other, more recent Whistler tales Owl and Rosa might be spinning. She decided that she'd heard enough.

'You've been with your brother the whole time then, have you?' she broke in. 'Since the trial – the end of November?'

'For most of it,' Rosa replied, switching neatly. 'Jonathan

is his name. He is most unwell, poor man. Delusions. A terrible torpor. He can do almost nothing for himself.' She folded her long hands atop her knee. 'I did actually return to London a week or so ago, if I am honest, but have been confined to my studio. Commissions to catch up on. Good things.'

'Your studio,' Maud said, 'that I have never even *seen*.' Her indignation flared; it was suddenly gigantic. 'You told me I'd be welcome. Whenever I liked. That I could bring my work. When we first met, this was. A – a year and a bloody half ago.'

'I shall take you.' Rosa made as if to stand up. 'My goodness, Maud, if this has brought you pain, any pain at all, then I shall take you right this minute. It isn't far.' She appeared to think. 'As a matter of fact, there is something on the stocks that I want you to see. An artistic question, you understand. I have a portrait nearly finished – a portrait in oils of one of Charles's associates – a most unfortunate-looking man, extremely like a hedgerow creature, a shrew or some such. He has requested a rose bower in the background, but I admit that this has me stumped. I simply cannot imbue the wretched flowers with any sense of life. They resemble the pattern on a dull piece of needlework. I was hoping that you'd be willing to suggest how I might improve them.'

Maud was thrown by this, rather expertly thrown, straight down into a deep ditch. She looked at the fire, thinking despite herself what it would be like to assist Rosa with an oil painting, with a paid commission. Surely it would be marvellous. Her resentment now seemed foolish and unwarranted. Might she actually be losing her wits, left up there in that hotel room with only Edie for company, who knew nothing of art or any of it?

'I can't. I – I just can't.' She rubbed her belly; she made a hopeless gesture. 'This could happen at any time.'

Rosa merely shrugged, then went for the bottle she'd brought with her: squat and inky black, the golden label flashing in the firelight. Brandy. After tracking down a pair of teacups, she joined Maud at the hearth, pulled an armchair close to hers and poured them both a large measure, even though it was scarcely ten. The liquor tasted of burned fruit and lint, with a trace of India rubber. It scalded Maud's throat and melted through her compacted innards; she seemed to sink a little into her chair, her fingertips tingling, her eyes fluttering shut.

When she opened them again, Rosa had paper and pencil and was sketching, sketching rapidly, recreating her shrew-man and his roses while asking a string of questions about colouration, arrangement and so on. Maud's replies sounded weak to her, formless and incomplete, but Rosa seemed well pleased by them; she nodded and sketched further, making notes at the sheet's edge.

'This is how it will be, Maud,' she declared, after a few minutes. 'Between the two of us – in the future. Assistance. *Collaboration*. This is where we are heading.'

They began to talk again of a shared house, that old

dream, but now sustained by their own earnings alone. Maud soon became so involved in it, in Rosa's company and the intentness of her conversation, that the everyday routine of which she was so heartily tired became something of a surprise. Edie entered without knocking, as usual, having been supplied with a key by the desk. Rosa stood as the door closed behind her, leaving Maud seated in the middle – wedged, it felt like, between the arms of her chair. She looked at Edie, then at Rosa, and then back at Edie again; and she knew that this meeting could only speed along Rosa's departure.

Edie's clothes that day were brown and soapstone grey, sensible in every regard, like all the clothes she owned. She removed her gloves, drawing herself up in the subtlest and most respectable form of confrontation. She was not unfriendly, not in the least; indeed, she was regarding Rosa with an expectant curiosity, almost as if her sister's visitor was a performer of some kind, who might at any moment trill out an aria or produce a dove with a flourish of her hand.

'Rosa,' said Maud, 'this is my sister. Mrs Edith Crossley.'

Rosa's smile was inscrutable – drawn curtains, a shuttered shop. 'I can see the resemblance,' she said.

'Miss Rosa Corder,' said Maud to Edie. 'My friend.'

'Miss Corder, that is a remarkable gown. May I ask where it came from?'

Edie was polishing up her accent, her manner, presenting what she imagined was her best self. It struck Maud as very stupid. She fought the urge to cover her face with her hand.

Rosa's smile did not waver; her eyes went, just for an instant, to her cloak and hat. 'Why thank you, Mrs Crossley,' she replied. 'Most kind. I made it myself.'

Edie seemed to find this fascinating, asking about fabric and patterns, and sources of inspiration – as if she, in the span of a dozen lifetimes, would ever wear anything so bold. Rosa's replies were brief, faintly evasive, those of someone preparing to leave. Maud asked if she'd join them for luncheon, which wasn't far off now. Different parts of her hoped that Rosa would accept and deliver her from tedium; or that she would refuse, and spare her further embarrassment.

'We can tell the hotel,' she said. 'Have them send up another plate.'

Rosa turned to Maud, the affection on her face revealing clearly that the offer was to be refused. She retrieved her cloak and pulled it on, fastening it at her throat. 'I must be off. All I wanted, dearest Maud, was to let you know that you are in our thoughts. That you never leave them. We shall talk more when this is done with. We have plans to make, you and I.' She looked pointedly towards the water-colours on the table. 'Beginning with next year's Grosvenor.'

Edie – still by the door, in her hat and coat – was listening closely. 'Plans?'

Maud tried to sit up. 'Miss Corder is an artist. She sells her work. She supports herself by it.'

Edie considered this. 'Can a woman really hope to make her livelihood in this way?'

Maud glowered over at her. Jimmy's mother had asked much the same question, but she at least had the excuse of age for her obsolete views. This had been coming for a while, Maud realised, accumulating throughout the days Edie and she had spent together at Sharp's Hotel: an argument written deep, impossible to efface or resolve.

'Rosa does,' she retorted. 'She has a studio, a studio of her own, not far from here.'

Edie was quiet for a second. Maud could sense her scepticism; her determination to say her piece. 'I take it, Miss Corder, that you are a follower of Mr Whistler?'

For once Rosa would not be drawn. She fitted on her hat, apologised, and said again that she really had to be going.

'It is you, I suppose,' Edie continued, 'who has been encouraging my sister to paint these flowers of hers. Does she think that she can become an artist like you? That she can support herself with sketches once she has exhausted her value as a model and is no longer wanted by Mr Whistler?'

This was new: open disdain, thrust forward, almost as if Edie had been waiting for an opportunity – for a culprit, perhaps, beyond Maud herself. Furthermore, it was now abundantly clear that she thought of her sister's life not only as shameful or unrespectable but *ridiculous*, brainless, a waste of time. It was similar to the scorn Jimmy endured from certain quarters of the press, and from the enemies who'd assembled at the trial. Maud stood, wobbling with the weight of the baby, and maybe the teacups of brandy as well. Edie came forward, ready to help; Maud stepped to the side, refusing even to meet her eye.

'I've changed my mind,' she announced. 'I will walk with you, Rosa. To Southampton Row.'

'Maud,' said Rosa – she sounded rather less sure than previously. 'Would it not be best to wait until you are—'

'It isn't far. You said so yourself. I'm perfectly fine.'

'You shouldn't be walking any distance at all,' said Edie. 'Think of the cold, Maud. The stairs.'

Maud wouldn't be deterred. 'Come,' she said to Rosa. 'Let's be off. I find that I cannot bear the thought of another afternoon cooped up in here.'

She readied herself to go, forcing on her boots, grabbing at her hat and shawl. Edie didn't protest any further; but as Maud struggled by her, out into the corridor, she said that she believed she would come along as well.

'You needn't,' Maud told her. 'Truly.'

Edie's stubbornness was a match for her own, however; her sister left the room after them, locking the door, and followed a few yards behind as they inched down the staircase. Maud clung to the banister with both hands. The stairs were steeper than she remembered. Her back was straining horribly; the child had selected this moment to shift itself into a yet more burdensome position. But she was determined. She would do this. Rosa was beside her, alert for mishap. There was a nervousness in her artist friend, though, a certain distance, that Maud hadn't seen before; she was like someone unused to dogs given the task of holding the chain of a growling mastiff.

As they approached the bottom of the staircase the concierge hurried over, looking for the signal to run for a cab.

'No,' Maud told him, shaking her head, 'no, just a stroll. Just a — a stroll.'

The women crossed to the hotel doors under the close scrutiny of the entire lobby. Once they were outside, Maud looked towards Pentonville Road, a hundred yards or so away, and had a sharp sense of how limited her energy was — of how it was being drained further by every halting step. She panted in the biting air; she licked her cracked lips. There was actually a very real chance that she would stumble, and slump, and be able to go no further.

Rosa saw it. 'Maud, much as it pains me, I don't think . . .'

'No. No, I'm well. Come on.'

Gradually, torturously, the main thoroughfare drew closer — the flow of hansoms, the omnibuses with their advertising placards, the endless people. Rosa was not as steady a support as might have been wished for, due to the unusually high heels on her boots, but the pair of them found a pattern of sorts. Maud began to divide up the remaining distance in her mind, into separate lengths of street and lane, having a half-formed notion that this would make it more manageable. Above, sparrows bickered atop a lamp post; she smelled smoke, blackly acrid, from a brazier across the road; and something seemed to fall from her, dropping away among her skirts. Warm liquid soaked the inside of her thighs and the back of her left knee, spreading swiftly through the stocking. There was a splattering sound. Maud halted, skidding a little, her grip on Rosa's arm tightening so much that she cried out. Together they looked down. The pavement was wet beneath her, one of her boots splashed to a shine.

Edie ran up, asking if she was all right, if she could hold on. She began calling for a cab, waving, moving to the kerb. Maud stood stock still, hands on her haunches now – staring at the wet pavement, listening to the dripping, trying to recall how it went last time and how long she might have. She made herself concentrate upon her body, upon the child – upon what was beginning to happen. That first slow squeeze.

A Hackney carriage was convinced to stop. Edie rushed back towards her, urging her to go over to it, to climb in – saying that they had to get to Camden, to the midwife.

'Rosa,' said Maud.

'She's not coming. She's gone.'

Maud gazed around her in confusion and then glimpsed a strip of turquoise, some distance along the street already. She couldn't make out very much more through her watering eyes. Was Rosa turning as she strode away? Was she waving them off?

Nothing could be done. Maud shuffled through the mud to the cab, keeping her feet half a yard apart, her saturated petticoats swinging heavily beneath her dress. She made it to the door – to the carriage's three cast-iron steps. The taste of Rosa's brandy was still in her mouth. She found herself thinking of earlier, of the heated words they'd exchanged before it had been poured – and realising with fast gathering force that something was amiss. Now that Rosa was gone, she could see it; she could *feel* it, like a burr in a glove. She blinked, rooted to the spot, unable to lift her boot.

'The locket,' she said.

Edie gave the midwife's address to the driver. She opened the door and pointed to the lowest step, as if Maud required direction; then she noticed the expression on her sister's face. 'What is it? What's wrong?'

Maud looked back at her. 'I never told her about the locket.'

Part Three
The Gold Scab

January 1879

'The shore forms a white curve,' said Jim, 'from midway down the right side to the lower left corner. Water and sky are the same shade of pearl grey, with just the slightest *soupçon* of blue.' He narrowed his eyes. 'The boats – those lighters there, dragged up onto the ice, and those barges with their masts – are darker, rather like wet slate; while that fog bank to the rear adds a haze of ochre, quite smothering the buildings within it. Their lights are merely dim squares, so dim that they are barely there at all.'

Eldon was nodding; he clapped his gloved hands together. 'You have it, old man,' he said from behind his scarf. 'You have it exactly.'

It was a while past midnight. They'd waited until the gas had gone out along the Chelsea Embankment, and something of the old calm had returned. Jim had then set about working to his method: locating the Nocturne and impressing it completely upon his mind. Eldon, there for company, was not one to complain, but he'd begun to fidget as the minutes became an hour and his extremities were numbed by the cold. Jim himself was reluctant to leave. It had been two years at least since he'd last done this. He had a fear that his memory, his burdened consciousness, could not hold another image, another arrangement of tones; that it was simply *full*, and once he turned his back the scene before him would be lost forever. He went, though. One had to have a little faith.

'Where's this for again, Jimmy?' Eldon asked as they crossed the entrance to the Albert Bridge, their boots crunching through frosty mud. 'Scotland, wasn't it?'

'A fellow in Edinburgh,' Jim replied – thinking of that barge on the right: the angle of the boom against the mast, the bunched canvas of the sail. 'A dealer. He attended the trial. Felt the injustice of it all. Tells me he'll be able to sell any Nocturne I send him, for fifty guineas or more. I'd have done him fireworks, *naturellement* – a summer scene, another *Black and Gold*. But time is of the essence.' The White House appeared ahead, like a distant cliff sliding from the mist. 'This is only the start. These picture dealers are always prowling around here, you know. All I need do is work, dear Eldon, and the gold will appear.'

As he made this claim, Jim felt the uneasy undertow that so often runs beneath wishful thinking, dragging at one's confidence even as one speaks. There was work, that much was true — etchings, this lone canvas promised to a man four hundred miles away — but it was a minute fraction of what was required. A cup of water tossed into a burning barn.

Eldon enquired no further, perfectly happy to believe him, and asked instead about the fortunes of *Art & Art Critics*. Jim revealed with considerable satisfaction that his pamphlet had reached no less than its seventh edition.

'It goes like smoke, *mon cher*. It disappears in its hundreds from the booksellers' shelves.' He hesitated. 'Which isn't to say that there's been any blasted money. Costs of production, you understand. A venture in *publicity*, that damnable word, and naught else.'

Eldon was nodding again, his shoulders hunched and his hands buried in the pockets of his coat. They approached the front door. Jim reached for his key; the metal was so cold he could feel it through his glove.

'Any word yet from the *Madame*?'

An unsurprising question. They all loved Maud, of course they did, and were understandably concerned for her. Eldon was especially devoted, Jim had noticed — like a loyal body-guard, albeit one of little practical use.

'She's as well as one can expect. Boredom is the enemy more than anything else. Her family are tending to her — and they are not, I believe it's fair to say, friends to art . . .'

'She writes to you, then?'

'Via Lucas. You know, my chum on the rue de l'Arc de Triomphe. And I write back by the same path. Spin my Parisian fictions. Nothing too specific.'

Was that *disapproval* on Matthew Eldon's mild, meaty face? A crease of censure between those blond eyebrows? 'And she suspects nothing,' he said. 'She thinks you are in France?'

'It had to be done. *Had* to be. Don't you dare try to prompt guilt, Eldon – not over a ruse as innocent as this. Tell me, have *you* ever tried to apply yourself to anything whilst sharing your abode with an expectant woman? It is impossible. Absolutely impossible. This I learned most memorably the first time around. And now, well – every last hour is precious, *n'est-ce pas?*'

As if to reinforce this point, the front door was opened to reveal Mr Sumner from Levy and Company. He'd moved a dining chair to the hall and sat there quite awake – waiting in the dark. As Jim and Eldon entered, he struck a match, touching it to a candle set in a holder at his feet. The effect was rather sinister.

'Hell's bells, Sumner,' said Jim, 'you are a strange beast. Will you pass the night down here, I wonder? A room was made up for you, you know, on the first floor.'

Sumner did not speak; he had the air of a man tired of speaking. He gestured for Jim to approach and went through his pockets. There wasn't anything of worth or interest within, Jim always made sure of that. Nightingale's writ of execution had been served a week before, and now there was a human filter set over his household, a net that would both catch any gold coming in and prevent any valuables from leaving.

The house was cold and cheerless, kept dark as a matter of financial necessity. Jim soon retired to bed; then awoke with the watery dawn, donned three shirts and a stained smock and went directly to the studio. Eldon was there already, sitting at the piano in scarf and gloves. The lid was up; he played the occasional idle chord, smoking a cigarette – coasting, as he tended to do, on the verge of complete vacancy. He'd plainly been there all night. Jim presumed that a bottle had been involved.

The canvas, prepared the afternoon before, had been covered with a light grey ground and set flat on the table to prevent the paint from running. By the light of a low winter sun, just coming in through the ice-sheened windows, Jim mixed the paint until its tone matched his recollection. He thinned it out with syrupy glugs of linseed oil, making it quite liquid – *the sauce*, he used to call it. The basics were laid in, using long, steady strokes of a broad brush; appraised with a hand on the chin; judged inadequate and wiped off. This was done again, and a third time. The morning advanced. Eldon slipped from the piano stool to the floor below, where he dozed gently. The fourth attempt was right, or at least not completely wrong: the shift in the surface of the water, the smoky coalescence of the fog, were perhaps just about acceptable. Jim left it, stalking around the chilly room. He peered down into the street, over towards the embankment, and smoked a couple of thin cigarettes. Then he returned to work.

Another bead of ivory black was stirred into the sauce

and one of the narrower brushes selected, so that a start could be made on the barges. The hulls were rendered in ghostly silhouette; the dark lines of the masts traced across the river mist. This looked so well, so close to his intention, that Jim almost didn't trust it. Straightening up with a wince, he dropped the brush into a soft-soap jar. He removed the eyeglass and wiped it on his sleeve; and jumped to discover Owl standing immediately before him, only a couple of yards away, in top hat and grey overcoat, grey gloves and cane – coming yet closer, craning his neck, regarding the morning's labour with great interest. For a large man who certainly knew how to underline his entrances when it suited him, the Owl was also capable of a really quite unnerving stealth. Why he would choose to employ it now was anyone's guess.

'That impertinent brute on the door,' he murmured, 'insisted upon damned well *searching me* before he'd allow me in. Is that legal?'

'So I am told,' Jim replied, masking his surprise. 'It is his work, Owl, you see.'

Owl had already moved on. 'A Nocturne, eh? Damn good idea. Would you have me place it for you? There's a dealer over in Marylebone who could get a healthy sum indeed for a new Whistler oil.'

This was annoying. Jim had been hoping to prevent Owl from learning about this picture, and his connection with that dealer in Edinburgh. There was a suspicion growing in him that the Portuguese *required* dependency, in an odd sort of way; that if the fellow learned he was enjoying any success whatsoever he'd simply disappear again, this time for good, taking his funds and his pledge of help with the litigious Mr Nightingale along with him.

'It isn't finished,' he said. '*Mon vieux*, it's barely begun.'

Owl accepted this with an incline of his leonine head, and instead reported that he had a sum of money for Jim, ready cash, that he'd managed to keep hidden from that blundering cur of Mr Levy's. How much exactly, and for what — a *Carlyle* proof? One of the drawings Jim vaguely remembered letting him have? An ornament, a Japanese print? — was not specified. There was nothing unusual in this. Owl liked their affairs to remain as obscure as possible; for Jim's own protection, he claimed, as what he himself did not know couldn't possibly be uncovered by the enemy.

From beneath his arm, Owl now produced the morning's post. It was composed entirely of bills: Jim could identify them now from the envelopes alone. He'd begun sending them on to Reeve unopened, in the hope that he'd be able to sink them in a sea of lawyerly obfuscation. They were trifling, for the most part, matters of a few pounds only. This did not lessen the terror they provoked, however, so damned thick and unrelenting was the swarm.

'I've had a couple of letters,' he said, laying the bills beside the new *Nocturne*, 'from a Mr Morse. You recall him, I'm sure — the fellow who took over Lindsey Row. He has a query about that Chinese cabinet he bought from me.

Says it appears to be missing its top section, and asks if anyone at our end might know of its whereabouts.'

'In for repair,' Owl replied. 'Morse knows this, the fool. Now – I have news regarding Nightingale. The legal types have had their powwow and the first payment is to be made. It should all be confirmed by the week's end. I'm afraid that the cockney Argus downstairs will have to find somewhere else to hang that sad little hat of his.'

And just like that Jim's weary irritability lifted away. He looked out at the last of the morning, and the intense blue of the January sky. The largest debt was to be cleared. The man evicted. His freedom restored.

'This,' he said, 'is good news indeed.'

'Furthermore,' Owl continued, 'I've been talking to a pal of mine at the Fine Art Society. Marcus Huish, the managing director. I believe you two are acquainted.'

Jim's spirits dipped somewhat. 'Huish,' he pronounced, 'is one of the *enemy*. Hang it all, Owl, he arranged that damned fund for Ruskin, after the trial, to pay the old vulture's costs. He and his cronies are among my—'

'Huish is no partisan,' Owl said. 'This you must understand, Jimmy. He did that thing for Ruskin, true – and now he seeks to do something for you as well. A new impression of the Thames set is what he proposes, to be displayed and sold on their premises. And the Society also wishes to buy the plates – which I need not tell you means serious tin. Things can be arranged, I believe, so that no payments are made until Levy's man is well and truly out.'

Jim considered the studio: the assembled artworks, held hostage to the bailiff; the scuffed furniture; the leak beneath one of the windows, staining the paintwork. 'The Fine Art Society,' he said.

'I understand it is difficult,' Owl continued, 'but there is real admiration over there, Jimmy, for your genius as an etcher. No one better alive today, they say. Certainly not in London. Possibilities galore, old man, if you only demonstrate an ounce of willing. Copper will be turned into gold.'

Jim said nothing. Owl was patient; he took off his hat and turned to survey the canvases.

Up here for the past few weeks, alone mostly, Jim had thought much about his life – where it was, what had been done with it and what looked likely to happen from now on. And by heaven it was difficult at times to feel very good about it at all. Forty-four years old at his last birthday, two years more than his own father had managed, and running out of clothes, of food, with no money even for coal or candles. His work was valued by some, yes, but reviled and ridiculed by many more. Behind the swagger, the defiance, had always been a conviction that one day, at some point in the future, he would *come through* – that his work would silence the critics, or convert them even, and his unswerving adherence to his own sense of art would find its reward. Now, though, as the trial's din faded away, he couldn't be rid of a creeping sense that this might not actually be the case. *He could fail*. Be ruined beyond repair. He saw it very clearly.

'Kindly inform Mr Huish – inform him—' Jim's attempt at hauteur grated on his own ear. He sighed, looking over hopelessly at the mortgaged piano and the still slumbering Eldon beneath it. 'I must accept. I have no choice. You see this place, Owl. You see the – the straits I'm in. We are so very close to the end, *mon vieux*. You know it. To dissolution.'

Owl was regarding him with deep sympathy. 'I understand, Jimmy. God knows I do. I've stared down the barrel of it myself, on far too many occasions. And I will do everything possible to save you from these dreadful bothers. The key, my friend, the bloody key is *management*. There is a way to keep the Sheriff's men from your house. To safeguard what is important. To preserve the best of yourself, come what may.' There was a pause, expertly weighted – the kind that comes before a revelation. 'Bankruptcy.'

Jim didn't move or breathe. He could feel himself staring; his eyeballs ached. Speech, for the moment, was beyond him.

Owl was not at all discouraged by this response. He seemed almost to relish it. 'I am just about to pay two hundred pounds,' he said, 'to induce old Nightingale to flap away, and am pledged to provide his people with two hundred and fifty more. So that's four fifty you'll owe me – and a damned good start.' He turned towards the piano. 'El-*don*!' he shouted, stamping his boot on the floor. 'Eldon you sot, rouse yourself.'

Eldon woke; he looked around in confusion. 'I seem,' he mumbled, 'to have been asleep . . .'

'How much,' Owl asked, 'does Jimmy owe you?'

'Owe me? I don't – he doesn't—' Eldon lifted himself up onto the piano stool. 'Why Owl, not a bean.'

Owl was shaking his head. 'I think you'll find, old chap, that it's a cool hundred at the very least. And you're expecting repayment in the near future.'

Jim recovered enough to speak. 'Owl, you fiend, what *are* you on about?'

'Here's how it is. Bankruptcy is declared, using old Reeve, at the London court. You get him to submit a sizeable bill of his own as well. Appoint an amenable fellow as the receiver. And all these petty demands will cease. No one can take any further proceedings against a declared bankrupt. The claims on the estate will be sorted and ranked, and those of your friends – being the most substantial – will be at the head of the queue. We'll be in control, don't you see? The others, these rodents who have gnawed at you so long, will have to make do with the crumbs. This is what the law dictates.'

Jim leaned against the table, inserting the eyeglass to get a better look at Owl's face. 'My things would be sold. My house.'

This was neither confirmed nor denied, but the Portuguese's enthusiasm increased yet further. 'The first claims would be ours. Mine and Eldon's. Reeve's. We would ensure that your work would be kept safe. That it was borne off to a sanctuary somewhere, held in trust for you – or used, perhaps, to generate the means for your recovery. This room – by Jove, this room is packed with treasure. I'm amazed, quite frankly, that the bailiff isn't more interested in it. We could claim these canvases here, don't you see, for low sums, and then sell them on for their true worth. Why, we could get hold of the lot, Eldon, between the two of us.' Owl crossed the studio to where *The Three Girls* was propped, the pale bodies and pink flowers lit up by the sunlight. 'Immortal artworks such as this one here should not fall into the hands of paint-grinders, or poulterers, or pastry-makers. It would be nothing short of a crime! This here is the *answer*, Jimmy. I feel it.'

'If I were to declare—' Jim found that he couldn't use the words. 'If I were to follow the course you suggest, would it not be the case that—'

Owl stopped him. 'I must say,' he declared, a gloved hand raised, 'that this room is really quite . . . *outrageously* cold. I take it there is no coal, or fuel of any kind? Very well. That is to be expected. It feels damp as well, don't you think? I thought this on the stairs also. That devil Nightingale has much to answer for, in all honesty.'

'Owl—'

'I propose a relocation, gentlemen, so we can discuss this further over a spot of luncheon. A cab to Piccadilly, to a French place I know – and then perhaps a wander over to the Strand, to call on Anderson Reeve.'

Shock still rang through Jim, humming in his toes and tightening his breath; even so, he couldn't help smiling a little at this suggestion. 'And how precisely,' he asked, 'would we pay for this repast?'

Owl took out his cigarette case; he'd reined in his eagerness a fraction, but continued to radiate an irrepressible good cheer. 'There's coin, as I said. More than enough. Come now – you aren't beaten, are you Jimmy? Shave that chin. Have John brush you a jacket. To hell with the man downstairs.' He split the case open and offered it around. 'We three are men of the town, are we not? Let us go to her.'

*

February 1879

So a sad farewell was bade to the silent Mr Sumner – oh yes, handkerchiefs out and no mistake – and a modest sack of gold supplied by the Fine Art Society. Thus assisted, Jim issued invitations to a fresh round of Sunday breakfasts, with an eye upon *consolidation*: upon reminding his allies in artistic society who they were, and what they would provide should the call come. He was now required to manage the culinary preparations himself, Mrs Cossins having jumped ship just before Christmas, being unable to survive on IOUs rather than wages, and well aware, despite the gin, of her own professional worth.

These, Jim perceived, were the last days. Yet another chapter was drawing ineluctably to a close, and this proposition of Owl's, this *bankruptcy*, was fast becoming inevitable. The sole remaining option. Everything he owned would be gone. The wardrobe that clothed him, the walls that he'd had built around him, the green-tiled roof, set at such an exquisite and original slope, that sheltered him from the incessant English rain. It couldn't be helped. A gentleman, he knew, could only meet such a fate in one way. He must revel in it.

An afternoon was spent roaming the streets of Chelsea, in search of a photographer he'd not yet used and had therefore incurred no debt with. Eventually one was found, and a pair of portraits taken, back to back. The first captured Whistler as he wished his friends to see him: a three-quarter view, seated with a hand up to his chin, wearing a deliberate, roguish smile.

'The eye must glint,' he instructed the fellow, 'as if with mischievous purpose.'

The second, however, showed Whistler as he was to his enemies: standing straight, hand on hip, glaring directly into the camera as if confronting it.

'Terror must be the result,' he said as he struck his pose. 'They must look upon it and know exactly what they deserve.'

Examples of each were displayed upon the mantelpiece in the White House dining room. They caused some rather gratifying consternation among his guests.

'Are you asking us to choose, Mr Whistler,' they enquired, 'which version we would have?'

He laughed along with them, and gave no definitive answer; but he *was*, most emphatically. There was an element of threat, almost, in these two photographs – a message that was pretty damned difficult to misinterpret. A couple of people asked who he'd been thinking of when standing for the enemy photograph – to whom it was truly addressed. He didn't trouble to reply. They all knew the answer.

It was impossible, Jim felt, to consider his situation, the way such a scattered crowd of creditors had moved in on him, and not detect a guiding intelligence. They had been rallied together. Bribed, or perhaps even bought out. This person, this *orchestrator*, would have to be a man of stature, or at least the sort of stature that would impress and intimidate a little fellow in his shop. He'd have millions to hand. A towering townhouse and a country pile. A fleet of vessels, say, bearing his name.

Could anything be more goddamned provoking? Frederick Leyland had surely found a way, a year and a half on, to wield his horsewhip. During the last week of January, stewing in embittered solitude, Jim became convinced that action was now the only honourable course. John lingered on in the White House's lower reaches, through a kind of animal loyalty Jim supposed; he'd demonstrated an aptitude for spying several times in the past, so Jim had him follow the shipbroker around for a spell. If he had some hard facts concerning Leyland's women, Jim thought, there might well be a way to expose the philandering swine for what he was. To bring about his disgrace and his eternal banishment from polite society.

Results came quickly, with John naming a restaurant in Mayfair that Leyland frequented (and had invested in, it was suspected, in return for absolute discretion) to ply a particularly favoured female, a Mrs Caldecott, with lobsters and champagne. Jim knew immediately what he should do. There would be a confrontation outside this establishment, before a smart crowd of onlookers, where a rapier remark about Leyland's choice of companion – about this shadow army he'd assembled, these ranks of painted ladies, and the demands he made of them – would slice away the villain's respectable visage once and for all. As tended to be the way with Jim's imaginings, this would be followed by a scuffle – instigated by the foe, naturally – which the righteous artist would win without any special exertion: a left hook, an uppercut, a boxing of ears, rounded off with a boot to that bony behind as the humiliated Leyland retreated, bloody and breathless, to his carriage.

This vision remained unrealised. Experiencing something confusingly like *reservation*, Jim did not march up to Mayfair. Instead, he brooded in his lonely home, trying to find consolation in what he'd told Godwin after the trial, out before the Courts of Justice. *There'll be a better way of doing it.*

Any further reflection on this matter, however, was prevented by a pair of reappearances. First, wholly without warning, came the bailiff. There was another writ of execution – something to do with unpaid rates, one he'd quite forgotten. But the result was the same. A man was placed in his hall, to check his pockets and watch his movements. He was obliged to rush about town, engaging in befuddling, futile arguments with solicitors and the Sheriff's officers, and to fire off endless urgent notes to poor Reeve. It was all a most senseless waste of his time.

And then, two days later, Maud was brought back by her sister. The sight from the studio window was enough to startle Jim from his ruminations and bring him to the door. She was pale beyond belief. Barely able to plant her own steps. As they descended from their four-wheeler and came across Tite Street, the sister kept a scowl fixed upon him – which grew yet more ferocious when she spotted the man, a weathered specimen named Donaldson, lurking in the shadows behind.

Maud couldn't speak, not really; she shivered in Jim's embrace. The sister took her up to bed at once, returning a while afterwards with a couple of questions to ask. Had Jim received her letter, informing him of his daughter's – his *second* daughter's birth? And if so, why had he made no response?

What could Jim say to this? He was aware of no such letter, but that wasn't to say that none had arrived. It would have got swept up with everything else. Lost in the drift of writs.

'The child was . . . well, I take it?'

Edith – was that correct? – set her lips in a cold line. 'Maud, her name is. That's what her mother chose. She's small and a little quiet, but the doctor was satisfied. His bill is on its way to you. The birth took nearly a whole day. Some complication. A lot of pain. The chloroform, in the end, left her quite insensible.' She took a steadying breath.

'It was easier. The fostering, I mean, the moment of parting. Easier than – than last time.'

The sister blinked dazedly, miserably, made vulnerable for a second by her exhaustion; then she looked around the silver grey parlour and seemed to remember who she was talking to. The remainder of her conversation was clipped and practical, little more than a list of Maud's requirements. She took her leave reluctantly, though, walking rather slowly to the door and casting a last worried look towards the staircase.

Jim sent straight away for Willie, having no confidence at all in the quacks of Kentish Town.

'There was injury,' said Dr Whistler, after he'd made his examination. 'Nothing too concerning, I think, but she's very weak. She needs to heal.'

Rest was prescribed, and peace, and beef tea; and having got past Mr Donaldson unmolested on account of his profession, Willie slipped Jim a couple of pound notes to defray their expenses.

It jarred the soul. Maud's robustness was her great gift, forming an uncommon partnership with her grace and artistic sensibilities. It had honestly never occurred to Jim that giving birth might lay her so low. The first time had been difficult, certainly, but nothing like this. Confined to their room, she slept and she wept; and she bled still, rather heavily he thought. He had Willie back, and the sister, but neither could tell him anything. He became steadily more concerned. Could bereavement seriously be on the cards here? The loss of Maud Franklin. The loss of his *Madame*. That really would be too much.

But no, thank God, this very darkest of thoughts actually seemed to push the girl in the opposite direction. One dull afternoon in the middle of the month, Jim discovered her sitting up in bed. He approached and she gripped his hand, her eyes open wide and uncommonly bright, and asked him in a faint, hoarse voice what the devil was going on with that man down there in the hall.

'Is he from Levy? Has that wretch done as he threatened, and served his writ? I thought he couldn't do anything while you weren't here. That's what you said.'

Damned near beaming with relief, Jim lowered himself beside her, reflecting that the truth could be an enormous and unwieldy thing; if it was mishandled, or dropped in the delivery, it could do grave damage. Maud was unwell. He had to be careful.

'No, dear girl, this is something else. Hughes is the company name. They arrived mere hours after my return from France. But you mustn't worry, not for an instant. There is a plan afoot. It is bold, I warn you, and it may sound alarming at first, but it is a truly great scheme. A way of shaking off the enemy's snares once and for all, and bounding off together into the woods.'

Maud waited. Jim looked into her face, so drained of health and colour; at the dark crescents pressed beneath her eyes.

'Bankruptcy,' he said, much as Owl had done to him.

She released his hand, fell back onto the pillow and pulled the blankets over her head.

'It isn't how you think,' Jim said to the heaped bedclothes. 'Listen, Maudie, it works like this. The declaration is made, the estate valued and claims entered against it. My friends conjure up debts, as large as they can make them, the largest being first in line. And then they claim our possessions – don't you see? – for us to retrieve afterwards. Every last thing. Every painting and print. Every stick of furniture. No further proceedings can begin. The enemy is frustrated. Caught in a stalemate. And a year from now we will wonder what all the fuss was over.'

From within the bed, Maud made a peculiar sound, midway between a gasp and a snarl. She threw the sheets off her, down almost to her waist, lying still for a moment with her eyes fixed on the ceiling.

'Well,' she said. 'All right then.'

February 1879

The worst of it was her memory. It was worse than the headaches; worse than the confounded treachery of her limbs, so weak and prone to collapse; worse even than the unthinkable state of her lower regions, where everything was so desperately, excruciatingly sore that simply passing water felt like she was settling herself against a strip of red-hot iron. No, the worst thing, the really distressing thing, was that she had no recollection of the birth, or of her child. Or at least nothing she could trust.

Edie had brought her into the midwife's house, through to a downstairs chamber used for birthing. There had been a bed with no board at the end. Lamps had been lit, the fire stoked and water brought. She'd been in pain by then – that great staggering pain that scooped all thought from your head and set you bawling with everything you'd got.

Her hat had rolled away across the floorboards. Her boots had been removed, then her stockings and her gown. The midwife's hands had charted the dimensions of her — of the baby inside her and the position in which it lay. Some time later a man had arrived, bespectacled and fat, a doctor she was told, and the drug had been administered. It had been measured in tiny drips — *grains*, the doctor had called them — but the dose had been generous. There had been a smell a little like pears, but far sweeter and stronger than any pear could ever be.

And after this the pieces became smudged together, their sequence quite lost. There was Edie's wax-white face, the jaw clenched so tightly Maud had feared for her teeth. The fierce redness of blood. The tug of the doctor's blade, like a bramble snagging on your coat. And the child. Maud had for so long now been accustomed to finding Ione in her dreams — Ione newborn, black curls caked to her scalp, letting out a scratchy mewl — that she truly could not tell if the images in her mind were of the new baby or of her first. Her efforts to examine them, to test them somehow, only deepened her uncertainty.

Clear sensations, rooted properly in a time and a place, began to return about two days afterwards. Fully clothed and feverish, she was sitting in a hansom beside her sister, feeling a sharp, agonising twist for each individual cobble-stone they traversed. She gripped the leather handle and pressed her forehead against the glass, concentrating very hard upon not screaming aloud. Edie explained that the child was already gone, away with the same family. They were going to register the birth, like they'd done the first time. As Maud had insisted they do.

'You must be on the certificate. That's what you said. So you can claim her later, if you wish it.'

So Maud gathered herself as best she could and answered the necessary questions. Her perception, however, was still lagging: when the registrar asked her daughter's name, she gave her own instead. She'd been thinking of Alexandra, should the child prove to be a girl, but didn't try to correct the error. Indeed, she promptly added Jimmy's surname, and his middle name also, to hear how it sounded – and then her own surname too, for good measure. *Maud McNeill Whistler Franklin.* It only just fitted on the page.

The registrar took down the father's name, and that he was an artist by profession; the mother's name; and then, after a pause, he asked the location of the birth.

'What about me?' said Maud. 'What of my profession?'

The fellow eyed her inscrutably; he indicated the boxes printed on the certificate with the brass nib of his pen. 'There is no place for it, madam.'

'Artist.' Maud jabbed at the sheet with her finger, beneath her name. 'Put that I am an artist as well.'

Before long she was home again, at the decaying, beleaguered White House. It was dark; it was so dark all the time and it was freezing bloody cold. Spring was on its way, that's what people kept saying, but it felt to Maud like the seasons were actually slipping backwards. Like spring was withering into winter. Dr Whistler left more chloral for her, with strict instructions about what to take and when. Despite this strictness, it turned out to be almost as liberal as the measure she'd been given in Camden Town. It slowed her to a crawl, to a condition of near imbecility; but the pain was so great otherwise, and the direction of her thoughts so disquieting, that she could not bear to put it aside.

On the bad days, which at first were plentiful, it was difficult not to resent Jimmy – to loathe him, even – when he rushed in to tell her the details of his latest wheeze, or some triumph he'd brought about up in the studio. He'd already moved to another bedroom, telling her that he needed uninterrupted rest, what with all that was happening. Simple meals he could manage, but changing sheets and linen was beyond him. With the departure of Mrs Cossins, Edie had to be summoned from Kentish Town for the most basic ministrations. Maud caught herself thinking, as she looked around and saw anew how everything seemed to be coming apart – well, why not them too? What was stopping it, in all honesty? The house was to be sold. Bills of sale had been pasted over those plain white flanks. It was ending. Why not end Jimmy and Maud as well? She'd left her last home, walking down from Kentish Town at the age of seventeen to become an artists' model. She'd left with nothing but a carpet bag and a few coppers and she'd been perfectly fine. Couldn't she be fine again?

By and by, Owl and Rosa came to call, arriving unannounced one morning. The Portuguese, Maud had gathered, was once more a near daily presence in Jimmy's life. He'd tell her of how the fellow was proving little less than a saviour, in fact – familiar with the ins and outs of this bankruptcy plan they'd settled on, and quite selfless in his dedication to their requirements. And they were concerned for her, Owl and Miss Corder both – keen to see her well, to see her recovering, as she so surely was.

'I can't,' Maud said, rolling over, pulling the sheets around her.

'You mean you don't wish to receive them right now, or—'

'I just can't.'

Jimmy hesitated, puffing on his cigarette; then he went downstairs and handled it for her. She was too fatigued, she heard him tell them. Too battered by it all. Understanding noises were made and they went on their way. He came straight back and sat on the edge of the bed, stroking her forearm. He didn't ask her to explain, saying merely that he understood it. God knows he did. He knew how things could go; how one needed, at times, to hold one's friends at a distance. In her gratitude, in this glimpse of their old union, Maud's mind and heart swung about yet again. For a few minutes her dissatisfactions lifted. She let herself lean against him, closing her eyes – and felt better, in truth, than she had in a good long while.

Rosa Corder, however, was not noted for her lack of

persistence. Three days later, around nightfall, she was back at the White House, laughing with Owl and Jimmy in the downstairs corridor. Maud was caught in the privy, where so much of her time seemed to be spent at present. Sitting there in the gloom, scarcely daring to breathe, she stared hard at the weight on the end of the chain – a cast-iron grasshopper about three inches long, bought from a dealer in Kensington for a sum so large Jimmy had refused to disclose it. After about ten minutes all was quiet. She opened the door a tiny fraction, looking for her chance to creep upstairs; and there was Rosa, standing silhouetted in the drawing-room doorway, still in her hat and cloak. Waiting.

Maud gritted her teeth and came out, aiming to cut past. The narrowness of the corridor meant that the two women were brought close, their skirts brushing together; Rosa's had the crunch of satin and was a rich colour that might have been opal. She didn't speak until they were level – at their nearest.

'You are well. Thank God. You look well, I should say. When Jimmy told us how you had suffered – how you are suffering still – I thought I might go quite mad with worry.'

Maud avoided her eye. Since Rosa and Owl's first visit, the Leyland locket had towered in her thoughts like the parliament clock. During a half-lucid moment, she'd even composed a theory as to how Rosa might have come to know about it. If she'd been on Southampton Row after all, on the day of the Albemarle, she might have seen Maud knocking and deliberately hung back, out of sight; followed her into High Holborn, keeping her distance; watched Mrs Leyland's interception and the visit to the pawn shop that came soon afterwards; gone inside once Maud had started for Piccadilly and extracted the details from the broker. Maud had been distracted, hot and sick, full of urgency. She could have easily failed to notice that Rosa had been there.

But how likely was this, really? How could Rosa have learned that the locket had come from Mrs Leyland? And then there was the question of motive. Why would she do it? What could she hope to gain, or to learn? If she'd only approached, Maud would have told her everything. She would have welcomed the companionship.

The one certainty was that Rosa had known. Maud was well aware that there would be an answer, however – some slick account that she wouldn't be capable of evaluating with any intelligence. Or Rosa would simply deny it, tell Maud she'd misremembered, and that such delusion was only to be expected in someone who'd gone through what she had. There was no evidence, after all. Only her recollection.

No, right then Maud wished merely to carry on upstairs. To be alone and away from Rosa Corder. At least until she was back to herself again. 'I must go,' she mumbled. 'I need to sleep.'

'Maud, please.' Rosa spoke like an aunt, a concerned elder. 'Stay with me just a minute. Come into the light, so I can see you.'

A hand found Maud's elbow, the fingertips closing gently around the bone – the same hand that had directed her around the Grosvenor, the Royal Courts of Justice and many other places besides. She shook it off immediately and made for the stairs.

By the time she reached the bedroom door Maud was aching, positively *aching* for chloral. Every last part of her was demanding it in a low, insistent moan. She could see the bottle so clearly. The way the liquid bent the light. The sound of the stopper as you drew it out. She could feel the effects of it, almost – that delicious numbness spreading through your blood, flopping you onto the mattress, slipping you out of the window into the blue evening, off across the wide, misty river, beneath an endless expanse of stars.

There was a sound somewhere below. It was Rosa, Maud knew it, peering up after her, perhaps considering giving chase. She swerved away from the bedroom door and the bottle beyond, heading instead for the studio – not really thinking, wanting only to reach the furthest point of the house. Getting up there proved a stern challenge. She had to pause on the staircase, for breath and a steeling of the will; and the instant she'd succeeded she realised that it was in fact absolutely the wrong thing to have done. They'd be climbing to the studio themselves at any minute. Of course they would. To see what paintings were left to pawn, most probably.

Panting a little, Maud looked about her. It was strangely light up there, despite the advancing hour; the studio was like a glass-fronted observation deck, set atop a dark barge. Several canvases were out. Rosa's portrait was off to one side, ready for that year's Grosvenor. Scattered among the rest was a short history of Maud's time with Jimmy. The one with the fur coat. The former portrait of Florence Leyland. *The Three Girls*. Several others, more recent, unfinished ones, at different stages of completion. Many hundreds of hours of labour.

By the table, though, was something new: a Nocturne, a still, spectral scene of boats and masts, set upon an icy shore. And by God it was beautiful. It held the deepest beauty that the river could provide. He hadn't painted like this for years, for nearly as long as Maud had been with him. Yet here it was. Whistler had returned.

Footsteps mounted the stairs, candlelight breaking through the doorway. The studio was suddenly dark, the new Nocturne disappearing into shadow. Maud considered hiding, she considered it seriously – over there behind *The Three Girls*, crouching in the triangular space between the canvas and the wall. Then Jimmy appeared, candle in hand, telling her straight away that they were gone; that it had been a business call, a brief but vital stop on a matter related to the show.

'More copyrights,' he said, coming to her side. 'The *Mother*. Miss Corder's portrait. Enough to preserve our hides for a short while longer.' His arm was around her hips; his moustache tickling the base of her neck. She had a keen sense of his concern for her. His need. 'I do hope, you know, that you will feel able to join us again soon. That you will recover your taste for Miss Corder's society. It would be good, would it not, to have things as they were? That day, do you remember, when we made those Thames prints? The four of us together?'

The prints, Maud thought, to which Owl helped himself. She didn't answer. Jimmy moved away, towards the new Nocturne. He asked her opinion of it.

Maud dropped her stoicism. 'It's a fine one,' she said. 'It's a fine one indeed. It's – well—' Looking at it now, lit by Jimmy's candle, something occurred to her: this was a scene of bleakest winter. 'When did you do it?'

'Upon my return from Paris,' he replied, rather rapidly. 'I gathered it in the very same night and laid down the better part the day before you yourself came home. I had so little luck over there, you know. Such rotten weather. I could not find a single blessed subject. And then I discovered the offer from this dealer in Edinburgh, so I went back to it. Back to the Nocturnes. It still has something, wouldn't you agree?'

A problem had been encountered, however, common to all of the paintings still up there. The bailiffs, damn them, these *men in possession*, would certainly prevent any attempt at removal. Right then, it seemed likely that this new Nocturne would not go to Scotland, but wind up on the block in some grubby auction – an unfortunate consequence of the Owl's bankruptcy strategy, and one of the numerous quandaries in which Jimmy's affairs were mired.

Maud went to bed soon afterwards, leaving him to work. A dose of chloral was prepared, but she stopped the spoon just as it touched her lips — setting it unevenly on the floorboards, allowing the drug to drip out and dribble away. Her mind was stirring at last, shaking off its torpor like a layer of frost. Ideas were beginning to form.

The next morning she told Jimmy of the tricks, well known in Kentish Town, that could be used against a writ of execution. Following this, the new winter Nocturne and a couple of the smaller portraits were taken from their supports and rolled up in rugs — which were then sold on the front doorstep, with much loud negotiation, to Eldon, to Willie, to Owl, with the modest sums raised being handed over directly to the nearest bailiff. Japanese teapots left inside toppers. Assorted cufflinks and tiepins were pushed into the lining of one of Maud's more punishing corsets, which she couldn't imagine that she'd ever need again. That grasshopper weight from the privy chain was slid into the toe of a dress shoe. This diffusion of their belongings had an unexpected pleasure to it, an element of the game. As Maud shed the worst of her debility, as she was released from her bed and steadily less of her was sapped away by the drug, she felt the glimmerings of a new, improbable harmony; the promise, almost, of something beyond. For Jimmy wanted her at his side, he really did — to drink down the last of the vintage, he said, as the cellar slowly flooded around them.

A Sunday breakfast was held in her honour, at Jimmy's

insistence, to mark her reinstatement at the Whistler table. He invited several people whom she liked, and who liked her; a couple of unknowns, eminently agreeable types, she was assured; and no Rosa or Owl. The Tuesday before, however, John informed his master that he was leaving, as a result of the continued lack of coin. He'd found a place as a steward on an Atlantic passenger steamer and was due to set sail at the week's end. Maud was rather less affected by this news than Jimmy. They were now without help, though; there would be no one to wait at table. Jimmy said that he would do it himself, but with scant enthusiasm — for it meant labour in place of gossip and aphorising, and a definite departure from his preferred pose.

Then, on the very morning of the breakfast, Maud saw an angle. She approached Mr Donaldson and an associate of his who happened to be on the premises, and asked if they would be so very kind as to assist with the serving of the buckwheat cakes. She'd taken care to charm them, even as she and Jimmy had pulled the wool over their eyes. Some people waged war on men in possession, putting horrible things in their food, their beds and so forth, but she thought it far better to be friendly. It could do no harm; it might well lower their guard. Accordingly, these bailiffs had come to like her. They passed no judgement on the domestic arrangements of the White House. They knew, furthermore, that her health remained precarious, and so they agreed to her request more or less at once. Thus began the rumour that Whistler had his *bailiffs playing waiter* — that he was the master of his ruin, laughing even as the bills of sale went up and the creditors stood in line for their slice of his estate. It spread swiftly throughout fashionable society. Jimmy would come home from dinner in his last remaining suit of evening clothes, cackling as he opened the front door, calling out Maud's name and announcing that she was, without any shadow of a doubt, an absolute goddamned *genius*.

Spring 1879

Jim was installed towards the rear of Lord Archie Campbell's box at the Lyceum, gazing up at the ornate ceiling rose, pondering the many injustices of his life. The box was a good one, naturally, with a superior vantage; Archie and his friend Addington were at its front, leaning upon the upholstered ledge, spotting acquaintances out in the wide, shadowy shelf of the dress circle. Irving's company were a quarter-hour into the first act of *The Merchant of Venice* when something was seen. Jim was waved forward; opera glasses were pressed into his hand, and his attention was directed to a box opposite, a tier below theirs.

'No husband,' Addington said. 'Your chum's elsewhere, Whistler.'

'In the finest company, surely,' murmured Lord Archie, 'that money can procure.'

Each of the children was present, Freddie included. Next to Fanny was an uninteresting-looking fellow Jim took to be the fiancé. And behind them, tucked in a dark corner, was Frances Leyland, appearing for all the world as if she was trying to sleep.

Jim returned the glasses to Lord Archie. 'Gentlemen,' he said, 'I must leave the premises. For the lady's sake. I must not risk embarrassing her, or giving the brute Leyland reason to strike at either of us. He'd never believe that it was chance. Not after everything that has transpired.'

His companions saw the sense in this, and were impressed, plainly, by Jim's keen sense of honour. After a brief farewell he slipped out. The corridor was empty. It curved around the back of the auditorium, lit by fittings with smoked glass shades, turned down low for the performance. He did intend to depart, honestly he did; to head to the White House and to Maud, perhaps via the good doctor's for a finger or two of brandy. But this was an *opportunity*, wasn't it, in a way – unlooked for and unlikely to be repeated. And his presence there was wholly innocent, after all. So instead of taking the stairs directly to his right, he followed the corridor for a distance, descended one level and located the box containing the Leylands. Then he settled down to wait.

Florence, Elinor and Freddie all left the box at a trot, while the applause for the first act was still sounding, heading out for refreshments. Avoiding their attention was a simple matter of positioning: stand six feet upstream, into the curve, and even with a bamboo cane, a crimson-lined cape and a chalk-white forelock, you were invisible. Fanny and her fiancé emerged a minute or so later, at the more stately pace of adulthood. Jim had painted the eldest daughter right at the outset of their connection. Aged fourteen, she'd been a restless, good-natured child, happiest on a horse she'd told him – she'd even chosen to be shown in a riding habit. He thought he saw discomfort in her, there in the Lyceum corridor; a chafing, perhaps, at the fashionable gown she wore. A last remnant of the girl he'd once known. She quickly overcame it, at any rate, taking the arm of the stolid gentleman who'd been selected for her and following after the others.

The mother was left alone, as Jim had predicted. This had been her preference back when he'd shared their box with them, rather than viewing it from across the theatre: the auditorium as it emptied, the rows of vacant seats, seemed for her to hold some mysterious appeal.

Mrs Leyland turned as he entered. Nearly two years had gone by since he'd last stood this close to her. He tried to hide his dismay at the pain and fatigue that marred her lovely face. His mind was knocked quite empty; he bowed, unsure now of what it was he'd come over to say. An avowal of sympathy for her plight and his continued loyalty? But what use was that? What help was he in a position to offer? An explanation of his bankruptcy, stressing that it was not defeat – how he was still fighting, and would win, the declaration being in actual fact the cornerstone of a devilishly clever plan? This seemed misplaced, even to Jim.

She spoke first, hushed and very fast, like someone running out of air. 'Please,' she said, 'go.'

'I am so glad – so very glad to see you.'

'Go,' she repeated. '*Now*.'

'Mrs Leyland, I—'

Her voice was lowered. There was anger in it, he realised, anger at his recklessness. 'The locket. He found out, Mr Whistler. Last Christmas. He found out and he *wields* it against me.'

'I do not understand.'

'The locket I used that day, as my excuse. For speaking with your – your friend. Freddie was made to confess. Poor boy, he had to. And of course Frederick knew at once what my intention had been. He regards it as a betrayal surpassing any of his own.'

Jim was frowning. Was this some ancient secret, shared at Speke, unwittingly jettisoned from his memory? Or was she confused – left half-crazed by the abuses she had endured? He wondered how best to ask her to explain.

Mrs Leyland's head dipped. Her dark auburn hair was plaited and wound up tightly; even in the dimness of the box Jim could see the grey in it. She was flagging, losing resolve, and yet at the same time finding a sort of nervous, confessional energy.

'And so now I am being punished. Oh, how he *flaunts* it. The days of disguise are past, Mr Whistler. He has these women of his ride about in our carriage. He has them wait in it – wait in the street, outside our door. Every day seems to bring evidence of more . . . *offspring*. Of payments made, enormous sums. Apartments kept. He invites my humiliation before all London.'

The old sense of alliance had returned to Jim, along with a compassion so acute that it brought an aching lump to his throat – and a deep hopelessness, for there was nothing to be done here, not really. Nothing more to be said. He tried, of course.

'I'll call him out. I'll do it. The demon cannot be allowed to do these things without consequence. I'll call him out on Prince's Gate and I'll beat him black and blue. You see if I don't.'

It was unclear if this was of any comfort. 'I have Fanny's wedding in July,' Mrs Leyland said, 'and then I will be gone. He won't divorce me, but I no longer care. Let him settle whatever terms on me he chooses. I can stand no more of it.'

A loud, mirthless laugh was heard, away somewhere in the cavern of the theatre. It sounded rather like Lord Archie; it occurred to Jim that those fellows may well have spied him through their opera glasses and were now conveying a warning. Sure enough, the first few people were filing back into the stalls below. The Leyland children would not be far behind. Jim was preparing to go, attempting to compose a halfway satisfactory farewell, when Mrs Leyland grasped hold of his sleeve.

'There is a plan,' she said sharply, staring towards the curtained stage. 'For your bankruptcy. He isn't finished with you, Mr Whistler.'

*

4 June 1879

The moment was precisely timed. Jim was up on a platform, seated behind a table, in a meeting room on the ground floor of the Inns of Court Hotel in High Holborn. It was the first really warm day of the year. The room's double doors opened onto a covered courtyard, each new arrival emerging from the dissolving glare of strong sunlight. Jim smoked cigarettes, awaiting the appointed hour, watching these people take their seats. Most were tradesmen. They conversed with one another, comparing their paltry debts and fanning themselves with newspapers, no doubt savouring this chance to lob a cobblestone at a famous man – to haul one of their betters down into the mud for a prolonged trampling. His people came too, of course. There was Maud, sitting at the rear with Eldon, looking distinctly tense; the Ways, major and minor, nodding over at him in respectful greeting; a couple of his more regular breakfast guests from the White House; and then the Owl, after everyone else naturally, claiming a chair in the very front row with empty seats on either side. He angled himself across the one to his left, laying an arm along its back, and gave Jim a sly wink. For perhaps thirty seconds, everything felt like it might just be manageable – under their control, as Owl had predicted.

A minute before three, however, the shark swam in, scattering the smaller fish: in black, as always, befrilled and alone. The doors were closed behind him. Those lifeless eyes swept the room, without any particular interest. All conversation ceased. Leyland went to the front row as well, to the leftmost end. He removed his topper and sat down.

This wasn't a surprise. All those who wished to make a claim against Jim had been required to present a submission ahead of the meeting. Leyland had plainly been monitoring the bankruptcy's progress, for he'd pounced only a day after the formal declaration with a claim of three hundred and fifty pounds, for those undelivered paintings: the missing portraits of his daughters and (most especially) *The Three Girls*. This placed him comfortably in the top tier of creditors, among the five largest sums. There had been no question in Jim's mind that he'd attend. He had a *plan*, did he not – isn't that what his poor wife had said? The British businessman wouldn't be there merely to gloat either. He'd be seeking influence.

Officiating that afternoon was Jim's new solicitor, George Lewis; for old Reeve, as requested, had finally submitted a bill for his years of patient service – quite a stunningly large bill, it had to be said, too large to feel remotely glad about, whatever the circumstances – and was now an interested party. Lewis was somewhat younger than Reeve, and a good deal more exacting. He now brought the room to order and commenced their business: the first meeting of creditors. The total sum of the debt was the headline – four thousand five hundred pounds, according to papers filed in the London Bankruptcy Court. Announcement of the sum raised a few gasps, some tutting and a snigger. It was proposed, and quickly agreed, that claims were to be settled by the liquidation of assets and a public sale to be held at the debtor's property on Tite Street, Chelsea – with all works of art in his possession to be sold at Sotheby's within a year of the present date. The approximate value of these assets, and the amount therefore expected to be reclaimed, would be determined by a Committee of Inspection.

Jim sat back, frowning into the middle distance. He'd been forewarned about all of this, but it was still extremely discomfiting to hear. A public sale. Good Lord. The mind-boggling *vulgarity* of it.

'This committee,' Lewis continued, 'is to be composed of three members, drawn from among the body of creditors. It is the business of this meeting to select the persons best equipped for the task.'

Owl promptly volunteered his services, as they'd arranged, saying he was a dealer in pictures, rare furniture and *objets d'art*, who possessed a deep familiarity with the debtor's holdings and could make a fair valuation of them. This passed without objection, as did Owl's proposal that Mr Thomas Way, printmaker of Wellington Street, take a place as well. Jim relaxed a fraction, absently considering the colours of the room – the shifting golden browns of a summer afternoon, the slanting square of fiery sunlight upon the opposite wall – trying to disregard the black note at its margin.

'And as a third member,' Owl continued, looking off behind him, 'might I nominate Mr Matthew Eldon, an artist from Putney, who can make an accurate assessment of—'

'I shall serve,' interrupted Leyland. His voice was loud and firm; he sounded a little bored. 'I shall serve on this committee. With all due respect to Mr Eldon, I believe that mine is the more significant claim. I am a businessman, and a collector of paintings now for nearly two decades. I believe I know the value of Mr Whistler's productions.'

The room agreed with exactly the same willingness that it had for Owl and Way. Leyland had reputation, galling though it was to admit. He had authority.

Someone would object. Jim was certain of it. Owl – his disdain for Leyland, the face of modern philistinism, was supreme. Or Anderson Reeve. The lawyer knew of the fellow's wickedness, of his scheming and manipulation. Way, even, meek mouse though he was. He'd heard Jim's tales and been horrified by them. Surely he had a limit.

But nothing came. The business of the meeting continued without complaint. Jim had been told that he was expected to remain silent, for the most part, unless directly appealed to for information. This, though, was too much. To have the British businessman's plan reveal itself so blatantly, to see it unfurl so very blackly and without the least challenge, was more than he could tolerate. And so up he stood, inserting the eyeglass, his chair scraping hard as it was pushed back from the table.

Jim had lost innumerable hours to declaiming Frederick Leyland: railing before that portrait in his studio, recounting the villain's crimes, detailing the scalding contempt in which he was held by so many. And now it was happening. The real Leyland was not ten yards away. There was an audience arrayed around them. Not an enormous audience, it was true – Jim noticed that nearly half the chairs were left vacant – but it was enough.

'And so we see, gentlemen,' he began, 'so we see here before us this afternoon the power of the plutocrat. This, mark you, is how he brandishes his influence – how he makes his grievances known. It must be distressing, must it not, to have arrived at the apex of one's life to discover that you are *only a millionaire*. That it is only because of an abundance of lucre, amassed in the very grubbiest of methods, that your fellow man takes you seriously at all.'

Jim could feel himself straightening as he spoke, his shoulders drawing back; was it an involuntary pride, he wondered, investing his person with the gravity of his words? No – Lewis was reaching around his chair and tugging on the tails of his summer jacket, trying to pull him back into his seat. He ignored this as best he could, throwing out his hand in a scornful gesture.

'*Enfin.* This is what it is to be an artist. We suffer the yoke of the rich. We are subject to their whims and their folly and their desperate, stifling meanness. We suffer it daily, *mes amis*. We suffer it *eternally*. Yet you have before you today the opportunity – you have in your hands the chance – the chance to upbraid – to halt—'

Lewis was persisting, finding strength in mortification. Jim lost a portion of his balance; he rocked up on one foot and was brought down, somewhat more heavily than was dignified. There was a shallow burst of applause, five people at most. Anger struggled with embarrassment. He brushed the curls from his burning brow, the eyeglass dropping out, and glowered away towards the door.

Dear Lord, it was difficult to sit through the rest of it – to listen to Lewis define what amongst his belongings, the painstaking accumulations of a lifetime, was eligible for inclusion in this public sale. Very little stuck; but Jim could hardly help heeding that of his artworks, the unfinished paintings were to be set on the block alongside the finished ones, and sold off just the same. His one reliable line of defence against the philistines had been stripped away.

At the instant of adjournment, Leyland left. Jim gave chase, hopping from the platform, darting back out into the greenhouse heat of the covered courtyard. Leyland was crossing the stone floor, marching over the ribs of shadow cast by the iron and glass roof. Overtaking him, Jim swivelled about to stand in his path.

'So there it is,' he declared.

The shipbroker stopped, resigning himself to an exchange.

He didn't appear triumphant, or even especially malignant, just like a man running short of patience.

'For all these years it has been you. You at the head of it, and you at the goddamned tail. Cheating me over my peacocks. Setting the Board of Works upon my house. Marshalling my enemies for the courtroom. And now buying up my debts – rallying this rabble to bring me down. For that's what you've done, isn't it? You are not *one* creditor, Leyland, but a whole throng of them!'

Leyland fitted on his topper. 'I don't have time for this.'

'It is characteristic, I must say, most *charmingly* characteristic, that you have appeared to claim your vengeance not with that horsewhip of yours but an account book. Punishment with the pen – *Bon Dieu*, very apt! And now, I suppose, London will see the Liverpool shipbroker in a perfect reversal of his patronage, extracting where once he bestowed.'

Now *that* was a line. Jim was sorry that there was nobody nearby to overhear. It was certainly wasted on Leyland. The fellow appeared to arrive at a decision, drawing near and lowering his voice, treating Jim to a close view of the frill, with its primped, creamy folds; the point of that perfectly barbered beard; the smell of his eau de cologne.

'You are a *fraud*, sir,' he said. 'An artistic Barnum. A charlatan pretending to a genius that he does not in the least possess. You deceive the simple-minded. You poison them with your mendacity and your contemptible posturing. I will open up your house and I will put your miserable existence on display. I will show you for what you are.'

A weapon was required, and in something of a hurry. Mind ablaze with blinding white, Jim reached straight away for the most deadly. 'Expose my true state, is that it? The hollowness of my claims to renown? Rather like, say, the serial adulterer, the brazen fornicator, who pretends to lead a respectable family life? Who will destroy a wife he does not deserve for the sake of his boundless lust – for the sake of eating lobster with his harlots? Fathering more bastards along the way than the – the city can contain?'

Was this a threat – an actual threat of action, of exposure? Jim lifted his chin and kept his eye locked with Leyland's; but saying it aloud, finally confronting the rogue with it, had made him uncertain. He knew how these things could go. Drag an Englishman's private arrangements out into the light for no reason but his shaming and you risked shaming only yourself. There would be talk of dishonour, of *ungentlemanly behaviour*, resulting in the disgrace of the accuser rather than the accused. Was it simply too hazardous, even for one teetering on the brink of the void?

Leyland knew all this as well. Of course he did. He stepped around Jim, making for the hotel doors. 'Whistler,' he said, 'you confounded ass.'

*

Jim had always enjoyed destroying his work. *Purgative* was the word, with all the usual analogies applied: the slate

wiped clean, the room swept bare, the dice gathered up
for another throw. Along with his favourite clutch of brushes
and the table palette he'd brought over with him from Paris,
the broad-ended knife was for him a truly vital piece of
studio equipment. The blade must have just the right width
and weight. One had to be able to slide it between the
canvas and the rubbery hide of the paint and really drive
it along – strip off everything, the ground included. He
considered himself to be rather expert at it. In the right
conditions, he could cut away a yard or more with a single
stroke.

This time was different. These were not paintings being
abandoned due to dissatisfaction, but obliterated in a spirit
of defiance. If anything, though, this increased Jim's vigour.
He'd stacked them against the studio wall – portraits of
friends, of Mitford and his wife; a few of Maud; earlier
canvases, nude sketches and little landscapes, that had been
hanging around for a decade or more – each one awaiting
its moment.

He'd returned home from the creditors' meeting in a
state of clear-headed fury. This he'd known for absolutely
goddamned certain: none of these works would have a price
affixed to them to be sold for the reimbursement of Leyland
and his surrogates. Their only worth, after he'd been obliged
to leave the White House and the committee had commenced
its valuations, would be as blank canvas. He'd gone upstairs
in trousers and shirt, rolled up his sleeves and set to it.

Owl had come over, and was watching from the studio

chaise longue as a full-length oil sketch of Maud in grey and blue was removed forever from the earth. He was talking as well, offering rueful reflections upon how completely Fredrick Leyland had blindsided them, along with schemes by which disaster could still be averted.

'Clever though our shipbroker is, there will be ways to regain the advantage. His ploys and stratagems can be turned, you know – flipped about and used against him. And we, as ever, have plans of our own. Those plates over there, for instance. We could value them merely by their weight in copper, and sell them to Eldon for safe-keeping. And of course any inventory we compile will make no mention of the paintings in pawn or away for engraving . . .'

Jim said nothing. He'd worked his way down to the bottom corner of the full-length. It held Maud's disembodied foot, clad in a slipper, like a black oyster shell against the biscuit brown floor. The blade slid beneath the layered paint, prising it free; it curled over, flaking away, lost at once amid the shavings heaped around his shoes. It was as pleasant as ever to listen to the cadence and timbre of Owl's fine rich voice, but the old sense of reassurance was not quite there. A new element had been introduced, Jim decided: a long-limbed, black-clad spanner jammed directly into the inner workings of the machine. The canvas before him was now clean, or as clean as he could be bothered to get it. He took it from the easel and tossed it beneath the piano. His feet dragged a little through the paint peelings – like dead leaves, he thought, fallen from his denuded career. He stood for a minute, a hand on his hip, gathering himself for the next one.

'Just promise me, Jimmy,' said Owl, seeing what was to happen, 'that you will spare your *Three Girls*.'

Jim looked around; the painting in question was off in a corner, on its side, which lent it an odd effect. 'That picture was done for Leyland. He talked, once, of hanging it in the Peacock Room. You can be sure that he'll have an eye out for it, when you come to do your inspection with Way. He'll want to grab it, Owl. A trophy, don't you see? Whistler's scalp, as good as. It has to go.'

Owl sat up, swinging his legs from the chaise longue, in such earnest that he actually put out his cigarette. 'My friend, this I cannot permit. These others are sketches, a mere flexing of your powers. But *The Three Girls* is a full and marvellous expression of them.' There was a significant pause. 'That, old man, is a five-hundred-guinea picture. History will condemn me if I stand by while it is erased.'

Jim firmed his hold on the knife's handle, both irritated by Owl's interference and relieved, undeniably, to have been halted. 'It is too large to be smuggled out,' he said at last. 'Even men as blockheaded as those downstairs would notice.'

Owl wasn't concerned. 'It won't be here – after you have vacated, when we perform our inspection – I promise you this, Jimmy. As your friend. Your devoted friend.' He grew regretful; contrite. 'You blame me for his presence on the committee. I know you do.'

Jim considered this. 'I suppose,' he said, 'that with your understanding of it all, and how it was to run, you might have devised some means to block the fiend's participation.'

'I didn't think that he'd try to become so directly involved. That I confess. But do not give him another thought. I will atone. I will save your *Three Girls*.'

Realising that he was going to relent, Jim set down his one absolute rule. 'He *must not see it*. That is the critical thing. He must have not the least sense that it might be available. Do you understand, Owl?'

Owl placed his hand upon his breast, upon that length of red ribbon pinned to his lapel, and the heart beneath. 'I will see it done. I will see you through this, my dearest old man, to the best of my abilities. We cannot save your fine house – that, alas, is beyond us. But everything of real worth will be salvaged. By the time of the public sale, nothing will be left but scraps and trash. It will be an embarrassment for your enemies, a rank embarrassment. Leyland will wish he'd stayed well out of it.'

The Portuguese leaned back, cracking open his cigarette case, his conversation now wandering off in another direction altogether, as he began to recount an extraordinary dinner he'd had the previous week at a restaurant in Piccadilly. It was a typically Owlish yarn – in which his party was seated and perusing the menu before they realised that the table next to theirs was occupied by a trio of old men with the faces of dogs; whilst just behind were midgets, half a dozen of them, arguing about wine; and across the room, in a tender tête-à-tête, were a young girl with a full ginger beard and a giantess who must have been twelve feet tall.

'A troupe of curiosities, they were,' Owl explained, a little unnecessarily. 'Engaged at the Egyptian Hall, which was only a street or so away. Turns out they took all their meals there. It certainly lent the place a rather singular atmosphere.'

Jim nodded, murmuring something, but his thoughts were on the public sale. He imagined a crowd packed into Tite Street: gentlemen of the press down at the front, his allies among them; a wooden platform, onto which item after item was wheeled out, through the front door, up the steps, for a full display. He went over to a bale of drawings, stowed behind the door, and began rifling through it. Close to the top was a cartoon of Leyland, done a week or so earlier in pen and ink. He'd sketched these things inter-mittently since the Peacock Room – usually during dinner, for the amusement of his companions. This one was unspar-ingly cruel, depicting the befrilled shipbroker as a blackened, reanimated cadaver – jaw gaping, skull bulging, eye staring dully. There was another behind it, similarly monstrous, in which he held a horsewhip in his claw-like hand; and another further back, where a peacock's plumage was bursting from his hunched shoulders.

Crossing the studio at speed, Jim crouched down and pulled a canvas from beneath the piano, one of the larger ones – for it would have to be large. He bore it to an easel and quickly fixed it onto the stocks; then he wheeled around, looking for brushes and paints, barely resisting the urge to leap up into the air.

'Owl, *mon vieux*,' he shouted, 'I believe, yes, I do actually believe that I have found the better way!'

4 June 1879

After the creditors' meeting, Maud found Jimmy in the hotel courtyard, wandering amid the potted palms in a state of some agitation. She told him that she wasn't coming back to the White House just yet, as she'd decided to visit the Grosvenor with Eldon, having only seen the exhibition once since it had opened the month before. A special point had been made of assembling a submission that year, despite their deepening difficulties; not least, Maud suspected, because it gave the exhibited works a safe berth, well away from the bankruptcy proceedings. There was also the matter of his name – the reputation that had to be kept up. Interest in his paintings, he'd been saying, had never been higher, with opinion split between acclaim and denunciation – the standard Whistlerian divide.

Jimmy nodded a half dozen times in distracted approval.

He didn't think to question the timing. 'Pay particular attention,' he instructed, 'to those before the portrait of Miss Corder. The mezzotint is underway, you know. Be sure to mention this to any who seem to like it.'

Maud said that she would. She waited until he was in a hansom, heading back to Chelsea, and then started north. Before Eldon could query this, she informed him that they were not going to see the *Arrangement in Brown and Black*, as it was now entitled, but its model.

No one answered the door. Number 93 seemed empty, just as it had when Maud called the previous summer, on the day of the Albemarle – the day that they'd learned of the second child. She took a breath. The walk from High Holborn had been only a couple of hundred yards, but the hot stink of the city had brought on a shade of fever, a deadening weakness in her back and legs. She'd pushed herself through it, though. This had to be done. Stepping away from the door, she looked along the dusty length of Southampton Row. Nearby, two carts were struggling to pass one another, with all the usual invective. Then she turned to Eldon.

'Matt,' she said, in preparation.

Eldon looked back at her from beneath the brim of his faded topper. 'Miss Franklin.'

The chisel was slender yet heavy, tapering to a sharp, flat end. Maud had bought it on the way, at an ironmongers in Red Lion Yard. She held it out by the blade.

Eldon saw her meaning. He didn't much like it. 'Miss

Corder is Owl's girl,' he said. 'And Owl is Jimmy's man.'

'This is for Jimmy.' Maud planted the chisel's handle in his palm and pointed towards the door. 'Stick it right there. Same height as the knocker. I'll keep watch.'

Despite his reluctance, Eldon proved a capable house-breaker. He bent over, leaning in, applying his weight; there was a groan, a splintering crack, and the door swung open into a dark little vestibule. Maud checked the street; the carts were still there, wedged in tightly now, the drivers almost at blows. Nobody had noticed.

'Wait here,' she said.

'But—'

'*Wait here*, Matt. Shout if anyone comes.'

Number 93 was small and astonishingly cluttered. The narrow hallway was lined with boxes, cartons and bags. There were canvases wrapped in brown paper, crates bearing the stamps of foreign auction houses, a bronze statuette of a naked child riding a goat, two dozen coal black teacups – Chinese, Maud guessed – lined up along the top of a low bookcase. It was like being inside an over-loaded drawer, with more objects than empty space. To the right, through a doorway, where one might expect a front room – chairs, a settee and so forth – was an artist's studio, as disordered and crowded as the hall.

Maud went in, walking cautiously to a tiny patch of bare floorboard in the centre of the room. The shutters were closed. There was a musty coolness, and the mingled smell of linseed oil, chalky dust and mice. The little light that seeped in from the hall fell on a small painting by the fireplace, up on an easel, one of half a dozen that Rosa appeared to be working on. It showed a baby in a crib, not much more than newborn: a round pink face against a patterned shawl. The style was loose, simple – French, Jimmy would call it – and the colours bright; the forms deliberately flattened, very slightly. Maud realised that she had never actually seen Rosa's work before, beyond the odd sketch. It was bewildering, at this stage, to discover the true extent of her talent. She found that she was pleased, delighted even, the result of some residual loyalty; cross, also, that this had been kept from her, like a secret withheld; and upset, yes, very upset, for the infant pictured here made her think with an abrupt and overpowering clarity of her own children. The two daughters that she had now surrendered to others. Those familiar feelings arrived – the nag of panic, that aching, crippling grief – like a load dumped atop a flimsy table, beneath which it swayed and seemed ready to break apart.

This was no good. Maud pressed her eyes into the crook of her right elbow, tears soaking into the grey poplin. They were well. They were in good health and being cared for. It was the only way. And *they were well*. Inaction and misery would not help them, nor would it help Jimmy and herself. She'd come here for a reason.

Lowering her arm, Maud wiped her face on the cuff and sniffed loudly. She was turning away when she noticed the words in the bottom right corner of the canvas, painted as if sewn into the hem of the shawl. It was a name, the name of the baby: *Rosalind Katharine Howell*. Owl's daughter, born to his wife Kitty a year or two before. The Portuguese had set his mistress to paint his child – the daughter that practically shared her name. Maud almost smiled. Now there was a neat bit of arrangement. No one could ever accuse the Owl of a lack of nerve.

The room ran the whole length of the house, from front to rear, with a folding wooden screen dividing it in half. Maud forced one of its central panels back about eight inches or so, fighting against the rusted hinges, to reveal an area that was a bit less dark and marginally more tidy. It was dominated by a dressmaker's dummy, upon which a gossamer thin gown, storm-cloud purple and very much Rosa's in its design, was in the final stages of assembly. Squeezing through, Maud emerged beside a broad desk that had been pushed up against a wall. Across it, gathered into loose piles, were sketches in pencil, pen and ink and watercolour. They ranged from the barest beginnings to finished studies. Some were of clothes, gowns and hats mostly; others, to her puzzlement, she found that she nearly recognised. A number portrayed identical glassy-eyed maidens, playing lyres and reclining on knolls, looking distinctly as if they'd been drawn by Edward Burne-Jones. One sheet, pinned to a board as if recently worked on, held an expert watercolour of a heavy-featured woman brushing her hair. The style was markedly different, richer and more earthly; it seemed to be by another hand altogether. The initials DGR were entwined in a corner.

Maud walked to the desk, standing by its chair; and on the far edge, beneath a jar of charcoal sticks, she saw a single sketch of Battersea Bridge, with the soft, clustered silhouette of Chelsea drifting mistily behind. She slid it from beneath the jar and picked it up. Along the bottom were several attempts to imitate the Whistler butterfly. She lowered it, looking around her in disbelief, almost reluctant to learn what else this part of the room might contain.

Upon a smaller, simpler table beneath the window was a line of photographs. They showed the Leyland children: a three-quarter-length portrait of each one, and then all four of them together. The images were no more than a year old. Rosa was in the early stages of applying a coloured tint; beside the photographs were half a dozen brushes standing in a glass of cloudy water and a ceramic palette smeared with paint. Maud was frowning now, frowning hard, but she was composed, her mind making the necessary connections. She had a strong feeling that something was still missing. Then she turned again, towards the interior wall, and there it was.

The portrait was a head and shoulders view, roughly life-sized. It was unfinished, the brushwork raw in places, but already Frederick Leyland appeared dignified and darkly handsome. You'd take him for a statesman or a great composer, lofty thoughts seeming to glow within that wide forehead. It bore little resemblance, in terms of temperament at least, to the person Maud had seen at the creditors' meeting only an hour earlier. Jimmy had tried to dissuade her from attending, saying that her health remained delicate; that the strain of it, the provocation, might prove too much. But she'd been determined. She'd wanted to hear every word, and to make notes too. As the White House underwent its painful disintegration and the shape of the future began to materialise, she'd resolved to stay on her damned toes. It'd be like the trial, she'd told him. She'd keep to the back, out of the way, and would leave if she felt herself ailing.

There had been a crucial difference, however. Beforehand, in the hotel's covered courtyard – after Jimmy had left, going on ahead to talk with his new lawyer, and before Eldon had appeared to escort her once more – she'd spied the great absence from the Court of Exchequer. The Owl, huge and pristine, had been cruising around the courtyard's periphery, making not for Jimmy but a public lounge on the building's eastern side. Maud had watched as he'd greeted someone within, rather more surreptitiously than usual, and had withdrawn with them to a nook away from the entrance. She'd shifted position, skirting a cluster of thin, cast-iron columns to lengthen her view into this lounge, and had seen something that at first had made no sense. No sense at all.

Owl had been with Frederick Leyland. Even at a distance of twenty yards, standing half-silhouetted by a bright window behind, the association between them had been plain. Leyland's attitude had been of slight complaint, and Owl's of deference, as he made an effort to explain something, tapping one extended forefinger against the other. It had been a dense exchange – that of men with a purpose of some kind and little time in which to lay it out. After only a minute they'd broken apart, Leyland leaving the lounge and stalking back towards the hotel lobby. Owl had selected an armchair and lit a cigarette.

Maud had met with Eldon soon afterwards and had gone into the meeting room on his arm. She'd made no notes. She'd heard Owl's voice, and Leyland's; and poor, fuming Jimmy, attempting a righteous reproof and being halted by his lawyer. She'd known then that she had to act. Answers were required.

Out in the street, Eldon said her name, as a warning; then she heard him address someone else, rather more casually, and a woman reply. It was quick, far too quick. Rosa Corder was over beside the baby painting almost before she could turn from Leyland's portrait. A stare ran between them, a line scored through the stale air. Each had caught the other red-handed: Maud in her trespass, her mistrust – Rosa in something rather deeper and darker. This is the moment, Maud thought. This is exactly it. But she stood absolutely still, incapable of movement or speech.

Rosa, of course, was not. She was wearing a sort of tailored habit, the colour of ground coffee, with folds gathered around the neck. Her hair was up, pinned in a wave; the hat in her hand sported a huge, snow-white ostrich feather. Her talk was light at first, making no comment on Maud's presence, or the fact that Eldon was posted on guard outside – asking forgiveness even, for her rapid entrance into her own home. She'd been taking her supper in an establishment across the road, she said, when the proprietor had told her that a couple were at her house and were going inside, which had put the fear of God into her as she'd thought that Maud might be her landlady, tired at last of the unpaid rent. Now she'd learned otherwise, she was acting as if she was pleased. As if she thought that Maud had called to rekindle their friendship.

'At last,' she declared, 'at long last, you are in my studio!' – and then she commenced a little bloody *tour*, describing how the sun's rays moved through the room, which work was suited to which area, and so on.

'I had to know,' Maud interrupted, after a minute of this. 'That's why we broke in, Rosa. I had to know what you were up to.'

Rosa swallowed; she shrugged, brushing the ostrich feather across her knee. 'I can't imagine what you think you have uncovered, Maud, but I—'

'Mrs Leyland's locket,' said Maud. 'The one she gave me. You mentioned it that day, back at Sharp's Hotel. Don't you remember? I hadn't told anyone about it, not a soul. And yet you knew. I couldn't work it out, not for the life of me.'

'There isn't—'

'But now I see.' Maud looked at the Leyland portrait.

'The husband must have learned about the locket somehow, from the son I expect. He told this to Owl, who passed it on to you – and you were so busy pretending sympathy, pretending concern and friendship and the rest of it, that you forgot what you were and what you weren't supposed to know.' Maud's anger was gathering pace. 'The whole thing was to get you two in Leyland's good graces, wasn't it? Win you his patronage and much else besides, I'm sure. Your blasted Owl heard that Jimmy and Leyland were in difficulty over that dining room, and so he went at once to offer his services. To become Leyland's spy. His *agent*.'

Rosa was studying her hat, picking at the feather. 'I don't know how you can say these things,' she murmured. 'It wounds me to hear them.'

'He's been steering Jimmy wrong, hasn't he, on purpose? The house. The bloody *trial*.' Maud had a sudden, chilling vision of a conspiracy, its tendrils stretching in every direction; a trap, almost. 'Did he *know* how that was going to turn out? Anderson Reeve said that the judge more or less told the jury what to decide. To award Jimmy that farthing. Was the damned judge one of Leyland's too?'

Rosa merely sighed, as if these questions were both irrational and faintly tiresome.

'Your Owl has been encouraging every mistake, every bit of foolish bravado – and taking whatever he could for the pair of you along the way. The prints that summer. This copyright business. All that missing furniture.' Maud realised that the sketch was still in her hand: the counterfeit Whistler, now a little crumpled. She held it up. 'And *forgery*, for God's sake. What were you going to do – try to sell it as an original?' As she spoke it occurred to her that this would be a rather strange course, given the present state of Jimmy's prices. She lowered the drawing and dropped it to the floor.

'That was an experiment only,' Rosa said. 'It was never my intention to—'

'And now bankruptcy. The grand finale of Leyland's revenge. The crowning bloody masterpiece. Jimmy Whistler ruined once and for all. And Leyland himself on the committee, granted leave to rifle through what's left of his possessions. I saw them, Rosa. Leyland and Owl – earlier, before the meeting. Planning it all out.'

'This is delusion.' A note of warning had entered Rosa's voice. 'I have accepted work from the man, yes. And Charles knows him. Of course he does. He knows everybody. We have to eat, Maud. We are still your friends.'

Maud barely heard her. 'I suppose that Jimmy is just your Owl's latest mark. There was Ruskin, whose every secret he's since spilled for the amusement of his companions. There was Gabriel Rossetti. We never did learn the reasons for that parting – although I see that you're copying him as well. He's a humbug, Rosa, a bloodsucking rogue.' She faltered, her train of thought reaching an unwelcome juncture; the rage, so bright and enlivening, dimmed to grey dismay. 'And you knew of it all. You went along with it. You talked to me of art. Of what we two might do together. You lied to me.'

'Come now, you really mustn't be so dramatic.' Rosa tried to meet Maud's eye. 'You've suffered. I understand this, far better than you think. You have been gravely unwell. Given up another child – two in as many years. That is a dreadful burden, Maud. I fear it has left you confused. It would do that to anyone.'

Lord Almighty, thought Maud, she's bloody well trying to make me cry. To sob my way into her forgiving embrace. Twisting about, ignoring the twinge that cut beneath her hip, she planted the hardest kick she could upon the easel bearing the incomplete Leyland. It was dashed down, crashing against the wooden screen. The canvas came free, flipping away like a playing card and clattering behind the tailor's dummy. A dog started to bark somewhere out at the back.

'I knew that something was wrong. I *knew it*. I'm not quite the idiot you take me for. Your absences. Your promises and plans. The way Jimmy first brought you in, to calm me after Ione. But I did not suspect that you were making fools of me and Jimmy both.'

At this, Rosa Corder's patience finally expired. She set aside her ostrich feather hat. 'I don't think you're an idiot, Maud, but dear God you are gullible. You drink down anything that's put in front of you. Don't you realise how Jimmy takes advantage of this? His wide-eyed girl from the lower orders?'

'You don't have a single clue about Jimmy and me. You don't—'

'If you aren't careful you'll end up in the same sad position as Jo Hiffernan. He'll have you living at his convenience, as a nursemaid for his bastards. As a supplicant, begging for coin, made to look on as his career advances and another woman replaces you at his side.'

'He would never do such a thing. You don't have a *single clue*.'

'Frances Leyland,' Rosa stated next, as if the name was an argument in itself. 'Your Jimmy would have left at once had she asked him to elope with her. He wouldn't have given it – given *you* – a second thought. Did you really not see it?'

'That was friendship only,' Maud countered, about four fifths sure. 'An alliance against that – that brute you're so damned pleased to be painting for.'

'Did you imagine also that he was actually in Paris last winter – when you were readying yourself for the birth?' Rosa, standing there in her disordered studio, was quite calm; rather frightening in fact. 'Dearest Maud, he never left Chelsea. He never left the White House. Those letters of yours, propped so nicely upon the hotel mantelpiece with their Parisian postmarks, were just another little falsehood. He forwarded them to an old friend of his over there, who obligingly sent them on to you. And you never for a moment suspected, did you?'

This time Maud could not frame a reply. She had noticed a certain vagueness in the letters. Jimmy's observations on the French capital had tended to be brief, a line or two at

most, and news of his friend Lucas next to non-existent
– the main business of the correspondence being to revisit
the Ruskin trial, and *Art & Art Critics*, and the wickedness
of Frederick Leyland, in typically forthright terms. Just
Jimmy, she'd thought. Just how he was.

Rosa softened. 'I have deceived you,' she said. 'I admit
it. But I cannot apologise for taking work from Frederick
Leyland. I must make my living, Maud, however I can.
Society barely tolerates a woman artist. You know this as
well as I do. I have no wealthy family to carry me along,
nor a list of Academicians willing to lend their influence,
nor an artist husband to further my interests. I have Charles
Howell.'

'You two are bloody liars together.'

Rosa's expression was almost pitying. 'Yet so much of
what I said to you was not deception, not at all. About our
kinship, Maud. About how we two can help one another,
and learn from one another. Those plans of ours can still
come to pass.'

Maud shook her head. The pattern was simply too obvious
now: an unsparing blow followed by a caress, by concilia-
tion and endearments. You are a hopeless blockhead – yet
we are alike, engaged in the same struggle. I have lied to
you, exploited you – but we can still be the firmest of
friends, allies in a lifelong fight. It suddenly became unbearable. She studied the mess for a moment, plotting a path
out to the hall that gave Rosa the widest berth. Then she
levelled a final glare at the woman before her, and was

amazed, quite honestly, by how unruffled she was, how very certain of herself and her assertions.

'Rosa,' she said, stepping past, 'just shut it, will you?'

Outside, Eldon had news. Owl – he was almost completely sure it had been Owl – had come along the street in a hansom, but upon seeing him standing there had instructed his driver to keep going, off into Bloomsbury. Maud veered south, towards the Strand, seeking only to put distance between herself and Number 93. She wasn't moving anywhere near as swiftly as she would like.

'Get us one,' she said. 'A hansom. Quickly.' We will be well, she told herself. There is an answer to this. We will be well.

'What's happening, Miss Franklin? What happened in there?'

'Quickly, Matt!'

*

It was early evening by the time Maud reached Chelsea. They'd had just tuppence between them, her and Eldon, which had meant no cab and a long walk, broken by stops on benches and low bits of wall so that she could recover her strength and wait for various little pains to subside. Next to nothing had been said; Eldon had seemed to understand where things stood, though, and carried on down the embankment with a tip of his hat. Maud approached the White House. She was desperately footsore, faint with headache and coated in dust, but she wasn't finished yet.

In the hall were two men – put there, she thought, by the building society: a terrier-like fellow called Watson, and another, square-faced and younger with rather red eyes, whose name she couldn't remember. They sat cross-legged on the floor, playing dice; as she entered they gathered up their coins and counters, rose to their feet and bade her a good afternoon. She returned their greeting, assuming an easy manner, assuring them with a wink that she had no cash concealed about her person. Watson gave a laugh; the red-eyed one grinned sheepishly.

'He in the studio, Mr Watson?'

'Where else, Miss? Hard at work on his pictures.' Watson put on a voice, high and strained – a passable imitation of Jimmy's drawl. 'Making gold, don't you know, Watson old chap. Making gold.'

The other one chuckled in a way that suggested he'd heard this before – that they both found Jimmy ridiculous. Here's the difference, Maud thought: for all their civility and lack of censure, they would never think to mock a man before his wife.

'Any sign of Mr Howell?' she asked next, a touch more sharply.

The good humour ceased. Something about the Portuguese prohibited mirth. Mr Watson started to sit, readying his dice for another round. That fellow had been there earlier, he told her, but was gone now. Mr Whistler was alone.

Maud climbed the stairs, her forced smile fading, her heart feeling like a lump of cold mud. Honesty was needed.

A straight account. This was where they had to begin. She would tell him about the locket, about Mrs Leyland's warning, and then about everything else, right up to that afternoon in Rosa's studio. The Owl would be knocked from his perch and chased away. They could confront this bankruptcy without any further confusion or falsehood. She'd collect together all the papers – take them to Edie perhaps, and Mr Crossley – and they'd progress from there.

After Southampton Row the studio seemed especially vast and empty. Jimmy was working in the soft evening light, so absorbed in a large canvas that he didn't notice Maud's arrival. Upon the table palette, in amongst the tubes and jars, was a four-pint paint pot, made from tin with a string handle. From the drips running down its side – from the smears on his hands and clothes, and the principal colour of the painting on which he toiled – she could tell that it was part of the stock of peacock blue left over from Prince's Gate. As she walked forward, light shifted across the picture's surface and there was a faint metallic flash. Jimmy was laying in coins with Dutch metal, weaving them once again into peacock plumage, the way he'd done in that mural of the fighting birds. The patterns used were the same, an act of deliberate reconstruction; but applied, she discovered, to a truly grotesque end.

Past Jimmy's shoulder was a face, a frowning golden mask with a black, pointed beard: the day's second portrait of Frederick Richards Leyland, and the precise opposite of the first. Full-length this time, the shipbroker sat hunched at a grand piano. He'd been transformed into a gruesome monster – a man crossed with a peacock, Maud supposed it was, made in part of money, the hands upon the keys being little more than a jumble of golden, coin-like feathers. The inevitable frill at his neck was mirrored by one sprouting atop his head, a peculiar, ugly comb; his long leg terminated in a peacock's bony claw. Drawing nearer, she saw that this creature's anger had a cause. At its neck was a barbed stinger, attached by a long whip of a tail to a Whistler butterfly hovering overhead, for which it looked around in vain.

This thing was a couple of hours' work at most, painted crudely on unprepared canvas. But it had a charge to it, a blunt force, its joyful malevolence shot through with a dogged sense of triumph and a seam of the very darkest bitterness. Maud's determination fled. It left her as if it had never been. How in heaven was she to tell Jimmy that his closest associate, his dearest friend, was in fact in league with his most hated enemy? That he had been all along, it seemed, for a matter of years now, undermining him on Leyland's behalf, encouraging him to act against his own interests, and surely gaining some secret satisfaction in the results?

For they were demolished. That was now beyond doubt. Very soon they would be *homeless*, for pity's sake. Maud began to grow fearful. How would the foster parents be paid? What would happen to their daughters? Bold action was called for. This she recognised. But they could not afford for Jimmy to be distracted any further than he was already. She had to think.

Jimmy turned around. The fretfulness of the Inns Court Hotel was quite gone. His sleeves were rolled up past his elbows, his moustache and eyeglass flecked with peacock blue paint. Seeing Maud, he smiled so broadly, with such unchecked glee, that despite everything she felt herself beginning to smile back.

'And how was Miss Corder?' he asked. 'Was she not stately – gazing down with queenly disdain upon the rabble milling about her feet?'

Maud froze for a second; then she realised that he meant the portrait in the Grosvenor. 'She was. Like a – a queen. It was a great success.'

No more was required, thankfully, as he wanted to move them on as quickly as possible to the canvas fastened to his easel. The title was the first thing he pointed out. It was written inside the book of sheet music propped open on the piano stand, with certain letters – an F, Maud noticed, and an L – festooned with little frills. *The Gold Scab*, it read, and beneath, *Eruption in FRiLthy Lucre*. The peacock feathers were next, and the coins tucked into the plumage; the bags of loot piled atop the piano; and then the stool – *Bon Dieu*, the stool! He almost hopped on the spot. It was the White House in miniature, with its double front and steeply pitched roof – the original design, prior to the involvement of the Board of Works. This hideous bird-like version of Frederick Leyland was literally perched atop it, his threadbare peacock tail fanning out over the façade.

Summoning the required response proved more of a challenge than usual. Before Maud could speak, however, Jimmy dashed past her, over to the far wall. There stood another two of these painted cartoons, each around half the size of *The Gold Scab* and rather less complete. One showed a pair of lobsters, bright red, cavorting in a black, treacly waterfall – making love, it looked like; the larger of the two had a frill at its neck, poking out between segments of the shell. The other depicted a great boat, wrecked upon an ochre hillside.

'Noah's Ark,' Jimmy told her, 'at the slopes of Mount Ararat.'

From a crack in the ark's hull streamed a procession of pale faced, black-clad people, winding down the mountain into the foreground. Every one of them, both male and female, had the same bulging forehead, the same staring eyes, the same tapering black beard and frilled shirt: an unsettling multiplicity of Frederick Leylands. Disappointed by her blank-faced reaction, Jimmy set about talking her through it, something about how just as Noah had repopulated the earth, so Leyland – with his reckless scattering of his seed – was in the process of repopulating London. Instead of bringing the joke alive, though, this account rather confirmed its death. Jimmy raised an eyebrow and admitted that it was perhaps slightly obscure, which was why he'd decided to make *The Gold Scab* a good deal more *direct* in its attack.

A feverish feeling still clung to Maud, her head thick and throbbing, but irritation was now keeping her alert. Why on earth was he submitting to distractions and grudges when so much else remained to be done? 'What are they for?' she asked.

'Why, Maudie,' Jimmy replied, 'they are to be left behind.'

'At the White House? In here?'

'*Naturellement*,' he said, casually sly; then his excitement flared once more and he rushed out an elated explanation. 'He'll march up, won't he, the instant he's admitted, to start rooting through the canvases for what he imagines to be his. And this is what he'll find. This is *all* he'll find. There are plans in place. Everything but these fine pictures will be gone – stored in safety with the doctor, with the Owl. With our allies. And these three here will be wheeled out before the whole city. Carried downstairs for the sale. Put on display in the street. Written up in *The World*, the *Athenaeum*, the *Art Journal* – even *The Times*. Word will circulate throughout the country. Overseas, I should think. He'll be exposed for what he is. A philistine who has driven out his wife. Disgraced himself with his greed and his faithless promiscuity.'

Maud swallowed. 'Isn't there a – Jimmy, isn't there a danger to this?'

'From Leyland, you mean?' Jimmy laughed. 'What would he do, precisely – *ruin* me?'

Maud couldn't pretend to any expertise on the codes and manners of wealthy society, but she knew how it could be with secrets – how they often ended up blackening all who touched them. 'Not from him. From everyone else.'

Jimmy was unconcerned. 'My dearest girl, I assure you that I understand very well what is appropriate. This has such a beautiful poetry to it, don't you see? And there will be much rejoicing at Leyland's discomfort. Seldom has a man been so widely scorned and reviled. Why, only last week a lady was telling me—' He was off now, slotted into his favourite groove, ready to run on indefinitely. But Maud had heard enough.

'I know about Paris, Jimmy,' she said. 'I know what you did.'

This stopped him, at least. He took out his eyeglass with the slightest trace of nervousness. He expected a detonation, plainly, tongues of flame, the righteous wrecking of his studio. And maybe he deserved it. Maud remembered Rosa's words on Southampton Row. *He wouldn't have given you a second thought.* She felt a sudden need to test him. To ask for something.

'We should go away.'

Jimmy stared; then he looked back to *The Gold Scab*, trying to disguise his relief. 'Away to where?'

'You said you'd take me abroad. Right back at the beginning, when I first came to you. Don't you remember?'

'Dearest Maud, I said a great many things.'

'You said that you'd take me to Italy, Jimmy. To Venice.'

He was considering it now. 'It might be a deft move,' he reflected, 'to absent myself from the country as the committee does its work. As the cartoons are discovered and my enemies rage. And Venice – it is true that I have long thought of passing a month there.' He sighed. 'The tin, though, my girl. The blessed tin.'

Maud found that she was ready for this; more than that, she had a *solution*, towards which Jimmy had only to be nudged. 'What about the Fine Art Society? They've done all right with your plates, haven't they?'

In truth, Mr Huish's payments had become the one thing keeping them from complete destitution. The connection was made, thankfully; the two parts fitted together. Jimmy stood very still for a while, his eyes fixed upon Peacock Leyland's scaly foot. Then he snapped his fingers.

'Maudie,' he announced, 'I have had the most marvellous idea.'

*

October 1879

There was a whistle-blast outside, and an unintelligible shout further along the platform; a white curtain of steam was drawn across the window as the train began to pull slowly from the station. Maud thought that she was to have the compartment to herself, but at the last moment a man climbed in. He was a priest, a wiry, vigorous-looking sort of about sixty; in a cassock and cloak, no less, with one of those black, broad-brimmed hats. Once his valise was stowed, he took the seat opposite Maud and introduced himself in serviceable English. Her hair, he explained, had enabled him to guess her nationality, there being scarcely any redheads in France; and before you knew it they were chatting along quite happily, about Paris, as the train left the city behind, and the different journeys that lay ahead of them. She removed her gloves as unselfconsciously as she could, in order to display the ring. It was cheap and plain, barely silver at all – but there on the relevant finger, should anyone think to check. She told the priest that after a stay with a family friend on the rue de l'Arc de Triomphe, she was joining her artist husband in Venice, where he was etching views of the city for a special society in London. Saying these things to such a person felt good; it felt pleasingly legitimate, after all these years of God knows what.

Everything had gone rather well. They'd had some luck at last – although Jimmy had grown cross when she'd put it like this.

'It is not *luck*!' he'd cried. 'By thunder, girl, it is my rightful goddamned due! Or about *half* my due, I should say – for they know what they're doing, damn them. They've got themselves Whistler at a bargain price.'

The money had seemed generous enough to Maud. The directors of the Fine Art Society had voted to advance Jimmy one hundred and fifty pounds on a set of twelve copperplates, with an option to purchase for seven hundred upon on his return. She'd known him turn out a plate in two or three hours. If Venice was as beautiful as everyone said, he'd be done in a fortnight. A few paintings could also be made; there was talk of pastels. They'd return with one definite sale on the cards and a good chance of very many others. They would have means. They could begin anew.

'He will want the views, then,' the priest said. 'It is a good field, oh yes, a very good field for painters. He will be wanting the sights.' The old fellow began, counting on his fingers. '*Le palais des Doges. La catedral de St Mark. Le Rialto.*'

Maud nodded along, trying to remember as much as she could. 'He's been studying photographs,' she replied. 'He will certainly have ideas.'

They parted at Dijon, the priest's destination. He blessed Maud before he went, crossing himself and so forth, which was sweet. Minutes later, though, wandering on the concourse with her carpet bag, the evening crowds streaming around her, she couldn't say that she noticed any benefit. Perhaps such things simply didn't work on the non-observant – or the actively sinful, which she supposed she must be. Perhaps they just slipped off like an ill-fitting shoe.

It was frightening, this journey, well beyond anything she'd undertaken before. She was absolutely alone, somewhere in the middle of a foreign country. There was no one she knew for hundreds of miles. Rosa came unbidden into her mind, urging courage, clear-headedness, self-reliance. Her brow furrowed. Looking around for a distraction, she spied a large, well-lit restaurant on the opposite side of the station.

The dinner she got there was unexpectedly good: two slices of rare beef; just-cooked beans that squeaked against the teeth, swimming in a sharp, oily sauce; a glass of rich red wine poured from an earthenware jug. Sitting by a window, she looked through the English art papers that Mr Lucas had bought for her in the Gare de l'Est. While in Paris, she'd been on the lookout for detailed news of the White House sale, now nearly a month in the past – the dispersal of effects, the sale of the building itself, its owner's flight overseas – but it had barely been noted, with a few lines at most. There had certainly been no mention of huge painted cartoons. She could find nothing in these issues either. It seemed increasingly likely to her that Jimmy's scheme to shame Leyland, of which he'd been so very proud, had been foiled somehow.

Maud paid and gathered up the art papers, dropping them into a bin on her way out. She made the next train with time to spare. They departed, and were quickly clear of the city. Outside now was darkness, broken only by the occasional patch of gaslight, illuminating a road crossing, a wayside tavern or the passing platform of a provincial station. It was quiet enough, her carriage being almost empty and a fair distance back from the engine, so she put her bag behind her boots, undid a couple of her corset's lower hooks and went to sleep.

She woke suddenly, her head knocking against the window frame. It was night still. The carriage was moving noisily beneath her, clattering from one set of rails to another – crossing the intersection, she saw, as they approached a large station. She turned to discover a man, rather fat and fast asleep, sitting directly across from her. They'd been two strangers together, six feet apart and dead to the world. This gave her an odd feeling. The sign for Modane slid by the window: her next change. Relieved, she rose from her seat and reached for her bag, patting the top to find the handle, taking care not to knock knees with the fellow slumbering opposite.

It was only the middle of autumn, yet Modane was freezing, the snow piled so deep and packed so solid it was as if the station had been dug out from under it. The change was quick, but the train into Italy proved disconcertingly popular. Parties were hastily claiming compartments for themselves – lowering blinds, making beds across seats. Maud had to settle for a coupé at the rear of a carriage, where it was cramped and rather cold. Giving up on sleep, she pulled her coat more tightly around her and concentrated on the view.

They were in the mountains now. The massive forms were just becoming visible in the deep blue of early dawn: the ridges and dizzying peaks, the black forests, the glowing veins of snow. Maud knew that she should be stirred, that she should reach for a sketchbook, or at the very least try to fix things firmly in her mind – the elements of a picture – as Jimmy would do. She felt more diminished, however, than inspired. Staring up at something that staggeringly huge seemed only to reflect her own unimportance. Her total nothingness.

The Alps had been top of Edie's list of great things, ahead

of anything she could think of in Venice. A strange dance had been done when Maud had called round to say goodbye. Beforehand, she'd vowed that she would be both detached and decisive, that she would not on any account allow her sister to make her feel guilty, or bereft, or anything else. This was being done for money, to improve a circumstance that had grown truly dire. It was what was required. She'd had fifteen pounds with her, in fact, taken from Jimmy's advance, to leave for the foster family – enough to see them through to the new year if necessary.

'Do you think you'll be away that long?' Edie had asked. 'I thought it was only to be for a month at most.'

And then there had been tears, great heaving sobs; for the fact of it was that Maud and Jimmy would have to remain in Venice until his commission was complete, and there was absolutely no way of knowing how long this might take. He had etched plates in two hours, it was true. But he'd also fussed over them for weeks on end. Maud hadn't wanted to go to Italy any more. She hadn't even wanted to go back to Chelsea.

'Just sight of them,' she'd said. 'Just for a minute. Surely that would be all right?'

Edie had refused, though, as she always did, stating that it would make everything more difficult and add to Maud's troubles; and then she had actually set about talking up the trip, in an attempt to repair her sister's resolve. The list of great things had been rolled off, with visible effort. The majestic mountains. Gondolas. Carnival masks. Maud had been told that she would be able to rest, and recover her health at last; that Jimmy would work, to begin rebuilding his fortunes; and that perhaps, when they returned, the situation could be different.

By Turin, Maud was heartily tired of solitude. She went out into the blinding morning sunshine, shivering her way along the side of the train. The carriages seemed every bit as full as they'd been in Modane. Putting down her bag, stamping her boots upon the icy platform, she looked off at the city's dense mosaic of terracotta roofs; at the horizon beyond, a jagged white line of mountaintops, unreal in its perfection; at the flawless sky overhead, only a shade more blue than black. She wanted to laugh aloud. What the *devil*, she thought, am I doing here?

English was being spoken somewhere on the train, among the Italian and French. Following it, Maud discovered a little family, a mother and her two adolescent sons, with a compartment to themselves. The mother – simply dressed, even-featured, capable-seeming – agreed to let her join them, introducing herself as Mrs Holt and her sons as Duncan and Richard. The boys fell quiet, both being old enough to be rendered mute and red-eared by the arrival of a young woman. Noting the intricate beaded pattern at the hem of this stranger's skirt and her tiny, fashionable hat, Mrs Holt was keen to establish her respectability. She was a widow, she said, journeying out with her boys to winter in Milan with her brother, who was a successful trader in cured meats.

'Italian hams,' she informed Maud, 'are quite without equal.'

Nestled in a warm corner, the chill beginning to leave her body, Maud suddenly felt quite exhausted – ready to nap and nothing else. The woman's expectant expression served as a prompt, however. She pinched the ring through her glove, rotating it on her finger.

'Mrs Whistler,' she said. 'I am heading down to join my husband in Venice.'

Mrs Holt didn't seem to recognise the name. 'To travel such a distance alone,' she said, acting as if impressed. 'Why, I don't believe I could do it. Although I must say that these two ruffians here are more burden than boon, the majority of the time. Do you have any children, Mrs Whistler?'

The steam whistle sounded up ahead. Maud stayed quiet for a few seconds, wondering if there was some kind of challenge concealed within this question; if an assumption had been made. She considered embellishing her fraudulent propriety – the daughters left with relatives, perhaps, to be collected before the year was out, when their father's work was done – but it was more than her weary mind could manage. She looked out at the platform, just starting to move away now, and shook her head.

'I do not.'

December 1879

Maud came in from the staircase and shut the door behind her, brushing powdery snow from her sleeves. Under her arm was a package wrapped in paper and string, a couple of letters collected from the Café Florian, and a loaf of bread shaped like a little torpedo. Jim watched her from their bed, on the far side of the dingy two-room apartment. Still too poorly to do very much, he'd passed the morning in dismal contemplation of the equipment and materials he'd brought with him from London. There were copper-plates and etching tools, barely touched; pastels and chalks, which had seen only a few days' use since his arrival nearly three months before; and the brushes, a dozen or so of his best, the heads as neat and dry as on the day they'd been bought.

The last of these, right then, seemed particularly vexing.

Venice was a place for Nocturnes. Jim had known it from his first evening in the city – when a winding lane, no wider than the span of his arms, had brought him to a stretch of moonlit water, looking out towards the dome of a distant church, almost lost in the mists of the lagoon. There was no money, though, for the necessary paints, and the quantities of linseed oil that Nocturnes required. Neither was there any blasted *space* – no room for a table, nor for the pacing and lunging that attended on such work.

And of course there was the cold. This Jim had failed to anticipate. One had an idea of Venice that stood quite apart from the season, derived from Canaletto, the lithographs of Lessore, and old Turner, he supposed: sun-bleached squares and shady canals, gondolas drifting in the still warmth. That the city also existed in *winter*, and was subject fully to its debilitating hardships, came as a most unwelcome surprise. It was a bitter one as well, worse than Chelsea by a considerable extent – colder even, he reckoned, than those he'd known in St Petersburg as a boy. It was a climate in which clothing served as no protection, and fire struggled against the chilling dampness that rose up from the water.

Money, however, accepted no excuses. The past few years had taught him that, at least. Huish's advance allowed only for starvation rations, and the meanest accommodation on the Rio di San Barnaba, but the president of the esteemed Fine Arts Society had known that the man before him had to take whatever was offered. There was only enough to last until Christmas, realistically speaking; any longer and they'd be subsisting on cat's meat and cheese parings. So he'd prepared his plates, readied his tools and forced himself out into it.

Yet at first – well, for weeks – this watery city had confounded him. It was like a knot of beauty: an entanglement of views pulled so damned tight that it simply could not be untied. The necessary immersion would not come, due to the nagging worry that there might be better just around the next corner. And then, when one did finally stop – sit on a ledge or step, pull the plate from one's pocket and slide the needle from its cork – both copper and steel would be like ice; rather colder than ice in fact, and painful to the touch. Fingers shook and grew numb in moments. The whole exercise had rapidly acquired the complexion of farce.

Inevitably, Jim had fallen ill, brought low by the most burdensome and tenacious of colds. Maud, still not yet entirely well herself, had become concerned and fetched in a troupe of local medics. During the course of their examinations, a number of bystanders had become involved – the landlord, the neighbours, a delivery boy with a parcel for upstairs – everybody providing opinions and arguing with the doctors while the invalid had sniffled somewhere between them, quite forgotten.

For there was a contrast, Jim had soon discovered, between the silence of the city, with its shadowy alleys and spectral reflections, and the great noisiness of its populace.

He found the language wanting in refinement and a degree of exactness; and the *religion*, dear God, the religion was accompanied by a clamour of bells protracted enough to rouse the dead. One Sunday, devilishly early, he'd been driven downstairs in nightshirt and coat to remonstrate at the church door. A group of deacons had emerged to fend him off, and they'd rowed for ten full minutes beneath a blackened painting of St Barnaba healing the sick.

In short, Jim had come to be dogged by a sense of the *opéra comique*, as if he was wandering unwittingly from one ridiculous scene to the next. His life appeared to have become some kind of allegory, an absurd and very cautionary tale.

Maud moved out of sight – to the dresser? To look out of a window? Jim craned his neck, asking in a hoarse and plaintive voice if she would be so kind as to pass the letters. She came through, impassively handed him two envelopes, then walked back. He could tell from the handwriting that they were from Way and Nellie, his brother Willie's charming wife, who was proving to be more inclined to correspondence than her husband. His hands were shaking a little at the thought of the news they might contain. This was the other great impediment: a really quite dreadful and unexpected homesickness. The painter of London, of its bridges and lovely fogs, had been uprooted, transported many hundreds of miles from his rightful province; removed from the clubs, the galleries and the theatres; from the hansoms, the fine French cuisine and the *luxury* – from all that he enjoyed and deserved. At times he wanted to paw the ground, like a racehorse kept from its race.

His people too, his boon companions – he missed every man-jack of them. In the depths of his illness, he'd fanned out his unused paintbrushes on the bed and named each one for his absent friends. There was Theo for block shapes, and Alan for details; Archie for certain highlights, like the spread of fireworks; Matthew, the very largest, for great sweeps of sky and water – for those Whistler fogs. And the trickiest, a brush with a triangular head and lush deep bristles, purchased for him by Maud from a colourman in Soho – which he'd found versatile, suited to all manner of tasks – he'd called Carlos.

The letters were torn open and devoured in seconds. Jim slumped back, the pages falling limp in his hands. They were dear people, Way and Nellie, and they meant well, but their correspondence seldom failed to disappoint. Jim was writing more than he had in his entire life – and receiving *nothing*, it felt like, in return. They dashed off a couple of pages, a few vague mentions of this or that, allusions and inferences rather than complete tales. No meat. No *spice*. He had never felt more away from things. From everything in the world that was important.

The state of the show, of course, was a matter of constant speculation. The White House had been sold, that much he'd discovered, to a dull dog on *The Times* named Quilter; which was enough, in large part, to chase the crows off his carcass. But the fate of his work, the paintings he'd been obliged to leave in the studio – and those he'd left there very much by design – remained tormentingly unknown. A further sale was scheduled for the new year, at Sotheby's, of drawings, canvases and so forth. But much more than that nobody seemed able to tell him.

Owl, as always, was the real mystery. He'd disappeared in the weeks prior to Jim's departure, another of those unexplained absences, not even showing himself in the last wild days when Jim and Eldon had careened around the empty White House. They'd scrawled aphorisms above the doors, sung rude songs at the studio piano, composed mordant missives to lawyers, accountants, receivers, and to every enemy on the books. Yet throughout, no matter how much liquor was consumed, both had been looking over their shoulders, half-expecting one of those famous, nonchalant entrances – and feeling a touch let down when it had failed to arrive.

All Jim had were rumours. A new life by the sea, somewhere down in Kent. Tours of the Continent, of Belgium and the Netherlands, in search of the usual opportunities. Rather more perturbing hints of meddling at the Fine Art Society – suggesting to the fellows there that their great etcher was neglecting his commission to perform other work. Jim had written to the Portuguese at some length, scolding him gently for his misinformation, and urging him to come out to Venice himself, where there were many chances indeed for Owlish enterprise. This elicited nothing. The letter might as well have been posted into the lagoon.

The lack struck him now, in his gloom and dissatisfaction. He looked to the paintbrushes, standing in an old vase atop the mantelpiece – to Carlos, the versatile brush with the triangular head. 'Owl, *mon vieux*,' he said. 'I have left you the show. Do be so kind as to tell me how it goes.'

Maud was listening – looking through from the other room. 'Perhaps he's avoiding you.'

Jim sighed. Maud had been down on the Owl for some time, since long before their departure from England. The cause of it he'd been unable to discover. 'He is my friend,' he told her. 'You do not realise, I think, what he has done for us.'

Coming closer, Maud leaned against the doorframe. She considered him for a moment, crossing her arms. She seemed unimpressed.

It sometimes struck Jim as perfectly incredible, given the extent of his reversals, that he still had this excellent young woman at his side. Her compassion astonished him. Her love gratified him. He was helpless before her, really. *Affinity*: yes, that was the word. Being here, alone in a land absolutely foreign to them both, had allowed them to rediscover their affinity. As he'd languished, coughing and sneezing and so on, she'd resumed her artworks, those flowers of hers – positively radiant in the colouring, if still a little naive in the forms. He'd provided her with guidance and correction, and they'd been master and pupil once more. In return she'd cared for him, and had him go out, when he felt well enough, on expeditions: walks on the

Lido, to marvel at the sunsets; or to acres of Tintoretto, hidden away in remote chapels, that had left him positively stammering with ecstasy.

And yet how, in total honesty, could one not grow weary with the constant company of another? Of being isolated with them – required to live with them in poverty, and in exile? It would be impossible. There was a simplicity to her, an *ordinariness* almost, that had come to infuriate him. Her remarks, at times, as they strolled through the city's sewer-smelling labyrinths, had made him damned near bite his knuckles in annoyance.

'So pretty here,' she'd say, 'isn't it, Jimmy?'

Signs could be detected as well of a melancholy cast to Maud's mind, worsened by the malaise that had lingered in her since the second birth. She was writing even more letters than Jim, to sisters and aunts – and to children, he'd begun to suspect. To daughters. Matters quite dealt with, as far as he was concerned. On her ring-finger, too, was that cheap bit of pewter bought for the purposes of her journey down from Paris – but she'd yet to remove it, even after he'd made a couple of rather pointed comments. He'd heard her on the stairs, in the alleys and the markets, introducing herself as Mrs Whistler. She'd done this back in London, it was true, with tradesmen and moral types, but only on occasion and where strictly necessary. Here it seemed her adopted name. Jim was not known for his perceptiveness when it came to the thoughts and feelings of others, yet he could detect a slightly fraught quality to his *Madame*, as she kept them both going through those desperate, frozen months – the faintest sense of strain.

Today, though, she was taking no nonsense. 'There's word at Florian's,' she said, 'of some English passing through.'

Jim tilted back his head, pressing the letters over his face. 'Who could it possibly be, this far out of season? A disgraced actress? An eloping earl?'

'The Leylands,' Maud replied. 'Quite the party, it is. The father. Fanny and her husband.' She looked at the floor, fiddling with the buttons of her well-worn coat. 'They say she's already with child. Due in the next few months. And the rest of the children too. Bound for Trieste, then away on a tour.'

Jim lifted off the letters and looked up. The last he'd heard of this family, Mrs Leyland had left, just as she'd said she would in the Lyceum, and requested a separation. 'When?' he asked.

Maud didn't know, but it made no difference; in less than a minute Jim was clattering down the stone staircase, a soft felt hat on his head, passing the bamboo cane from hand to hand as he pulled on his coat. He rushed onto the Rio di San Barnaba in amongst a sparse early evening crowd, heading left – no, right – no, it *was* left – towards the nearest footbridge. He'd not been out much on his own, in truth, and had stuck mostly to the Dorsoduro. As a consequence he had only the vaguest idea how to locate the railway station.

Maud was at his elbow. 'What are you doing? What d'you think—'

'I shall be there to *greet him*, Maudie!' he cried, jabbing his cane into the air. 'I shall be waiting at the goddamned gate! Our dear friend Leyland must be congratulated on his – *ha!* – his new-found freedom. On his liberation from the marriage bond that he regarded with such contempt.'

Years before, one Christmas at Speke, they'd talked – the family and James Whistler, then their *cher ami* – of embarking on a tour of Europe, of the places they could visit together. And here the fiend was, having dispensed with the troublesome painter and driven out the blameless wife, embarking upon it without them. It seemed at that moment like an insult. Yet another inexcusable affront. The notion came to him, there in the grey Venetian twilight, of a duel. Why the blazes not? Such a thing could happen here in a way it could not in London: a fight with pistols, or swords, or some other instrument of death. Or at the very least there could be a good solid punch-up in a square somewhere. A dunking in one of those marble fountains. A whipping – yes, a whipping! Give Leyland a dose of his own medicine. It was the stuff of which legends were made, quite frankly. A bit of poetic goddamned justice.

'Jimmy,' Maud said, tugging at his coat. 'We don't have the first idea when the train gets in. Which train it is, even. Are you just going to wait in the cold all evening? How long—'

He shook her off, plunging down a canal-side path, over

the hump-back of another little bridge; then he paused at a junction, beneath a gas jet, and screwed in the eyeglass as he realised he had no idea at all where he was.

'I can't miss him,' he said, starting off to the right. 'Don't you see, Maud? I simply *can't*.'

The street widened, becoming a small campo with a white statue in the centre, some saint or other, besides which five or six men in heavy winter coats were smoking pipes around a brazier. Halfway across, Jim got a sense that this was in fact leading them in the wrong direction – that it went off to the north-west, towards the main loop of the Grand Canal. He circled the statue to find himself facing Maud, panting up behind him, obviously close to her limit.

'This is useless,' she gasped. 'God save me, Jimmy, but I – I honestly don't understand what it is you hope to do.'

Jim glared up at the darkening, colourless sky. A crescent moon was shining behind a thin sheet of cloud. Droplets of ice were clustering in his moustache, he noticed, and at the corners of his mouth. There was a fierce tickle at the base of his throat – a cough building.

'How the *devil*,' he croaked, 'did you imagine I would respond?' He flexed his fingers around the end of his cane. 'Hang it all, Maud, why in thunder did you tell me this?'

Maud approached, her breath misting around them. She took his arm, his shoulder, gathering him in. 'Come,' she said. 'Let's go back. It's bloody freezing out here.'

This was evasion, of course; something in her manner,

usually so guileless, brought Jim quite abruptly to the verge of an overwhelming insight.

'But then,' he said, 'why is Leyland in Italy at all? A tour will take weeks, surely. Months. He's on the damned *committee*. He made a special point of joining it, didn't he, so he could get at my paintings – *The Three Girls*, and others as well no doubt. But if he's out here he'll miss the sale. The one at Sotheby's.' He looked again at the frozen moon; at the saint, his marble head bowed, his arms outstretched. 'Why in heaven's name would he miss the sale?'

Maud pulled in her shawl, trembling against his side, saying nothing. And there it was. She wanted him to ask these questions. This was the reason she'd told him.

*

With the advent of the new year, Jim's cold finally retreated. Away went the extract of malt and the throat pastes; back came that old sense of wanting to *show them*, to show them all. The best revenge, so the saying went, was living well. Jim could not completely agree: he'd always felt that the best revenge lay in some form of exquisite public humiliation, or a good thrashing. Nevertheless, he still found plenty to like in the thought of victory, of artistic triumph and soaring prices – in buying back everything that had been taken from him. As he was too poor for oil, and the city too chilly for copper, he decided to pick up his pastels instead, venturing outside with a drawing board and a few sheets of coarse brown paper.

And all at once, it seemed, the secret places of Dorsoduro were revealed: alleys, courts and bridges; decayed marble-clad palaces and passageways of ancient brick; the wide, sweeping skies. They came to him quickly, three or four studies a week, in flaming reds, dusky blues and oranges, and those cool, soapy whites that only pastel could supply. And they were good. He was sure of it. He felt again the bellows' roar of pride; his soul leapt high and wild. Whistler was restored.

Maud saw it too, bless her heart. She laughed when he showed her the first ones, a gleeful little hoot, and declared them the most wondrous things; then she squeezed him tight and planted kisses on his jaw, his neck, his earlobe.

'They'll sell, you know,' he said into her hair. 'I really don't see how they can help it.'

Along with Jim's self-regard returned his sociability – initially centred at first, rather to his bemusement, upon the American Consulate. The consul and his wife, having discovered him at work one day and learned who he was – having *known* who he was, actually, and been most pleased to make his acquaintance – took to inviting him to gatherings in their splendid dwelling at San Maurizio. From this, other invitations inevitably sprang, at palaces up and down the Grand Canal. Jim was unused to spending time with Americans, beside his brother and mother and a couple of others, and the directness of their manners required some adjustment on his part. At times, he could not quite escape the sense of being under examination – of being before a board of inspection perched alertly upon a sixteenth-century sofa, attempting to get the measure of a character rather resistant, it had to be admitted, to easy definition.

Thankfully, not all the people encountered in these American palaces were of a diplomatic cast. As the winter eased, writers and composers and even artists began to stroll onto the scene. These young men, it transpired, had all heard of James McNeill Whistler as well; they were rather in awe of him, in fact. He soon discovered that they needed very little convincing to lend him money, and were glad to provide artistic materials gratis – meaning oils at last for Matthew, Alan and the rest of them. Several were regular visitors to the watery city also, and knew where fun was to be had. Venice slowly took on a rather different aspect.

Details from London, however, remained unforthcoming. The whole show had collapsed into shadow. Jim decided to be philosophical about this. There was little left to be lost in England, in truth, and everything to be gained in Italy. And of course now he knew the reason for it; for one question led inevitably to another and the natural conclusion was reached – or confessed to, it felt like, somewhere deep within him. A number of weeks still had to pass before he was able to speak of it. He was at the Rio di San Barnaba, out on the narrow balcony with Maud. It was late; he'd just returned from a reception at the consulate. He wasn't sure if he'd woken her or if she'd been awake already, but she'd put on her coat to join him for a cigarette.

'I mean, it's obvious,' he said.

Maud pursed her lips to exhale and looked at him enquiringly.

'Leyland has someone there. To watch his interests. Leaving him at liberty to tour the Continent.'

Maud stayed quiet. She smoked, shivering slightly as she stared up at the stars.

'He has lawyers, of course,' Jim continued. 'Lawyers by the dozen. But that isn't it. My fellows would see them off one way or another. It was shown in the Court of Exchequer, was it not, what a lawyer knows about art. No. Maud, I – it—' He stopped. 'It must be treachery. And there is really only one culprit.'

There was a short silence. Maud bent down to grind out her cigarette in a broken saucer, then leaned against the wrought iron balustrade.

'I suppose we shouldn't blame him. What's the use? The Owl is a creature of coin – drawn irresistibly to its deepest reserve.' Jim pulled at his moustache. 'The duplicity, though, Maudie. It is deuced hard to take. That he stood at my side and spun me his stratagems, whilst trafficking all the while with the enemy. With *Leyland*, for God's sake. The things he told me and had me do – to think that in reality—' He glanced at Maud. She'd been waiting for him to make this deduction, he saw. She'd been waiting for some time. 'Great heavens, you knew,' he said. 'What did you know?'

Maud shrugged. 'Nothing really. A feeling.'

Jim sensed omission here, but was too damned blue,

frankly, to go after the full story. He had begged this person for their aid. He had been so grateful when they had seemed to offer it. With Owl he'd been at his most vulnerable — and yet the fellow had been sniggering to himself, more than likely, as he'd extended that helping hand.

Very well: now he was angry. This was firmer, more familiar ground. He strode back inside, emerging a moment later with that triangular-headed brush. He felt its weight, studying the long, supple stem and the bright metal band at the base of the bristles. Then, gripping the rounded end, he bent it way back over his shoulder and sent Carlos spinning down into the canal.

March 1880

Mr Bacher was a tall man – good-looking and sandy-haired and very *full*, Maud thought. Walking by his side, she felt like an invalid once more, frail and sallow, worn down by the winter and sliding back slowly into the ailments of the previous year. She found herself leaning in on him, allowing herself to be guided, firming up her hold upon his arm. He came to Venice every spring, he told her, usually staying until what he called *the Fall*, and was entirely comfortable with the place – Maud couldn't quite think of it as a city – in a way that she knew she never would be. She'd realised the other day that she hadn't seen a horse, hadn't smelled manure or heard the clip-clop of hooves, in nearly six months. There was something uncanny, also, in those chipped, floating palaces, striped with pink and white; the stone saints with missing fingers, gazing down lovingly from their alcoves; the shadowy little churches, their plaster crumbling, inside which you'd come across a gigantic painting by Titian or one of those other swells. It was like a dream at times, and not necessarily a pleasant one. It set the mind going in all manner of unexpected directions.

Venice was cold that day, as usual, and overcast; it was also busy, busier than Maud had yet seen. Vegetables by the crate-load, chickens in cages and countless other things were being unloaded from boats, with much shouting and gesticulation. Mr Bacher navigated it easily, while asking her endless questions about Jimmy. He was only slightly older than Maud, from the city of Boston he said, and an artist and etcher, set up in a large, ramshackle house on the Riva San Biagio with half a dozen of his countrymen. All of them were perfectly fascinated by the artistic celebrity – the *American* artistic celebrity – that they'd discovered in their midst. As they went on, she began to suspect that Mr Bacher had offered his assistance – with an errand to a stationer's and a couple of other shops – merely so that he could subject her to some uninterrupted quizzing.

'Why, then, did more men not come forward to take the stand? He's popular, isn't he, in London – with the great painters there?'

Maud stepped around a confused goat. She didn't answer.

'He's told me that a number of his friends disappointed

him. But why on earth would they do that? Surely it would have been an honour – for such a noble cause—'

'He received a lot of poor advice,' Maud said. 'There were people he thought loyal who have proved themselves otherwise. The whole thing was – it needn't—' She gave up. 'Honestly, Mr Bacher—'

'Otto,' he murmured, 'please.'

'Otto. It was a peculiar time. A most peculiar time.'

'He showed us the damages at Florian's last night. That single farthing, on the cord around his neck. There was much ominous talk about how he wasn't finished with them – with Ruskin and his crowd. What d'you think he intends to do upon his return?'

Good Lord, Mr Bacher, Maud wanted to say, he doesn't *know*; he doesn't have the foggiest bloody idea! She was tempted, also, to reveal that the coin on the cord was merely the latest of several Jimmy had claimed were *the* Ruskin farthing. Shortly after her arrival, in fact, she'd watched him flick one defiantly from the Rialto, into the waters of the Grand Canal.

Instead she said, 'Another pamphlet, I'd imagine. Perhaps some kind of public address. He's been talking about that a fair bit.'

'My dear Mrs Whistler,' laughed Bacher, 'he's been dashed well *doing* it, every night this week. Why, they nearly ejected him from the Orientale, he was making so much fuss!' With that he embarked upon an affectionate imitation: crowing, unmistakably pompous, but self-mocking as well.

'The Masterpiece, *mes amis*, should appear to the painter like a flower. It has no reason to explain its presence. It has no mission to fulfil.'

Maud tried to smile, wondering why it was that people always thought she'd want to hear their impersonations of Jimmy. It was true, though, that this tendency of his to pontificate – to deliver his rules and edicts, of which there seemed to be so very many – was becoming more marked. A fresh and willing audience had been stumbled upon, its knowledge of the trial and everything afterwards limited to a handful of brief newspaper reports, which meant he could remould the legend in any way that suited him. Furthermore, this group from the Riva San Biagio was especially keen to laud a countryman who'd raised the standard for art, for the practitioners of art, in one of the great nations of Europe.

'Nothing in the least bit great about it,' Jimmy had declared once, in Maud's hearing. 'It is the land only of damned ignorance. Of coal-smoke and parsimony.'

For along with his passion for lecturing, a new stridency had appeared in Jimmy's sense of himself as an American. It was something he'd made very little of previously, back in Chelsea, beyond his buckwheat cakes, Edgar Allan Poe and the occasional mint julep. His accent, around his young artists at least, grew noticeably riper, shedding some of its careful imprecision. And in a really rather dizzying turnaround from his initial homesickness, he now bowed to none in his monumental scorn for England and the English – for the Academy and the Grosvenor both; for Queen Victoria, the foundlings in the boot-black factory and every godforsaken soul in between. It was difficult for Maud not to resent it; to be concerned by it for a whole host of reasons. Even Jimmy realised this.

'I don't mean *you*, Maudie, of course,' he'd told her a couple of days earlier, 'when I say these things. You stand apart. You and one or two others.'

'You talk as if you'd never go back.'

He'd laughed. 'Oh no, my girl, I shall certainly go back. There are scores to be settled, are there not? Heavens, you know more of this than anyone.'

'When, then?' she'd asked. 'Just so I know.'

And here he'd grown vague, and talked for a while about the work he still had to do: more pastels, Nocturnes in oil. 'We must empty the treasure chest, mustn't we, before we haul anchor and sail away?'

It was baffling. Maud had thought that once Jimmy had realised the truth about Owl he'd be looking to return home as soon as possible, to set everything straight. Cause a bit of fuss, as he so liked to do. But this just did not seem to be the case.

'What about Mr Huish? The Fine Art Society? Aren't they expecting their plates?'

'The Fine Art Society,' he'd snorted, 'has us living out here on pennies. They can wait.'

Thwarted, Maud had fallen quiet for a moment, chewing on a fingernail. Then she'd decided simply to come out with it. 'What about the others – those you trusted with the show? Don't you wish to—'

'*They can wait.*'

The stationer's shop was as busy as the canals. It had a long marble-topped counter, rather like a tavern bar, with goods arrayed behind. Maud was known there. She stood out, she supposed – even more so today, with Mr Bacher beside her. The one clerk who spoke capable English took her order: material for correspondence, pens, ink and paper, much in demand on the Rio di San Barnaba.

As Maud was going through her lire, trying to hide from Mr Bacher how precisely she had to count out the lire, the clerk was called away, a few yards down the counter, to attend to another English-speaking customer. She glanced over. A clean-shaven man in a dark suit and a short hat was addressing the fellow in the loud, excessively clear voice used habitually by the English with foreigners. Mourning paper was under discussion: four different options, with various widths to the black border, and weights to the paper itself – and on one, the most lavish, sad little *putti* perched in each corner. The clean-shaven man turned, his voice lowering, to consult with someone standing a step or two behind him: a woman, dressed in black, with a black hat and veil. The style of both was Italian, albeit modestly so, and they looked new. She came forward – she was young, Maud saw, and very slim – to consider the paper laid out on the counter, lifting the veil from her face.

Maud started, coughing rather hard, and dropped several

of her coins on the floor. She crouched at once to retrieve them, as did Mr Bacher, almost knocking heads as they pinched the thin discs from the floorboards. The American helped Maud back up and returned the lire to her hand.

'What is it, Mrs Whistler? Are you well?'

'Thank you, Mr Bacher. It's nothing. I am – it is only—'

He was no fool, worse luck; he'd noticed where she'd been looking. 'Do you know them? Are they from London?'

There seemed no point in denying it. She nodded.

'Shall we . . . talk to them? Do you know who they are mourning?' Mr Bacher had an enthusiasm in him, for all his solicitousness, as if he thought he'd landed in the middle of an authentic Whistlerian drama. 'I shall find out.'

'*No*,' she hissed, 'No, Mr – no, Otto, don't—'

Too late. Mr Bacher would not be halted. Maud turned away, but watched his progress reflected in the glass doors of a display cabinet. He started with the clean-shaven man, a servant it appeared, yet soon gained an audience with the young woman, who, she saw now, was quite indisputably Florence Leyland. The tall American removed his hat and bowed. From the dips of his head, and Miss Leyland's weary gratitude, Maud could tell that he was offering his condolences. Her order was ready; she paid, sliding coins across the counter. Mr Bacher was back at her side before she'd finished stowing the package in her canvas shopping bag.

'I regret to report,' he said, 'that Miss Leyland has lost her sister.'

Maud thought of the Royal Courts of Justice; of the two

daughters berating their mother as they led her back to their pew. Of the portraits – the riding habit, the close-fitting gown, the child in the blue dress – all of which she believed Jimmy had now destroyed.

'Did she say which one?'

'She did not. But her party is only stopping in Venice for a couple of hours, to change trains on their way back from the north-east. They are returning home as quickly as possible for the funeral. Letters are being sent ahead so that preparations can begin.' Mr Bacher put on his hat – dark blue felt, rather like Jimmy's. 'Hence the paper.'

Maud looked along the counter once more. Miss Leyland and the servant were leaving the shop. He was going outside, holding the door open for her; they were heading left, back towards the railway station. Maud pushed past Mr Bacher and started after them.

'Who is she?' he asked, falling in behind. 'Was she a part of the trial? A – a patron?'

'Otto,' said Maud, 'just be quiet for a blasted minute, will you?'

The station was not far – over a small square and across the Grand Canal. Six trains were lined up within, beneath the iron and glass roof, the engines at alternating ends. There was a large, mobile crowd; musicians playing somewhere, a violin and a trumpet; the smell of coal-smoke and roasting chestnuts. Part of the Leyland group was assembled on a platform in the centre, an assortment of bags and packing cases piled beside them. Maud stopped a distance off. She could see Florence; her brother, red-bearded and lost-looking, a black band on his sleeve; and several others, similarly attired, who she couldn't identify. As she was taking it in, a whisper passed through them and they all turned towards the concourse – almost to where Maud and Mr Bacher were standing. She tensed, and nearly fled; then she spotted the true object of their attention.

A wet-nurse was approaching, Italian from the look of her, clad in black lace with an infant in her arms – a babe that couldn't have been more than a few weeks old, its little pink face peeping from the swaddling. Another woman, also a servant, walked a few feet behind the nurse; and there, trailing to the rear, was Frederick Leyland. Maud could almost hear Jimmy's voice, railing on about counting-house rats, philistine businessmen, befrilled barbarians. No frill could be seen that day, though – only a long black frock coat buttoned up to the Adam's apple and a dull black topper pulled low over the brow. Leyland passed close to Maud, within six feet, but he didn't notice her. His eyes seemed bruised, so deep were the shadows beneath them; his beard was growing ragged.

As the wet-nurse reached the party, another of the Leyland girls emerged from a railway car. It was Elinor, the youngest, as drawn and dreadfully despondent as the rest of them – meaning that it must be Fanny, the elder sister, the new bride, who was dead. The father carried on to his son; a couple of words were exchanged, then Leyland senior climbed aboard the train. He reappeared in the window a few seconds later, directly above his surviving children and his grandchild, removing his hat, sitting in darkness.

It was like a painting, Maud thought – one of those huge modern scenes by Mr Frith or Mr Fildes, so prominent in the Academy and despised so fervently by Jimmy and his friends. *A Death Abroad*, it might be called. *The Unscheduled Return*. The millionaire's party, with its retinue of servants, dazed by their loss. The listless confusion of the surviving children. The widower, that older man from the Royal Courts, standing a few yards apart to smoke a cigar – given charge of the infant whose birth, it would seem, had killed his young wife. The raw misery of the father, up there in the carriage, a hand now pressed across his brow. The aching absence of the mother. It was too awful. Dear God, too awful.

Mr Bacher, hurrying to keep abreast, managed to offer Maud a handkerchief. She snatched it from him, mopping at her eyes as they left the station, then blowing her nose noisily as they crossed back over the canal. She'd lain on that same bed. Sheets soaked through with her blood. Death stretched out beside her, silently waiting. Fanny Leyland's fate was so very nearly hers as well. She found a wall, a rounded stone ledge, and clung to it; a sob shuddered through her, buckling her knees.

'My dear Mrs Whistler,' Mr Bacher was saying, 'I – I honestly did not realise that there was a personal attachment here. I should have listened to you earlier, in the shop. I am an idiot. This is a self-evident fact. I apologise, truly I do.' He paused. 'These things are tragic, terribly so. I had an aunt who died in such circumstances. My uncle, afterwards – he couldn't forgive his son. Not ever. It – it shaped them both.'

He fell quiet, thank the stars, for a minute or two, sunk in his recollections. Maud stood upright and wiped her burning eyes on the last dry corner of Mr Bacher's handkerchief. She was wondering if she'd have to offer some kind of explanation when he spoke again.

'Was that older fellow the one from Whistler's photograph, over at the Rio di San Barnaba? The patron who refused to pay for his dining room?' He lowered his voice a little. 'The peacock fellow?'

Maud stepped back from the ledge. More than anything else, she felt enormously tired. It would be best, she knew, for Jimmy to learn about Fanny Leyland's death in the fullness of time, through his usual channels. There was no possible benefit to them telling him now. She sniffed hard; she shook her head.

'You've got to be careful, Otto. With Jimmy, I mean. You must've noticed how he can be. Finding out about this won't help him. He'll become angry. Or morose. It could halt his work completely. The prints, the pastels. The lot of it.' She looked into Mr Bacher's open, eager face. 'Do say that you'll keep this between us. Please.'

The American was nodding. Maud saw that she'd played this just right. The fellow revered Jimmy, as so many young men seemed to do. He wanted to be trusted. Her appeal, the mystery of the whole incident, had left him intrigued and deeply gratified.

'I will, Mrs Whistler,' he said. 'I will.'

*

'*Mes élèves*,' cried Jimmy, as they arrived back at the Rio di San Barnaba, '*au moment parfait! Ici*, Bacher, *ici!*'

He was over at the dresser, its top cleared to make a narrow etching desk. The eyeglass was inserted; the acid feather poised between thumb and forefinger. Various bottles and bowls were arranged around the dresser's edge, and in the middle was a copperplate, one of the first, which he'd brought home the previous day. It bore a view across the lagoon to San Giorgio Maggiore, in which the great church was nearly lost behind a mesh of masts and rigging. He waved Bacher over, ready to demonstrate the Whistler method of biting the plate. Jimmy had always been generous with both time and advice, and supremely unconcerned about professional secrecy; and besides, Otto Bacher had his own press and considerable knowledge of the art shops of Venice. He was a good friend to have.

Maud left them to it, going through to the back room. She took off her hat, gloves and jacket and sat on the bed. Jimmy's pastels were on a low table beside it, in a folder now quite full, each study preserved carefully between two sheets of tissue paper. A new one, that morning's work, lay on top, left there for her to admire. It was lovely, as lovely as all the others – a curved canal lined on one side with empty gondolas, a white wall reflected perfectly in the water – yet she did not call out to him, as she might usually have done. She felt a flat fatigue with it, with everything here; with giving Jimmy what he needed; with her own work, to which she might now choose to apply herself. This lay on the floor beneath the table – a rather smaller pile of drawings in chalk and pastel, and a couple of watercolours. They were of flowers, as always, whatever she could find in the markets. Jimmy had been kind about them, offering praise and a fair bit of guidance. Right then, however, she couldn't even look their way. Instead, she filled one of the new pens and began a letter to her sister.

> Dearest Edie –
>
> Forgive me – it has been only four days I know since last I wrote and I have not given you the chance my dear, with all you have to do, to write back – but the question of their well-being weighs on me – it weighs on me most dreadfully. I know I should not ask you – that I have no right to ask you – but might you think for my sake that you could pay a visit to

There was a crash from the other room, something glass being knocked over; an exclamation from Mr Bacher and a curse from Jimmy; her name shouted loudly. She set aside the letter and went through. Mr Bacher was in the middle of the room. He'd taken off his jacket and was examining it – holding it up to the light, and also away from his person. Jimmy was still by the dresser, upright and quite motionless. The wet feather was in his hand; the eyeglass swinging on its ribbon. Maud saw that the acid solution had gone over, the bowl tipped somehow, its contents running fast across the surface of the dresser and dripping down into a wooden box used to store his shirts.

'Maud!' he yelled again. '*Maud!*'

'Yes. Christ. Yes, Jimmy. I'm here.'

The top shirt had been heavily splashed and was beyond salvation. Maud plucked it out, folding it over to guard her hand before using it to wipe the dresser's acid-streaked flank; then she started on the top, pushing back bottles, jars and instrument cases to mop up the spill. Bacher laid his jacket on a chair and came to help her. He removed the empty bowl and gingerly lifted out the plate – it seemed to be unharmed, luckily – holding it level to protect against any accidental biting. Soon it was done. Maud made a quick check for damage – the dresser's varnish was starting to bubble in several places. She realised that Mr Bacher was staring at the wall behind, where the room's only decoration was to be found.

Two large photographs were pinned to the plaster: two lurid illustrations of Jimmy Whistler's most ferocious side. There was a portrait of himself, one of that odd pair he'd had done at the start of the year – the harsh one, standing aloof with a cold snarl – as if ordering someone thrown in a dungeon, it always seemed to her. Its kindly counterpart had been presented to dear Mr Lucas back in Paris.

Beside this was an image taken in the very last days of the White House. It showed that cartoon, *The Gold Scab*: Frederick Leyland, half peacock, hunched at the piano, being stung by the Whistler butterfly. It was from this hideous likeness that Mr Bacher had recognised Leyland at the railway station. He kept his word, though, meeting Maud's eye for only a second before turning to Jimmy – who remained fixed in place, the acid feather raised – to ask a question about retouching.

The shirt was discolouring, its fabric breaking apart. Maud slid between the two men, opened the doors to the balcony and stepped outside. The sunlight was unexpected. For a few seconds she could see almost nothing; she blinked, glancing about her, as the world reformed from blinding whiteness. An empty terracotta plant pot stood just to the left of the doors. She dropped the shirt in it and doused it with rainwater from a small watering can.

Honeysuckle covered one end of the balcony rail, wrapped tightly around the patterned metal. The plant was beginning to bloom, its thick scent mingling with the chemical odour that seeped from the shirt. Maud cupped one of the larger flowers in her hand, collecting together the long, curling petals; it was so loaded with colour – a deep, luscious orange, those spots of vivid crimson – that it seemed to hum against her skin. She released it, letting it bob back among the leaves, and leant on the rusty rail, feeling the light on her hair, on her shoulders, through the thin cotton of her gown. Here at last was a real, suffusing warmth. She squinted along the greenish canal below, at the boats and mooring posts; then she closed her eyes and lifted her face up to the sun.

Autumn 1880

After a spell of resistance, the cork surrendered to the screw with a rich, round plop. The blood-like liquid glugged into the triangle of little glasses, the waiter then retreating, setting the black bottle at the table's edge. Thomas Way, Way Junior and Jim Whistler each took one, chinking them together before raising them aloft.

'To you, Mr Whistler,' said Way, in his honest cockney tones: *Mistah Vistlah.* 'Things have been deuced dull without you, sir. A year late!' He looked to his son, and both laughed. 'An entire blessed *year* late!'

They drank. Jim winced at the taste: port, sickly sweet and slightly warm. England.

'What did Mr Huish say when you walked through his door? Did he throw things, perhaps?'

'I cannot deny, my dear Way,' Jim answered, wiping his

top lip with a forefinger, 'that in the very first instant he was not overly pleased to set eyes upon his wayward etcher. But, as you know, we artists have a great advantage in these situations: our work. When I told him that there were three times more plates than we'd agreed, and damn near one hundred pastels also, all of which were surpassingly fine and set for exhibition at his place – well, let us simply say that his anger diminished somewhat.'

The printers laughed again. These were staunch fellows, Jim reflected. They'd hailed him exactly as he might have hoped: as a returning hero, a lost adventurer. The shop had been closed at once, the father removing his apron and visor and instructing his son to do the same. They would celebrate, he announced, with a fine luncheon. Jim suspected that the establishment – a restaurant hotel named Hummam's, in a corner of Covent Garden market – had been selected long before, with him very much in mind. It had a bohemian air, with gilded Arabian arches and ornate, low-hanging lanterns, and a clientele that seemed drawn mostly from the theatres – not really Thomas Way's sort of place at all. Still, the little chap had conducted himself with confidence, asking for a table at the front, by one of the windows, knowing this to be Jim's favoured position. He'd ordered the port as they sat – the '47, he'd said, was an uncommonly strong year. Jim had bowed to his expertise on this matter.

Both Ways emptied their glasses, and the father promptly poured another – filling up Jim's as well, even though he'd drunk barely a quarter, until the wine formed a perfect plane across the top. They urged him to talk of Venice; so, stirred by their warm welcome, he told them something of the summer that had just passed. A glorious vision was evoked. There was Whistler, roaming through crooked alleys and secluded squares. Drifting about the shadowy waterways in a hired gondola, in search of his scenes. Finding friendship and respect with a vitalising circle of young Americans, in whose company he swam in the canals, diving from boats and bridges; dined beneath the bright heavens on St Mark's Square, and in a sequence of charmingly decayed palazzos; held great rollicking debates on artistic matters, from which he'd invariably emerge the victor.

'We were poor, of course. Oh, quite crushingly so. It was a return to student conditions. But Venice was harvested, *mes amis* – its treasures gathered in. The fruits of that year, on plate and paper and canvas too, will change the game.'

'There are paintings as well?' asked the elder Way.

'Nocturnes, yes, a half dozen,' said Jim carelessly. 'The cathedral. The lagoon. Works of the finest delicacy. Paint, you know, should be no more than breath upon a pane of glass. I told this to the boys out there a hundred times.'

The waiter appeared, and food was ordered: a side of beef, naturally, *à la maison*. Jim rolled a cigarette.

'But enough of new works. What, my dear Way, of the old? What of the sales, man – the Committee of Inspection?' He lit the cigarette and inhaled, savouring the tingle of tobacco; he sat forward in his chair. 'What the devil has been going on?'

At this the Ways changed, becoming hesitant, a little of the pleasure draining from those spaniel faces. The elder drank down more port. There was a plain sense that his enthusiasm to hear about Venice had been induced to some degree by a desire to delay this particular point in the conversation.

'I tried to stop them, Mr Whistler,' he said eventually. 'Mr Eldon helped me a good deal, really he did, but too much authority was arrayed against us.'

'What d'you mean?' asked Jim. 'What authority?'

'I mean the money, sir. His millions. The lawyers – that receiver too. Defected, the lot of them. To Leyland.'

This was Jim's suspicion, gleaned from his correspondence. The fortress had been overrun; the guards, upon the outer walls at any rate, had turned their goddamned coats. It had been an overwhelming action, impossible to resist, and one there had seemed little point him returning to England to witness.

'What of the cartoons? What became of them? Did he see them, at least?'

Way nodded, but the details Jim craved – Leyland's anger, his powerlessness and humiliation – did not follow. 'He sued to keep them out of the first sale – the public one, at the White House. The matter was decided so quickly that by the time I heard of it everything was already settled in his favour. The two smaller works, the lobsters and the boat, disappeared not long afterwards. All sorts of things were going by that stage. Indeed, sir, it was only by shifting the large one to your brother's that I prevented it from going too. It made it to Sotheby's — didn't I tell you this?'

'I understand that there was a lot called *The Creditor*, but—'

'That was it.' Way's voice was quick with shame. 'That was the one. I don't know who gave it that title. A man called Dowdeswell bought it. Printseller on Chancery Lane. I'm sure that he'd consider selling it back, Mr Whistler, should this be required.'

Jim looked at his cigarette; he'd quite lost the taste for it. *The Gold Scab* had been created with a very specific purpose: to mortify Leyland, mortify him publicly and remind the villain exactly who he had affronted. Who he had cheated. How grave the wound was, and how unhealed. And yet it had been swept aside. Slipped out into the world with barely a murmur. There was a sense of a failed joke: a bucket of water balanced above a door that had fallen the wrong way, or a chair with a loosened leg that no one had sat upon. The cartoon had been made to fail. Why on earth would he want it *back*?

He couldn't face explaining this to Way. Keeping up a show of unconcern, he asked after *The Three Girls*. This drew a single deep nod from the father, and a series of shallower but no less emphatic nods from the son.

'Oh yes, Leyland was certainly hunting for that. Before he went abroad, that is. Yes, he was after that one especially.'

'Mentioned it many times. Said it was his, he did. That he'd paid for it.'

'There was an arrangement,' Jim said, 'with Mr Howell regarding that picture. We'd agreed that he was to shield it from Leyland. Transport it from the White House. Save it from the sale.'

Way Senior set down his port glass. 'It was nowhere to be found, sir,' he said. 'That's for sure.'

Jim was almost amused. 'Are you telling me – my dear Way, are you honestly telling me that the Owl was true to his word?'

The Ways exchanged a lengthy look. The son seemed to be urging the father to stick to an earlier resolution – to say something it had been agreed that they had to say. Although reluctant, the father accepted it. He turned back to Jim, but couldn't look at him directly, choosing instead to study the silver salt cellar, sliding it an inch across the tabletop with his forefinger.

'Mr Whistler,' he said, 'I believe we need to talk about your Mr Howell.'

*

It took Owl just a week to track Jim down. The reunion occurred on Regent Street, some fifty yards from the two-room workshop that had been rented for him by the Fine Art Society. He was with the younger Way, whom he'd been granted as an assistant, walking back from supper at the Café Royal. An evening's labour lay ahead; for inevitably, that which had looked wholly perfect in Venice seemed a good deal less so when unpacked, cleaned of sawdust and viewed in the hard light of London. Jim was now engaged in an intensive round of alterations and rebitings, ahead of printing out a completely fresh set of proofs.

Owl's approach was direct: he stepped before them, into a stripe of gaslight, and boomed out their names in robust salutation. The Portuguese was as spruce as ever, with checked trousers, a watch-chain and new kid gloves, and that crimson ribbon, that obscure decoration, pinned to a spotless grey overcoat. He was a sleeker beast than formerly, and somewhat thicker in the mid-section; his plots and manipulations were clearly paying off.

Jim felt a plunging sensation – a bristling of hairs, a quickening of the blood – but managed to limit his immediate response to asking young Way to go on ahead to light the fire and perhaps apply some grease to the press. The lad obeyed, giving Owl a glance that suggested he'd like nothing more than to plant a boot against those checked trousers and send the fellow careening into the gutter.

Owl didn't notice. 'It warms my heart,' he declared, 'to think that Jimmy Whistler is at work on something entirely new. A set of Venetian etchings! Lord above, I cannot wait to study them.' He hesitated, allowing for an invitation to come up and see what was underway. None came. 'There's word about town, among the dealers and so forth, that there are pastels as well. Is this so?'

Jim leaned back on a heel. After Venice, after all the

Italian and French, and the various burrs and brogues of his American friends, that Portuguese accent rang slightly hollow. The Owl was even sounding false. His attitude, too, was mystifying. He must, he simply *must* have realised that there would be difficulty here. Did he really not know that his victim, his dupe, was onto him? He gave no sign of it, though, seeming unperturbed that his greeting had not been returned. That nothing, in fact, had been said to him at all.

'I mean, if this is true, it is a genius move. Pastels, by God! A perfect fit for you, old man. All the finest qualities of your art: the looseness, the sureness, the colours. And each one unique. I smell coin, my friend, and a tidy bit of it.'

On he ran, with that old fluency, about how very long Jim had been away; it was November already, did he realise? How this absence might be played to his advantage. How all artistic London was wondering what had become of their pugnacious butterfly. How the time was right for a *renaissance* – for the show to begin anew.

After a couple of minutes Jim could take no more. He rapped the end of his cane smartly against the pavement. 'What is it that you *want*, Owl? What brings you here, precisely?'

Owl's brow lifted. 'Merely the concern of a friend,' he replied. 'Of an ally in your bothers, who rejoices to see you rising out of them.'

Jim regarded him sceptically.

The Portuguese saw that he must make an offering. 'I

have it,' he said simply. 'I did as I promised, Jimmy. I saved the large canvas for you – *The Three Girls*. Maud and the others, there in the altogether.'

This was news, at least. Jim asked him where it was.

'Over at Rosie's. I say, though, old man, you'll never believe the wheeze that got the thing out. It was mere hours before the sale. Certain parties were poised, if you follow me, and means of egress closing fast. The yard of the White House was filled with—'

'Come then,' said Jim, turning towards Piccadilly. 'Let's be off.'

A hansom was taken. Many of their most diverting chats and serious conferences had occurred within those neat little vehicles. This time, however, Jim held his tongue and let Owl talk for them both. The Portuguese spoke for a while about mutual acquaintances, and all that Jim had missed, trying to trap him in conversation. He said nothing, looking out at the darkening city, refusing the cigarette case that was held open between them; so Owl moved on to a subject he knew his companion could not ignore.

'I expect you'll have heard about Leyland. He's finished, they say. His heart shattered. Even his famed rapacity in business is said to have tailed off almost completely. The sad tidings did reach you, didn't they, over in Italy? Of Fanny?'

Nellie had reported the death in one of her letters, early in the summer. It had quite confounded Jim for a while. He'd thought of the happy child he'd once known, with whom he'd played on the lawns at Speke, whose portrait he'd painted – and who'd drifted away, and grown, and hardened against him so lamentably. His final sight of her had been in the corridor of the Lyceum Theatre, when he'd last seen them all, parading awkwardly with her fiancé. And now, less than a year afterwards, she was in her grave. It seemed absurd, and so pointless – like something left cruelly unfinished, for which they were all owed a damned good explanation. Maud had known already. Jim could only guess how – gossip among the English in Venice, perhaps – but she'd still wept when they'd spoken of it. She'd been ill again by then, confined to bed for much of the time, and crying at all sorts of things.

'Have you seen Mrs Leyland? Written to her?'

No territory was forbidden here, plainly. Jim shook his head.

'Word at first was that she'd found a house in St James's. That there was an agreement giving her five thousand a year.' Owl struck a match and smoked; he picked a shred of tobacco from his lip. 'More recent reports have her back in Liverpool, though. Living in lodgings, making no show of any kind. You know that he refused her permission to attend their daughter's funeral?'

This Jim hadn't heard. His grip tightened around his cane; he shifted on the hansom's upholstery.

Owl noted his discomfort, with the slightest satisfaction at having broken through at last. 'The essential character of the man, I think, was revealed in that proscription. His villainy shines out, even in his own darkest moments. It cannot do otherwise.'

The journey was a short one, thankfully, half a mile at most. Jim climbed from the hansom, leaving Owl to pay, and peered down the gloomy channel of Southampton Row. A fog was settling, slowly filling the long, straight street, snuffing out its lights one by one. Owl threw away his cigarette and fished the key for number 93 from his pocket. Jim followed him inside, waiting while he lit an oil lamp that had been left by the door. Having called there several times before, usually while trying to locate the Owl, he thought he knew what to expect. But the lamp flared to reveal a barren hallway. All the clutter was gone, along with the rugs and the pictures on the walls and most of the furniture. It was as if it had just been vacated.

Owl pointed to the front room. Jim went through, thinking of Frances Leyland, of her suffering, wherever she was; he imagined vaguely what he might do, whilst knowing full well that the honest answer was nothing.

The sputtering lamp found *The Three Girls* before anything else. It stood diagonally across the room, barely fitting within it. After many months of prints and pastels, of paintings no more than a few feet square, the thing was staggering – you staggered in there, quite literally, as you tried to take it in. That he had painted this giant caused Jim some brief amazement. Once he was accustomed to the basic fact of it, however, its appearance rather dismayed him. The harmony of the colours had been thrown off.

There was a sickly hue to the nudes — a deadness to the paper screens behind. Was it dirt, he wondered as he inserted the eyeglass, some amalgam of grease and dust gathered during its escape from the White House and subsequent storage? Or merely the yellowing effect of Owl's lamp? He glanced around the shabby little studio. As with the hallway, it was denuded, stripped almost bare — a dismal scene indeed.

Owl was talking again about the campaign he'd waged to secure the painting. A clever switch had been performed, apparently, using a small rough copy that Jim had made in the months before his departure for Italy. The original was then removed from its stretchers and rolled up tight inside a length of drainpipe, so that it could be smuggled from the premises with the help of a roofer Owl had bribed for this purpose. It had been a nerve-racking affair, the Portuguese claimed, requiring all his skill, and undertaken in constant fear of discovery and arrest — for he would have been criminally liable, a thief bound for gaol. The whole business had cost him nearly a week of sleep.

'I swear that I have not taken such pains to retrieve another's work,' he said, 'since my time with Gabriel. Have I ever told you, Jimmy, what I did for him?'

While Jim continued his examination of *The Three Girls*, Owl spun out a tale that was outlandish even by his standards. He told how Gabriel Rossetti, half-mad with grief and remorse, had insisted upon burying a ream of his verses with a departed lover — Elizabeth Siddal, the suicide, already dead by the time Jim had moved through the Cheyne Walk set back in the 1860s. As the years had passed, though, and so much of his talent was planed away by chloral and brandy, Rossetti had come to regret this gesture most keenly. So it was, after much probing of his conscience, that he'd charged Owl with *exhumation*: with both the necessary paperwork and the process itself, in the depths of night, while the venerated painter-poet had cowered tearfully at home.

'Strange to relate,' Owl said, 'that although she'd been in the earth for several years, and was thus corrupted to a more or less complete degree, she retained an otherworldly beauty. Her hair, old man, that red hair – it had kept growing. It overflowed from the coffin, shining there in the candlelight. Upon returning to Gabriel, I told him—'

'Owl,' Jim interrupted. 'You must surely understand what has happened. I have a blasted brain in my head, you know. I have talked with Way and received a full account. He has been watching you. He has observed the obvious collusion between yourself and Leyland.'

Owl's face remained quite bland, revealing nothing. He twisted a corner of his moustache. '*Collusion*,' he sighed, after a pause. 'Such an unsatisfactory word. If you would merely—'

'He told me about my cartoons. How you worked with Leyland to keep them out of sight. How you allowed him to carry off great bundles of studies, and that copy of this painting here. All of which he has since been selling on at devilishly low prices, to do his best to depress the market for my productions.' Jim was growing vehement, properly so; although well seasoned in enmity, blatant treason was new to him. 'He told me how you attempted to claim the *Mother* from Graves the printseller. To settle two hundred and fifty pounds of your debt in that way, in the place of money from the sale of the house. *You*, who said the paintings in pawn were safe! Who knew my particular attachment to that work! It looks black, Owl. It looks damned black.'

The Portuguese wouldn't go down without a swing or two of his own. 'But then, Jimmy, then the *Mother* would have been mine. Don't you see? I could have handed the thing straight back to you. If old Way hadn't poked his beak in – if the damned receiver hadn't been alerted to it – that painting would be standing in here tonight, next to this one.'

Jim wouldn't hear it. 'Way also spoke of mounting suspicions that your debt – the money you'd provided me with, to ward off Nightingale – hadn't in fact been yours at all. That the vast fortune paid by the Metropolitan District Railway had gone to another person altogether, who'd turned out to be the true owner of that house of yours. That the cash you fronted came from a rather different source.' He adjusted the eyeglass, as if to focus his glare. 'A *Liverpudlian* source.'

'Jimmy—'

'It makes me re-evaluate your labours. The chaos and fire that has consumed the show. Everything that you've made sure I've lost track of. Have I been played for a fool, I wonder? Has my dearest friend – my truest ally, so I believed – been *milking* me all the while? Is this, when one casts an eye over his career, actually his game? His own particular art?'

Owl placed the oil lamp on the floor between them, lending the studio an eerie, cave-like ambience. He put his hands in the pockets of his checked trousers. Beneath a front of enjoyment, of affection for Jimmy Whistler and the tripe he could be made to swallow, was now a definite unease.

'Old man,' he said, 'you are a great and dear friend. And, by God, a bloody *genius* of art. This is why I so exerted myself to obtain this painting here, to keep it from the fellow you imagine me so bonded to. And once we've agreed our terms, I'll return it to you with a gladdened spirit – an unburdened heart. I still think it one of your best. A five-hundred-guinea picture. And as you're riding so high after Venice, no doubt the sum will climb yet further. Why, together we could—'

'You wish,' said Jim, 'to make terms.'

The Portuguese tilted back his hat. 'Well, the picture is in *my* possession. I went to pains. And it was removed – it could be easily claimed – in my capacity as debtor and a member of the Committee of Inspection, from the property of an absent bankrupt.' He gave a short laugh. 'I mean, it will be *reasonable*, Jimmy, you don't have to worry about that! An exchange of some kind, I was thinking. Proofs from Venice, for instance, would be most excellent – those you're printing with young Way. Perhaps one of each, say, from the first Fine Art Society set? And the pastels. I hear there are sixty, so . . . four of those?'

There it was, laid open at last: an appraisal for the sake of personal gain. It had always been there, Jim saw, wound around their connection like a climbing vine. He looked to *The Three Girls*, his studio companion of so many years – his masterwork, he'd thought once. The colour effects might be impaired, but that composition was still quite perfect: the placing of the parasol and the spray of cherry blossom, the slender bodies arranged like notes on a sheet of music, with such a gentle rhythm to their forms. And there was Maud, of course, positioned to the left. So fresh then, so innocent. Before their trials had begun.

Owl was still talking away, about how he'd be able to sell on whatever they agreed to for great sums, boosting those Whistler prices no end. Calmly, Jim studied his bamboo cane. They were crude these canes, carried principally for the sake of distinctiveness, the hollow stems sawed into lengths in a workshop somewhere, and that was that. Their ends, accordingly, could be rather sharp; he'd scratched the leather of several pairs of boots with them, along with innumerable tiles and varnished floorboards. He tested the present one with his thumb. Yes, that would do it. If one raised the thing above one's head *so*, with one's hands set about two feet apart, and plunged it in *so*, spear-like, with all one's strength, it should – yes, it *had* punctured the canvas, poked clean through, making a hole the size of a sixpence close to the centre of the parasol, as if it were some form of target. He shifted his grip, reversing the position of his hands – feeling like a goddamned whaler, there in that Holborn sitting room, straddling a longboat in the open ocean, working his harpoon into the flank of a leviathan.

Pulling it down was more difficult than he'd anticipated. The weave of the canvas proved resistant; the oil, even the thin coats he used, slowed him yet further. He persisted, snarling, the eyeglass swinging free – but could not, in his excitement, his sudden overriding rage, exert much control over the direction of the tear. It veered sideways, through that right-hand girl's loose *contrapposto*, jerking nearly to the base of the picture; then the entire thing popped off its support and fell like a curtain, a great flopping tarpaulin, wholly enfolding Jim and his cane. He thrashed about, stamping at the heavy, stiffened sheet until he was free and *The Three Girls* was but a tangled rag beneath him.

Owl had picked up the lamp and retreated almost to the hallway. He'd gone a little pale. 'Jimmy,' he said. 'This is most unnecessary. Surely we can—'

Jim's topper had been knocked off in the commotion. Retrieving it from among the painting's trampled remains, he pulled it back on and straightened his collar. 'You may,' he panted, doing his best to assume a sardonic sangfroid, 'you may keep the picture, Owl. Consider it a gift.'

The departure was to be vintage Whistler, a swoop

through the hall and then out; his momentum was interrupted, however, by the sight of a slim woman standing halfway down the stairs, in virtual darkness. It was Miss Corder, dressed in one of those habit-like coats of hers. Jim wondered how long she'd been there, and how much she'd seen – what she could see right then, through the studio door, of the ruin he'd left strewn across the floor. He couldn't discern very much of her face, of those peculiar, plain-pretty features, but when she spoke her voice was warm with pleasure.

'I hear that congratulations are in order, Jimmy. That the Venice work is beyond compare. I knew it would be so. I simply knew it. Such a venture could only be the most rousing of successes. Perhaps one day soon you might allow us to—'

'You were part of it, weren't you?' he said, his fury supplying an almost startling lucidity. 'And Maud found out. That's why – *that's* why she would see you no more.'

Miss Corder descended another step or two. She seemed unsurprised. 'Maud misunderstood. That's all. It was a misunderstanding. I will write to her. I've been meaning to for months. If you could just tell me where you are living, I—'

Jim nearly laughed. They worked fast, these two, damned fast! He tipped his hat and turned on his heel, continuing on his way. Owl was giving chase, forsaking dignity, making his justifications – trying to appear amused by Jim's feat of destruction and the fighting spirit that had driven it. There was a pleading note now, though, a whine on the edge of his baritone.

'My dearest Jimmy, you know I – come, really – this is a failure of communication only – the – the intention was as pure as, as – I sought simply to *further* you, don't you see, to help you to the comfort you deserve . . .'

A hansom was close by. Jim hailed it with his cane-harpoon and hopped inside, snapping the workshop's address to the driver. Owl instructed the fellow to wait, to allow them a moment, crossing the pavement as if he would climb aboard as well. But Jim shut the doors against him, and held them shut, leaving the Portuguese with a boot set uselessly upon the step. He removed it, peering in through the window; then he opened his arms wide in a final appeal.

The driver slid back his hatch, up above the top of Jim's hat. 'What am I to do, then? Is the other gentleman coming?'

'No,' said Jim, sitting back, tucking the eyeglass into his breast pocket. 'Drive on.'

Autumn 1880

Maud swivelled on her chair, shifting the hem of her gown, which was tight enough to make standing up something for which you had to prepare. She looked across the room, assessing her exit. Luncheon was over, the atmosphere above their long table loaded with smoke. Plates held only bones, slicks of sauce, the odd unwanted vegetable; the party's earlier energy was giving way, pleasantly, to a well-fed, boozy languor.

Being without lodgings at present, Jimmy was obliged to play host in a restaurant – a French place, of course, just off Shaftesbury Avenue, swell enough but not overly concerned with social form. Maud was at one end, with Matthew Eldon on her left. The poor fellow wasn't doing well, that much was plain. Godwin had told Jimmy that he'd dropped away while they'd been in Venice, and had been labouring under some mysterious malady. There was a new sullenness to his manner – a blackness of spirit akin to that with which Jimmy himself was afflicted from time to time, and that she'd known too – but more severe, she perceived. A good deal more severe.

'Well, Matt, here we are,' she'd said as they'd sat down. 'Together once more.'

He'd given her only a small, pained smile and had barely spoken since.

To Maud's right was Mrs Godwin, a dark-haired, dark-eyed woman, small and smart – pigeon-like, she couldn't help thinking, in her neat roundedness – with an air of natural refinement that made Maud feel like a factory girl. She was happy to talk, though, soon revealing that she was an artist, or rather an art *student*, since marriage and motherhood had obliged her to relearn everything. Maud had looked at her inquisitively, inviting an explanation. She hadn't supplied one.

Overhearing something of this exchange, Jimmy had swept down upon them. He liked this woman, Maud saw, the young wife of his oldest friend; he liked her immensely. Made munificent by a sense of impending success, by the universal laudation of his friends, he'd declared that they both surely stood at the absolute forefront of London's female artists. Their work, although very different, was equally admirable, and it needed to be displayed.

'You are ready, I think, the two of you. Ready for the Grosvenor, and many other places besides. When the Venice etchings have been shown, and the pastels as well, we will go through your work and make our selections. We will have it seen by the necessary people. Miss Franklin's flowers, Mrs Godwin – the honeysuckle, you know, that she drew in Italy – *Bon Dieu*, they are the finest examples of such things that you will ever find placed before you.'

His hand had settled upon Maud's shoulder, his thumb rubbing up a tiny fold in the fabric of her gown. She'd turned to protest; and he'd given her a confidential, sidelong look, the brow above the eyeglass twitching slyly.

'Indeed,' Mrs Godwin had replied. 'I should certainly like to see them.'

Jimmy was now back at his seat in the middle of the table, among Campbells, Coles and Mitfords, spinning yarns of Venice – of nights at the Café Florian and elsewhere; of swimming in the lagoon, and sketching from his gondola; of various minor foes engaged and bested. The showing that afternoon was good, with nearly all of the wider Whistler circle present. Several of the more daring, such as Godwin, had even brought wives or sisters. A new face or two could also be found among the gentlemen. Most notable was a fleshy, rather flamboyant young Irishman addressed by all as Oscar, who appeared to be listening closely to what was being said; he was a poet, Mrs Godwin had told her, and already of some renown. In fact, there was but one really glaring absence, which the company was now starting to discuss. Maud hesitated, releasing her hem. She decided that she could perhaps wait a minute longer.

'I told you,' said Bertie Mitford. 'Did I not tell you, Whistler – months, nay, *years* ago? The Owl is a robber!'

Everyone looked at Jimmy. He puffed on his cigarette, gazing thoughtfully at the ceiling, counting out each second of the pause. 'Well, my dear Mitford,' he replied, flicking ash onto his plate, 'so was Barabbas.'

Lord, how they laughed. All poise was forgotten; they beat their fists upon the table, and rocked back hard in their chairs. It was impossible not to get caught up in it, but even as she smiled Maud was frowning a little too – for wasn't Barabbas pardoned and released, while Jesus went to the cross?

Jimmy was moving on, however, his self-satisfaction so great he was practically aglow. This was the Whistler who had slapped on the Prussian blue at Prince's Gate, taken John Ruskin to court, painted *The Golden Scab* – and who was applying himself now, without mercy or restraint, to what he termed *the scalping of Master Howell*. The lines were well rehearsed, and the topics carefully chosen. The business concerning Disraeli, with whom the Portuguese had claimed, ridiculously, to have a personal connection. The furniture declared lost, or in for some programme of protracted repair – but really put in pawn or even sold, with Owl pocketing the cash. The lies and obfuscations that had issued forth in an unending stream.

'When the running of one's show is given over to Howell,' Jimmy proclaimed, 'it acquires the wild farce of the panto-mime – the clown stealing the clock, *mes amis*, and sitting on it while it strikes.' He raised a hand to stem the mirth. 'But beneath this, lest we become indulgent, there is a focused and voracious aim. This cannot be forgotten. Never again would I dream of presenting Howell to anyone without explaining in the same breath – the Owl, *bird of prey*.'

This brought forth another shout of laughter, the thump of fists upon white linen, the chimes of shaken crockery. Again, Maud caught herself grinning, while Mrs Godwin suspended her gentility to release a vindictive giggle.

Matthew Eldon was the only person who did not join in. His arms were crossed, a penny cigar burning quite forgotten between his fingers; there was a deep line scored an inch out from the corner of his moustache that Maud hadn't noticed before. He seemed to have edged back from the table, from the party, as if sliding his chair slowly into the shadows. Maud moved closer and asked him softly if anything was wrong. She realised that a part of her actually wanted him to be annoyed by all this, and to object to it in a way she could not; to stand up and state that Jimmy's venomous display really went too far. That it sailed extremely close to malice.

This would never happen. Eldon was too loyal. Instead he sat motionless for a while, a rough statue hewn from wood, the cigar smouldering on in his hand.

Then he sighed. 'I know that he's a louse, Miss Franklin,' he said. 'I know it. I just miss him, that's all.'

*

442

The meeting was arranged for three o'clock, at the refreshment lodge in Hyde Park. Neutral ground, Maud supposed, in case events took an unexpected turn. There might be hysterics. A snatching. All sorts of desperate nonsense. Such things must occur.

It was a fine late autumn day, cold and crisp as new sheets. Maud met Edie beforehand at Marble Arch and the sisters walked diagonally across the park, on a path half buried by leaves. With her usual perversity, Edie appeared to think that she could soothe them both by working her way down a list of Maud-related worries. Health was foremost. Was she looking after herself properly? She still looked so pale, so thin; she was wheezing like an old woman. Was she completely sure that she was out of danger?

Yes, Maud replied, all was well, or reasonably so; Dr Whistler had seen her three times since her return and had pronounced that she was recovering. It was the damp in Venice, he'd surmised, and the rather wretched places they'd been obliged to live in. Such a relapse had been nigh-on inevitable. He'd given her a special paste, and some kind of cordial to drink. There was no cause for concern.

Mention of the Whistler name brought Edie to her next item: the state of Jimmy's finances. Had the bankruptcy been resolved? Were they able to feed and house themselves, and cover their responsibilities? They were, Maud told her firmly – going on to relate with the faintest irresistible trace of told-you-so how the Fine Art Society had paid up in full and were going to exhibit the pastels early in the new year.

'Everyone says they are sure to sell. Jimmy says they won't be able to help it.' Maud looked ahead to the Serpentine, now visible between the trees, the coppery sunlight catching upon the water; her nerves suddenly sharpened, sending a shiver through her shoulder-blades. 'It looks good, Edie,' she added, more quietly. 'Honest it does.'

The refreshment lodge was long and low and doing a surprisingly brisk trade for mid-November. A family was sitting outside, on a bench next to the doors: a man and woman, plainly but respectably dressed, with a small girl playing close by, hopping back and forth in a game known only to herself. Maud's eyes fixed immediately upon this child, upon the auburn locks that spilled from beneath her simple bonnet, upon the shape of her face, the motion of her little limbs, the movement of her lips as she whispered under her breath. It was only when she and Edie actually arrived at the bench that she noticed the infant, fast asleep, held in a sling across the man's back.

There was an impact almost, something seeming to whistle in at tremendous speed and clout her about the head, dulling her senses, setting the world at a distinct remove. The couple rose. Both were tall and lean, and slightly guarded. She was introduced to Mr and Mrs Walters, the foster parents, and then to Ione, to her own daughter, now three and a half years old. She said something in return, she must have done. She began to cry. She apologised to the Walters, to Edie, several times over. She took hold of herself somehow and crouched before the child, before her Ione – thinking that if she is scared, if my tears upset her, if she asks to be taken home and away from me, *I will die*.

But no. The girl was curious. Confident, even. Dear God, she was like Jimmy.

'You are my mama,' she said.

'I am,' Maud managed to answer.

Ione pointed at Maud's gown. 'Your dress is blue.'

Maud looked down, abruptly aware of how the gown clung to her beneath her coat and how rich the silk was; how conclusions must surely have formed in the minds of the foster parents about her, about her circumstances, her character, her motives in——

Ione held out her hand. Maud accepted it, her head swimming with gladness and gratitude. The child's grip was firm. Maud could feel the warmth of her palm through their gloves. Without consultation, she was led off towards the broad curve of the Serpentine.

It was growing cold, properly so, the sun's rays now broken by the skyline. They talked about the handful of ducks that bobbed upon the water, agreeing that they looked very chilly indeed, poor things; and then the rowing boats, moored along the lakeside in a jagged column, covered for winter. Ione confided that she liked boats, but had never been out in one.

'Perhaps we shall do that,' Maud said. 'You and I, in the summer. Perhaps we shall.'

The girl gave a serious nod. 'And Maud,' she said. 'Maud as well.'

Maud blinked. The baby. The one she'd barely seen. The one she'd never held, or called by her name. 'Of course. Yes, of course. Yes.'

'And Mrs Walters.' Ione stopped; she looked over her shoulder, towards her foster parents, who were walking with Edie a dozen yards behind. 'She'll come too, won't she?'

'I don't—' Maud faltered, overcome by a dark feeling, a deep sense of shame; by a consciousness, acutely painful, of her own unsuitability. Her hopeless inadequacy. You are no kind of *mother*, she thought fiercely. You are no more than a damned stranger. She swallowed. 'I – I don't see why not.'

Soon afterwards they retreated to the lodge, to a booth near the fire, for sweet tea in tin mugs, a plate of buns with a waxy glaze, and a rather stilted conversation – with which Edie was no help at all, remaining at the margins in what she probably imagined was a considerate silence. Ione had picked up a bun, which looked enormous in her hands, and was busy attempting to work a corner of it into her mouth. She'd sat on the bench beside Mrs Walters. The woman was friendly enough, but with a hardness about her also; it was there in her wide-set eyes as she considered Maud across the table and asked if she'd had far to come.

Maud had an answer ready: only from Wimpole Street, she said, where an apartment had been leased. She thought it best not to reveal that she was actually back at Sharp's Hotel, while Jimmy stayed with his brother and plotted their next move. She spoke distractedly, however, unable to stop looking at the children. It scarcely seemed real, after all her yearning, to be sitting there with them. Ione had Jimmy's nose, she noticed, and his brow – the nose and brow he himself shared with his mother. And baby Maud already had a head of coal black curls. The infant was stirring now and was brought round off Mr Walters' back – rather to his relief, for she was a solid little thing, with plump red arms, a Franklin chin and a decidedly grumpy expression. Set upon her foster mother's lap, she reached at once for the pieces of bun left on the plate before her.

They looked like a family. You couldn't deny it. Ione leaned against Mrs Walters, finishing off her bun, scrutinising her mother – who sat there in all her supposed elegance, in her fur-lined coat and her dainty little hat, as if she'd wandered in from a far-off, unknowable, slightly ridiculous land. The dark feeling returned. You have no right to be here, Maud thought. No right at all. The best thing you could do would be to leave them alone.

Mrs Walters tried to interest the infant in her; in going over to her, perhaps. Baby Maud looked up – this child for whom she'd bled and screamed, for whom she'd come so sickeningly close to death – and her chubby face was empty of recognition, of concern, of anything really. She gave a single shake of those black curls and returned her attention to the bun.

447

Do not rise, Maud told herself; but she rose. Stay here, she commanded, at this table; but she made to leave, muttering yet another apology. Edie had plainly been expecting this and started to get up as well.

'No,' said Maud. 'Don't. I won't be long.'

Outside, the sun was almost gone, the colours of the park fading with the light. Maud went around a corner of the lodge. She stood for a minute; then, after checking she couldn't be seen, she took out tobacco and papers and removed her gloves to roll a cigarette. As she struck a match to light it, the flame glinted on metal – on the ring, still there on her finger, proclaiming her Mrs Whistler. It had gone unmentioned at the luncheon, but surely wouldn't here – not by Edie at any rate. She thought of what her sister might say and let out a short, bitter laugh. Her lip trembled. A hot tear popped onto her cheek.

Dabbing her eyes on her coat cuff, Maud dragged on the cigarette and gazed into the park: at the mist beginning to creep above the waters of the lake; at the trees and shrubs sinking into shadow. There were few people about now. Before long she noticed a woman standing alone beneath a tall elm, off towards Rotten Row. The face couldn't be seen, but that hat – an impractically large smear of lavender, bright against the surrounding greyness – left no doubt as to whose head it sat upon.

Maud dropped the cigarette and started towards her. She'd thought that if she ever saw Rosa Corder again – at the Grosvenor, say, or one of the colour shops about town

– her reaction would be an angry one: a glare, a couple of words about betrayal, and that would be all. And there was anger now, oh yes – what was she doing there, exactly? Was she following Maud around? Why in heaven would she be doing that? But mingled in with it was something peculiarly like relief – dear Lord, like *happiness*. For Rosa was the one person who knew everything. The one person who might understand.

As she walked, Maud was also queasily aware that right then Jimmy was attending a concert organised by some grand society lady, during which he would certainly take the chance to reprise the performance he'd given at the luncheon; and again later on, when he'd been invited to Lord So-and-So's for dinner. By the time he was finished, the Owl's well would be permanently poisoned. There'd be scarcely a person left in London who'd do business with him. It was deserved, of course, in the strictest, harshest sense. A wrong had been done. A great lie told. And yet at the same time Jimmy's vengeance would leave a father and husband with no way at all to make his living. It would deprive a penniless female artist of her protector. Maud realised that Rosa could well have followed her to the park to ask for clemency. To beg for her assistance. She didn't know quite what she'd say to that.

When she was about thirty yards away, however, crossing an avenue, the figure suddenly stepped back, swinging a bag of some kind onto her shoulder and heading off in the direction of Brompton Road. Despite her promises to Edie,

Maud was still weak; reaching the elm under which Rosa had been standing, she slowed and began to cough. Something pale was poking from the trunk – a sheet of paper, tucked into a cleft in the bark. Left for her. A note, she thought at first, pulling it out. A plea for help.

The paper bore a sketch, made from that same spot. Fluently drawn, rather more detailed than Jimmy's tended to be, and far surpassing anything Maud herself could ever hope to do, it showed a woman, in fashionable clothes and a touch too thin, strolling hand in hand with a young girl in a bonnet: Maud and Ione, over at the Serpentine, as they'd been barely half an hour earlier. It was a moment of awkward beauty. They were sharing a shy look, smiling just a little, angled towards one another. The mother was leaning down, as if she was listening.

A tear patted against the paper. Maud shook it off. She wiped her face, staring hard into the gloom, at the shapes of the trees around her and the yellow seam of gaslight that ran along the street beyond. But Rosa Corder was gone.

Author's Note

After Whistler's death in 1903, the American art critic Elizabeth Pennell and her etcher husband Joseph set about writing the first complete biography of the artist. They'd known Whistler since the late 1880s and had spoken with him at length about his life and work. Interviews were conducted with as many of his surviving friends and associates as they could find. The intention was to set down the definitive history of James McNeill Whistler and establish him once and for all as a great genius of American art.

But certain details proved elusive. As always, there was a question mark over Charles Augustus Howell, who'd died in suitably mysterious circumstances in 1890. The Pennells knew that he'd been embedded in Whistler's affairs during the desperate years prior to Venice, and had been extracting a measure of profit for himself, yet could ascertain very little beyond that. They were struck, however, by the admiring affection with which Whistler still talked of the Owl, more than two decades after their rupture. He was, the artist told them, 'the wonderful man, the genius ... splendidly flamboyant, the real hero of the Picaresque novel, forced by modern conditions into other adventures, and along other roads.'

The Pennells were also convinced that something was missing from the saga of the Peacock Room – something involving Whistler and Frances Leyland. Frederick Leyland had died in 1892, suffering a heart attack in the carriage of an underground train. The 70-year-old Frances agreed to talk to Elizabeth, but dismissed any suggestion of impropriety; the rumours of an affair, she maintained, of an elopement, were absurd. The Peacock Room itself remained unchanged in the dining room of 49 Prince's Gate until 1904. The next owner of the house, Blanche Watney, thought it 'hideous' and at one point considered having it torn out and destroyed. Fortunately, the American industrialist Charles Lang Freer intervened, offering to buy the room from Watney for eight times the amount Whistler had been paid, before having it dismantled and shipped to his home in Detroit (it's now in the Freer Gallery of Art, Smithsonian Institution, Washington D.C.). Freer's price, appropriately enough, was named in guineas.

Maud Franklin refused to meet with the Pennells at all. After her return from Venice, she exhibited water-colours of flowers at both the Grosvenor Gallery and the Society of British Artists, under the curious pseudonym Clifton Lin. None of these have survived. In 1888 she separated acrimoniously from Whistler, almost literally forced from his home by the widowed Beatrice Godwin, who he married the same year. She moved to France, seeking sanctuary in Paris with the sales agent George Lucas, and later married a wealthy American, John Little. Her daughter Maud appears to have died in childhood, but regular contact was established with Ione, who married Warwick Tyler in 1899 and emigrated to America. Maud's letters to her are deeply affectionate, full of maternal concern and requests for news – and conspicuous in their failure to discuss or even mention Ione's father.

By the time Elizabeth Pennell tracked Maud down she was a widow, living in some style near Cannes; Pennell noted that a 'motor' stood outside her country house. When Elizabeth rang the bell, however, her subject's erstwhile *Madame* would not even come to the door. She tried calling again the next day, with the same result: a maidservant making apologies, saying that her mistress wasn't at home. Reluctantly, the biographer departed, convinced that she was being watched from behind the blinds of an upstairs window. Shortly afterwards Maud wrote to the Pennells, explaining simply that she did not like to speak of the past. Everything she knew of those days would die with her. As the Pennells themselves put it, with barely contained frustration: 'Maud could tell the whole story, but she will not.'

It was in this absence that *Mrs Whistler* first began to take shape. Maud's experience is a striking gap in a history that is elsewhere immensely detailed, albeit filled with contradictions and inconsistencies. My manipulations are largely those of focus, various minor spats and skirmishes having been omitted or consigned to the edges of the narrative. It should be pointed out, though, that Whistler's long-suffering lawyer was in fact named James Anderson Rose, a change decided upon to preserve the distinctiveness of Rosa Corder. The fate of *The Three Girls*, also, has never been discovered – although a picture fragment later came up for sale at Dowdesdell's Gallery that showed a young woman in a near-transparent shift and a red headscarf crouching beside a potted cherry blossom (now on display in the Courtauld Institute of Art). She bears a close resemblance to a figure in the rough, smaller copy of *The Three Girls* that Whistler made before he left for Venice (now in the Tate Gallery collection), and looks very much as if she might have been cut from the remains of a larger composition.

Numerous books were consulted during the writing of this one. Particularly useful were Linda Merrill's authoritative accounts of both the Peacock Room and the Whistler-Ruskin Trial; a fascinating if rather forgiving study of the Owl by Helen Rossetti Angeli entitled *Pre-Raphaelite Twilight*; and the excellent online archive of Whistler's correspondence assembled by the University of Glasgow, from which many of this novel's best lines were lifted.

Heartfelt thanks are due to everyone who has worked with me on this book, at its different stages: Euan Thorneycroft and all at A M Heath; Suzie Dooré, Charlotte Cray, Ann Bissell, Dom Forbes, Katie Espiner, Cassie Browne, Ore Agbaje-Williams, Jane Robertson and the team at HarperCollins. I am also indebted to Jacqueline Riding, Hallie Rubenhold, Ros Wynne-Jones, Nikita Lalwani, Natasha Lohan, Brian Fantoni, my mother Christine Plampin and my ever-supportive family and friends. And Sarah and Kester, of course, who put up with a lot.